F · DAY

THE SECOND
DAWN OF MAN

Colin R. Turner

Published by Applied Image, July 2016
ISBN: 978-0-9560640-2-8
First edition 2016
Text version 1.2

With thanks to Sarah McIver, Krisztina Paterson and Stephen Turner.

Book news and updates may be found at:
freeworlder.com
facebook.com/colinrturner.author

Also available from this author:

Into The Open Economy – How Everything You know About The World Is About To Change. *(Applied Image, ISBN: 978-0-9560640-4-2)*

Typeset in Minion Pro, Arial & Garamond Pro on OpenOffice

For Luka, a giraffe, and a lion.

F-Day | *n. abbr. 'free day' or 'World Freedom Day'*
A hypothetical date in the future when the world's
largest economies devolve money and the market
system in favour of an open- or open access economy.
(see: gift economy, The Free World Charter)

PART 1
A PERSONAL AWAKENING

"*She is free in her wildness, she is a wanderess,
a drop of free water.*

*She knows nothing of borders
and cares nothing for rules or customs.*

*'Time' for her isn't something to fight against.
Her life flows clean, with passion, like fresh water.*"

Roman Payne – *The Wanderess*

F·DAY -18057 DAYS

I t was almost like a standard issue childhood memory. Karl was standing barefoot in the shallow water, watching tiny fish flitting this way and that around his feet, reacting to his movements. The sun was beating down on a beach somewhere in Ireland, where Karl and his older brother Ben were standing in the river, looking down, faces aglow in the diamonds dancing on the water.

Karl was hot, but he was happy and the world was new – almost five and a half years old in fact. It was a warm, safe place, full of new things to be discovered. Here and there, small flat fish were appearing suddenly in little flurries of sand, then darting away a little before disappearing into the sand again. Karl was transfixed.

It was summer, sometime in the early 1970s. Karl and Ben had left their parents to go exploring the far Northern end of the beach. Their mission? To discover the estuary that lay there. Karl had no idea what an estuary was, so Ben debriefed him for the mission. So, rivers all come eventually to meet the sea? Karl pondered. OK, that sounded cool.

Karl was a quiet and curious boy, and idolised his big brother. Ben was cool, strong, funny, and he knew things – lots of things. Even though he was almost seven years older than Karl, they had great fun together, talking in their own language – a kind of silly talk that no-one else understood.

Now they had reached the estuary – A River Meeting The Sea – and were both bent over, hands on knees in the warm, shallow water. Karl watching, Ben pointing out and naming the tiny darting creatures whose world they were dominating with their giant feet. Miniature molluscs, crabs, urchins and fish, all playing hide and seek in the sand. The sun was hot, the sand golden, and the water clear, teeming with life.

The world truly is a magic place, thought Karl. *This is going to be amazing...*

F·DAY -5694
(34 YEARS LATER)

Most people are awoken by noise, but for Karl Drayton it was the opposite. It was the sudden onset of silence that made him jump up in the bed. *That bloody machine has stopped again!* He sighed, threw his legs out of the bed, pulled on a pair of trousers and went downstairs to tend to the stapling machine.

The auto-stapler that he had paid so much money for, would – supposedly automatically – whir away in the room below his and Gill's bedroom, apparently just waiting for them to fall asleep before jamming and going silent.

Karl entered the packing room and saw the flashing lights. He cursed, turned on the light, and removed the two booklets from the machine that had attempted to bind themselves together in an awkward amorous embrace. He wrenched them apart, threw them unceremoniously in the bin and hit the reset button. The machine thought about it for a moment, then beeped and whirred itself back into action.

Karl sighed, stretched himself and reached for a cigarette. He had had just about enough of this business. Printing and packing books in the middle of the night for corporate clients – multinational companies, banks, government offices. Dreary end-of-year financial reports, consultancy reports, technical manuals, staff manuals – all paid for with dreary end-of-year budgets.

He picked up one entitled, *'Health And Safety First: In The Food Factory'.*

"Hmmph! Probably has a whole chapter dedicated to banana skins," he muttered, tossing it away.

He knew most of these dull books would probably never even be looked at. They existed just to fulfil a legal requirement, and each would probably sit idly on some shelf for twenty years until a cleaner came along to release it back to the wild.

He found some matches under a pile of papers and lit the cigarette.

He didn't have much right to complain though. After years of struggle and the robbery that had nearly destroyed him, Karl had managed to completely turn the business around. Since taking the decision to move everything to his house, operations were cheaper and easier, turnover had doubled, and now, finally, he was earning himself a very good living.

Three years ago, those enterprising thieves had driven *his* car through the front door of his print shop in the middle of the night and taken anything they thought they could get a few Euros for. Printers, packing machines, computers, stock – even a sandwich toaster for god's sake. Gone. Then to cap it all, the insurance company said they would only pay out a small percentage of the value – because he had left his keys in the car that they used.

Karl was furious at the time but ultimately powerless. He eventually had resorted to taking what money he could from the insurance and, with a bank loan, tracked down his equipment through some dubious contacts, paid their premium ransom, and had most of it 'magically' returned to him. Karl would never forget the wild look in the boy's eyes when he handed over that fat envelope of cash. The fear, the anger, the desperation were all imprinted there. Karl actually felt like he was doing them a favour – whoever 'they' were.

He flicked on the computer screen.

But they were the bad old days, and he had bounced back – even managing to regain some of his insurance losses from the insurance company, who, unbeknownst to them, were now also his print clients, and paying him rather over-generously for his services.

But it sucked.

He checked his emails. One spam, one customer query.

"Will answer that in the morning," he muttered in a plume of smoke, then looked out the window.

A black cat was threading its way silently through the dark bushes outside. It stopped and stared back at him.

Karl felt unsatisfied. He had always been a curious and creative boy. He loved nature, he loved playing music, making things, building things, fixing things. If anyone had a problem, he would do his damnedest to help them solve it, and wouldn't give up until he had. Yet for his entire early adulthood, he seemed to be trying to solve his own life. How to make a living? What did he want to be? What did he want to do? He was good at lots of things, but it seemed impossible to make money from all of them. He didn't want to specialise. He wanted to do everything!

He felt at odds with the world. He had had no interest in school. He had never seen the point in memorizing stuff he wasn't interested in and had failed all his exams. He then watched his friends all go through college and get good jobs and nice wives and babies, and he was left behind.

After years of falling in and out of various jobs, Karl had eventually decided to start his own business. It had been tough getting off the ground, but now, here he was, almost forty, with a successful business, a girlfriend, a nice home – and it sucked.

Why? Why did he find it so hard to be happy?

The cat outside looked away in scornful disinterest and moved on.

Karl was thirty-nine, with a scruff of strawberry blonde hair and pale blue eyes. He was handsome, but years of struggle had taken its toll. He smoked and drank too much and never regarded his appearance. He was stooped and lacked confidence. He had always found it difficult to meet women, and the ones he did didn't stay around for long.

Gill had been his first real long term relationship. He had met her over ten years ago in a bar in Dublin. She was bottle-blonde and her face bore the same battle scars from years of smoking and rancour.

Together they had shared a common interest – drinking. Karl, the middle-class boy, feeling like a castaway, adrift in a world which didn't belong to him, and Gill, who had come from a poor family, and had suffered a litany of abuses at the hands of her alcoholic father.

Despite being from very different backgrounds, together they had escaped and shared solace in a world that was acutely hostile to them. They had pulled through the hard times and were finding their way in the world at last.

But if this was success, Karl mused, then he didn't want it. Neither of them were happy. There had to be more to life than just working to buy things.

Lying back in bed, with the familiar humming of the machines resumed below, Karl's mind began to wander. His thoughts raced. His mouth wet with the acrid taste of nicotine. He felt uncomfortable. Remote. He reached over to Gill but she was fast asleep – sedated under a heavy gin-scented breath. He knew this couldn't continue.

Whirrr Whirrr

F·DAY -5414

The following winter, Karl and Gill were driving home late from a print delivery. It was a dark country road, wet from the afternoon's rain. Gill was driving.

"I think I'm going to sell the business," Karl suddenly announced. Gill almost swerved the van.

"What?!" she shouted.

"Yeah I'm going to sell up. I've had enough. It's time to do something else."

"What are you fuckin' crazy?!" she retorted. "Things are just getting good and you're gonna quit?" She was speeding up now.

6

"Hey, take it easy," Karl said leaning forward. "I don't know Gill. It just doesn't feel right. I need to do something else. Maybe get back into music, play some gigs or whatever..."

Gill slowed down and shook her head.

"For fuck's sake Karl," she pleaded finally, "you've just spent the last few years turning the business around. We're making good money now. You'll never make that kind of money from music. Why not give it a few more years anyway?"

Karl snorted. Typical Gill, he thought, always trying to put off the evil day. He lit up a cigarette and opened the car ashtray.

"No," he said firmly. He pulled on the cigarette. "These book jobs I'm doing are all going to go to the internet soon. In a few years time, no-one's going to be printing this crap. I need to sell it while it's still worth something. In a few years, this whole business could be worthless."

He was trying to be logical about it, but there was no rationale behind his decision. It was nothing to do with the money. He just wanted out. Karl usually took forever to make up his mind, but when he did, there was very little would stop him.

Gill fell silent and was getting agitated. Karl knew what that meant. She was going to hit the bottle the moment they got home.

"Well, let's see what happens." he said finally and stubbed out his cigarette in the ashtray.

Karl never imagined for a minute just how accurate his hunch about selling the business would turn out to be. His business sold quickly, earning him enough money to clear his mortgage, pay off all his loans, and take the next three years off.

Three months later, the global economy crashed.

For the first time in their adult lives, Karl and Gill were completely debt-free and stress-free. They had a golden opportunity to take time out and explore the world that most people could only dream about.

Little did Karl know just what direction that exploration was going to take him.

F·DAY -4923

A gentle summer wind was billowing in the bedroom curtains when Karl woke up. He immediately smiled, then tried to get up.

Ouch.

His head felt like a kicked basketball, his stomach like a bag of soap, but he didn't care. He jumped out of the bed. He was very happy with himself.

Last night had been his test – a late night festival. Laughing, singing, drinking beer with all his friends in the great outdoors – all without smoking a single cigarette! He was very proud of himself. Those social nights had always been his Achilles' heel. A few beers was usually all it took to wash all his willpower away – until last night!

Gill was still asleep. She had bought him that quit smoking book that had sat on his bedside table all these months. He had put off reading it, assuming it to be full of tiresome self-hypnosis exercises. He wanted to give up smoking all by himself, and last night he triumphed! He got dressed.

He was just leaving the bedroom when he looked again at the smoking book and paused. Mind you, he thought with renewed curiosity, what would be the harm in reading it now? He had already beaten the cigarettes alone, so he had nothing to lose.

He picked it up and turned over to the back cover. The author, Karl read, was an ex-hundred-a-day smoker, who, based on his own success, had decided to try and cure the whole world of smoking! Whatever method he was using, it was doing a good job by all accounts, since the book had apparently sold tens of millions of copies. So, what was the big secret? He brought the book downstairs, put on the kettle and began to read.

The book's message turned out to be really simple: *I am not going to brainwash you into quitting smoking because you have already been brainwashed by smoking. I am going to help you undo that.*

For Karl, this was an epiphany. The author was right – smokers fooled themselves into enjoying something that's actually disgusting, just to get the nicotine. To quit, the author suggested, you only had to face down that tiny physiological craving, while at the same time 'waking yourself up' to the true, foul taste of the cigarette.

The book was playing with Karl's head for days after he had read it. Whatever his feelings about quitting smoking, the book thoroughly cemented it. No doubt there. But there was something else – something unsettling about the book that he couldn't shake from his mind: if he had been brainwashed by smoking – and been blissfully unaware of it – what else was there that he might be brainwashed about?

Little did he know that after reading the book, not only would he never smoke again, but he would never see the world in quite the same way again either.

F·DAY -4903

The music sounded like it was inside out. The huge echoey space was sucking up the beats and melody and swirling them around like some giant acoustic blender, then spewing the resulting drawl out in all directions. Karl was in a strange night club. He had no idea where. It was like some alien, futuristic space – a giant hall tastefully lit in subdued indigo light, filled with exotic plants, moths and birds. The central glass dome was filled with a magnificent oak tree, looking even more incongruous being splashed by the insane laser show from the dance-floor around the corner. There were soft paper lanterns lining a stairway that went up the tree. Karl could see some shadowy figures kissing high in its leafy canopy.

This place is amazing, Karl thought, but not very busy. How the hell do they make this pay? He turned and walked over to the bar, a giant slab of black rock. A guy quickly appeared and Karl ordered something, but he didn't recognise the name. His words were lost in the slushy music diving around him like some music-breathing dragon, chafing the air from his lips.

A few minutes later, the barman served up the most spectacular looking cocktail Karl had ever seen. An enormous, heavy crystal glass about thirty centimetres tall, the top bowl holding a thick green juice, fading to red at the bottom, then threading down inside a complex series of glass stems – a twisted lyre of iridescent blue, copper and yellow liquids.

Karl thanked the barman and was fumbling for his wallet, but the barman just walked away and went back to where he had been sitting with his friends. It was a little strange, Karl thought, but raised the heavy glass to his lips while waiting for the barman to return. He drank a large mouthful of the green liquid and suddenly stopped. It was beautiful – like nothing he had ever tasted. It was like juice but it wasn't heavy. It was like alcohol, but it didn't sting. He felt an immediate sensation of his head clearing and his loins soaking up the fluid like some long-craven elixir. It was having an immediate effect on him, but not like being drunk, it was more like coming back from a long hill walk in the rain, puffed up with a sharp sense of nature, brimming with endorphins. It was satisfying like no other drink he had ever tasted.

Something about the music suddenly changed. The beats were getting louder? No, it was a cracking sound. Karl looked back towards the central dome and the tree. It was gunfire. A police raid? He could see uniformed men rushing around the tree, firing indiscriminately. The music suddenly cut out. People were shouting.

Now there was another noise. The sound of a chainsaw, getting louder. Rasping the air like an angry bee. Drilling into Karl's brain. The heavy glass slipped through his hand and fell to pieces on the floor. His feet were soaked in the liquid and lumps of crystal. Then they saw him.

"Over here!" one of them shouted. Karl couldn't believe they were talking about him.

The tree shook suddenly. Screams came from the branches as the great tree started to creak and snap. It fell gracelessly to the floor. They were running for him now. He had no idea why, but he had to escape. He looked for a door but they were almost on top of him. He tried one door, but their hands were on him. Shouting, accusing, hating him...

Waking. He jumped in the bed, like the sound of breaking glass. He gasped. His heart was exploding in his chest.

"What happened? Are you OK?" came Gill's sleepy voice. She was awake. Karl was glad. His terror and confusion started to subside. He looked around.

"Yeah. I'm OK" he sighed. "I'm OK..." He lay back down and could hear the swirling music again. What the hell was all that about, he thought.

F · DAY -4902

The next day, Karl was woken up at 7AM. The phone was ringing.

"Hello?" he said blearily, squinting at the clock.

"Hi Karl, sorry to wake you," came a very gentle voice.

Karl sat up and looked again at the clock. "No problem Ben, what's up?"

His brother sounded very strange – like Karl had never heard him before. He was talking very quietly and sounded like he was shaking.

"I need to ask you a big favour Karl..."

"Of course," Karl replied instantly. "Shoot!"

Like Karl, Ben had found adult life challenging at the best of times. He was an actor – and a damn good one – but, having met Barbara young and starting a family, Ben had had to settle for a string of menial jobs just to keep food on the table, while waiting for his big acting break. So far, it hadn't come. Now he was forty-seven and delivering pizzas.

"Karl, I... I... don't really know where to begin... Barbara and the kids have gone to her mum's..."

"What? She's left you?" Karl shouted incredulously. Gill looked up at him.

"No, no, no... nothing like that..." Ben was fumbling for words. "Er, things are very bad here Karl... We got behind in our mortgage..."

"OK..."

"Well, quite a lot behind..."

"For god's sake, why didn't you tell me, Ben?"

"Yeah I thought I could handle it..."

"How long are we talking about?" Karl asked, beginning to see where all this was going.

"Er, a couple of years..."

"A couple of years??" Karl exploded. Gill was up and walking around now.

"Yeah, I know, I know... well anyway, I got back from work last Tuesday night and there were two guys from the Sheriff's office at the door..." Ben was breaking up. "They served me a court order. They gave me a week..."

Karl looked at the clock. Today was Tuesday.

"They're coming today at 8.30, unless..." Ben said quietly.

"OK, Ben. Yes. Of course. What do you need?" Karl was making shrug gestures to Gill.

"Five thousand. Today... Well...now..."

"OK...no prob-"

"...and another ten thousand next week," Ben quickly finished.

Karl sighed.

"OK. Of course Ben," he said at last. "Give me half an hour."

In twenty minutes Karl was in the car. It looked like his and Gill's life holiday was going to be cut short, but he didn't mind. Ben was Ben. It was just a pity he hadn't got the recognition he deserved.

F·DAY -4897

For the months following Karl's 'de-brainwashing' epiphany, he had developed a rabid thirst for knowledge – reading up on the internet, soaking up the best and worst information on secret societies, conspiracies, aliens, lizards, alternative medicine, media hype, social engineering and psychology. The smoking book had proven to him that not all you think is what it seems, and sometimes it's worth taking a second look for a different perspective.

He didn't have much time for conspiracies in general, but he loved the way they offered a different compelling angle on mainstream thinking. Karl's curiosity was feverish. During his searches, he came across an interesting movie called *Truthfest*.

Truthfest was a veritable cornucopia of conspiracies, most notably the 9/11 terrorist attacks on the US having been perpetrated by the US Government. This was perhaps the king of all conspiracies, because of the potential ramifications if it were true, and the compelling evidence supporting it.

But for Karl, these kind of conspiracies were no more than playthings for the mind. Tantalising to believe, but, true or not, they didn't really offer anything positive or useful. As far as Karl could tell, whether foreign extremists or local politicians are bombing you, it didn't really make that much difference. Neither option is good or desirable. But Karl found something else in *Truthfest* that was far more interesting.

Since the banking collapse in 2008, people everywhere had been talking about debt and the economic crisis. Every news channel was full of celebrated economists offering their commentary and solutions to the banking mess as it was unfolding. *Truthfest*, however, offered a totally different take on the money system which Karl found fascinating.

> *"...since money is no longer backed by gold or other tangible value, this means its only value is in Government say-so. Also, it may be surprising to most people that the vast majority of new money is not even created by Government, but rather out of private commercial banks making new loans...*

> *"This means, effectively, that all new currency is subject to interest – and since the money to service that interest doesn't even exist, new money and loans must continually be created to make up the shortfall..."*

It sounded crazy. For the first time, Karl was seeing money for what it really was: a giant game based on nothing but confidence. Did this stuff that was ruling everyone's lives only have value because we say it does? It was starting to sound more like a belief than anything else. Could money actually be nothing more than a religion?

Another website that intrigued Karl was *The Earth Project* which presented an impressive alternative vision of a future world, where large-scale automation and engineering were utilised to create a world of high-technology and abundance. It reminded Karl of *Star Trek*. They had been working on designs for years to create a blueprint for the future – a future which had no use for money.

To Karl, sucking up all the information from these sites, and watching the global financial crisis get deeper and deeper, everything seemed to be pointing in one direction: Money – do we really need it?

The more he thought about this, the more it occurred to him how things might be a lot better without it. But was it possible?

He clicked another video called *'Just Imagine'*.

> *"Imagine a world without money... No more working in a job you hate. No more having to pay rent or bills. No more obscene greed or poverty. No more low quality food or products sold just to serve a bottom-line and keep a company in profit. No more consumer culture with all its waste of resources and pollution. No more poisoning the environment with cheap but dirty ways of generating energy. Imagine a cleaner, better world for all with zero financial stress."*

Wow, who wouldn't want that? A world without money would certainly be highly desirable. It would be nothing short of a new age of mankind.

But if everyone didn't have to work, wouldn't things just stagnate? The video suggested making better use of technology to do all the heavy lifting, but surely there would always be some work for people to do. Would they do it?

Karl was trying to reason it out.

Presumably, anyone who loved their jobs today would most likely continue doing them, albeit more on their own terms. And what if the jobs that technology couldn't provide for were just spread among the community? Surely that would be a minimal commitment?

It was starting to make sense to him now. If no-one had to work or worry about putting food on the table, then they would have more time and energy to dedicate to community work and projects. If a community needed a small team to fix a burst water pipe, who from that community would refuse to help since everyone benefited from the work? Also, work that strengthened community bonds would surely create its own social incentive.

It seemed to Karl that once people's basic needs are met, they *like* to help out, to work together – for the social experience, the learning, or for the sense of achievement. In fact, didn't people always work together in times of crisis, sometimes through the night until they are exhausted? He guessed this was because a crisis puts everyone on the same level, and with a common purpose. People *want* to help.

He thought back to when his own printing shop had been burgled. Almost all the other business owners in the block had come to help him clean up the mess and offer whatever assistance they could to get him back on his feet. He never forgot it.

Families too. People help each other unconditionally. In fact, maybe the only reason people compete in the world now, is because they are working for their survival? Isn't it only natural for people to compete or be greedy when they are faced with scarcity?

To Karl Drayton, it was starting to look more and more like that scarcity wasn't even real. It was actually only *financial* scarcity. There's no scarcity of water, food and shelter in the world, he thought. It's just hoarded and kept under lock and key by a market system.

Karl was always acutely aware of the great luck he had had in selling his business just before the bottom fell out of the world economy. He also knew time was precious because this money was not going to last forever. As someone who loved solving problems, this new thinking about money and the world was irresistible – and now he had an opportunity.

Just like the guy who had written the quit smoking book to cure the world of smoking, could he, in some way, help cure the world of money?

F·DAY −4886

Karl had spent many days and nights pondering this concept during his regular beach walks. He loved the sea. Both he and Gill had bought their house five years ago in the South of Ireland near the beach, far away from Dublin city. He loved the silence and the solitude there and often walked the beach, sometimes in the middle of the night, enjoying the moonlight and fresh air.

It was a beautiful golden beach, very popular with tourists in the summer, but Karl preferred to have it to himself during the long winter months. Sometimes he even felt a little indignant during the summer when everyone was out with their towels, ice creams and naked babies, taking over *his* beach!

This morning Karl was up early and decided to go for a stroll. It was a bitterly cold, windy day, and the sea was frothing and foaming over the sand. The beach itself was being whipped up by the wind, and small, elevated streams of sand were threading their way along as if following some pre-determined course.

He was leaning, pushing forward into the wind, the tails of his collar flapping madly. He started ruminating over the news item he had just read over breakfast. Ireland's *Hibernia Trust Bank* posting profits of over a billion Euro for the previous year. Karl couldn't believe it. Not only was Hibernia Trust one of the main recipients of the post-crash bailout money, but it was also Ben's bank – the bank that he had just handed over fifteen thousand Euro to a few months before to stop them putting Ben out onto the street.

"Why the hell are we all participating in this lie?!" he shouted suddenly to the wind. "All the problems in the world and these people – the politicians, the bankers and economists – they have no real solutions to offer! They just patch over things with laws, or by juggling figures.

"They talk about injustice, inequality and climate change – but all these things are the product of the scarcity-based system they are upholding! They just keep regurgitating infinitesimal changes within that status quo, and filling everyone's head with technical jargon and nonsense.

"Everyone is like, 'uh it's complicated, so I guess they're right. What's on the telly then...'. What a load of bollocks! Life isn't complicated.

Sharing and respect isn't complicated. Trying to maintain control over a false system and pretend it's working *is* complicated!"

The wind roared, bringing him almost to a stop.

"Are they really that incompetent? Or that short-sighted? Or, are they actually keeping this crock of shit going deliberately just to look after themselves?"

It was incredible – there was Ben, a married man with three children, doing his best, almost becoming homeless – in the name of arbitrary *numbers*. People all over the world – starving, dying from curable diseases and suffering – for the want of *numbers*.

To Karl, that's all money was now – just a bunch of abstract numbers attached to a belief that gave them value. Yet the suffering, stress, hunger and curable diseases were all *real* – because of this shared belief. If everyone stopped believing, its value would simply disappear – along with pretty much all those unnecessary problems and injustices.

He stopped to wipe some sand from his eye. The roar of wind in his ear was deafening. He pulled up his hood and continued.

He started thinking back to the moneyless world idea. Karl was a realist and wasn't falling for the whole utopia thing. He knew there would always be problems in the world. The world was never going to be perfect. And yes, a world without money would have its own problems – but it would still be a hell of a lot better!

"It's got to be a step in the right direction," he shouted again to the wind, "we should at least try and make it the best world we can, right?"

The wind abated a little, as if considering this new proposal.

Karl decided to just go as far as the river that day, as it was very cold and he had work to do at home. When he reached the river, he suddenly stopped and stared down. He saw something there that he had never noticed before.

The wind stopped and his face warmed, like a dawn of realisation.

The water was dead.

He recalled the river of his childhood beach memories – all those years ago when he and Ben were watching the fish. The water had been clear, deep and full of life. The river before him now was a piteous brown trickle, dull, streaked with algae. Why had he not seen this before? Years of over-farming, and the river he had played in as a child was now nothing more than a sewer.

The wind stirred again.

"Oh my god, this is happening in my lifetime!" he shouted, his words whipped and stolen by the wind. "Water is life – and look what we're doing! We are already dying!"

He put his collar back up and walked away. He didn't have a choice any more. It was time to do something.

F·DAY -4396

Karl was obsessed now, feverishly writing notes, recording ideas into his phone, trying to formulate the flood of inspiration he was having. He had experience designing websites for his business, so was thinking about creating an online movement or petition.

He liked many of the sites he had seen around the idea of a moneyless society, but felt they all lacked something. Some were just too futuristic or unrealistic looking, some were too convoluted or complicated, and others were too entangled in religious or spiritual mysticism of one kind or another.

He wanted something simple, something neutral. To take the best ideas of each and distil their combined message into a concise format that anyone could understand. He needed to find the lowest common denominator.

It didn't take him long to figure out that that lowest common denominator was freedom. It made sense. Even if money was just a shared belief, it still constricted people's behaviour and prevented them from being free to reach their full potential.

But freedom on its own was not enough. Freedom required responsibility. If no-one or no thing was governing your actions but you, then responsibility was paramount. Responsibility towards nature, other species and each other was essential.

Finally, he hit on the idea of defining a base set of requirements for such a free society – the minimum behaviour required to make it work – and to arrange these requirements into a formal document or charter that people could endorse. It was brilliant. He was super-charged now.

He took a clean sheet of paper.

The principles, he felt, should be founded on the importance of nature first and foremost. Because the Earth is a closed, living system, then surely the combined common good of *all* its creatures has to be respected above solely human considerations – even religious or ideological aspirations. He started writing.

> *"The highest concern of humanity is the combined common good of all living species and biosphere."*

> *"Life is precious in all its forms and free to flourish in the combined common good."*

Great! That was a good start. Now to declare equal ownership of the Earth's natural resources:

> *"Earth's natural resources are the birthright of all its inhabitants, and free to share in the combined common good."*

Then, the recognition of the human community as an equal, inseparable entity, not limited or constrained by borders:

> *"Every human being is an equal part of a worldwide community of humans, and a free citizen of Earth."*

Perfect. He was trying to use minimal, simple words. Next, a human community that supports its members unconditionally, and seeks to use the best methods at its disposal to create a better environment and quality of life for all species:

> *"Our community is founded on the spirit of cooperation and an understanding of nature, provided through basic education."*

> *"Our community provides for all its members the necessities of a healthy, fulfilling and sustainable life, freely and without obligation."*

> *"Our community respects the limits of nature and its resources, ensuring minimal consumption and waste."*

> *"Our community derives its solutions and advances progress primarily through the application of logic and best available knowledge."*

It was becoming an impressive document. A final word on responsibility towards the vulnerable and the future:

> *"Our community acknowledges its duty of care and compassion for members who are unable to contribute."*

> *"Our community acknowledges its responsibility to maintain a diverse and sustainable biosphere for all future life to enjoy."*

After a few edits, Karl was happy with the final text. There were ten principles in all.

"Ha! The new commandments!" he chuckled to himself.

Now all he needed was a name.

Since his ten principles were all about bringing freedom as the ultimate goal, the title needed to reflect that. Freedom was a simple concept that anyone could understand, and hopefully one day the whole world would truly realise it.

It hadn't taken him long. *The Free World Charter* was born.

F·DAY -4386

Within a couple of weeks, Karl had the bare bones of a working petition website. His idea was to find as many people as possible who would back the charter principles for building a better society. It wasn't really a petition site. Karl had no plans to direct it at anyone in particular. His idea was that if enough people backed it, it would manifest itself. Surely if such a site had several million people supporting it, it could no longer be ignored as a way forward?

The idea was tantalising, but he felt something was missing. His website was so far just a dull looking document – like a legal statement – sterile and unattractive. It needed something to lift it up – something positive and inspiring.

One day, he was passing the door of his spare bedroom when he heard a strange flapping sound. He walked in. The room was dark and dusty with cracks of sunlight coming through the blind. He rolled up the blind in a great plume of dust, and there, sitting on the window ledge was a beautiful creature. Trying to hold back his cough, Karl put out his hand. The small tortoiseshell butterfly alighted on his finger. Wings twitching, mottled brown, with bright patches of orange, white and blue.

"Well, hello there..." Karl said.

Trapped inside the house and hopelessly out of season, the poor creature had been launching itself against the glass trying to get out. It was winter and he wouldn't survive long, but for Karl, the symbolism of the butterfly and the work he was doing was immediately obvious.

A butterfly as a logo, symbolising freedom, metamorphosis, fragility and beauty. It was perfect. Karl put the insect gently back on the ledge and reached for the camera.

"One last job my friend," he said gently, "then you can go free..." He took a few pictures then opened the window. He watched the lost creature – now immortalised – flutter and tumble away in the cold breeze.

F·DAY -4380

"Yes!" Karl whispered to himself, punching the air. The video was finally uploaded.

Karl's video was a basic animated presentation outlining his idea of a money-free world. Using some images he had got from the internet and voicing a basic script over them, the video was clear and concise. He had given it a simple name: *Let's Make Everything Free'*. That should be sufficient to get people to start thinking, he thought.

After many days of tweaking the design, adding in the new video and new colourful butterfly logo, everything was finally ready. Karl hit return and *The Free World Charter* went live.

He signed it himself, then posted links to it on all the social media he could get his hands on. Twenty minutes later he got a second signatory – all the way from Thailand.

"Woohoo!" Karl shouted. "Go Thailand!"

F·DAY -4374

Signatories were coming in steadily. Karl spent the next few days promoting his site and video on various internet forums and social media. Within a week, he had almost two hundred signatures, but there was also a dark side.

The YouTube page was also alight with criticism. Karl was trying to answer them as best he could, but comments like "Fuck your communism!" or "What a load of bullshit!" or "Retard!" were coming in thick and fast. He spent time replying to each comment and trying to argue his points positively, but the more he debated, the angrier they got – some even threatening.

> *Gidgeon96: "you so fucked up man i going to come teach u a thing r two bout pain straiten ur mind a little. me and bro got*

23

your ip address now gonna come find you fucking homo commie"

Karl pushed away from the desk. He was feeling sick. He was now starting to realise that being popular is also when you make enemies. He vowed to be more careful in the future and not to fuel their anger. If the comments were nasty, it was probably best to just leave them alone. Time to do something else.

Suddenly his phone rang on the desk beside him. Karl jumped in his seat. He picked it up and clicked answer.

"Hello?"

Silence.

"Hello?"

Silence. Karl's skin suddenly started crawling up his back.

The phone went dead. He checked the screen. Unknown number.

He stared at the phone, then back at the computer where the nasty commenter's threat was still hanging there.

"Surely he can't have..." he began.

Suddenly the phone rang again. Unknown number. He went cold. This time, he said nothing.

"Hello, am I speaking to Karl Drayton?" came the distant voice eventually.

"Who is this?" Karl demanded.

"Good afternoon, Mr. Drayton, my name is Bob Stein from PhonesForever. Can I ask you if you are happy with your current phone provider?"

Karl laughed, hugely relieved.

"Haha! Yes! I love my phone provider! Mwah! Mwah!" He shouted, kissing the phone then hung up.

"Why are people so defensive about money?" he later posted to his newly formed Free Movement discussion page. Within minutes he got three answers:

> *Steve Green: "It's survival mate. People still need money to survive. You're threatening their means to survive. Fuck with that and they'll fuck with you..."*

> *Johnny Gonzalez: "Hi Karl. Money is everything to most people. We're trashing their whole belief system."*

> *Sarah Jason: "Karl, try parachuting into the Vatican and announce to everyone that Jesus is the Anti-Christ and see how many friends you make. LOL xx"*

Karl smiled. He was proud of his new little band of freedom warriors! They were right. If money was a religion, then what he was proposing was in fact nothing short of heresy. Was he going to be the new Galileo?

Despite the harsh comments from the naysayers, the signatories to the charter were still going up and up. Karl's Free World Charter was beginning to turn from a website into a movement.

Though he was not aware of it yet, his website was not the only thing moving in his life.

F·DAY -4245

Having spent so many months and late nights working on the site, he and Gill had almost become strangers in the house. Though neither of them were working, they rarely saw each other, busy in their own lives and only meeting briefly for meals before going back to their business.

Karl was becoming obsessed, not just in the website, but in a different way of looking at things. Most of the time he dared not speak to his friends or family about his ideas, as the few times he had broached the topic, they had instantly poured fire over them, and were even starting to gently distance themselves from him.

Gill didn't agree with his ideas either. They had argued so many times and now both just avoided the subject entirely. Getting rid of money was too crazy for most people, and Gill's obsession with shopping and filling the house up with useless trinkets was getting unbearable for Karl.

Karl's emerging view of the world was, he had to admit, not just an obsession. He was changing. It took him a while to realise it, but almost everything he knew about himself and his life was becoming obsolete. He was finding less and less in common with his old friends and his entire way of life.

He couldn't watch television any more. The advertising, brainwashing and media manipulation was so blatant to him now that it was unbearable. It was like someone had lifted a veil of what was really going on behind the scenes and it made watching the programs impossible. The product placement, the ever-exploding graphics, force-feeding you the next program before the current one is over. The advertising – how they try to entice you with evocative imagery for some products; with fast moving imagery for others; with shocking pictures to make you feel guilty or insecure; for charities which are really businesses; the absurdly insipid catchphrases like 'caring for you' being regurgitated over and over again. Karl realised what advertising had really become: a constant barrage of images and ideas to undermine your confidence or instil fear until you finally succumb.

Even shopping was becoming irritating. Garish signs with sales always, everywhere. 50% off! 70% off! Hurry, hurry, hurry! Don't miss out! Last chance offers! Closing down sales for shops that never close.

Money has made us crazy, Karl thought. The strategy, he guessed, was that marketeers figure that most people are too busy with their everyday struggle to question the sense or validity of the crap they were being asked to buy. If it seemed like a bargain, then that was enough.

No sense of the environmental or human cost behind the product. Confusion and insecurity were vital weapons in the profit machine.

He felt like he was on the outside looking in at the zoo of human life at feeding time. A species obsessed with numbers, he thought. Money, debts, bills, wages, prices, profits, accounting, balance sheets – numbers that we had assigned mystical importance to. The entire notion of exchange, Karl was realising, was something alien to nature. We were actually the only species who restricted ourselves in that way. Nature gives freely and expects nothing in return. The monkey takes the banana but never owes the jungle. Everything evens out in the end.

In some ways, it was satisfying for Karl to have this new-found alternative perspective, but it was also getting increasingly lonely. Gill didn't see things the way he saw them. Maybe she was getting lonely too, he thought.

Karl felt like he was now a hapless passenger on board an express train, on a journey into some unknown, uncharted country – and he was loving it. The only problem was that Gill was still at the station.

F · D A Y − 4 1 8 6

He did it. He couldn't believe it. He felt strange; guilty and elated at the same time. Last night, he had jumped in with both feet and told Gill their relationship was over.

She was shocked, but it wasn't a huge surprise to her either. Her only shock, Karl figured, was that he had had the gumption to do it. But when Karl opened his mouth, he suddenly found he couldn't stop. Everything that had been on his mind poured out. How he had changed so much, that he couldn't continue his old life, how he had found a vital new purpose, how he wanted to travel, how he wanted to have other relationships, meet new people, how unhappy he had been. He had no choice. He cared about her, but couldn't love her the way she wanted.

They cried, but both knew it was inevitable. Karl was resolute. It was his life, and he was now taking charge. For too many years he had drifted along with the flow of other people and it had left him miserable.

His desire to free the world had had an unexpected effect on him. He also needed to free himself – for better or for worse. For too many years he had been confined to the prison of struggling in business, low self-esteem, and a loveless relationship. Now he was free in every sense to do as he wished, and the feeling was indescribable!

He felt light – even dizzy, like a child spinning around and around. He was energized. He had money. He had a mission. He had no ties. For the first time in his life, the world was completely open to him.

And he was ready.

PART 2
A GLOBAL AWAKENING

He sees her.
He knows her.
But she looks like shit.

Squashed in her chrysalis,
the dark winter of her soul,
fingers bent; long scratching nails
forgotten during the freeze.
Yet still alive.

Her shrunken heart - hollow in her chest,
still murmurs, and tells of its weak existence.

Too weak to fight back; too sore to feel pain,
trapped in her translucent world
weeping inwardly.

Suddenly a miracle happens.

A yellow blade of light appears -
cuts through the undergrowth.
Finds the angle, hitherto unfound
plays heat on her brittle shell
Cracks.
Splits along a seam.

The tiny heart stirs.
The heat stings.
The air smells.
She flickers involuntarily.
Then she remembers...

Colin R. Turner – *Unfolding The Butterfly*

F·DAY -4000

feeds.theguardian.com/france:

FURTHER RIOTS – 16 PEOPLE ARRESTED

Riot police arrested 16 people and fired tear gas in violent clashes with protesters marching in Paris as striking workers continued to blockade refineries and nuclear power stations in an escalating stand-off over labour reforms.

Police fired tear gas at about 100 people on the edge of a protest march through Paris. Several masked people charged shop windows, smashing them, and cars were damaged near the route of the march. There were skirmishes at Place de la Nation as riot officers cordoned off protesters, some of whom complained of heavy-handed policing.

Read more >>

feeds.aljazeera.com:

PROTESTS IN KENYA AS OPPOSITION MARKS 'DAY OF RAGE'

At least two dead in police firing in Kisumu city as opposition supporters protest against electoral body.

At least two demonstrators were killed in police firing on Monday, as opposition supporters in Kenya blocked key roads and set fire to tyres in 'Day of Rage' protests aimed at overhauling the country's electoral system.

Protests took place in several towns but in Kisumu, an opposition stronghold in western Kenya, police opened fire before using tear gas and water cannon to quell the protests.

Read more >>

feeds.bbcnews.com/environment:

AUSTRALIA'S GREAT BARRIER REEF HIT BY 'WORST' BLEACHING

Evidence that Australia's Great Barrier Reef is experiencing its worst coral bleaching on record has renewed calls for the UN to list it as 'in-danger'. The National Coral Bleaching Task-force says 95% of reefs from Cairns to Papua New Guinea are now severely bleached due to ocean warming.

It says only four reefs out of 520 have no evidence of bleaching. UNESCO voted not to put the reef on its World Heritage in Danger list last year, but green groups want the decision reassessed. Coral task-force convener Prof. Terry Hughes told the BBC his team was yet to find the southern border where the bleaching ended.

Read more >>

F·DAY -3564

Two years had passed since Karl had jumped into the abyss. It was the first time in his adult life that he had found himself truly alone. Having always craved the company of others, fearing the silence of solitude, he had come face to face with himself at last. And he liked it. He lost the fear. He overcame the craving of attachment. After years of exile, he was beginning to like himself again.

The house that he had shared with Gill, and from where he had run his business for all those years, sold quickly. They settled their financial affairs amicably and remained good friends. Gill had a new partner, and Karl could immediately see how much happier she was. After all the heartbreak and wasted years, true love's patience had been rewarded.

Karl was also thrilled to finally see his brother Ben on television, who, after all his efforts to become a serious actor, had landed himself a ridiculous job hosting an American TV game show called 'Eat My Shorts!' – a slapstick quiz show with semi-naked contestants. Ben would never in his wildest dreams have dreamt of being a quiz show compère, but had been head-hunted for it from one of his dozens of screen tests. He loved it – and was getting very well paid. He had wasted no time in paying Karl back the money he owed him, before he and his family headed off for their new American life in upstate New Jersey. Karl was very happy for them – and also very glad to receive the money as his own had been running low.

For a while, Karl's new life had been dizzying – like being pushed out of a spacecraft without a line. He had been disorientated. No up, no down – just a universe spinning madly out of control. Finally, he had steadied himself and found the way forward: travel.

His childlike curiosity about the world had reawakened in him, and he wanted to see more. He now had almost fifty thousand signatories to the Charter in almost two hundred countries, and many offers of help from people. He would love to meet them. So he had an idea.

Could he travel around the world without using money – just relying on the generosity of people? It would be a great way to spread the message and use his own life to set an example for people. It was worth a try.

He set to work trying to enlist support and sent emails to all the signatories asking for their help with food, accommodation and transport. He was overwhelmed with the response. He had over a hundred offers of support from people all over the world, inviting him to their homes with open arms. For Karl, this was a humbling experience – to find strangers who were offering him so much. It was a seminal moment that confirmed what Karl had always thought, that people everywhere were basically good.

He enlisted the help of his friend Rob, a PR guy and Charter supporter to help promote the story. Rob put a press release together and sent it out. It worked a charm. Karl, now dubbed the 'freeworlder', made several daily papers with a feature piece announcing his plan to travel the world without money. All the lights were turning green.

That was when he met Abby.

F·DAY -3388

Abby Moore was a driven person. She had met Karl through one of the many Freeworlder chat rooms that had sprung up. She shared Karl's ideas but was also the perfect antithesis to him – over-achieving, passionate and brave. She was from Dublin's inner city, street-smart, vegan and super-fit.

A former company executive, she too had turned her back on the rat-race and began working as a life-coach cum social-worker to people in the inner city tenements, mostly for free, but sometimes through sponsorship from the local council. Like Karl, she was passionate about helping people and was already considered something of a local hero.

He and Abby had met under the Dublin Spire one cold, rainy night on Dublin's O'Connell Street and fell intensely in love. Karl had never been happier, and soon, like Abby, he became vegan too. The Charter was to promote life – and using animals for food when healthier alternatives were readily available made no sense anymore. Like Karl, Abby was also keen to travel and immediately agreed to join him on his moneyless odyssey.

Within a few months, they had left Dublin hitch-hiking, bound for Scotland on a ferry paid for by Karl's father. So began a six-month trek that brought them all across Europe, through Turkey and Iran, into Asia and India, the beautiful Sri Lanka, then through Malaysia, across to Australia and New Zealand, catching a cruiser to the Americas, Chile, Bolivia, Ecuador, Mexico, then north to Georgia, New York, Quebec, before finally landing in Iceland.

The practicalities of travelling solely without money had proved impossible at times, yet they spent little and enjoyed spectacular generosity and hospitality from people everywhere they went. They made great friends – supporters and non-supporters of the Charter, and had a great time. The world now felt like their back garden, and its people their extended family.

During their travels, they had been discussing a lot with people the

36

subject of how this moneyless world would come about. Karl was convinced that if there was ever going to be a moneyless world, it would most likely begin in one country first and spread out from there. For Karl, that country was Iceland. Being almost entirely energy self-sufficient and having a small, tightly-knit population, Iceland was perfect. Now here he was, finally, on the ground in Iceland!

As a child, Karl had always had a fascination with this place, which only grew the more he discovered. The volcanoes, the great waterfalls, the geysers, the glaciers, all filled him with awe when he was young, but no pictures from his boyhood encyclopedias measured up to the experience of actually being here.

One of Karl's Freeworlder contacts in Iceland ran a car hire company and offered Karl a free car for two weeks. He just had to supply the petrol.

"That's about as close to free as I can get," he quipped and accepted the wonderful offer. So Karl and Abby went on a fascinating tour of Karl's boyhood dreams. And Iceland delivered.

Iceland's wonders, to Karl, were not just the volcanoes, waterfalls and glaciers. The space in between them was a treasure in itself. The raw landscape, the vast, barren lava fields covered in frozen dollops of rock, carpeted with thick green moss, here and there punctuated by thin threads of rising steam telling of the restless inferno not far below.

The multicoloured heaths that wrapped the hills in wintry muted colours while the small, tough plants battled it out for the attention of the scant pollinators. The fields, eerily still and seemingly bereft of bird or animal life; the impossibly clear, clean air that quenched your lungs and charged your soul.

The warm, subdued cafés and taverns of Reykjavik bathed in candle glow, rich in the free heat from underground. Iceland was, without a doubt, one of the world's greatest treasures. The energy in the island was palpable – and not just underground.

Karl had set up meetings with some of the protest groups that had been burgeoning in Iceland since its spectacular banking collapse of

2008. He was invited to join in one of the protests on Parliament to which he agreed. What he saw there disappointed him a little.

There had been fresh elections a couple of years before, and the old Government had been ousted in favour of the opposition party, The People's Party, who promised to help out hard-pressed people with their mortgages whose repayments had almost doubled since the collapse.

Of course, this never happened. Though most people readily accepted that politicians love to make alluring false promises before election-time, Karl, unlike most of his contemporaries, felt that most politicians were actually earnest in their intentions, but get tangled up in the red tape outside their control, which ultimately chokes the life out of their idealism.

Today, the newly elected parliamentarians were filing out of the church on their way to the Alþingi, Iceland's parliament, for the first time after summer recess. What Karl saw disappointed and saddened him. Outside the steel barriers that had been installed for the event, a group of around two thousand people had assembled and all began booing, banging the steel barriers with their feet, name-calling and blowing football sirens, under the watchful gaze of the armed police. But what he saw on the other side of the barriers disappointed him even more.

He saw ashen-faced, scared people – the politicians – watching the protests as they walked by just metres away. Karl could sense not just their fear, but also their own sense of helplessness and disappointment in the impossible situation they had found themselves in. Karl quickly realised that the answer to Iceland's problems didn't lie on either side of those steel barricades. It looked liked no-one really knew what to do.

Karl met with several of the protesters afterwards. One man, Vern, was something of a local hero. Having successfully overturned a mortgage judgement against him, his case had become widely publicised. He was a curious, tall and distant character who always had the appearance of thinking deeply about something else when you were talking to him.

"So you think that maybe these people would go for the moneyless idea?" Karl had asked.

"Well, yes and no..." Vern said, fading out and looking at the rooftops.

Karl followed his gaze over to the rooftops, but couldn't see the attraction.

"What do you mean?" he asked.

"You will need to ask them, I think," Vern said finally.

Karl couldn't imagine this guy being any sort of role model or leader to mount a campaign.

Another protester, Mikkael, a teacher and prominent eco-activist, spoke very well to Karl and politely listened to the moneyless idea, but didn't seem to want to stay around to hear the details. Karl was disappointed.

Finally, he met Jeni and her husband Gunnar, a struggling middle-class couple with teenage children. They were strong environmental activists who had a particular issue with the Icelandic Government's apparent blasé attitude to their beautiful country. After talking to them, it wasn't long before Karl understood what the problem was with Iceland.

"How can you suggest such a thing when we are already having so many difficulties paying our bills?" Jeni had burst out. "Things are already bad – and now we're to have no money? Isn't life hard enough already?"

Karl gently tried to explain but she was belligerent.

"These fucking politicians and bankers have ruined this country and our lives and no-one is doing anything about it. We're all suffering here while they are just doing nothing!"

Karl understood now. He felt sorry for Jeni, but he realised what the real problem was. The people were more intent on blame than in problem-solving.

Iceland, as Karl saw it, had the answer right under its nose – underneath its very rocks in fact – a practically infinite store of free energy just waiting to be unleashed, but people couldn't see past the blame and retribution.

"No," Karl explained, "the real problem is that people think money is some unmovable certainty – something we can't live without, but we can't truly solve our problems unless we start to consider money as optional."

Jeni didn't look convinced. Karl continued.

"Once people have the flexibility to see money as optional, not required, then the mind begins to find solutions in surprising ways. We all use money to survive, so we naturally assume that survival is not possible without it. Almost every single human thought, word or action is based around money as the central pivot on which society hinges – but if we can break that connection, we will discover the limitless possibilities for our species that lie beyond."

Karl and Abby stayed in Iceland for two weeks enjoying the spectacular scenery before finally heading home for Ireland. They had been travelling non-stop for six months and they had had enough. It was time to settle down for a while.

Karl had had plenty of ideas during their travels. He was still optimistic, despite all the negativity of the islanders, that Iceland could potentially be a pioneering moneyless state. The potential for it was too tantalising – even if the locals couldn't see it themselves. He decided to set up a Facebook group and call it 'Iceland: the world's first money-free country' to see if he could get more support for the idea. Maybe if Icelanders saw the interest in it they might consider it?

Secondly, he had been toying with the idea of building a countdown clock into the site to 'World Freedom Day' – the day the world would declare itself free of money. He felt both ideas could complement each other and offered a unique way of focusing on the 'free' idea. He was going to be busy again, but he loved it.

Things were going to get a lot busier for him than he thought. Abby had another little side project for him that was busily growing in her tummy.

F·DAY -3260

MEET GAMA – THE ONLINE AI DOCTOR

Researchers at Gray's Biotech Inc. in Massachusetts have unveiled the world's first online AI doctor, GAMA. G.A.M.A. – which stands for Grey's Analytical Medical Adviser, is an artificial intelligence that draws medical knowledge from various sources and applies it to user queries. GAMA has already 'read' tens of millions of medical books, journals and papers from open access repositories.

Keen to emphasize that GAMA is not a doctor replacement, CEO Mark Staedlar said: "GAMA is just a medical assistant, designed to ease the work load from the local GP and physician. GAMA already has all the knowledge of every medical specialist combined and is also continually learning. Users can ask GAMA any medical question and GAMA will return all the pertinent questions to move towards diagnosis and/or test recommendations. Patients can then take a printout of GAMA's findings to their local doctor to proceed to the next stage."

Read more >>

MOSCOW 'TATSY' GATHERING DISPERSED

Police moved in late last night on Red Square to remove the 'Tatsy' gathering that had begun camping there three days ago. The group of around 150 people and their equipment were moved by police without incident. Tatsy, the free food cooperative that began in London, had set up five makeshift kitchens on the Square run by volunteers, offering an assortment of free meals and soup to passers-by.

The police later issued a statement praising the Tatsy group for their peaceful cooperation but warning the public of the dangers of accepting food from unlicensed vendors.

A spokesman for the London Tatsy, Tom said, "Ask yourself, which is more outrageous? Giving away free food? Or stopping someone from giving away free food?"

Read more >>

F·DAY -3212

With all the excitement over their impending new arrival, Karl and Abby had never felt closer. Soon after arriving back in Ireland they moved to seal their relationship.

On a spring morning, they eloped to a far-flung corner of the island and engaged the services of a local pagan druid to officiate their union in a Celtic hand-fasting ceremony – their only witnesses the local flora, the hidden fauna, and the open sky. It was the perfect union and they both felt truly blessed.

After enjoying a few days holiday, they got busy organising their home in Dublin, in readiness for their new family member. Karl had managed to organise some gigs and was playing music again on the weekends.

Since settling back, Karl had created the Facebook Iceland group and devised a working countdown clock to his hypothetical day of world freedom. His idea was to count down to an arbitrary date in the future, then to subtract or add seconds to the clock according to relevant world events. Day zero or 'F-Day' would be the day when the world's largest economy decided to give up money. He set it to fifty years.

Soon after going live, the F-Day clock started getting lots of interest from the other similar free movements. *Truthfest* was the first to react and they posted links to the site on their Facebook pages and websites all over the world. Karl had included a version that people could embed on their own pages and it was already getting plenty of embeds.

Karl included *Truthfest* as the second official contributors to the Free Day Clock. They too would be able to deduct seconds from the clock as they saw fit. That fact alone was significant enough, Karl reckoned, to deduct the first round of seconds. It was all guesswork of course, so he subtracted five hundred thousand seconds from the total clock – almost six days. It would be a self-organising system that would improve over time.

It wasn't long before word about the clock was spreading. Its cheeky, perpetual certainty made people curious. That's exactly what Karl wanted. In a world where most people seemed asleep or oblivious to what was really going on around them, this offered the perfect jab of altered consciousness. While they toiled away in their jobs, this innocuous little clock was busy ticking them into a completely different reality.

The comments section was alive with both the highest enthusiasm and lowest scathing criticism. But criticism or not, the viral effect of the site was way more than Karl had expected.

It was also a lot more than Mike Ross had expected, who, without even blinking, swept the F-Day Clock off his giant touchscreen and started googling. In two minutes, he had Karl Drayton's mobile number.

F·DAY -3199

Mike Ross was a wiry red-headed man, who described himself as "the closest thing to a fortune-teller without stealing". He was a freelance media guru. To say he had his finger on the pulse would be grossly inaccurate – he had usually finished writing all about the pulse before it even happened. His job – and what his clients paid him obscene amounts of money for – was to find the next big thing.

He wore heavy-rimmed red framed glasses as if to exaggerate his carrot-colour hair, only to then complement everything with blueberry dungarees and a green cheesecloth shirt. He was, quite literally, an industrial strength nerd. He spent every day in his shabby New York office with the blinds closed in front of half a dozen screens, surrounded by empty paper cups and take-away boxes. He was a hunter, prowling the back alleys of the net, cloaked in a thousand different user identities and misdirected IP addresses. Usually he never even knew what his prey was, but he sure knew it when he found it. Today, Karl Drayton was it.

Mike had signed the Free World Charter some months before under one of his many identities, just to get himself on the mailing list to see if anything interesting popped up. He did this with dozens of sites every day. It was just a chore and the dullest part of his job that he usually did while talking on the phone. Mailing lists, he had discovered, were where news happened before anyone else knew about it. He had all his email programs set up with keyword triggers to monitor the thousands of newsletter emails he received every day. Three such words were 'era', 'arrival' and 'countdown'. The more keywords hit, the higher up the email got in his 'readable' list.

A few days ago, Mike – or rather his pseudonym 'Jake' – had received the email announcing the Free Day Clock:

> *"Hello Jake, F-Day is excited to announce our very latest initiative: The Free Day Clock. We are counting down to a new era. Check it out: f-day.org/clock.*
>
> *"We believe The Free Day Clock will help raise awareness of the impending necessity for a money-free world, by quietly announcing its arrival through a simple countdown. We have set the clock to begin counting down to an arbitrary date fifty years from now, but with a provision for time to be subtracted from the clock as world events dictate. For example, if a single country decided to go money-free, we could subtract some years from the clock to bring the countdown closer.*
>
> *"We are defining Day Zero as the day when the world's largest economy goes money-free. Please check it out and share the*

website around if you can.

"Thank you,

"Karl Drayton, F-Day."

Mike was pleasantly piqued by the email's confidence and brevity, so he followed the link. What he saw was a large old-style digital clock counting down the seconds, minutes, hours and days to just over eighteen thousand days from now. Beside it were links to F-Day and other information, but what got his attention immediately were the likes and comments:

> *'114,508 people like this page*
> *89,012 comments'*

Mike had a nose for this kind of thing – and now every hair in his nose was twitching. Somewhere in this was a hot story. He googled around to do some basic cross-checks, then went for Karl's number and dialled.

Karl had just got into the shower when the phone rang. He cursed, threw on a towel and ran to the bed.

"Yeah hello?" he said breathlessly.

"Hello, is that Mr. Karl Drayton?" came the voice.

Karl was intrigued by the soft, nasally New York accent.

"Yes, Karl here."

"Good morning Mr. Drayton. My name is Mike Ross. I'm calling from Redross Media Associates in Brooklyn New York. I have a few questions about your..." he woke the screen "...F-Day Clock I'd like to ask you if I may?"

"Er yeah, sure thing. Shoot," Karl replied, sitting down on the bed and folding his arms for warmth.

"Thank you. I saw your clock page has over a hundred thousand likes but it seems to be only active since two weeks ago. Am I right? Can I ask how you got those sort of numbers to your page?"

Karl was chuffed. "Sure," he said. "Yes, that's right. I have a large mailing list of signatories from the Free World Charter, and we've had a lot of help from The Truthfest Movement. Are you familiar with those sites?"

"Yeah, I know the Free World Charter and I'm checking out the other one now. I've been looking down through some of the comments and I gotta tell you it's pretty freaking crazy in there. So much love and so much hate, all together. What's the deal with that, do you think?"

"Ha ha!" Karl burst out. "That's par for the course I'm afraid. What we're proposing freaks most people out – until they get it, that is," Karl added wryly.

"So let me see, you're proposing a moneyless society, where no-one works but yet everyone helps each other out, is that right?"

"Er, no not quite. We're proposing a society that has evolved beyond the use of money through a re-prioritisation of human values and efficient use of technology and education, as a replacement for the broken, unfair and unsustainable model that we use today." Karl could feel himself getting a little annoyed, but he thought he had summed it all up quite well nonetheless.

"Cool. Mr. Drayton, would you be interested in doing an interview with one of the majors here in the States?"

Abby had walked in and gave Karl the questioning 'who's on the phone' look. Karl looked at her and shrugged.

"Er, yeah sure," he said, then quickly added, "what have you got in mind?" which was really his oblique way of saying he had no idea what a 'major' was.

"Er, leave it with me for now and I'll see what I can set up. I have your email address anyway. If you don't hear from me they'll probably get in touch with you themselves. Thank you very much, Mr. Drayton. Have a nice day."

"OK sure, thank you. You too." Karl pressed the phone and stared at it for a moment.

"Who was that?" Abby asked.

"Dunno... something media associates. I'm not sure. I think they want to interview me," Karl said vaguely. He threw down the phone and towel and bolted for the shower. He was freezing. Abby picked up the towel in his wake and put it on the radiator, shaking her head.

"They're in New York," he shouted from the shower.

Mike Ross did something he rarely did. He stood up, walked over and opened the blind. His office was like a set from some 70s TV detective series. He was quite proud of that fact. He felt he was a detective – a world detective, working for the big media giants, sniffing out the next big scoop before it happens. He loved and lived by that old catchphrase: 'If you can see the bandwagon, you're already too late'.

He stood straight and stared out the window at the Manhattan skyline, the cars, the people, the sleepy Hudson below – the view that people pay big bucks for – that he was paying big bucks for. He found himself looking down at the seeming futility of people rushing around through their busy lives and never seeing the bigger picture – the picture that he could see, the picture that now, through his work, he had some considerable control...

Mike was the consummate workaholic, single, obsessed, living on junk food, living to work. He rarely checked his bank accounts, but they were pretty sizeable. He could retire today if he wanted to, but for what? He would have nothing to live for. He loved his job. He loved the chase. Maybe that's why the free world idea resonated so much with him today.

For him, the money was irrelevant. For most rich people it's everything, and they're still not happy – not because the money doesn't make them happy, but because it takes them away from what does make them happy. Most parents say their children make them happy, but they spend the best part of their day being away from them, doing shit for money that doesn't make them happy.

The free world idea made Mike realise how lucky he was – and how lucky most people aren't. He wanted to talk to Karl for no reason other than to see if he existed, to see if he was a normal person, to get a sense of the man who was single-handedly trying to dismantle the largest ever social edifice: the monetary system.

Mike's sense was sharp and he worked quickly. Karl Drayton was ripe. It was time to make some calls.

F·DAY -3193

Karl was busy in his home office. Abby was downstairs painting. He was typing up a press release for his PR friend Rob all about the F-Day Clock. Rob was a great guy, who had helped Karl on his moneyless travels the previous year. He had got him an interview on BBC and with two of the big press agencies. Of course Rob was doing it voluntarily, which was great, but unfortunately, in this world, it made things slow.

Karl decided to talk to Rob about the release, so he opened up his video chat, saw Rob online and called.

"Hey," Rob said. Rob was a chunky, cheeky guy, with a deep Yorkshire accent, very relaxed about life and happy in his own skin.

"Hi Rob," Karl said. "How are you?"

"Pretty good, my friend," Rob said cheerily. "How's the new house coming?"

Karl smiled. He and Abby had just moved in a month ago and were still doing up the place.

"It's looking great, my friend. Abby's doing some painting in the hall."

"Oh keep her busy fella... keep her busy," Rob quipped in his adorable accent, winking.

"Ha, yeah!" Karl grinned, while looking down at an email that had just come in, "Listen Rob, about this press release, that last paragraph..."

Karl cut off.

"Yo..." said Rob.

"Mm"

"Mm? Hello?" Rob urged, looking side to side. "What's up lad?"

"You won't fucking believe this..."

"What?? Speak up man!" Rob boomed in a theatrical voice.

"I'm on CNN next week. The *FutureNow* programme!!"

"..." Rob was open-mouthed.

"Exactly..." Karl read it again. "'Dear Mr. Drayton... would like to interview you at our TV centre, New York for our feature-piece *FutureNow*... to be aired July 18th ...to include flights to and from Ireland, hotel, transfers and expenses... please respond as soon as possible to confirm arrangements... 'This is amazing!!"

"Oh you won't be needing me anymore then," said Rob as he robotically lowered himself down and off the screen.

"Ha ha!! This is brilliant Rob! Amazing! And don't worry, your job is only beginning..."

"Really?" said Rob, head sliding back up the screen hopefully.

"Ha! Got to go tell Abby. Ciao dude!"

"Chow mein Fuhrer," said Rob, hands together, head bowing.

"Abby!" Karl shouted.

F·DAY -3180

Karl was nervous. He had kissed Abby goodbye and was queueing at the terminal to board the plane. For some reason, this trip was making him nervous. It wasn't the flights or the travelling. That was fine. He couldn't place it. It was like all his unseen work in the last few years was suddenly being pulled out into the daylight for public scrutiny. He felt an uneasy weight on his shoulders. It was all very easy to sit in your home office formulating ideas and putting it up on a website, but sitting down in a TV studio to argue those points with experts live to millions of people was a different ball-game. Hmm, maybe the Americans would appreciate that 'ball-game' metaphor?

He was very confident with his subject material, but now he was being put to the test.

He got on the plane and was shown to his seat in business class. Wow, he thought. This was another life. Lots of space. He looked around at his fellow business class travellers, mostly guys in shirtsleeves on their iPads, and the occasional young, well-heeled family travelling in the style to which they are accustomed.

Arriving at JFK airport, Karl was immediately plucked from the crowd by a highly efficient liaison officer for CNN. None of your grubby handwritten signs, Karl thought. This girl had done her homework.

"Good morning, Mr. Drayton" she beamed. "My name is Laura Mills for CNN."

She offered her hand and shook his.

"Hi Laura, lovely to meet you."

"Likewise," she said warmly. "We have a car waiting outside and I'll fill you in on the way."

"Thank you."

Outside a large black Lexus was parked in the VIP section and Laura ushered him inside. After the satisfying 'chunk' of the door closing, the driver moved off and Laura began.

"Welcome to New York, Mr. Drayton. We'll bring you to your hotel now as I'm sure you need some rest. Tomorrow the debate goes out at 4.35pm, but we need you in the studio by 9am to go through rehearsals and show you the format. Our driver will pick you up at 8.15 from your..."

"Hang on – 'debate'??" Karl interjected. "No-one mentioned anything about a debate?"

Laura looked puzzled. "Er, yes. It's a standard format for this show. *FutureNow* is a show about the future, but we have a 20-minute debate segment where we get people together with different ideas about the future to debate the possibilities with each other. I'm sorry if no-one told you. I hope it's OK for you?"

"Well, yes... I guess," said Karl distractedly. "So who am I up against?" he asked wryly.

"Ha ha, don't worry, it's not a boxing fight! Tomorrow we have yourself and Dr. James Fallon, an economist from Michigan who has invented a system of open-source banking which he claims can solve global economic problems by decentralising bank ownership."

"Nice," Karl muttered and immersed himself in the passing madness of 42nd Street.

F·DAY -3179

"...thanks for that Maria, let's watch that story and see how it develops," said Norman, the square-jawed programme compère in his musically-perfected TV voice. "Now it's time for today's FutureNow Spotlight!"

The studio speakers suddenly exploded into life with the ridiculously excessive jingle marking the beginning of the programme segment, while the VT went to a cheesy spinning-globe and spaceship motion graphic. Karl was not in the least nervous. In fact, he wasn't even particularly interested anymore. He was just going to use this as an experiment. He was disappointed about the debate format and didn't really care much about this interview anymore.

"Today we have in studio Karl Drayton, founder of F-Day, a movement that proposes the abolition of all money and trade, and Dr. James Fallon, economist and inventor of OpenTeller – an online bank which has no owner. Both gentlemen believe that they hold the key to the future of economics. Here they are to tell us more. Welcome gentlemen."

They nodded and mumbled simultaneously.

"Dr. Fallon, if I can start with you. OpenTeller – a bank with no owner? What is it and how does it work?"

"Thank you, Norman. OpenTeller is a software bank that is the sole property of its depositors. There are no shareholders beyond the depositors themselves. We have devised a fully autonomous banking system that regulates itself based purely on the data and transactions that are feeding into it.

"As you know Norman, many times in the past we have seen how the actions and mistakes of banking directors and leaders, under pressure from shareholders, have crashed banks and even wrecked countries' economies. Today, we have enough artificial intelligence technology that can eliminate this kind of human error forever and have a bank that is run fairly for its depositors only."

"That sounds fascinating Dr. Fallon. Let's discuss it in a moment. Mr. Drayton, your idea is even more far-fetched. No banks, no money, no trade? Nothing? Tell us about the theories behind the Free World Charter."

"Good afternoon Norman. It's great to be here. Well, the theories behind the Charter are nothing new, nor are they even mine. I just put them together in one place. The concept of a money-free society has been around for a long time, and of course, was used in practice for many thousands of years before money existed.

"Now this idea is coming back into the fore now for a few reasons. First, our global economy is grinding inexorably to a halt as it needs so much debt just to sustain itself; second, we are now beginning to understand that our prioritisation of profit over nature is clearly not going to work out well for us long term, and third – where perhaps myself and Dr. Fallon will agree – our technology has now reached a point where all manner of incredible things are possible. There is..."

"Thank you, Mr. Drayton," Norman cut in surgically. Karl froze mid-syllable. "If I could come back to you, Dr. Fallon..." Karl relaxed. "Why would I put my money into OpenTeller? What makes it different for me as a customer?"

"Well, there's no difference in what facilities OpenTeller can offer," Dr. Fallon answered. "We are taking deposits and loaning money just like any other bank. The only difference you will see is in our stability, and of course our fees. Since there are no employees except technical staff to pay, our overheads are a tiny fraction of a traditional bank – and of course our bank is far more efficiently run..."

Karl was feeling mischievous. "*Our* bank?" he said. "I thought your bank had no owner?"

Dr. Fallon darted a glance at Norman who again expertly interceded, "You'll have a chance to debate in a moment, Mr. Drayton. Dr. Fallon, you mentioned your bank even gives out loans. How does that work? Who makes the decisions on loan eligibility?"

"We have built a series of AI-based algorithms for making loan decisions that take account of many factors and input from the client. This also eradicates bad human decision-making which ultimately protects the other depositors. We haven't had any problems so far. Similarly, we have a set of algorithms that govern interest rates and fees based on our internal data and live external data from the markets."

"So OpenTeller is up and running now?" asked Norman.

"Yes, we currently have over five hundred active accounts, eighty of which are successfully performing loan accounts. The service is still being tested, but we will begin rolling out a national campaign later this year."

"It sounds like a great idea. The very best of luck with it." Norman chirped, in his musically-perfected fake enthusiasm. Karl was starting to think about his dinner.

"Mr. Drayton, how does a moneyless society work? Will it work?"

"It will work, just as soon as we *want* it to work, and break away from our current cultural conditioning. Money, and the whole idea of exchange comes from a time of primitive technology and scarcity. We have now outgrown these limitations.

"We have technology today that can provide for everyone on the planet easily, yet we still use this archaic idea of exchange for people to access their basic requirements. The only reason we are still doing this is because the people who benefit most from that system are the ones who control it and, of course, see no reason to change it.

"I should point out that while the Free World Charter *does* advocate a money-free society, it is not the highest or sole purpose of the Charter. We are advocating first and foremost the urgent need for mankind to realign with nature and to understand his *true* place and purpose in the world.

"As a species, we have become detached from nature, from our own community, from each other – even from ourselves. The endless race for arbitrary numbers that we call 'money' is literally consuming us."

Norman sat back a little in his chair and nodded barely to Dr. Fallon.

"With all due respect Mr. Drayton," Dr. Fallon began, "you didn't answer the question. How can a moneyless society work? Why on earth would anyone do anything?"

"Because they want to. If you want to talk about algorithms, our human conditioning is itself an algorithm – a set of instructions that tells people how to act based on a given input. We believe that we only do things if someone pays us, for instance. We believe we can't have an apple unless we pay for it. We believe hard work will give us greater rewards, even if it makes us miserable. These beliefs have no basis in reality. All of this human 'software' is loaded into us through our cultural conditioning, but really this is fluid and changeable. Most people can't see that because all their thoughts exist only inside that algorithm."

"I don't think you can compare humans to computers, Mr. Drayton," Dr. Fallon said dryly. "People want to gain an advantage. If money gives them that opportunity, then so what?"

"'*So what*' is precisely the attitude that is poisoning our land, water and air, Dr. Fallon," Karl snapped. "And is the reason God knows how many millions will die from starvation and curable diseases this year; the reason we are blindly facilitating the mass extinction of thousands of species every year, the destruction of our oceans,..." Karl could feel himself starting to get angry so he checked himself a little.

"Look," he continued, "people believe capitalism is the driving force behind progress and efficiency, but this is an illusion. We only attribute progress to capitalism because we are simultaneously doing both. We are progressing anyway. Can you imagine the guy who invented the wheel refusing to share his invention until he received payment? No, me neither.

"People do things because people *want* to do things. We like to improve our situation, we like to improve ourselves, we like to be stimulated, we like to meet people, we like to work together. It's not complicated. People do the things they love – because they love doing it."

Dr. Fallon was silent.

"People shouldn't do things they hate, Dr. Fallon, but they do. In fact, almost all of human misery is people doing things they hate because they believe they have no choice. We are prisoners of our own minds – because we are only conditioned one way – and usually the way that benefits the one doing the conditioning."

Karl was starting to get angry now at himself, but not because he was getting so impassioned, because he didn't like the approach he was taking. He was starting to come across preachy – and he hated that.

They were going to go for the jugular – and they were right.

"So you believe that some dark force or 'Illuminati' is controlling people for their own purpose?" Norman asked, vaguely smiling.

"No," Karl said quickly, glad of the question. "I certainly don't believe any organised malevolent force is seeking to enslave mankind. That's an absurd notion, which if you think about it, is itself centred on the belief that money is an immovable certainty. Our problem is not people, but a system that *rewards* people for greedy behaviour.

"We have to dismantle that system urgently – start seeing beyond money and focusing on the things that really matter: life, nature, our community, our relationships, the future, progress, technology, freedom. That's what the Free World Charter is proposing – how amazing we can truly be if we just base our society on what's actually important.

"Money is an invention, based loosely on the law of the jungle: eat or be eaten. We can do a lot better than this now. I believe mankind is ready to transcend this animal state and become true adult citizens of the cosmos. We are breaking out of our chrysalis."

"...to boldly go where no man has gone before?" Norman quipped, with a faint grin to James.

"Absolutely," Karl said defiantly. "Why not?"

The studio speakers suddenly burst into life again. "Thank you, Karl. We'll be back for more on this right after these messages. Don't go away." Norman chirped.

F·DAY -3178

Karl woke up with a headache. The hotel room was so stuffy and his mouth was dry. Maybe it was the late glass of wine he had had when talking to Abby before bed. Or maybe it was the interview.

He felt bad about the interview. He was too angry, too preachy. He imagined most American families watching him open-mouthed, wondering what trip he was on before they changed the channel over to cartoons. His 'opponent' James Fallon and Norman had shaken his hand politely after the interview and left him standing in the studio – maybe to go grab a beer and discuss Norman's giant investment in James' 'unowned' bank, Karl mused. He had felt a little deflated and like a lost kitten afterwards, until some kindly camera assistant came and showed him where to go and what to do next. He had been glad to get out of there.

Karl got up and put on his dressing gown and decided to indulge himself in a little capitalism before breakfast, so he rang the desk and ordered breakfast to his room. Why not, he thought to himself. Everyone else was doing it and he felt a little despondent.

He picked up his tablet and checked to see if anyone was taking him seriously last night. He logged on to the Charter website and was astonished. Over eleven thousand new signatories in the last twenty-four hours – and climbing! The interview had gone out live, but was repeated later in the night and had gone to the web too.

"Fucking hell! Wow!" Karl shouted. He threw the tablet on the bed and went to brush his teeth. A minute later he came back with toothbrush foaming in his mouth and went to check his YouTube channel. He had gotten over a hundred thousand views in the last day!

"Mmmmnnhhh!!!" he shouted through his toothpaste. It was incredible. He was delighted. He hadn't watched the interview himself but it looked like – preachy or not – he had pressed quite a few peoples' buttons last night. Karl's campaign had just taken a giant leap! The game was beginning to change.

And his phone was ringing. Karl ran for the sink.

"Mr. Drayton?" came the voice.

"Speaking."

"Good morning Mr. Drayton, this is Anna Gúzman, business affairs reporter from ABC News. Are you still in New York?"

F·DAY -3166

Karl had had an exhausting few days in New York. He had done a very polished fifteen-minute interview with ABC that he had been fully prepared for this time. He had been calmer in his approach, finishing with what he thought was a great answer to how such an idea was going to happen across the world if different countries didn't agree on it.

"Bob, we don't need everyone to agree straight away. There are many countries where this could happen now, today. Iceland, for example, is a perfect choice for an open economy. They're small, energy self-sufficient and a have strong sense of community.

"Ultimately all these borders are meaningless anyway. We are all human. We share the same lands, waters and air, and we need to start working together to preserve them. Isn't it time we all stopped being prisoners inside imaginary lines drawn by dead people?" he had said defiantly.

It was one of those sentences that hung very nicely in the studio air for a moment, and Karl could feel it hitting home.

He had some hours to kill before going to the airport, so he called Podge.

Karl had met Podge online – a keen Charter advocate. He had been involved in the Occupy Wall St. protests but, like so many, had eventually came to the realisation that the banking system was not just corrupt, but in fact entirely obsolete. He was telling Karl that the Occupy protests had almost completely disbanded. People had lost interest and, of course, the economy was turning around, so people were getting more work too.

"Don't you think it's bizarre," Podge asked, sitting cross-legged on his apartment floor, "how quickly people lose sight of the problems once their own needs are satisfied? Do you think it's because they don't really care as long as they are OK, or is it just that they are too busy and have less time to think about wider issues?"

Podge was one of those characters that you would run a mile from if you met him in a back alley. Well over six feet tall, covered with tattoos and piercings, wild grey eyes and completely bald. But like many people Karl had met along the way, his dirty punk appearance belied the sweet soul and dark intelligence beneath.

"Hmmm," Karl pondered. "Yes, I've often wondered that myself. But then I wonder how would I act in that situation. I think, for me, being busy wouldn't change my attitude about things, but it would change the amount of time I give to it. I'm sure you know how easy it is to get people to agree to something that makes great sense, but getting them to act on that information is an entirely different matter – especially in a minority cause."

"Absolutely," Podge said as he stood up to help himself to more coffee. "More?"

"Yes, please." Karl offered his cup. "There is another possibility you know."

"What's that?" Podge asked, as he poured the coffee and placed the floral tea cosy back on the coffee pot.

"What if it's not that people are too busy? What if the reason the Occupy movement is petering out is because, deep down, people don't believe it is the solution?"

"Go on..." Podge squatted back on the floor.

"When I was travelling, meeting lots of other freeworlders and strangers, I got a huge sense that almost everybody believed that we – society that is – were on the edge of something big. Everyone, even inadvertently, was talking like some big change was coming down the tracks very soon. It was like some subconscious foreknowledge that everyone shared."

"Yes! I've got that too!" Podge said, becoming animated. "People are talking like it's the end of an era or something. It's weird."

"Yes, it's very strange, but not surprising. There's so much information floating around out there that flies in the face of generally accepted reality. Wikileaks, Piratebay, The Truth Movement, Occupy, Open Source, all the climate change and other eco warnings. It's easy to see, either we decide to change, or nature will decide for us. It's an easy subconscious calculation to make."

"True," Podge said.

"What if supporters of Occupy inwardly believe the answer lies deeper than just banking reform? What if we try and get their support for a post-money system altogether?" Karl was getting animated now. "What if we try and start a Free Movement from Occupy? The network is already there, the precedent is there. It could happen easily."

"I'm not so sure," Podge said, "a lot of the Occupy guys were looking for bankers' blood on the sidewalk! I'm not so sure those guys are ready to call for complete abolition of banks. They'd rather send them all to the chair and watch them fry."

"Yes, sure, but maybe a fresh tide of free, non-violent sentiment will dislodge these guys and we'll create a new movement altogether from the ashes of Occupy?"

"It sounds awesome dude."

"Can you help? Can you talk to some people?"

"I'm on it. I can think of around twenty people I know from Occupy who were always on with this angle. I'll connect with them and see if we can spread things from there. It's not such a big leap for the others. I'm sure we can make something move."

"Brilliant!" Karl was really excited. "I love recycling!"

"Ha ha!! Bring it on, bro!"

Karl was on fire when he left Podge's apartment. A combination of too much coffee and inspiration was making him giddy. He hopped into a yellow cab and started heading for JFK. On the way, he got a text from Rob: 'The game is afoot in Iceland dude! Have you seen the Facebook page?'. Karl took out his tablet.

"Ha!" he shouted. The taxi driver looked up in the mirror, but Karl couldn't stop smiling. "The game is afoot!"

The Indian driver frowned fleetingly, then quickly resigned himself to having yet another crazy fare in the back. But for Karl, the game was afoot indeed. His Iceland page had overnight gained another twenty thousand followers.

`f-day.org/feeds/update:`

US INTERVIEWS AND GROWTH [-1000 DAYS]

On foot of the recent US interviews and gains in signatories for both the Charter and the Iceland page, I am deducting 100 days from the F-Day clock.

F-Day.org >>

F·DAY -3164

President Baldur Reyksson was a cheerful, optimistic sort. That was probably what had got him the job. Having been one of the few businessmen in Iceland completely unaffected by the economic crisis, his positivity had been more than refreshing when he had decided to run.

An organic farmer from the north of the island, Baldur worked his farm almost without using any money whatsoever. He was known for his great produce, and, in Iceland, where temperatures rarely go up into double digits, anyone who can successfully farm grain and vegetables is held in an almost supernatural awe. He was famous for his barley, which he gave out liberally and freely to the people in his community. For that, he had earned himself the moniker 'Captain Barley'.

Going into politics had been something of a game for him as he was a playful soul, but he had also been gently shouldered into it by his fellow villagers, not least because of his charisma, but also because of his supernatural air. They were of the opinion that if anyone could sort their country's mess, Captain Barley can! Of course, what never occurred to them – as Reyksson rode to an overwhelmingly decisive victory – was that complex economic problems were not the staple of the humble organic farmer. He was a practical problem solver, that's all – not an economist. And that is precisely what would make the difference to Iceland.

As he sat in his dressing gown, eating his barley porridge, there was Karl Drayton staring right back at him from the front cover of yesterday's Reykjavik Grapevine. The headline read 'I want YOU to go free!' He knew the face, but couldn't place it. He started reading the article, then he remembered. Of course, he thought, it was Karl, the guy he had read about travelling the world without money. He read on to see what it was all about.

He was due to give a keynote speech at lunchtime in the University, so he had a little time to find out more. It appeared that Karl and his Free Movement had set up a Facebook page suggesting that Iceland go money-free as a pioneering experimental state for a money-free world. He would have easily laughed off the idea until he saw that the page had almost fifty thousand followers – that was a considerable chunk of Iceland's population. He read on.

At first, Baldur thought the idea of a moneyless country was completely barking mad, but it wasn't long until his farming mind kicked in and he started to see the practical sense in it. Iceland was a wonderfully resourceful country. If anyone knew that, it was him. Everything that Karl was saying was making sense. "Iceland has all the free energy it will ever need, the population is small, resourceful, closely knit, very eco-aware and tech-savvy. It's an ideal place to begin."

He went on, "We are calling on the people of Iceland to consider becoming a pioneering state for an entirely new social model based on nature, community and happiness, rather than on some numerical growth at the expense of these fundamental human requirements."

Baldur tossed the magazine away and began to do some googling. As he checked into some of the sites mentioned, he found the web opening up to him in a way that resonated strongly with his thinking on lots of levels: self-sufficiency, organic, natural health, alternative energy – all these ideas dovetailed seamlessly with the thinking behind

Karl's free movement, and, of course, grated enormously with conventional economic thinking.

He had time for a coffee, then it was off to college. He pondered the idea of mentioning the article in his keynote address. Maybe it was a bit of fun, maybe he felt a duty to mention it – who knows? Well, let's see what happens, he thought.

Later, during his speech to the students, the President was of course driving home his usual message of how Iceland was such a great country, how its students were among the brightest in the world, how the university was one of the most respected – all of the standard rhetoric that politicians use to infuse people with a sense of common purpose, thus giving themselves the appearance of being somehow responsible for it.

"...and who knows," he quipped light-heartedly at the end, "Iceland might even become a world-leader in freedom if this man Karl Drayton is to be believed." He held aloft a copy of the Grapevine. "Thank you all, and good luck to each of you in the future."

This was followed by that special half-hearted applause that students reserve for visiting politicians – polite and begrudging – but there was a confused timbre to it too. The students had no idea who or what Karl Drayton was, except for one. Sheila Campbell, a budding biologist and Truthfest activist from Australia, who, being the diligent student, also happened to be recording the entire speech on her phone.

When the president of a country mentions a mysterious person specifically by name – for whatever reason, everyone suddenly takes an interest. Perhaps Baldur Reyksson hadn't been fully versed on correct Presidential etiquette, or perhaps his rural pragmatism was just too strong. Whatever the reason, within just a few hours his university speech 'calling for a free world' was all over the internet.

F·DAY -3159

The one thing they don't teach you at NASA Space Academy is that space is boring. Perhaps you can't blame them for that – they might have considerably less uptake for their astronaut training program if they did, or more significantly, less Federal funding. Flight Commander Joel Robbins was now in a position to confirm this, having completed his 'sleep cycle' for the sixtieth day in the International Space Station: he was excruciatingly bored.

Of course, the view of Earth is breath-taking, but after a couple of weeks it starts to get a bit samey. Robbins found himself looking more towards the stars, moon and other planets than at Earth these days, as there was more variety in that direction. He was especially fascinated by the stars – tiny, fixed points of light, unwavering in the vacuum, smaller than on Earth but so much more intense and teeming in their billions. The other American co-commander had returned home last week, and Robbins' conversations with his Russian counterpart, beyond the magnetic chess set, were stunted at best. So he took to writing instead.

As a boy, Joel had loved writing poetry about his cat and his budgerigar. Unfortunately one day – perhaps in an effort to spare the arts world – the cat ate the budgerigar, thus curtailing young Joel's poetic aspirations for a while. Until now. Joel could feel the muse stirring inside him once again as he sat there suspended four hundred kilometres over the giant blue globe. All it needed was time, and boy, did he have lots of that.

He pulled himself over to the whiteboard and began. After an hour he gave a little chuckle to himself, then went to fetch the video camera. He managed to persuade his Russian friend to hold the camera while he positioned himself beside the window and began to recite.

Blue Dollar Boy – a poem by Joel K. Robbins.

There's a big blue ball in my sky,
that's passin' my window by and by

if I had a dollar mama
she makes me cry
every time this marble fills my eye.

I'm a country boy mama,
through and through
just ekin' a livin'
floatin' in the sky.

I've been floatin' out here
eight weeks and some
waitin' for my baby shuttle
home to come.

Back to good ole Kentucky
Somewhere way down below
where the gooses should be layin'
and good people a-prayin'.

It's easy to be blue mama
in this wild blue yonder
but this big blue world
jus' keeps passin' by and by.
If I only had a dollar mama
she makes me cry
every time that big blue marble fills my eye.

He rounded his recital off with a proud grin and a thumb-up salute. His Russian friend, completely oblivious to the poetic atrocity that had just occurred, smiled, handed him back the camera, then went back to his chores. Joel gleefully popped out the memory card and started setting up the uplink to Houston.

Before lunchtime the next day, every American and most Europeans knew the name of Commander Joel K. Robbins and his 'honest, heartfelt poetry' – at least that's how they were politely portraying it on all the big news channels in their 'and finally' sections.

Within a few days, the video had over ten million hits on YouTube

65

and was the top trending topic on Facebook and Twitter for almost a week. Of course, the terrible, clumsy poetry was what had given the video its initial prominence, but there was something else about it that was affecting many people in a mystical, almost religious way.

Commander Robbins had inadvertently framed the Earth's crescent beautifully behind him, and the sun's reflection on the atmosphere was caught at the perfect angle, giving the most wonderful, dazzling lens flare to the shot. This contrast of the remote, naked beauty of the planet against the drab, clumsy poetry of Robbins was sparking something of an awakening for many people – the human lamenting his desire to earn a dollar versus the infinite majesty of nature. There was simply no comparison – and all the spiritual, ecological and free movements were ready to take full advantage.

Of course, Joel Robbins was delighted with his new-found fame and took all the criticism of his poetry in very good spirits. On his return to Earth, he was inundated with chat show invitations and book publishing offers – though strangely not for poetry books.

"It's sure good to be back on ol' big blue," he told the waiting media throng that had gathered for his arrival, giving them his now trademark thumb-up salute. Joel had mistakenly become the most celebrated, most unlikely, yet lovable cultural icon of his time. Blue Dollar Boy became the first awakening point for millions of people.

F·DAY -3157

President Reyksson was furious. He felt like he had been tricked. He felt stupid. He was pissed off with his girlie crew of advisers trying to tell him what to do. They were trying to find ways to fire-fight the exploding story, to manage him, to get him to do some godawful soft-focus interviews – gently retracting everything he had said about Iceland dropping money and replacing it with the usual meaningless wordy pap to muddy things up and get things 'back to normal'. They had even handed him suggested scripts which he had flung across the room before ordering them out of his office.

Since the video had gone viral on the net, Baldur had hardly slept – and it wasn't just to do with the stress. He was changing. His point of view about the world was changing, and it felt like there was no going back. The more he learned about the possibilities of a money-free society, the more he could see how absurd was the alternative that he and everyone else was still living under.

The Icelandic media had been merciless. Some were questioning his sanity. The cartoonists were having a field day – one depicting him in caricature as a naked emperor in a clothes shop with no money to buy clothes. Of course, the way the video had been presented on YouTube was not exactly what had happened, but it was close enough that he had no reason to refute it. Sheila, the ever-diligent biology student who posted the video, had cut to the last couple of minutes of his speech where he was seen to be extolling Iceland's many virtues then holding up the Grapevine magazine and saying Iceland could even be world-leaders in freedom.

He looked, he had to admit, far more like a revolutionary than a president. He knew the previous twenty minutes of his speech would have shown the true context of what had really only been a witty remark at the end – but he also knew that trying to explain all that to the media was not going to convince anybody. A speech can be about anything, but it only takes five or six words to make a great headline.

He called his secretary. It was time to act.

"Mel, can you please call the party leaders and ask them to come to the meeting room at six o'clock?"

"Sure thing," came the reply.

At five past six, Baldur walked into the meeting room. The voices had been animated but shut off the instant Baldur entered the room. His expression of grim determination silenced them all.

"Gentlemen, sit down," he gestured.

The four party leaders took their seats and looked at him

expectantly.

"I'm going to make this as simple and brief as I can," he started. "I'm sure you are all wondering why I blurted out those remarks. Let me tell you first that that video was severely edited and does not reflect the tenor of that speech in any way accurately. However, I did make those remarks – somewhat in jest – but not entirely in jest either.

"We all know only too well how videos can be manipulated to create a desired opinion, but it is not far enough removed from reality that I can refute it as false. Those are the facts for now."

He paused for a drink of water. The party leaders looked briefly to each other but remained silent. They knew something was coming.

"Gentlemen, I believe the Free Movement is right and we should now begin working towards making this happen..."

The room erupted. Finally, one voice came through. It was Thorarinn, the leader of the main opposition party.

"Baldur, these guys are just a bunch of communist upstarts who are probably unemployed. They don't have a clue about economics or how things work in the real world. You know that. You're not seriously suggesting that we turn over our beautiful island to a bunch of..."

"...fucking hippies?" the Green Party leader suggested with a smirk.

"Frankly, yes," Thorarinn continued. "No-one on this island is going to take this idea seriously. No-one is going to take you seriously..."

"That's fine gentlemen," the President replied. "I am not here for myself. I am here to try and get the best deal for everybody on this island. I have looked into this idea at length over the last few days, and I can assure you it is entirely credible.

"This is possible in Iceland. I apologise to you for my careless remarks but I believe this is not a problem. I think it may actually be a fantastic opportunity to try something remarkable and we should embrace it."

The room erupted again. This time, the quiet voice of the Green

Party leader came through.

"Baldur, if you proceed with this you are looking at probable impeachment, and worse, ridicule for you and your family. You know we can't do this. You know Icelanders will never sign up to something that will effectively rob them of all the wealth they've fought so hard to achieve. Please, as your friend, don't do this."

"I appreciate all your concern Jo, and the rest of you. The fact is, I can't go back to the media now and lie about what I feel is right. Too much of that has been done in the past for the wrong reasons.

"I believe the free society can work in Iceland and I believe the people will go for it, because we are such a strong community, and we are innovators." he puffed his chest out proudly.

"I suggest you all go back and do what you have to do. If you want to impeach me, that's fine. I won't hold it personally against you. I will take all the risk and responsibility for whatever happens. At worst, I just get to go back to my barley in the peace and quiet – and that's something you know I can very easily live with."

The small laughter broke the tension in the room.

"At best," Baldur continued, "Iceland gets to make history and to do something extraordinary!"

After some friendly words between them all at the door that was not entirely unlike his friends saying their goodbyes as he was on his way to be executed, Baldur closed the door and called his secretary in. For now, he was still the president and every minute was precious. He was very glad that he had made peace with his old friends, but now it was time to meet his other not-so-old friends in the media and give them the hottest story since the air traffic-stopping volcano of 2010.

F·DAY -3153

Karl was very glad to be back in Ireland. New York was nice for a while, but not somewhere he could ever imagine living. There was a strange solitude about the place. He had made some good friends over there, especially Podge, and it was really nice to see things beginning to happen on the ground. After his interviews on CNN and ABC, his website figures had gone through the roof. The Charter had almost reached a hundred thousand signatories. These were heady days indeed, but something was missing.

After the initial fervour of his two interviews, the phone and emails had gone eerily silent. He had just done two interviews for the two biggest news channels in the US, but there had been no knock-on effect. He wasn't complaining, but he had thought that he would have been a little more in demand after the interviews.

Finally, his curiosity got the better of him, so he set about chasing up the guy who had got him the interview in the first place. He took up his phone and started looking through the last caller list. After a while, he found the first number in his phone from the States. It must be him he thought, so he dialled the number. Answerphone, with a robot female voice and generic 'the person is not available' message.

"Hello there, er, this is Karl Drayton here. From Ireland. You rang me a few weeks ago in connection with an interview. Can you please ring me back on this number?"

He put down the phone and stretched himself on the kitchen chair. Abby had just made some coffee and sat down beside him.

"Karl," she said in her strong Dublin accent. "You'll never guess what came..."

The phone suddenly danced into life on the table. The piercing ring and rumbling vibration was too much for the cat who made a quick exit.

"Hello?" Karl inquired.

"Hi, Mr. Drayton, this is Mike Ross from Redross Media Associates in New York. You rang here earlier?"

"Ah, hi Mike. Sorry, I couldn't remember your name."

"No problem. How was the interview?"

"Fantastic, listen thank you for that. It's made a big difference, but..." Karl felt almost rude now complaining to the guy who had got him the biggest interview of his life. "I don't know, I thought there would have been more callbacks or knock-on effect from other media channels..."

"Really? You got ABC too, right?"

Karl was impressed by how clued in Mike was. "Er, yeah, but since then it's been complete radio silence. Not a dicky bird. I'm not complaining really, but it seems a little odd, no?"

"Hmmm, hang on there..." Karl could hear him feverishly tapping away on the keyboard and mumbling to himself. After some seconds Karl could hear a distinct 'Oh', then the typing stopped. Karl imagined him scrolling down through some long screen. "Mr. Drayton?"

"Yes?" Karl said looking at Abby, who was now blowing over her coffee and stroking the cat.

"Well, it seems you've gone and got yourself an NSI."

"An NSI? What the hell is that?" Karl sat up straight in his seat.

"It's a Homeland Security order. NSI means 'Not Suitable for Interview'."

"What...?" Karl gasped.

"It's a standard blocking order used by Homeland Security to stop terrorists getting media exposure."

"What, so I'm a terrorist now? Seriously?" Karl gasped again. Abby was now looking at him very seriously.

"Ha! Yeah, it looks like it. Look there is an appeal process but I can't really do anything for you, because I gotta stay neutral, otherwise I start losing my clients. What I'll do is I'll email you a link for you to read up and lodge your own appeal, but..."

"But?" Karl repeated.

"Well, you're not hearing this from me OK?"

"OK..."

"Well you can use this to your advantage I think. You follow me?"

"Er, I think so..."

"Censorship is the crooked stepmother of great publicity," Mike surmised proudly. "You can get some viral mileage with this – especially in a grassroots, internet movement like yours. Just be careful though. Don't get too cocky! These guys can make life really difficult for you."

"OK right," Karl said. "Time to get the video camera out you mean?"

"Yeah," Mike laughed. "Time to get the video camera out. But be smart. Don't overdo it."

"OK, sure. Wow. Listen, thanks for your help Mike."

"No worries, but no mention of me anywhere, OK?"

"Sure. Got it! Thanks a million!"

"Don't mention it," Mike said, then hastily added, "literally!"

Karl laughed and turned off the phone.

"Did you get all that?" he said to Abby taking up her hand.

"I think so. Are you OK?" she asked, searching his eyes.

"Yeah. Wow. I guess." Karl was rubbing his face with his hands, trying to get his head around what he had just heard from Mike.

"What am I going to do?"

"Well, you can start by packing your things." Abby announced proudly.

"What?" Karl stared at her blankly for a few seconds. Abby's smile slowly widened, then she handed him the letter.

He flicked it open.

"Wh-what?" he shouted, standing up. "What?"

Abby, getting teary-eyed, nodded and instinctively placed his hand on her big belly. Karl leaned over and put his arms around her.

"Oh my god, this is amazing Abby! Amazing!"

They stood there in a silent embrace for some minutes until finally, the cat decided enough was enough and it was time for some food instead.

F·DAY -3152

In all the excitement Karl had completely forgotten about making the video as Mike Ross had suggested. As it turned out, he didn't need to. As had become something of a frequent occurrence since his 'awakening', life had conspired to bring him something infinitely better – a letter from the President of Iceland.

'Dear Mr. Drayton,

'Baldur Reyksson, President of Iceland, would like to invite you to participate in a three-day socio-economic seminar to be held on August 2nd, 3rd and 4th at the Ion Hotel in Selfoss, Iceland.

'The three-day seminar will be a small, private focus group for exploring the possibility of creating an alternative socio-economic system for the island of Iceland. Since a forum of this nature deals with sensitive issues that could greatly impact matters of public interest, your utmost discretion is requested.

'We look forward to meeting you there.

'The Office of the President of Iceland.'

Karl was chuffed. He sent a reply back immediately saying that he would be going, stopping only momentarily to consider whether he would have to pay for flights and hotels, then realising that surely no president invites you to his country, then expects you to travel in steerage and stay in bed and breakfasts at his behest. He chuckled to himself, clicked send and went to tell Abby the news.

As he walked out of the room another email arrived on his screen which had a small video attachment. There, frozen in the small video pane was Commander Joel K. Robbins sitting in front of a window overlooking Earth with the subject line 'WE NEED TO TALK'.

Some minutes later, Karl rushed back into the room to grab the laptop and switch it off when he saw the email. He was intrigued, so he sat down, opened the email and played the video. After regaining his composure from the shock attack of atrocious poetry, Karl looked up Rob, his PR guy, for a quick video chat.

"Hey, just on my way out and I got this email from some Commander Joel K. Robbins saying we need to talk. Who is this guy? This... crime against poetry has over a million hits!"

"JKR? You don't know him? He's the latest internet sensation, lad!" Rob said as he was busy picking something from between his front teeth. "Basically: astronaut, wrote a shite poem, popped it up on YouTube, popped back down to Earth, now he's the cat's pyjamas. Don't ask me mate. The world is a strange place."

"Ha ha!! OK. Sounds like we do indeed need to talk! Cheers Rob. Gotta run, talk later."

"Cheerio lad."

Karl sent a quick reply back to Commander Robbins including his Skype name and snapped the computer shut.

F·DAY -3150

Podge stopped, kissed his beloved photo then stepped outside, gently closing the door behind him. Two years earlier, his girlfriend Tanja had lost her battle to leukaemia. Every day since, his heart ached so badly. He had been with her every second right up to her last drawing of breath, which, he was sure, she had used up entirely just to make the faintest smile for him. He had been so strong for her, so she could go peacefully and happily, but for him, it had been like his entire insides had been scooped out with a cold claw, leaving a raw, aching emptiness that he wouldn't have wished on his greatest enemy.

These days the sadness was more manageable, but that was all. Manageable. He would never get over losing the greatest thing ever in his life, nor the hurt feeling of injustice that something so beautiful could be taken from the world in such a cruel way.

Podge's apartment was only blocks away from Wall Street, where he had arranged to meet some of his old buddies from the Occupy protests. As he rounded the corner he could hear the hubbub coming from just down the street. As he walked on, the crowds were getting thicker and thicker. Was this another demonstration, he wondered? After a few more paces he was now having to push and squeeze his way through. Some girl was shouting through a megaphone and the crowds were answering but it was too jumbled to discern any meaning in it yet. He looked around at the people standing there. He asked one man what was going on as they were being jostled together.

"I have no idea sorry," the man said, "but I think they're burning something."

That was true, thought Podge. He could smell paraffin. He pushed through a little more. Finally, he could hear what the girl was saying:

"This is a fucking big lie," she was screaming into the mouthpiece. "Bring up your dollars now and let's show these fucking assholes what they are really worth... You sir... have you got five?"

Podge could see what was happening now – and he recognised the girl. It was Anna, one of Tanja's closest friends – and she was burning money! Holy shit! She was getting people on the street to give her five, ten and even some twenty dollar bills, then dowsing them in paraffin and setting them alight. The effect was electric. Podge just stood on the sidelines soaking it up. Anna was amazing! This was not just a great protest, it was engaging and entertaining the public too! Protest meets art, he thought.

His thoughts were broken as he suddenly found himself being shouldered out of the way by a news crew, eager to get to the action.

75

"Ha ha!" He laughed aloud. "Karl," he said, looking skyward, "you're gonna love this!"

Of course, Podge knew well, destroying currency is a serious felony and sure enough, it wasn't long before New York's finest came along to restore law and order to the proceedings. Anna suddenly beamed in recognition of Podge as she was being dragged away by both arms towards the police van.

"Hey Podge," she yelled. "How the hell are you? Haven't seen you in ages. Where the hell have you been?"

With that, the door was slammed shut. Immediately, Anna's face popped into the window and she smiled and gave Podge the universal 'call me' sign with her hand. He smiled back and replied with a Commander Robbins-style thumbs up!

F·DAY -3148

Karl was smiling to himself as he watched the Wall St. videos of Anna burning the dollars. She was a fiery girl, he thought – literally. That was exactly the kind of peaceful and powerful demonstration people needed to jar them into thinking again. Podge had sent him the link and was arranging to meet her – just as soon as she was released.

He stood up to go and finish packing his bags for Iceland when suddenly a Skype call came through. It was an unknown contact. He clicked 'answer' and was met with a bright screen with a dark face.

"Hello?" came the twangy Kentucky voice.

"Ah, Joel?" Karl enquired.

"Yes, it's me. How are you?"

"Er fine, but I can't see you..."

"Oh hang on..." the Commander replied, then made some adjustments that wobbled the picture frantically for a second, until it settled with an image of Commander Joel K. Robbins in stark relief with the bright lamp just beside his left ear. "Is that any better?"

"Er, yeah that's fine..." Karl said half-heartedly. "How are you, Commander? It's great to see you."

"Thank you, Mr. Drayton..."

"Karl, please..."

"Karl... nice to talk."

Karl could start to see the features of the celebrity astronaut better now, although he had a long beard now and looked much skinnier than he had done in his famous video. Maybe it was the lighting, but he got the sense that this was a man who was not well.

"I wanted to get in touch with you Karl because I was watching your videos and reading your words on the Free World Charter."

"Yes, did you like them?"

"Yes, I did sir, yes, I did," Joel answered. "But there's one thing I gotta tell you..." Karl suddenly felt the onset of some petty criticism that he had heard probably a million times before and started to sigh inwardly for having taken this call. However, his sighs quickly evaporated when he heard what the commander had to say.

"There's folks here talking about shutting you down."

"What? The website? F-Day? Or the..." Karl began.

"No, not the website Karl," Joel said evenly. "You."

Karl felt a cold shiver travel right up his spine and across his scalp. The commander leaned into the camera.

"They want to put you right out of business entirely son – if you catch my drift."

Something about this man's strong American accent gave his words an extra menace. He sounded like some wayback sheriff warning him about a lynch mob that was coming after him and advising him to get out of town by sun up. Karl began to feel scared.

"Who exactly wants to 'put me out of business', Joel? And for what?"

"Well son, last week I was guest speaker at a shareholder's lunch for T.P. Hartnett, one of NASA's top tech sponsors. They're a prospecting company, part-owned by two of the energy majors. They supplied equipment to NASA for surveying the Moon and Mars in the 90s."

"Go on..."

"Well, last week, on account of my video, I was guest of honour you see, so I gave 'em a little speech about being in space and suchlike. After my speech, I sat down next to a gentleman called Barnes, and he was getting pretty tanked up and talking to the fella beside him..."

The commander stopped as if checking that no-one was listening. Karl was leaning into the speaker now.

"...and?" he prompted.

"Well, the guy he was talking to didn't have no name badge or nothin' but he was young, fit – and very sober. They were talking about this thing that the president said there in Iceland, about you and the whole Free Movement thing. Anyway, this Barnes guy was laughing about the whole idea over his glass of Chardonnay, joking that America should take Iceland as the fifty-second state just as soon as the Iceland president declares it to be a free country... He was all giggles, saying that Iceland can then be America's power plant..."

"Go on..." Karl said as Joel took a sip of water.

"...and this young guy wasn't laughing much at all, but says to Barnes: 'Don't worry that won't be happening anyway...', and Barnes says what does he mean, and this young turk says straight as a die: 'this whole free movement thing – we're taking it down in the next few weeks.'"

Karl's jaw dropped. The commander continued.

"'Taking what down, the free website? Who is?' Barnes asked him, wiping the tears of laughter from his eyes and getting serious. The guy just replied coolly: 'Everything – lock, stock and two smoking barrels –

if you know what I mean. It's already fixed.' Barnes asked him 'who was he, the Mafia?' But he wasn't laughin'... just drummed his fingers on the table, shrugged and said: 'No, I'm just a problem solver that's all.'"

Karl was struck speechless. He felt like he was reading some movie script. Was there really some malevolent 'they' who were plotting to kill him? The idea was absurd.

"I'm a fan of your ideas by the way." Joel suddenly broke through Karl's thoughts.

"What?"

"The free world idea – I think it's great. Not sure how it'll work, but it's sure worth a try. This thing we're doing sure as hell ain't working anyway."

Karl couldn't believe he was being so light-hearted considering the dark message he had just dropped on him. He started becoming distracted. Joel continued talking but Karl wasn't listening any more. He was thinking about Abby and their baby. He can't tell her this – not while she's pregnant. It's better that way. Then what about his trip to Iceland? Would they be safe?

"...you know what I mean?" Joel's voice suddenly came back into focus. Karl had no idea what he had been talking about.

"Er, yeah... listen I gotta go finish packing now... I'm in the air in three hours. Thanks for the call Joel. Keep in touch. If you hear anything more, please let me know OK?"

"Oh. OK. Sure thing, Karl. You take care now."

"Thanks, I will."

Karl sat on the edge of the bed for a minute rubbing his head in his heads. He was trying to think, but think what? He didn't even know what to think. Was it even OK for him to fly? Bloody hell...

F·DAY -3147

Circling over Keflavik, Karl felt an unusual sense of homecoming. He and Abby had been here a year before, mistakenly thinking – like so many others before them – that they were landing in Reykjavik and ending up having to hitch-hike the unexpected fifty kilometres into town in the middle of the night. The last time they were here, Karl had somehow felt that it would not be his last time. Abby had chosen to stay in Ireland, preferring not to risk the flight while pregnant, so Karl was flying alone.

For Karl, the place was magic. His last trip to Iceland had covered half the island in just over two weeks and he'd only met a handful of desperate protesters. Now he was back for more, but on a mission that he could only have dreamt about: a high-level meeting with the President to see about bringing about a money-free society to his childhood wonderland.

In the end, he had told Abby about what Commander Robbins had said, but had played it down a little. He hated to lie, but he didn't want to worry her either. He had no idea how to deal with this kind of threat – except perhaps something he was going to try and discuss with the President over the next few days.

On exiting the passport control in Keflavik, Karl was chaperoned efficiently away through a VIP channel by a police officer. Outside a car was waiting for him to drive him directly to Selfoss. Karl was becoming accustomed to this kind of royal treatment, but wasn't particularly impressed by it. He would prefer to make his own way, rather than be wheeled around by someone else like a shop dummy. After a pleasant hour's drive, Karl arrived at Selfoss.

Set in the rugged rockscape overlooking Iceland's largest lava field, the hotel boasted a view like no other in the world. In fact, it was not even like this world at all. It was more like something you'd expect to find on one of Jupiter's moons. Sharp, jaggy rocks forming steep black cliffs rising up from the lava field. The hotel itself looked – perhaps deliberately – like some prefabricated Martian colony building straight out of an Asimov novel. Thick, rounded windows were set into the grey building, jutting incongruously out of the rocky terrain on concrete piles. All that was needed to complete the illusion was a handful of men in the foreground wearing pressure suits and carrying scientific instruments. Karl loved the place immediately. Iceland never failed to surprise or surpass expectations.

When he got to his room, he was a little disappointed with the side view overlooking the car park, but wasn't intending to spend too much time there anyway, so he didn't mind. He set down his bags and there on the desk was an envelope addressed to him. He opened it. It was from President Reyksson – but not on Presidential headed paper, it was just a scrawl on a note block:

'Karl, can you meet me at the Stjörnu meeting room at 4 o'clock? Welcome to Iceland! Baldur.'

The seminar didn't start until the next morning but Karl was glad of the opportunity to meet the President beforehand, so he went for a quick shower, then set off in search of the Stjörnu room.

When he got there the door was slightly ajar, but he knocked anyway out of respect. There was no answer. He pushed the door slowly open and there, on the other side of the room was Baldur Reyksson, alone, looking at his phone and deep in thought.

"Mr. President...?" Karl offered, not really knowing how to address him properly. Baldur suddenly jumped from his reverie and waved to him.

"Karl! Come in, come in," he said enthusiastically, waving to a chair.

The two men shook hands warmly and Karl sat down in a meeting room chair opposite the president. It was a small conference room with all the chairs and tables stacked up over to one side.

"'Stjörnu' means star by the way," Baldur said, sitting down after shaking Karl's hand and nodding up at the ceiling. Karl looked up and saw the entire ceiling was made of glass.

"Oh wow! Perfect for the Aurora," Karl said. "It's really nice to meet you, er..."

"Baldur," Baldur insisted good-naturedly. "We're not in Washington, Karl. Iceland is a small place. We're all family here." He smiled and winked. Karl felt at ease. Baldur looked nothing like a president, he thought. He was wearing a long sleeve casual t-shirt and jeans. His eyes were grey and wild, his face weather-beaten and his manner basic. Perfect, thought Karl.

"Karl, we have a problem," he said. "In fact, we have a couple of problems..."

"OK, let's see if we can fix them," Karl said enthusiastically, then quickly added, "I have a problem too actually."

"Oh?"

"Well, we can talk about that later," Karl said dismissively, sensing the President's slight irritation.

"OK, well here's my problem. The first is that all the parties in our Government are seeking my impeachment. I knew this would happen, and I know these guys personally. It's nothing personal against me, they are just trying to keep their parties and government together. They held a secret ballot of no-confidence yesterday which was upheld and they're now seeking my impeachment through the high court."

"OK, well..." Karl began.

"It's not that important for me Karl," Baldur continued. "I don't like it or anything, but I know these guys are doing what they have to do and we'll all still be friends afterwards when I am back out in the wilderness."

He gave Karl a warm, wry smile.

"But the real problem for me is that it means we don't have much time. This impeachment thing could take only two to three weeks. Normally, any president would just resign in my position, but not me, because I don't really care too much about trying to save my name here, whereas I do care about what we might be trying to do, and I want to stick around as long as possible – to do as much as I can."

Baldur's thick Icelandic accent and defiant demeanour gave Karl the impression of a noble viking warrior, heading gloriously into a battle he can never win. He was really beginning to like him.

"OK, I understand," he said, nodding. "Time is of the essence. What else?"

"I just got a phone call before you came now, confirming what I had feared most about our little seminar here. The Grapevine magazine are onto us and are sending over a reporter tomorrow. Now I'm pretty sure they don't realise the scale of what's going on here, but when they do, all of Iceland is going to be here on our doorstep by lunchtime."

"Shit."

"Exactly. Shit. Maybe you don't fully appreciate what this means Karl. Once our little meeting goes public – whatever the outcome – people will draw their own conclusions. Businesses will draw their own conclusions. The markets will draw their own conclusions."

"Yes, of course. Financial chaos."

"And public chaos," Baldur said grimly. "I don't see any way to avoid it."

There was a momentary silence while both men were trying to envisage possible scenarios.

"Who else is coming here, Baldur? For the seminar?" Karl asked.

"Em, Hans Satter, a forward-thinking Austrian economist; Susan Briars, the eminent British sociologist; Max Bergan, Norwegian philosopher and author; erm... John Scott, American author and economist... he wrote 'From Boom to Ker-Boom – and back'..."

Karl let out a laugh. Baldur continued, "Jeffrey Ollsen, retired financier with Bank of Iceland; Jeni Tryggvadóttir, Icelandic ecological activist; Baldur Torvik, a well known Icelandic entrepreneur. There's also a small team of Swiss scientists who I contracted to do some geological and agricultural surveying a few weeks ago. Then there's you and me and a couple of secretaries to record the meeting. That's it, I think."

"So, apart from you, there's no-one coming from the actual government?" Karl quizzed. "Isn't that er, a bit strange?"

Baldur gave a wry smile again.

"Yes, but not because they weren't invited, Karl. I asked all the party leaders. They all declined to have any involvement."

"I see. So it's not that many people really. Are you thinking of cancelling the event? Or moving it?"

"It's too important to cancel. Not an option. It crossed my mind to move it, but it won't make that much difference. Word gets around here pretty fast. It's not called the Grapevine for nothing you know..."

"Ha! Yes, I'm sure. Ireland is a bit like that too," Karl replied. "So we can just keep the press locked out if they come."

"No, that will make the speculation even worse. There's only one thing we can do. We'll have to schedule a press conference."

"Really?"

"Yes, and I want you on the panel, Karl. To face the press with me and whoever else wants to do it. But I want you there. Will you do it?"

"Well, yes, of course, but..."

"This meeting is only going to go one of two ways Karl. Either we break incredible new ground and make real progress towards Iceland becoming a free country, or we all just make silly fools of ourselves in front of the whole world and go home. I don't know about you, but if I'm going to make an ass of myself, I'm going to at least give it my best shot! What do you say?"

Karl laughed. "Absolutely. Totally agreed. There's nothing to lose, for you with your impeachment, and for me, well, I make a fool of myself with this stuff every day of the week so it's water off a duck's back," he said brightly.

"I knew you'd be like that. That's why I wanted you here. Your positivity is rare, Karl. Don't let anyone beat that out of you."

The two men stood up.

"Thanks, Baldur. I really admire your gutsy determination. Whatever happens, this will be the first official meeting of its kind to explore the free society philosophy, and I can't think of a better place. This place is truly magic. I'm so happy and honoured to be here. Thank you for inviting me."

"Let's see what tomorrow brings Karl. Go and relax, have a hot spa, massage and dinner and we'll see you here tomorrow morning at nine o'clock."

"Thanks, Baldur," Karl said, shaking the proffered hand warmly. "I will. See you in the morning."

Karl had only gone ten paces down the corridor when he suddenly remembered his own personal dilemma. He stopped and thought for a few seconds, then turned straight around and back in to the Stjörnu room.

"Baldur, I need to ask you a favour..."

F·DAY -3146

The next morning, Karl had a fascinating breakfast, meeting the other delegates for the first time. There were quite a few that the President hadn't mentioned. Vern, the activist guy who had had his mortgage overturned was there, there were two guys from The Truthfest Movement who he had met before in Germany, and he had a fascinating conversation with Susan the sociologist and John the 'Kerboom' book guy. Karl's opening question to her about humans being a social species gave him some interesting insights.

"Yes, we are social, but normally in small, separate groups," she said cracking open her egg, being careful not to damage her red nails. "It's not clear how well we perform autonomously in larger groups, or as one planetary group. The reason is that once groups grow to a certain size, governments and hierarchies tend to spring up, which, for good or bad, mask the effect of the large group being autonomous without those controlling forces. So there is no decent proof either way that any large autonomous group can conduct itself successfully."

"So," said Karl. "perhaps the bigger question is, do these governments spring up in large groups through necessity, or are they just ego-driven subgroups whose main interest is to wield control over the others and/or monopolize resources?"

"No. No subgroup in a truly autonomous large group would ever achieve that level of control without some precedent or moral right to that position. That could be, say, some outstanding achievement or service that person or group made to the community that would hold them in high esteem from the rest."

"OK, that may be true of early tribal communities, but what of now? We all know most politicians never actually do anything before they get into power – or afterwards for that matter." There were a few sniggers around the table. The other diners were enjoying this banter too. "They get into power solely on the strength of wordy promises of all the good things they will do when they get there. That's pretty unusual wouldn't you say?"

"Ha ha, yes it is, now that you mention it," Susan replied, catching some egg dripping from her lip. "but I guess now we live in such a media-driven world, people can just pretty much advertise themselves into power. They just keep throwing money at it. And of course, if they're all doing that, someone has to win regardless, even if all the people are apathetic and only a few vote."

"Hmmm..." Karl still wasn't happy with that. "Supposing," he said, "that hierarchical systems do come about organically in groups, say where some individual has done a great service or whatever, but once that person dies or is no longer useful to the group, people – preferring the lazy option – merely forget to dismantle that hierarchy, leaving a vacancy for other, less worthy people to fill the space."

"That's pretty good Karl," she answered. "That would account for pretty much all the assholes in Westminster."

The table burst into laughter.

"The point is," Karl continued, "is the status quo. Why do we insist on keeping the same thing over and over, just because it's there, even if it defies all logic and sense? How do we beat the status quo?"

"Well, that's what we're here for today, isn't it? To change the status quo. Psychologists say people are lazy thinkers. It sounds sad, but it's true. It's easier to just repeat the same behaviour rather than change it. Also, people hate to let go of their precious beliefs and ideals. Icelanders, in particular, are tough cookies, I heard. That can be either good for us or bad for us, I don't know. But we're going to find out very shortly I think," she said raising her eyebrows.

"Yes," said Karl. "We sure will."

Slowly the group of delegates filed out the breakfast room and made their way along the corridor to the meeting room. Karl hadn't spotted the President at breakfast, but thought perhaps he was coming from Reykjavik. The Stjörnu room had been transformed into a board room for the day. In the centre was a large, oval mahogany table set out with water glasses, pens, paper, and to one end was a large screen hooked up to a laptop. It looked like a British Cabinet meeting, Karl thought, except for the window on the far end which was overlooking the extraterrestrial landscape.

It was a beautiful morning and Karl could sense a positive anticipation among the group. He had noticed that everyone in the group was completely for the free idea. There was no-one against it. He wasn't exactly sure if this was a good thing or not. Though he was certain of the principles himself, it was always good to have some critical input to keep things grounded.

They were all sitting down now and there was still no sign of the President. Karl thought that was unusual, having met him the day before and seeing for himself how important this was to him. John Scott, the author, began to make some jokes instead and quoted from his book to pass the time. He was something of a comedian Karl realised, but also a brilliant mind. He could sum up in a few words the whole world's economic circus that would usually take Karl a whole day to write. He consistently referred to money as numbers, not money.

"The debt crisis," he read from the back of his book, "mankind's Great War on Numbers, is being fought not with weapons but with giant calculators that decide who eats and who doesn't. We need to unplug from this numerical insanity, stop measuring and start living again!".

"Hear hear," came the reply from Vern.

"I love the title, 'Boom to Ker-boom'," laughed Jani the eco-activist. "Is it for sale, or free or what?" she asked testily.

"It's for sale," he replied meekly, "but hell, I need the money. It ain't ideal, but maybe we can use this free market system to eat itself from the inside."

"What do you mean?" Susan inquired.

"He means that by using the current system to market and sell the book it could potentially reach more people that way, and make more of a difference, is that right?" Karl suggested.

"Yes. And I need the money," John repeated.

Everyone laughed, not noticing the small woman who had just walked into the room.

"I'm sorry to disturb you," she said, quickly quelling the laughter with her Icelandic accent, "but Baldur is delayed and will be along shortly. He said to start without him and perhaps Karl could chair the meeting?" All eyes turned to Karl.

"What?" Karl couldn't help himself. "I can't believe he's not here. What could possibly be more important than this?" he asked her.

She looked down, paused for a second then repeated, "Mr. Reyksson will be along shortly and has asked that you start without him. That's all I can say."

She turned around on her heel to go out when Baldur suddenly appeared at the door and motioned to his secretary to follow him outside. He made no eye contact and said nothing to the waiting assembly, gently closing the door shut behind them.

There was silence in the room.

"What the hell is going on?" asked Dieter, the guy from the German Truthfest Movement. No-one answered.

Karl broke the silence and said, "Well, I think maybe we've got to trust Baldur on this. Maybe he's got a family situation or something. I met him last night and I can tell you no-one wants this more than him, so I reckon he's got a good reason."

They looked at each other and shrugged their general assent. Karl stood up and said, "Well, shall we just get on with it? I guess whatever's on that laptop is where we're supposed to begin..."

"Yes," broke in one of the Swiss scientists, Jorge. "It is our presentation of the survey of the island. Will I play it?"

Karl looked around and everyone seemed to be in agreement. "OK, let's roll it," he said, sitting down.

Jorge stood up and went over to the laptop. The big screen popped into life with a satellite image of the island overlaid with the words: 'Iceland: A Geothermal Survey'. Jorge began to speak and everyone started settling into the presentation, completely oblivious of the drama that was going on just outside the door.

"Iceland," he began, "is one of the most geothermally active land masses on Earth, as it sits between both the American and Eurasian tectonic plates. These plates are moving apart at a rate of two centimetres a year, the resulting friction and activity ensures Iceland's estimated harnessable energy is over four hundred thousand times its current consumption. Iceland has long been aware of this potential and has utilised this to attract energy-heavy industries, which are a strategic part of its overall economic affairs. These multinationals account for approximately fifteen percent of Iceland's GDP."

He changed the slide to a graphic showing a house with red underground piping.

"Throughout southern Iceland, where volcanic activity is greatest..."

The door suddenly opened. It was Baldur.

"Gentlemen, stop the presentation!" he ordered, walking in quickly and dropping a bunch of papers on the table. This was not the man Karl met last night. He was totally wild looking now, his hair was tossed and he looked like he was about to eat someone. He stood at the top of the table leaning on his fists, looking down at the papers.

"Gentlemen... and ladies..." he added with a gesture to Susan and Jeni, "events have suddenly taken on a life of their own..." He looked over to Karl almost pleadingly. Karl frowned. Baldur pulled out the chair and sat down. He was starting to compose himself now.

"I've just been speaking to the Governor of the Bank of Iceland and the heads of the other two main banks. They are all refusing to open today."

There were gasps from the delegates.

He continued, "earlier this morning, traders on the Tokyo Stock Exchange started shedding Icelandic Króna like it was a toxic substance. This contagion spread to China, India, the DAX and now London. The Eurozone is now selling off Króna at eighty to the Euro, half its value yesterday. When the US opens in a few hours, our currency will probably be completely decimated."

There was a respectful silence while everyone was taking in the bombshell.

"It's because of us, isn't it?" said Susan, putting down her pen.

"Yes," Baldur said gravely. "Yesterday I discovered that the media had found out about our little meeting. I guess word spread a lot further than I thought. As we speak, our national currency is being ditched because traders think that Iceland as a trading nation is over, or soon will be. As a result, our banks are now refusing to open, fearing, quite rightly, that there will be a run on them today. I have to go back in to Reykjavik now for an emergency meeting with the Prime Minister and the other heads of departments. Frankly, I don't know what to do. There are standard measures that we can take to protect our banks, but I'm wondering..."

"...if maybe this is actually an opportunity, and not a problem?" Karl finished. Baldur looked surprised, then nodded, giving him that warm, wry smile again.

"Do you mind if I speak for a minute?" Karl asked.

Baldur waved his assent, and Karl began.

"No one in this room, I'll bet, has ever imagined that the shift from money to no-money was ever going to be easy or straightforward. I'm sure some of you, like me, have imagined that some sort of resource or class war would be a feature of the final days of transition, possibly with a lot of people being hurt or killed along the way. I have long thought this myself, that it will probably take some genocidal or environmental catastrophe before mankind wakes up to the fact that the way we're living cannot continue.

"That was one of the reasons why we were thinking about trying to establish a free society in one country first, to try and spread transition from one country to the next by example. Once other countries saw it working, then their people would likely seek to adopt the same system.

"It sounds to me like events have overtaken us and we don't even have a choice now with Iceland, except to try and follow through, because if – as I'm sure all your ministers will be suggesting Baldur – if Iceland tries to stop the rot now and rescue the economy, the damage done is so severe that it may take years of austerity to make Iceland economically viable again – if ever."

"Agreed," Baldur said. "Iceland is now in economic free-fall. No-one really knows what will happen when we reach the bottom..."

"...well, I think we're about to find out," Karl finished.

Baldur's phone rang.

"Yes, what?" he answered. "Yeah, in two minutes... What?... Really?... OK."

He turned off the phone.

"It's happening already..." he said, nodding to the big screen. Jorge, who was still standing there, in the now vain hope of continuing his geothermal presentation, started fumbling with the remote and eventually found the TV channels. He switched over to RÚV.

There were hundreds of people gathering outside each of the banks in Reykjavik, there was a small crowd assembling outside the Parliament too. It was reasonably peaceful looking. Some shops on the high street had closed amid the uncertainty, and you could see footage of the owners standing outside looking up and down the street.

"All very civilised looking," Karl said in an upbeat way.

"For now," growled Baldur. "Wait 'til they find out what is happening..."

"So, you're going to Reykjavik now, Mr. President?" Susan asked. "Aren't we going to do a press conference or something?"

Baldur thought for a moment.

"I have to meet all the leaders and ministers. I will try to persuade them to back me to push things forward, but I know they won't. For them, this impeachment can't come quick enough. Perhaps they will even find a way to speed that up. I wouldn't be surprised, but my main concern now is trying to avert panic on the streets. I'm still President and I owe it to the people to protect them as best I can, for as long as I can. I'll announce a press conference for twelve o'clock. That should keep things in order until then, but I imagine the ministers will be busy doing their own press management now so I'll be flying solo on this one."

"No you won't," Karl said. "I'll be there with you."

"Me too," chimed in Susan.

"Brilliant, thank you," Baldur conceded, smiling. All eyes slowly drifted to John.

"Aw, OK, what the hell..." he conceded. "No-one's buying my damn book anyway..."

Within half an hour, the President, Karl, Susan and John were up in the air in Baldur's helicopter heading for Reykjavik. It was eleven o'clock and the low morning sun was casting long shadows on the rocky ground below. Only the occasional car threading its way along the road, glinting in the sun gave a sense of the scale of the landscape below. Susan was transfixed.

"The government still haven't called a press conference," Baldur shouted over the microphone. "I think they're waiting to talk to me first. I'm going straight to the Parliament. I've arranged our press conference at the Central Hotel. Mel is doing all the media now. I can tell you now, it's going to be packed."

Everyone nodded. He continued, "I remember a similar press conference in 2008, after the collapse. The press conference was completely mobbed – not even standing room, and a pretty tense atmosphere too. The police were there, lots of shouting, but no trouble."

"So we're the only ones doing the press conference? Not the Government?" Susan yelled.

Baldur shrugged. "We'll find out quick enough when we land."

No one spoke for the remainder of the journey. The chopper landed on the lawn behind the Parliament and Baldur got out with a nod and a wave, then the chopper lifted off again, heading for the Central Hotel. There was quite a crowd outside the front of the Parliament below, everyone looking up at the chopper, many of them shouting something inaudible.

"I guess they're not wishing us good morning," John shouted.

Two minutes later they touched down on the roof of the Central. There was no one there waiting for them, which Karl was glad about. The three delegates found the door and made their way down to the conference room. A hotel manager spotted them in the corridor and ushered them into a small side room, where they could compose themselves. Outside they could see the room was full already and lined with cameras at the back.

"Wow," Susan said. "It's pretty intense out there. Is this your first press conference?" she asked Karl.

Karl was fiddling with a small TV in the corner.

"Yes. You?"

"Yeah, I'm pretty nervous actually," she replied, clearly understating the fact.

"Really?" Karl asked. "Na, don't be. It'll be fun," he smiled. Suddenly the TV sprang into life.

"...just giving you that story again. We're hearing that President Reyksson has just been arrested outside Parliament. Rose, can you give us any more details?" came the booming voice.

The three delegates looked at each other in horror. The screen flicked over to the reporter outside the Alþingi.

"Hello Jan, yes a helicopter carrying the President arrived here a short time ago and within a minute or so, two senior police officers entered the building, and could be seen speaking to the President at the back for a minute, then they escorted him away from the building into a waiting police vehicle out the back gate. They drive off in a high speed escort, appearing to be heading south on the ring road..."

There was a sudden kerfuffle and confusion behind the reporter as people began shouting. The reporter was looking back over her shoulder.

"I think maybe... yes I think I see Mr. Johannson, the Prime Minister, coming through the front door... yes it looks like he's coming over to talk to us..." Her voice was drowned out by the rising clamour of the other journalists and yells from the crowd. The camera was being knocked about and the screen cut back to the studio, where the news anchor was intently looking on.

After about a minute, the camera began to settle and a lone voice came through.

"...in due course, yes, but for now we are just issuing this short statement. I understand there are lots of questions, but we are dealing with a highly unusual and sensitive situation that is unfolding minute by minute... here is the statement: The Icelandic government, in light of the extraordinary events that have taken place in the last twenty-four hours, have taken steps to stabilise the situation, and are continuing to review the situation on a minute by minute basis. I can confirm the following: On the best legal and economic advice we have received in the last few hours, all Icelandic banks will remain closed until further notice, however, we have asked that banks continue to service accounts normally and operate ATM machines on a limited basis. Account holders will still be able to withdraw money from their account at any ATM, up to a value of eight hundred Króna, or one hundred Euros a day until further notice..."

There were deafening cries of journalists all asking questions at once.

"I can also confirm..." the Prime Minister continued, motioning with his hand to be allowed to continue. Finally, the shouts subsided. "I can also confirm," he continued, "that President Reyksson was detained earlier by police pending an investigation into incitement, abusing the privileges of his public office and bringing that office into disrepute. He is being held at an undisclosed location pending the result of those investigations..."

Again, the throng of journalists burst into a million questions. One female voice cut through.

"Mr. Johannson, will you or the members of this Government be attending the press conference at twelve o'clock?"

"As I've said, this is an extraordinary situation that is unfolding as we speak and we are monitoring the situation minute by minute. It is hardly time for a press conference now as we are investigating all our options and liaising with some of the best minds across the world to help us deal with the situation. Let me assure you we are doing, and will continue to do, everything possible to bring this situation under control. That's all we can say for now..."

Another burst of questions, this time resolving to another female journalist.

"Is the government actually considering the proposal of the Free Movement as a solution?" The Prime Minister just smiled and raised his hands against any further questions and started moving away from the camera. The questions erupted again as he shrank away.

Karl turned down the sound. Susan looked out again at the conference room. It was half empty now.

"They'll all be back soon," Karl said. "The Parliament is just around the corner from here." She nodded, looking uncomfortably nervous.

"So we gotta get up there and go it alone?" John piped in. That didn't help Susan a bit.

"Well, it looks like it, doesn't it?" Karl said, annoyed that he had not considered Susan. He tried to lighten things up. "Tell you what, let's go out there and give them the best damn press conference they've ever seen! Let's go and be amazing."

Susan laughed a little.

"Yeah," she said, "let's go and do something amazing!"

Some minutes later, after a few false starts and last minute tweaks from the camera crews, Karl began.

"Good afternoon, ladies and gentlemen. As I'm sure you've heard, President Reyksson who was due to present this conference today has been detained pending a police investigation. I just heard it on the news myself, so I don't know any more about that than you do.

"Anyway, we've decided to go ahead with the presentation ourselves in light of the extraordinary unfolding events that might help to give some background to what's going on. My name is Karl Drayton, a social activist from Ireland. I run several online campaigns, the most notable of which is F-Day – or the Free Movement. To my left is John Scott, author and former economist at MIT from Michigan, United States, most famous for his book 'From Boom to Ker-boom and back'." There were some stirs of laughter in the audience. "And on my right, Susan Briars, senior sociology professor at King's College, Cambridge, UK.

"Because of the rapidly unfolding events and detention of President Reyksson, I hope you can understand that we have made no prior preparations for this presentation. What I would like to do instead is to talk a little bit about why we are here in Iceland, what we are hoping to achieve and then perhaps answer some questions at the end."

There were no murmurs of dissension, so Karl figured everyone was in agreement. They were clearly enthralled. Having got almost nothing from the Prime Minister, the journalists' appetites were voracious. They dreamed of days like this, being in the centre of the storm of potentially the biggest story of their lives. They weren't going to miss a thing. Karl went on.

"Many of you will know that there is growing global movement that is calling for an end to money and the profit system, in light of the serious damage being done to the environment and the human experience as a whole. These problems take the form of climate change, pollution, overuse and waste of resources, greed, poverty, social injustice, needless starvation and death from curable diseases. The Free Movement recognises that all these malaises on human life are unquestionably linked to the profit-motivated money system. Because we all need money to survive in this system, it has unavoidably become prioritised above all else. Since nature and community do not produce profit, we tend to forget them, but of course, we physically cannot live without them. We – and President Reyksson – believe that not only is it possible to live without money, but our lives will be many times better once we move beyond it.

"Just to clarify, we are talking about an end – not just of money – but to all forms of trade, borders and other imaginary social divides." He paused to see if he was hitting the spot. He was. There was complete silence in the room.

"A couple of years ago," he continued, "myself and a few others in the Free Movement concluded that most likely the easiest way for the world to start moving beyond money was to do so in one country first. After checking out a few candidate countries, we discovered that Iceland was the one that ticked the most boxes. The criteria we were looking for were: independence, self-sufficiency, neutrality, low population, good existing industry and infrastructure, high community values, physical isolation. Iceland, having a particularly high level of self-sufficiency in terms of energy became, in our minds, the prime candidate. So, we set up a Facebook page to see if we could get other people to agree with the possibility and to try build up a following. As you might know, today the Iceland Free page now has over a hundred thousand followers.

"I'm sure you also know that some weeks ago, the President mentioned this initiative in a college speech which got bounced all around the net. We had no idea that the President was interested in, or had even seen this idea until he invited me here for the seminar. I should make it clear at this point, that this seminar was intended to be held in secret, as the President just wanted to explore ideas and look at their feasibility. For this reason, he had asked each of us attending for our utmost discretion because he realised the sensitive nature of the proposals."

Susan and John nodded silently in agreement.

"So somehow," Karl continued, "word got out about the meeting and it now looks like investors all over the world started getting nervous about Icelandic stocks and currency, which have subsequently gone into freefall.

"President Reyksson asked me to come here today to try and help him explain the situation. Now that he's not here, I want – we all want – to make it clear that it was never our intention to cause the disruption or chaos that we see unfolding today. We came here for a private meeting with the President, that is all."

There was some stirring around the room now. Karl looked up and saw a man standing at the door flanked by police officers, giving him the universal throat-cut signal to stop. There were other police officers behind them. Karl's pause and gaze caused many of the reporters to turn around in their seats to find the source of the distraction. The man, now realising his presence was revealed anyway, began to speak up.

"Ladies and gentlemen, can I have your attention, please? I'm very sorry for this interruption but I'm afraid we have to call an end to this press conference early. Can you please gather up your things and start moving outside to the reception area?" He then started repeating his instruction in Icelandic.

"I beg your pardon," John announced over the microphone with an authoritative tone. "We are not finished here yet, sir."

"Sorry sir," the man said, "we have orders from the Chief Inspector and Mayor to wrap up this conference now. There's been a new press conference scheduled for four o'clock." The police officers were starting to move into the room around the sides. The man shouted again, "I'm sorry folks, can I please ask you to gather up your belongings and make your way towards reception... thank you."

Some people had begun to move, but most were still sitting confused in their seats, looking around. Karl had no idea what to do. Suddenly a young reporter from the front row said, "No, let's hear them out." People turned to look at her. "Let's hear them out," she repeated louder.

"I agree. Let's finish the conference first..." said a second older man who had stood up.

"I'm sorry sir," the officer repeated, "we are under orders from the Mayor. "We've got to clear the room now. If you can please make your way along..."

"No... no, fuck you. We're staying," another girl shouted. "I wanna hear what they're saying..." There was a murmur of 'yeahs' around the room.

"I'm sorry madam..."

"Screw the Mayor!" she cut in defiantly, waving her hand at the top table. "Let's hear them out first."

That was enough for most people. Anyone who had stood up now sat back down in their seats. The young police officer, now left standing alone and speechless in the middle of the room, dropped his arms down onto his sides in despair and waved the other officers out of the room. A spontaneous applause erupted.

Karl, keen not to show any disrespect, said into the mike, "Sorry, we'll just be a few more minutes OK?" The officer didn't turn around but shrugged and walked out slowly as if to maintain some semblance of authority.

"Ladies and gentlemen," Susan piped up, "we all appreciate the extraordinary circumstances surrounding this press conference. We had no idea this was going to happen any more than you did, so it's understandable if people are a bit jumpy. It looks like our presence on this island has had an effect that none of us could have predicted. At least give us the chance to tell you guys why we are here, so we can clear up any confusion and people can decide for themselves."

There was a warm applause from all the reporters. Karl looked over at Susan and winked. "Good work!" he mouthed to her. Karl looked back at John who gestured that he would speak. Karl nodded.

"Iceland," said John, "as you guys know, has quite a history of rebellious acts. I have to admit the way you guys handled the banking crisis was one of the main selling points for me. How do you guys feel about being rebels against the rest of the world?" There was no response. He went on, "What we're proposing is an independent, pioneering community that works together and uses the best of technology to make life better for everybody. This means you make the decisions that are best for you, for the environment and for the community – not for any bottom line or for the government. You are limited only by the amount of human labour and physical resources you have at your disposal.

"This numbers game is bullshit guys. It's based on nothing, only someone else's idea of getting rich off your back. I was an economics lecturer at MIT for fourteen years. One day a kid came up to me and asked me if you could have an economy without banks. I gotta admit it stumped me and made me wonder what would happen if the banks disappeared – and the truth is, nothing would happen. The sun would still come up in the morning, there would still be children to feed, things to wash and shit to be done. Why would all these things stop just because the bank didn't open? The point is, if we all kept doing our job as before, we would all continue to get what we need out of society even if no money was changing hands. And if we didn't like our jobs, then hell, we could go find ones we do like instead. Imagine how much more productive we would be then? And besides, all those shitty jobs in stores and offices that no-one likes would disappear anyway.

"I gotta admit, that kid's question woke me up and eventually caused me to leave MIT – well – before they ran me out of town," he confided. There were some laughs. The atmosphere in the press conference had changed completely. Maybe it was the camaraderie of the police officer being given the heave-ho, or maybe it was John's relaxed style, but there was a closer fabric among the group that had not been there before. It was palpable.

"We came here to discuss these ideas," Karl said, "now events have overtaken us with the Icelandic currency and stocks being wiped out. No-one wanted this to happen, but maybe this could turn out to be an exciting opportunity?"

Karl let those words hang in the air for a moment.

"OK, has anyone got any questions they'd like to ask?" Susan asked at last. The group of reporters stirred slowly. Eventually, the young woman who had put the police officer in his place stood up.

"Hello, I'm Lisa from the Iceland Review. Karl, Iceland may fit all of your criteria, but what makes you think that Icelanders would actually agree to having a free society?"

"That's true, we don't know. That's what we came here to find out. I still don't know if Icelanders will go for it since we haven't even had the meeting yet!" There were some laughs around the room. "Yes, it does fit the criteria, but I guess that's just the starting point. Making it happen is another matter entirely."

An older woman beside Lisa stood up. "A question for Mr. Drayton: you say we get rid of all the shitty jobs. So who's going to clean my drains when the toilet backs up? Is some guy who loves cleaning shitty toilets going to dance into my home holding a golden plunger?" Everyone erupted into laughter, including the panel.

"Haha! Well, yes and no. Look at it this way: if we can make a machine that can solve that problem for everybody, then we'll make it. But for those kinds of jobs, it's probably easier for a human to do it, and, as you say, you probably won't find a toilet genie, no."

There was another ripple of mirth.

"But," he continued, "what you will find are lots of people in your community who are only too glad to help.

"Remember, we are a social species, but money has disconnected us from each other. When you pay someone to come and unblock your toilet you don't need to interact with them. But we all love to help. It's built right into us. And when we no longer have monetary demands on us, we will all have more time and more compassion to help each other more."

The woman didn't seem fully convinced so Susan continued.

"Another idea being considered for operating a free society is to introduce service days. These are days that people would offer to their local communities on a regular basis. For example, depending on the local population and requirements, people might offer one day a month to serve their community. Once properly organised and rotated, you would always have people on hand to get things done in the community..."

"And clean shitty toilets." John finished.

"Exactly," Susan said. "The point is, in a free society, we could spend most of our time doing what we love and living well by automating the jobs we don't want to do, and rotating among the community the jobs we can't. I, for one, would have no problem giving several service days a month to a community that supported me in this way."

This seemed to satisfy the woman. Another reporter from the far left of the room chimed in.

"Hi, Einar from RÚV. What makes you think that everyone is going to pull their weight to make this society work? Aren't people just lazy? Won't they just all sit around waiting for someone else to do the work?"

Susan looked to Karl for help.

"That's one of the most common questions," Karl answered, "because we believe that we are only motivated by money. The truth is we are mostly motivated by money, but only because we need it to survive and live well in a monetary society. It's directly linked to survival, our strongest instinct. However we are also motivated by other urges too: the desire to be creative, to be productive, to help others, to learn, to improve ourselves and our surroundings, to meet people, to travel, to be popular, to be loved, to be sexually attractive, to have children, to look and feel good, to be healthy, to be happy and live long – all of these are genuine motivators of people.

"The problem is that these are drowned out by the giant money motivator that keeps us working for our own survival. But, once you take that away, and we agree as a community to guarantee ourselves all the requirements of a healthy and fulfilling life, then these smaller motivators will become our greatest motivators, and just imagine what we can become then?

"Every person will be able to aspire – and endeavour – to become their heart's desire without the restrictions of today. Aspiring artists, scientists, mathematicians, doctors, writers and musicians will be able to realise the pinnacle of their natural abilities; parents will be able to enjoy life in their communities watching their children grow; wandering spirits will be able to travel the world without fear of want; great thinkers, philosophers and idealists will be free to conjure up the next chapters for mankind's adventure on this planet and beyond.

"Humans are ingenious creatures. Our motivations and expectations of life are complex. Ask yourself, if you never had to work, would you really lie around on the sofa all day? Wouldn't that get just a little bit boring? I've no doubt that in a free world, some people probably would choose to do nothing, but so what? Let them. The fact is that people, by and large, are far happier when they are being productive in some way."

"Ab-sol-utely!" came a booming voice suddenly from the back of the room. Everyone turned around. There was Baldur Reyksson filling the open door with his stocky frame.

"And some people even like to lie around in police cells, but not this boy!" he said as he came marching up towards the podium. The room was full of whispers and gasps of astonishment. Finally, it grew into an applause that went on for at least a minute. Karl, Susan and John stood up to greet their friend, who shook their outstretched hands warmly.

Finally, after some adjustments to the top table, Baldur was sitting in the middle, flanked by Karl and John.

"What happened?" Karl asked under his breath during the reshuffle. Baldur adjusted his papers and was staring out into the camera lights with that mischievous twinkle in his eye.

"Bloody idiots," he muttered, "I had to ring their mother!" then launched into his prepared press speech.

Karl sat back, completely unable to stop smiling to himself. What a day, he thought.

F·DAY -3145

feeds.bbcnews.com/world:

ECB OFFERS EURO RESCUE PACKAGE FOR ICELAND

The Governor of the European Central Bank, Miguel Sanchez

today issued a Euro rescue package proposal for Iceland's troubled economy. The package is offering to guarantee Iceland Government bonds to their equivalent Euro value. Iceland's independent select economic committee are meeting with Government officials later today to discuss the proposal. If accepted, it is widely anticipated that it would spell the end of the Icelandic Króna.

Read more >>

REYKSSON APPEALS FOR CALM

President Reyksson of Iceland spoke for the first time yesterday after his release from police custody. He warned of people 'losing their heads' in the face of what he called 'exciting opportunities for Iceland'. Reyksson, who is currently undergoing impeachment proceedings, was detained by police yesterday during an investigation into improper official conduct and misuse of Government property, but was later released without charge.

Read more >>

POLISH PARLIAMENT ON THE BRINK OF COLLAPSE

15 members of the Polish parliament walked out in protest today after the court ruled that the recent election of Daniela Balcerak from the recently formed Free Party was valid. The opposition had contested Ms. Balcerak's results as void, accusing her of 'an illegal campaign to undermine the national security and sovereignty of the republic'. The central theme to Ms. Balcerak's campaign was a pledge to begin proceedings to disband the Polish parliament.

Read more >>

f-day.org/feeds/update:

ICELAND MELTDOWN [-3000 DAYS]

On foot of the recent events in Iceland, the F-Day panel has agreed to subtract 3000 days from its official countdown, bringing F-Day to just over forty-two years away.

F-Day.org >>

Karl had hardly slept. The previous day's events had caused a logjam in his consciousness. It was a day of historic twists and turns, under the watchful gaze of the world – and he was in the middle of it all. He felt really privileged. The atmosphere around the hotel and the island in general now was filled with that strong sense of camaraderie that blooms during times of crisis. People were stopping and talking on the street about what was happening. Shop and business owners were outside huddled together on the streets having coffee, trying to figure out what was going on. The people were visibly coming together, and life was already becoming a social experience. This, thought Karl, was how life should be all the time. It proves how well we act together when we are all forcibly brought to the same level.

Baldur's spectacular working of the press had been awesome to watch. A man, determined, sweeping aside all adversaries at a syllable's stroke. Somebody, somewhere had inadvertently pressed his Viking button, unleashing the fearsome Norse warrior within – conqueror of hinterlands, a plunderer of truth, sailing out into the dark unknown.

Baldur had cared little for the police – being puppeted by God knows who – with their sham of an arrest and farcical attempts to mute him. People tended to forget the tiny degrees of separation between all people on this island. Baldur, who knew everybody, had talked his way through their cell walls in seconds, leaving their arrest documents a smouldering pile of ashes in his wake. He was the farming President cum Norse hero riding a growing wave of public adoration. The more they were trying to cut him down, the more powerful he was becoming. He knew it. Now they knew it.

The architects of President Reyksson's impeachment were now starting to look like spoiled children telling tales in class, whose tables were now so irreversibly turned that they were beginning to incur the wrath of everyone else. In tough times people need a hero, and in a land where fighting convention is the norm, President Reyksson fitted the bill perfectly. There was no way they could impeach him now.

Karl felt deeply proud of the man he now called his friend.

President Reyksson fixed his moustache and scanned down through the paper again.

"Are you ready, Mr. President?" the cameraman said.

"Mmm," Baldur nodded. The cameraman gave him the five finger countdown and point. "Good evening everyone," Baldur began, "I don't need to tell you that the events of the last forty-eight hours have been shocking, unprecedented and quite incredible. I realise that my own actions in the office of President have been perhaps a little unconventional or eccentric, but I think you all know me well enough to believe me when I say I have never been dishonest or less than honourable.

"At this time, myself and some members of various forward-thinking groups around the world had scheduled a meeting to discuss the future economic possibilities of Iceland. This meeting was to be held in private as we were acutely aware of the sensitive nature of our discussions. The meeting was to be purely exploratory. Obviously, someone leaked out this information and speculation as to the nature of our talks spread around the world like wildfire, leading to the ditching of our currency and economic freefall that we have been experiencing.

"At this moment, our Government is considering a rescue package from the European Central Bank which will effectively bring us straight into the Eurozone. I'm sure many of you will have mixed feelings about that, but I want to tell you about a third option, that your Government will almost certainly not be presenting to you.

"I'm sure all of you will have noticed that the sun did rise today," he gestured casually towards the window, "that you woke up this morning and pretty much everything you knew about the world yesterday was still here today? Too easily we are led to believe that economic catastrophe is just that – a catastrophe. But as you can see, there is no catastrophe. We are all still here, very much alive, no bones broken, the sun is shining, the food is still growing in the field, the children are still laughing and playing, there are still things that need to be done. Life is still going on as before.

"Ask yourself, how much of our economic life is actually adding anything that contributes directly to our happiness and well-being? Most of us spend so much of our lives worrying about money, that we nearly miss the whole show. What if we changed the rules of the game? What if we changed the game entirely? What if the game was called 'get happy', instead of 'get rich'? What would we do differently? What are you doing now to be part of an economy that you wouldn't be doing if your only objective was to be happy?

"Imagine if, today, instead of thinking about our economic shock, we thought about our economic freedom? Freedom from economic slavery. As an organic farmer who has battled with all kinds of problems and setbacks, I soon came to realise that if I saw each problem, not as a problem, but merely as a gateway to a different option, life became so much easier for me.

"Iceland has been given an extraordinary opportunity here to do something truly amazing. Never in all modernity has a country or population come so close to the possibility of breaking with our self-imposed economic servitude forever. No more loans or mortgages, no more reckless pursuit of profit for profit's sake, no more living somewhere you hate and working at something you hate, no more worrying about your future or your children's future. No more cowing to Europe or external economic powers controlling our destiny.

"Iceland is one of the richest enclaves on the planet – resource-rich that is. We have all the free energy we can ever use, we have the brains, we have a great community. All we need to do is stand together, work together, for each other. We have done it before. I say let's do it again. Let us dare to be different. Let us dare to become the brave pioneers of mankind's future beyond money.

"Tomorrow, I will be walking the streets of Reykjavik to meet people between twelve o'clock and three o'clock, then onto Akureyri between six o'clock and eight. Come out and join me, walk with me, talk with me. Just like our ancestors did, let's define the future of our great little country out in the open air! We have nothing to fear and only great things to discover. The future is ours to make, so let's begin!"

"OK, you're off," the cameraman said at last. "That was pretty good chief."

"Hmmph, thank you," Baldur said wiping the sweat off his brow. He sighed and sat there for a moment. Yes, he thought to himself, that was pretty damn good!

F·DAY -3144

Karl wished he could have stayed but Abby needed him, and anyway he felt there was nothing else useful for him to do there. The two Truthfesters and Susan had stayed back to help out with the town hall meetings that were now being planned across the island. It was becoming like election time, but without the election. There was talk of a referendum on the money-free policy which seemed to be a good idea.

He was very happy to be home, to see that Abby and her little passenger were growing well. Together they tuned into the Iceland news channel in the afternoon, and there was Baldur – his friend – being mobbed by wellwishers along Reykjavik's Laugavegur. People pushing through and jostling to shake his hand. Baldur was repeating 'thank you, thank you so much!'

The camera panned out to show the streets completely choked with people. Shops were open, but, according to the commentary, no money was changing hands. People were on the streets offering hot drinks, soup and bread they had made, musicians were busking. It was like Christmas Eve, but without the shopping.

It was not entirely without protest of course. Many shop and restaurant owners were carrying signs and heckling the President as he was making his way through the throng. Some of the signs read 'my business is none of your business', or 'fight for the right to work'. One sign intriguingly said 'Free Snakes'. Baldur looked to be doing his best to debate with them, but the crowd was so loud and heavy that he was getting jostled along himself. It seemed to Karl that the dissenters were a very small minority and overall the atmosphere looked positively electric.

"He looks so happy," said Abby.

"Absolutely," Karl said almost tearfully. "he is one amazing guy. Look at that reaction! In just a few days this guy has woken up a whole nation purely by his guts and charisma. I can't wait for you to meet him."

"Really? We're going back?" she asked.

He shrugged. "Maybe," he replied, smiling at her. "Afterwards of course," he finished, putting his hand gently on her belly.

She laughed lightly, causing her baby to kick.

"Hey!" Karl shouted jokingly, pulling away his hand and looking down, "don't worry, you can come too," he said to the bump. He hugged Abby and they laughed together.

Karl was still tired and decided to go to bed for a rest. Yawning, he flicked open the computer screen to check the F-day website.

Web page not found, came the unhelpful response.

"Oh, bloody dodgy connection again," he muttered. He was too tired to think, so he closed the curtains, stretched himself out on the couch and drifted into a peaceful sleep.

In Karl's dream was a lake, a frozen lake surrounded by trees. Out in the middle of the ice was a frozen fountain. The water jets were frozen in mid-air. He walked out to it, but the ice under his feet was shaking, vibrating up and down like someone was waving the sheet from one end. He looked up and the frozen water jets were breaking off the fountain, first in little pieces, then big pieces, causing a metallic tinkling sound that was getting louder and louder...

Suddenly reality invaded the dream as the tinkle of his ringing phone was getting more insistent.

"Hello?" he answered in a bleary voice.

"Karl, the sites are down," came the voice.

"What?" he said sleepily. "Who's that?"

"Haha, Karl it's Podge. From New York. Sorry, did I wake you, buddy? All the free sites are down. I just checked. Is there a server issue or something?"

"Hey, hi Podge! Yeah was just having a little kip. I just got back from Iceland this morning."

"Oh yeah wow, we've been following it here..."

"Look Podge, can I call you back later? I'll check the site and see what the story is."

"No worries buddy, take care."

"Yeah cheers," Karl managed before throwing the phone on the chair and giving a big yawn. He put the screen back on. F-Day – not found; Free World Charter – not found. "Holy shit, what's going on?" he muttered. After some minutes he found the sites' error logs.

401 – unauthorised access
401 – unauthorised access
401 – unauthorised access
401 – unauthorised access...

He felt a cold wave come over him, from his feet, right up his legs, back and over the top of his head. Just at that minute, Abby walked in.

"Hey I thought I heard you," she said smiling. "Are you ready for some dinner?"

Karl looked at her blankly for a minute.

"What's wrong?" Abby inquired. "You look like you've seen a ghost."

Karl snapped back to it. "No, it's... OK. Just some problem with the website..."

"Oh OK," she said and started walking out of the room. "Come and have some dinner then you can look at it after OK?"

"Yeah sure," he said, looking into the distance and trying to hide the dread that was rising up in him. "Sure," he said to himself.

F·DAY -3133

feeds.bbcnews.com/world:

VIOLENT CLASHES IN POLISH PROTESTS

There were violent clashes last night in Gdansk as Poland's protests entered their second week. Riot police were called in to disperse crowds that had gathered at the symbolic shipyards to commemorate the 1980s protests. Police used tear gas and water cannons to clear the blockade that had effectively closed the shipyard for the past three days. 14 people were seriously injured including 4 police officers.

Read more >>

ICELAND'S ECONOMY TO BE FROZEN IN TIME

After yesterday's TV address to the nation, in which he'd urged Icelanders to become "brave pioneers of mankind's future beyond money", Iceland's President Reyksson took to the streets of Reyjkavik to meet the public. An estimated ten thousand people also took to the streets to meet the President and show their support, with some instead showing indignation.

There were some small protests from business owners, who were heckling the President, accusing him of committing 'economic treason', but Mr. Reyksson repeated his assurances that Iceland was an experiment and that the economy would be 'frozen in time', to be restored later in the event of an unfavourable outcome.

"Worse case scenario," he said, "we abandon the experiment and resume our economy exactly where we left off. There is nothing to lose – and everything to gain."

Full story and pictures>>

'EASTERN RISING' SHOWS NO SIGNS OF ABATING

The spate of protests across Eastern Europe is now at 'crisis levels' and has also spread to parts of Russia and Georgia, according to AP newswire. They are saying it is "difficult to determine a common thread to the protests, apart from the protest itself." The protests range from 'anti-austerity to pro-socialist and pro-equality' demonstrations. Russia's President Mendev today said that he welcomed "peaceful protest" and "meaningful dialogue for change" but warned that "social disorder or violent protest would not be tolerated".

Read more >>

SWISS GOVERNMENT TO VOTE ON BASIC INCOME

The Swiss parliament are to vote later tonight on amending the Welfare Act to include a basic income guarantee for all Swiss citizens. After a two-day marathon debate in the lower house, politicians will decide whether to adopt the new measures, widely seen as a progressive step in social justice and equality. The system has already been piloted in the city of Basel successfully for the last two months, which, supporters claim, has resulted in an immediate drop in crime rates.

Read more >>

F·DAY -3129

It was a warm, bright autumn day in Donskoy, downtown Moscow. In other words – a bracing ten degrees. Andrei Lagunov, his nine-year old son Tapac and seven of Tapac's classmates were walking silently in the morning air towards the city centre and Red Square. Tapac was a quiet boy with milk-white skin and coal-black hair. Sometimes Andrei worried about him. He didn't eat very much, was too skinny, and always seemed to be thinking. Thinking about what, Andrei wondered. He seemed to live in his own world, hardly spoke to him or his mother, Dominika, yet strangely, he was really popular in school. Andrei thought that maybe Tapac completely changed when he got to school, but his teachers also remarked on his quietness too.

Tapac was quiet, but he was not shy. He was just very calm and thoughtful which is what had made him popular. He was something of an enigma to his classmates and they were drawn to his aloof composure. He seemed to know things. He seemed to be one step ahead. He was like an adult and they all looked up to him.

Andrei turned to his son, "Are you sure about this Tapac? You know what they said on the news this morning?"

"Yes, I know Papa," Tapac replied. "This is why we are going today. Today is the right day."

Andrei sometimes felt out of his depth, like he was deprived of some special knowledge that Tapac had mysteriously acquired. What did he mean, 'today is the right day'? Does he know something I don't? he thought. The news earlier had warned of a striking protest by Russian miners in the city today. There seemed to be a protest every few days now it seemed to Andrei.

He was a bus driver, so he knew all about them. To him it meant huge traffic disruption and irate passengers. He was glad that today was his day off, but now here he was bringing Tapac right into the centre of it. He would have forbidden it, but Tapac had that strange sense of omniscience that was difficult to argue with. He seemed to know exactly what he was doing, and it was just better to let him do it.

They reached the edge of Red Square and saw the rows of police lining up and setting up the metal barriers ready for the day's work. Andrei suddenly felt sick. He got down and took Tapac by the shoulders.

"Son, listen to me. This is not a good idea. These men are dangerous and the police maybe even more so. Someone could get hurt today, and I don't want it to be you – any of you," he added looking around to the other seven boys. They said nothing but looked to Tapac.

"Papa," Tapac said, "the real danger is if we are doing nothing while our friends suffer. It's not about you or me or Mama. It's about all of us. Today, all different worlds will meet here, the past, the present and the future." He waved towards his friends. "We are the future, and the people need to know that we are here – that our voices count too." The boys nodded.

Andrei searched his son's face for answers, but he couldn't find any. He didn't know what he meant, he just saw the danger.

"Okay son, I will be with you," he said, "but promise me one thing..."

"What Papa?" Tapac asked, looking puzzled. His father didn't want to scare his son, but he couldn't find another way to say it.

"If I say run, we all run, okay?" Tapac looked a little annoyed. "Okay?" Andrei insisted.

"Okay Papa."

"Great!" his father said, kissing him on the forehead. "Let's go."

On the far side of the square a huge crowd was gathering now. A police cordon was being set up at the exit for the Kremlin. Andrei went over to talk to one of the Politsiya officers.

"Good morning, Officer, do you know what is the planned route of the march today?"

"Good morning. Yes they are planning to cross the river into Red Square, then to have a public rally here and afterwards march on to the Kremlin. Excuse me please..." he said while placing another barrier into position.

"Thank you," Andrei replied, "but this is the road to the Kremlin. Why are you blocking it?"

The officer glinted a smile, then shrugged.

"We have orders today that the crowd is too big, so no march to Kremlin." He turned and headed back to the truck.

Andrei felt a cold shiver. He looked down at the boys.

"Boys, I think we should move over to the East side in front of the store. It will be better there."

"No Papa," said Tapac coldly, "we'll stay here." He walked over to the wall, put down his sign and took his thermos flask out of the bag that Mama had packed for him.

Andrei sighed and shrugged and motioned the other boys over to sit by the wall too. As they sat there, they were becoming faintly aware of a low throbbing sound. Andrei looked at the boys, then at Tapac. The boys were afraid. He could sense it, but Tapac was cold and distant, sitting there wiping and inspecting his glasses as if out on a picnic. Andrei wanted to be a good father and give Tapac all the opportunities that he had never had with his father, but he wondered if he had gone too far this time.

On the far side of the river the miners were marching fast. They were being led by a twenty-strong drumming troupe, whose deafening pulse permeated the flesh and organs of all before it like some primitive war cry. The miners were carrying the usual array of signs, demanding better hours, more pay, more rights, a new government, decrying hate figures who they had singled out as the cause of all their grievances, but there was something else.

For a start, they were all dressed completely in black, and they were walking too fast. They had a strong momentum. They had purpose. They had hate. They had huge numbers.

Back on Red Square, it appeared as though the Politsiya had also felt the menace of the approaching black parade. Lines of armoured vehicles were rushing in now, more jeeps, more steel barriers, more personnel carriers unloading black-clad officers suiting up for riot duty. The throbbing was getting louder.

Andrei and the boys were watching the new activity with growing anxiety. Finally, the officer that Andrei had spoken to earlier ran over and told them they had to move and to get out of the square. They nodded and moved away, but they couldn't leave the square now. They were too invested in the unfolding story. Whatever happened now, they would be part of it.

They headed towards the huge crowd that had now assembled in the centre of the square, where a large stage and loudspeakers were being set up and tested. The crowd was a strange mix of serious, shady looking activists, mixed with happy but slightly unnerved foreign tourists who had inadvertently got caught up in the drama, security personnel talking on microphones, and local Russian onlookers who just came out for the show.

The heavy, distant throbbing suddenly came into sharp focus as the marchers rounded the final corner approaching the square. The dark mass of people approached, now shouting in coordination with the drums. The square erupted with cheers from the sympathetic crowd, and the man with the microphone enthusiastically heralded the arrival of their heroes. The crowd began to echo the shouts of the oncoming miners. The Politsiya were busy getting into formation. Armoured vehicles and water cannons were getting into position. It was like nothing could stop it now.

And nothing could.

Among the confusion of the next couple of minutes, there was so much movement of people and vehicles that Andrei never noticed the disappearance of the boys. It had already been decided that no dignified rally would ever take place. Everyone was here to fight. The marchers, realising the avenue to the Kremlin was being blockaded by Politsiya, were too fired up already. They wanted blood. The Politsiya could smell the rage and they too were intoxicated with the bloodlust now. They closed ranks. The miners surged. Missiles came from their pockets. Chaos opened up.

In the melee, no-one noticed the tiny group of young boys that had entered the arena, carrying small signs and chanting 'free our future'. In the noise of war, the report of automatic weapons, the explosion of molotov cocktails and popping of tear gas canisters, the sirens and car alarms, the shrill pre-pubescent cries of the small boys were brutally crushed.

Andrei, himself bleeding in the crossfire and unable to hear himself scream, was running about grabbing anyone, members of the Politsiya, protesters and terrified tourists.

"Where's my boy? Tapac! Tapaaaaac!"

Then he saw them. An ambulance in the centre of the battlefield had suddenly created a halo of calm in the now-dying battle. People had slowed and formed a circle. They were looking down at the ground. Andrei was pushing through the crowd of heads with animal strength.

"Tapac!" he cried.

He finally got to the circle and found a female ambulance worker, kneeling on the ground tending to his son, who was splayed out on the ground like a ragdoll dropped off a roof. Glasses smashed, leg twisted, blood coming from his ear and mouth. Tapac was shaking involuntarily, his homemade sign saying 'free our future' snapped in half beside him.

F·DAY -3128

feeds·bbcnews·com/world:

RUSSIAN BOY PROTESTER STILL CRITICAL

Tapac Lagunov, the nine-year-old Russian boy who was caught up in yesterday's baton charge in Red Square, Moscow is reportedly still critical and in a coma. Doctors at the Botkin City Hospital say Tapac suffered 'extreme trauma' to the back of the head, chest and legs, and may have suffered 'significant' brain injury. He is still undergoing tests.

Tapac and seven of his school friends had been staging a free demonstration during yesterday's violent anti-government protest by miners in which 40 people were seriously injured. Russia's President Mendev said he was 'deeply shocked' at the news and has been in touch with the Lagunov family.

Read more >>

ICELAND'S PRIME MINISTER DECLARES STATE OF EMERGENCY

Eric Johannson, Iceland's Prime Minister last night gave a televised address declaring a national state of emergency. Reacting to the mass walk-out of workers in Iceland's retail, industrial and civil institutions yesterday on foot of the recent currency crisis, Mr Johannson issued a stern warning to Icelanders: "The current groundswell of support for a free society in Iceland will quickly evaporate when our shops have no food, our homes have no power and the trash is piling up in our yards." He appealed to workers to "stay focused" and not to "become victims of mass delusion in these uncertain times".

Video and more >>

MILITARY TO INTERVENE IN POLISH POLITICAL VACUUM

The Polish Parliament was formally dissolved today after the elected parties failed to create a government. The outgoing ruling party met with military chiefs of staff who agreed to maintain a temporary military rule until fresh elections are held. The parliament fell into disarray following recent elections, after several members began legal proceedings and counter-proceedings contesting their respective electoral campaigns. A new election will be held on July 25. Meanwhile there were further protests in major cities last night, with some arrests in Warsaw.

Read more >>

'BIG MOMENT' TO BE ROLLED OUT OVER NEXT TWO YEARS

The Swiss Department of State announced that its new Basic Income Guarantee (or 'BIG Moment') will actually be rolled out over two years. The Minister, Alain Proust announced that the scheme would be introduced on a phased basis, starting with those 'most in need' and will run in tandem with the existing welfare system until the welfare system is phased out in two years. The final figures are yet to be decided but they are widely expected to reach eighty percent of the current Swiss average industrial wage. (about €24,000 pa.)

Read more >>

Karl snapped the computer shut and lay back wincing at the ceiling to get his eyes accustomed back to reality. He and Stef, the Dutch tech guy had just spent the last few days upgrading all the websites to prevent against future attacks (he hoped). They had discovered several rogue IP addresses that were targeting all his sites and had succeeded in shutting down their server. The IP addresses were registered to servers in Egypt, The Philippines, South Africa and Canada. Their attempts to try and locate the owners of these servers was interesting, but ultimately proved fruitless. They were registered under bland company names such as SMA inc., or Polytech, or ITC, all of which seemed to lead up blind alleys.

Since they were more interested in getting services back online, they didn't spend too much time investigating. Whatever conspiracies they were imagining, they could wait until later. First, they had to get things back up and running, then they had to try to figure out how to prevent such attacks in the future.

Stef was a brilliant computer technician from Holland who Karl had met through his website. They had been coordinating their efforts online for the last few days. Stef managed to configure the sites to bounce randomly from among a list of IPs and to block consistent direct IP requests to the sites. Also, he coded in some limitations for anyone accessing the sites too frequently. As an added precaution, they agreed to set up mirror sites and databases, so if one went down, they could quickly redirect to another. It was something Karl should have done years before, but he never imagined the site would come under attack in this way.

Since his return from Iceland, Karl had been so busy that he hardly kept up with the news, and was only vaguely aware of what was going on in the world. So when Podge called him, he felt a little like he had just crawled out from under a rock.

"Hey bro, how's it going?" said Podge, bald as ever, his anarchy tattoo caught in a chink of light in the Venetian blinds.

"Podge my friend, it's great to see you. Sorry I've been so busy lately. All the sites went down. We got hacked..."

"Yeah I know, I told you," Podge smirked.

"Oh yeah," Karl smiled. "Sorry. Thanks dude. So I've been doing all that and not much else. What have you been up to?"

"Dude, you're fucking with me, right?"

Karl couldn't tell if he was serious. "No, what's up?"

"Maaan, you're unbelievable!" Podge shouted, laughing.

"Sorry, I guess I've been out of the loop..."

"Yesterday we had the biggest motherfucking money-burning protest yet right here in Wall St. It was unbelievable. We reckon we burned over two hundred thousand bucks!"

"Whaat? Two hundred thousand bucks?" Karl shouted.

"Yeah I reckon. That Hilton girl was here opening up a new shoe store just around the corner and the place was packed. Loads of paparazzi and the rest. So lots of Occupy and Free guys turned up to try milk the crowd. Me and Anna started asking people to take out some notes. We had oil and matches to light them. We took out ten bucks each and started to look for more from people. It was incredible! The whole thing turned into a circus. All the Occupy guys were throwing in five and ten bucks, then the tourists started giving us tens and twenties! There was a reggae band busking and some samba guys joined in and they all got fired up. Next thing you know, we had bankster guys chucking in twenties and fifties on their lunch breaks. It was all over the net. Check it out."

"Hahaha! That's incredible! Brilliant." Karl exclaimed. "Will check it out later. It didn't make news though. I was checking that."

"Yeah, can you believe those guys? There were crews down there filming the whole thing, but not a dicky bird on the nationals. Total blanket job!"

"No matter, the net stuff is great! I was checking the site stats here from yesterday – we got a big spike in the States from around 7pm here. Now I know why!" Karl laughed.

"Excellent, so you got the sites sorted out then?"

"Yeah it was weird. It was an organised attack. No idea who, or what though." Karl felt that he should say something more to Podge about what Commander Robbins had told him, but again he bit his tongue. He didn't want to make it any more real by discussing it.

Podge was silent. "What kind of an attack?" he asked at last.

"Er, there was a group of IPs from all over that were overloading the server with requests. They brought the whole thing down. The only thing we know is that it was coordinated. All the requests began at the same time and ended at the same time. It was deliberate and well-organised."

Podge was deep in thought.

"Why?" Karl asked.

"Man," he said, wincing and frantically rubbing his bald stubble.

"What's up?"

"Dude, someone was in my apartment yesterday."

"Oh?" Karl said casually, trying to mask the cold shiver that had just passed through him.

"Yeah, it was the weirdest thing. Me and Anna got back here after the protest. We were high as kites coming in the door."

"Yeah, you and Anna?"

"Sorry, Anna is my new girlfriend. She was a good friend of Tanja's."

"Okay, right..." Karl said, wondering whether sympathy or congratulations was appropriate.

"Anyway," Podge continued, "we came into the apartment, but the door wasn't deadlocked. We always deadlock it. We thought that was really weird and went in, expecting to find the place turned upside down and our laptops gone, but no. Everything was exactly as we had left it. So we started to think we had just forgotten to deadlock the door, grabbed some food and headed for bed. I was taking some cream for my scalp from the drawer when I noticed my passport was gone. It was freaking gone. I started freaking out and looking for it, but it wasn't there. Anna was asking me if I was sure, so then we checked hers. It was gone too.

"Well, fuck me man, we couldn't sleep for nothin' then. We was checking everything in the apartment from the teaspoons to the sugar to the freakin' toothpaste. Anna was totally freaking out cos she's an illegal anyway from Cuba. Why the fuck would anyone want a Cuban passport, man?"

Karl was overwhelmed with a sense of duty now.

"Dude, I have to tell you that you might be in danger." Podge stared at him, still shaking with emotion. "A few weeks ago I got a call from Commander Robbins of all people..."

"JKR?" Podge asked with a weak, involuntary thumb-up.

"Yes JKR. He overheard a conversation at a business lunch. Podge, something is going down here. We might be in danger. All of us." Karl was beginning to scare himself, but talking about it was also making him feel better somehow. He had brushed this under the carpet for too long. "The websites weren't taken down by hackers. It was too organised. Stef said he had never seen anything like it before. Someone somewhere wants to put us out of business."

"Fuck me man," Podge shouted, "if they want to kill me they'll just shoot me right? Why the fuck would they sneak in here and take our passports?

"I don't know. They don't want you to leave the country. Why?" He thought about it for a moment, then said, "Look Podge, why don't you go find out what you can about who came into your apartment. Maybe you can ask a neighbour or something?"

"Sure, do you think maybe they bugged me too while they were at it?"

"Good point. Maybe. We can't rule it out. Maybe we should use encrypted chat from now on, just in case?"

"Shit. The computer," Podge said suddenly. "They probably fucked about with the computer. It was here all day. Still works perfectly, but maybe they added something... Shit..."

"Okay maybe. I'll ask Stef to get in touch with you and he can walk you through what you can check for on the computer. If they left something, he'll know how to find it."

"Okay cheers bro. I wish I could say I feel better, but I'm seriously fucked up now. We gotta move out of here..."

"Well look at it this way, if anyone wanted to hurt you they would have already done it, so there's no immediate danger. I'd say keep your head down for a while anyway, just in case."

"Okay thanks man. You stay safe too, okay?"

"Yeah I will, take care Podge."

Karl stood up, trying to figure out what the hell was going on, when suddenly a chilling thought occurred to him. He could hear Abby preparing dinner in the next room, so he went over to their locker and edged the top drawer open slowly.

"Phew!" he sighed, much relieved. The two passports were still there.

F·DAY -3125

feeds·bbcnews·com/world:

ANARCHIST PROTESTS ARE 'UNDER CONTROL'

London Metropolitan Police Assistant Chief Inspector, Bernard Camble, claimed that the ongoing protests at Parliament Square, Trafalgar Square and Oxford Circus, now in their second week of escalation are "peaceful" and "under control". The protests, some of which have seen public money-burning episodes similar to last month's protests at Wall St. in New York, have been largely peaceful. Inspector Camble praised the members of the Occupy and Free movements for their cooperation with police and local businesses.

Read more >>

ICELAND IS 'REMARKABLY STABLE'

Iceland's premier Eric Johannson has described Iceland's situation as remarkably stable in spite of the recent striking off of the Króna from global currency markets.

'We are still officially in a state of emergency,' he said, 'but on the ground, there is no emergency anywhere. Icelanders are a proud, hard-working people and most people are still working at their jobs in spite of wage uncertainty. We will be able to ride out the storm and get our economy back on its feet again.' There were hopeful signs of recovery for the beleaguered currency as it began to rally once again against the Yen last night.

Read more >>

feeds·shoutoutuk·org/world:

MONEY BURNING SPREADING LIKE WILD FIRE

Looks like this money burning thing is turning into a Europe-wide bushfire! We have reports from London, Newcastle, Berlin, Dusseldorf, Hanover, Madrid, Milan. Check out the videos below. Lots of small groups, but the bigger demonstrations like Berlin and Madrid has seen the wanton destruction of unknown thousands of Euro! One demonstrator, Tom from London, described it as being like an "exorgasm". "It's like something that seems so important, and you watch it go up in flames – to let it go like that is an awesome liberating experience. I challenge anyone to try it – even just a fiver. To feel the pain of letting go, followed by the exquisite release."

Videos and more >>

feeds·grapevine·is:

OMG! LOOK! NOTHING HAPPENED!

Looks like our national meltdown is really not much faster than our glaciers. What happened? The sky was supposed to fall on our heads and we were all supposed to run around screaming and diving for cover. Er no, not quite. A civilised bunch, we decided we'd think about it first. One could be forgiven for thinking that we frosty people are either in mass shock-denial or, dare I say it, are quite warming to the idea of being a free society. Psst, don't tell my friends, but I actually turned up for work today here at Grapevine HQ and, er, so did everyone else. Well, we love our jobs, so it's easy for us, right? Right?

Here's some more misty photos of Iceland>>

The centre of Moscow hadn't been that quiet since Lenin's funeral. The stark white ground set against the dark clouds gave the whole monochromatic scene an epic, historic feel. Through the chilly evening air, only the muffled sound of footfall in the snow could be heard as crowds gathered at the hospital gates to pay their last respects to Tapac, who, just hours before, had lost his fight for life and entered that immortal realm of martyrdom.

Nine-year-old Tapac Lagunov was a national hero now, beyond all reproach, beyond all harm, forever an innocent child victim of a greedy adult game. There were few among the miners or Politsiya that weren't riddled with shame. For many of those, Tapac's death would be their own defining, awakening moment.

Even the media, always keen to amplify and exploit the emotions, were silenced in reverence as they filmed the ordinary working people of Moscow filing past the hospital gates, many of them carrying large signs left completely blank. It was the ultimate expression of sympathy and contempt. There were no words.

The silence and reverence was short-lived however. After an ill-conceived condolence speech from the Russian President on TV, describing Tapac as 'a brave young spirit adrift in a sea of rage and cowardice', this was the last straw for the protesters who could maintain their reverence no longer.

Hell opened up onto the streets of Moscow that night. The anger had found a route. The first petrol bomb hadn't even hit the ground when the whole sky in Red Square appeared to begin raining fire. Police were overwhelmed by tens of thousands of protesters, as hundreds of cars and shops across the city were trashed and burned. Groups of masked gunmen ran through the streets, chanting and shooting into the air. In what would later become known as the 'Night of a Thousand Fires', fourteen protesters and four policemen were killed, with many hundreds of people injured.

As daylight crept back in, Moscow was spent. Looking like the aftermath of a nuclear holocaust, the streets slowly began filling up with citizens from all the rural, outlying parts of the country. Over a million people, many of them children, began their sit-down vigil on Red Square holding candles and pictures of a smiling Tapac with his own words, 'Free our future!'

Some three thousand kilometres away, however, Karl Drayton had other things on his mind as he watched Eli Drayton come into the world for the first time.

She was perfect, just like her mum – with thick black hair and a stubby nose. They all huddled together in a group hug in the fading twilight of the hospital room. It had been a long day. The Drayton family was now complete.

F·DAY -3124

In America, in her usual suave, perfectly timed delivery, President Carley appealed for calm in Moscow and offered her sympathies to the Lagunov family. In her State Of The Nation address, she paid tribute to Tapac and the wider Free Movement for highlighting the 'many problems of our Western way of living', but added firmly that 'complex problems require complex solutions' and that she had 'full confidence in her administration to clean up the economy and get America working again!' To drive her point home, she announced that Congress had agreed to an extra twenty-five billion dollars in funds to be invested in education and social housing over the next year, with a further commitment to increased funds in subsequent years.

The American media suddenly went into a crazy spin with the unexpected announcement, spending the next few days analysing data and poring over pie charts about the budget increases.

Jean Carley was probably one of the most admired presidents in American history – not just for being the first female president, but also for her former TV chat show career. Carley's People had been a cable hit from the get-go. She was America's darling chat show queen for twelve years running, asking the tough questions in her effortless, charming way. However, her frustration in dealing with politicians had finally got the better of her, and she decided to enter politics herself. With her legendary shoot-from-the-hip style, she went from cable hit to runaway polling booth hit overnight.

Jean was originally just an average all-American mom from Nebraska, but her rise to fame began after a chance interview she did on Fox News back in 1992. Her husband Jeb had been killed in action the year before in the Gulf War, but had died a hero, having saved two large personnel carriers from booby-trapped mines in Kuwait – at the expense of his own life. Jean, who had arrived in Washington, along with their two children, to receive Jeb's posthumous Purple Heart and Presidential Honours, had been accosted by an over-zealous young reporter afterwards:

"How do you feel being here today? You must be so proud of Jeb." she had proffered.

"Jeb was a beautiful and kind man who loved his family and his country, and who we were blessed to have in our hearts." Jean had said with steely pride and resolve. "Jeb was and always will be our hero, my hero. He died to protect his family, his country and his fellow troops. No-one could ask any more than that of any man."

"Wow, amazing words, thank you" the reporter gushed, "he sounds like an amazing guy. His father also served, is that correct?"

"Yes, Jeb's father Dale served in Vietnam. He also received a Purple Heart for bravery. He's recently retired as general – and his father fought in World War 2 as well. America owes a huge debt to the service and bravery of the men from this family. I know General Carley is enormously proud of Jeb today too."

Jean's almost mocking defiance and pride had stirred the hearts of many other soldiers' widows in the face of their terrible grief. Shortly afterwards, Fox had asked her to do a special one-off show for the fallen soldiers' wives and husbands. She agreed. Her calm yet strong interviewing style quickly gained the confidence of her interviewees and audience – and the attention of Fox's head of programming, who wasted no time in offering her a show and a deal she couldn't possibly refuse.

Carley's People went on the air a few months later, became an instant hit and was quickly moved to prime time where it sat resolutely for twelve years. Jean loved the show and the success, but something troubled her. All this time Jean Carley had been harbouring a dark secret – a secret that was tearing her apart. All her years of success had been based on a lie, and somehow she knew she had to make things right.

Jeb had hated the war, his obnoxious overbearing father, the army and all the bullshit that went with it. He had been terrified when he was called for duty in Kuwait – a twenty-seven-year-old corporal who had been bullied into service by his tyrant of a dad. He had wept in Jean's arms and had even planned to desert, but she had talked him out of it. She talked him out of it and sent her beloved husband off to his lonely, pointless death in the desert. How many nights she had cried herself to sleep in her empty bed for what she had done to Jeb.

Jeb, beautiful innocent Jeb, who had smiled at her as he walked away that morning with a casual wink and "see you later", smiling as he had caressed Sarah and Thom's sleepy heads in their beds before tiptoeing out of their room. Those had been his acts of true heroism for Jean – smiling in the face of his own sinking despair – not blowing himself to pieces in some fucking godforsaken sandpit. Jeb just wanted to live in peace and be with his family. Oh, how she missed his strong arms and pale blue-eyed gaze...

She had been through all the blame, grief and self-effacing as any widow could do until she could do no longer. She was cried out. Instead, she became a tough raconteur and a mouthpiece for social justice. She had dealt with more spineless, warbling politicians than she could bear. She had decided to quit the show and try and make a difference herself. In just a few years she was now sitting in the Oval Office. It was a plan that had worked very well, she thought.

But she wasn't done yet.

F·DAY -3121

For Podge and Anna, it was becoming almost like a day job. They were even getting to know some of the beautifully suited people scurrying in and out of their Wall St. offices for their lunch breaks, always on their phones.

"Who the hell are they talking to all the time?" Podge asked Anna suddenly, lightheartedly nodding and smiling at the impeccably dressed Italian man who was walking by, talking loudly to himself. "I mean they probably spend all day in the office shouting down the phone to some hedge-fund guy, then come out for a bagel and they're still with the phone. Don't they need a break?"

"You wanna break from protesting babe?" Anna inquired, then seeing his puzzled look, grabbed him by the arm and put her head against his shoulder. "No, of course, you don't. You know why?"

Podge shrugged.

"Because you're obsessed. Just like these guys. This is what you do best and you love it. So, this is what these guys do best and they love it too."

"Yeah," Podge conceded, "then there's all that thrill-of-the-chase stuff that goes with closing the big deal. I can see how it could be exciting." He smiled and put his arm around her waist as they turned the corner onto Wall St.

"Get back!" yelled the big red face that greeted them at the corner. Podge and Anna stumbled back in fright. "Back!" the mouth shouted again. Podge regained his composure. The face belonged to a S.W.A.T.

officer wearing body armour and helmet and holding a small automatic weapon. The officer motioned them to move back down the street.

"What's going on?" Anna shouted.

"Please move back folks. There's a shooter on the street ma'am..."

"Hey!" Podge shouted suddenly pointing past the officer. "That's Mattie..." He looked at Anna.

"Oh my God, you're right..." On the first floor balcony of a shop just inside an open window, Anna could barely see the skinny figure of a bearded man wearing a purple check shirt.

"You know him sir?" inquired the officer. "That's our shooter."

"What?" Podge was incredulous. "Mattie? Mattie wouldn't hurt a fly. He's one of our..."

Podge was interrupted by two piercing cracks of gunfire. The officer instinctively huddled behind the corner, shielding them back with his arm. They could hear the sound of falling glass.

"Do you know the shooter sir?" The officer asked again.

"Yes, has he shot someone?" Podge said.

"No, not yet, sir, I need you to go talk to the Situation Officer. We believe he may have hostages in there." He pointed over to one of the black jeeps that were now scattered across the entrance to the street. The officer spoke into his collar mike. "I have a friend of shooter here. Sending him over now, over."

"Roger that," the voice replied.

"Sir, you need to go and talk to the Situation Officer."

"OK." They ducked and made a wide circle over towards the jeep. Podge was still reeling in disbelief. He knew that Mattie dabbled a bit too much in 'illegal substances', but he was a gentle, loving guy. What the hell happened to bring him to this?

The Situation Officer was not what they were expecting at all. He was a small, slight man in jeans and t-shirt, sitting in one of the jeeps.

"Hi, I'm Brice." He turned smiling and offered his hand to both of them as they sat in the back seat of the jeep. "Tell me what I need to know about our friend here..."

"Em..." Podge was totally caught off guard by the man's calm, friendly approach. "His name is Mattie...Mattie Lynch I think. Lives on East Side, somewhere around Canal Street. Lives with his mom I think. Not married..."

"Subject on balcony again..." the radio cut in. Brice leapt from the jeep holding a microphone in his hand. Podge and Anna peered up and could just see Mattie standing on the balcony with the gun hanging down in his hand.

"Sir," Brice boomed through the megaphone, "we need to know if you are holding any hostages inside..."

Mattie looked over and shrugged weakly. He looked dazed Podge thought. Like he was tripping or something.

"I just want to go home," he said finally, rubbing his brow.

"M-13, I have a clear shot," the radio burst in.

"M-12, clear shot, awaiting signal," said another voice.

"Sir, I need you to throw your weapon on the ground, so we can all go home," Brice said reasonably.

"If you kill me, she will die. She's gonna die! You hear me?" Mattie screamed, suddenly sobbing.

"All agents stand down, repeat stand down," Brice said quickly into the radio. "Fuck! He's got a hostage. Fuck!" he cursed to himself.

"Let me talk to him," Podge said.

Brice turned around and looked Podge up and down.

"Does he like you? I mean does he trust you?" he asked.

"Absolutely," Podge said. Brice stared at him for a moment. Anna nodded.

"Yes absolutely," she agreed.

"OK," Brice handed Podge the mike.

"Mattie?" Podge called. "Mattie, it's Podge."

"Podge?" Mattie said faintly, looking up, shielding his eyes. Podge stepped out of the jeep holding the mike and waving the other hand up in the air.

"Yeah man, it's me."

Mattie looked to be shaking. Podge looked to Brice who signalled him to keep talking.

"Listen man, what's going down? We need to end this." Mattie was still shaking.

"He's in bad shape," Podge said, leaning into the jeep. "Let me go over and talk to him and we'll end this."

Brice looked doubtful. He looked from Podge to Anna.

"He's right," Anna said. "Mattie will listen to Podge. Podge is like a big brother to him."

"And if he kills you?" asked Brice matter-of-factly.

"That's not going to happen," Podge said.

Anna shook her head in agreement. "No way."

"OK but listen, sounds like he's got a female hostage in there, and as far as I'm concerned she's the most important person here now. You follow me?" Brice looked at him sternly and picked up the radio. "I don't care what happens to this guy, and you're going at your own risk as far as I'm concerned. I can't guarantee your safety, but if something happens and she dies or if he's got her wrapped up in some explosive, I'm going to be seriously pissed, you follow?"

Podge nodded. "Sure," he said.

Brice paused then pressed the radio. "OK, we got friend of suspect going over to negotiate. Male, bald, wearing black leather jacket and jeans. Please stand by." He motioned to Podge. "OK, go, go..." Podge leaned over and kissed Anna, ran to the edge of the cordon, then walked under and towards the balcony.

As he got close to the balcony, Mattie visibly relaxed.

"Hey," Podge said casually.

"Hey man," Mattie broke into sobbing. Podge was standing below the balcony.

"What happened, dude? What's this all about?" Podge asked, waving his hand around the deserted street – a surreal scene for Wall St. on a Monday afternoon.

"My mom," he sobbed. "They said they're going to kill her."

"What? Who? Who's going to kill your mom?"

Mattie was sobbing uncontrollably now. "The guys that I owe the money to. I owe them fifty grand man. If I don't pay up they said they're going to go after her..."

The street suddenly exploded in thunder and lead. Mattie and Podge's bodies both shook violently as they stood, being mercilessly pummelled with bullets, then dropping lifelessly to the ground in the smoke from the burning air.

Then silence, except for the distant screams of Anna.

In the front of the jeep, Brice looked down at the radio in his hand in shock, while Anna was running and screaming through the cordon to get to Podge. She knelt over him, screaming his name and lifting his head, but it was too late. Podge was gone. She cried up to the skies with Podge's head on her lap.

Brice slowly stepped out of the jeep, as all his gunmen were running back to their starting positions. They were all eyes on Brice. They were standing there looking at him, while two men went over towards Anna. As soon as one of them touched her on the shoulder, she jumped up and raced towards Brice.

"Why?" she screamed. "You bastard! You bastard..." She was trying to punch and kick him. Brice moved back and two of the officers stepped in to restrain her.

Brice was still in shock. "I... I didn't..." Then, slowly realising what had happened, he started looking around and up and down the street. All the officers and Anna were staring at him now, confused. He looked horrified.

"I didn't give the order," he said quietly.

F·DAY -3120

feeds·abcnews·com·au/us:

WALL ST. SHOOTOUT ENDS IN TWO DEAD

A shootout earlier today in New York's Wall St. has ended in two anarchist protesters being shot by Police. The two armed 'Free World' protesters had apparently seized control of a small office at the Wall St. accountancy firm Godin & Wallace where they had been holding one female hostage. One of the gunmen opened fire at police through a window shortly after police arrived. After a tense stand-off, both men were shot by police marksmen.

New York's Mayor Sam Gould arrived on the scene shortly afterwards and praised the law enforcement officers for doing their job, saying in an interview, "I have a lot of sympathy for the people of the Free Movement and what they stand for, but of course, you still gotta have law and order!"

Read more >>

Karl and Abby were having a wonderful time with their newest family member, Eli Drayton, who was full of gurgles, chat and cuddles. She was a happy child and liked nothing better than to sit there in her chair flinging her bear on the ground for Daddy and their dog Kylie to go chasing after.

Abby shook her head as she nearly tripped over Karl crawling along with the bear in his mouth to Eli's ecstatic screams.

"Come on, dinner's ready," she said. "Can't you just play fetch with the dog? You know, like in normal families?" she joked.

The phone saved him.

Karl was surprised to hear from Podge on the phone, since they always did their calls online. He answered the phone breathlessly in a cheery voice.

"Heeeeeeeey!" That cheerfulness was short-lived.

"Oh my God." He sat down. Anna's voice was hollow and shaking. He waved to Abby to go ahead without him and went to his office.

"They took him..." Anna burst into tears again. "And now they're calling him a criminal..."

Karl couldn't say anything. There was nothing he could say that would have any meaning. He was just sitting, nodding his head, being there.

"He wouldn't hurt a fly... you know that," she sobbed. They sat in silence for a few moments.

Finally, Karl felt a wave of conviction come over him.

"OK. Look, we both know how passionate Podge was for this movement. Someone is trying to break us. I've no idea who – maybe they're even listening to us now, but I know one thing, Podge would want us to continue. Now more than ever."

"Yeah, I know."

"But we have to be smart. Let's keep a low profile for now. I'll issue a statement denying the press claims and make a quick video, but that's all I'm doing. I'm not going to give any more oxygen to this hostage crap."

"Oh yeah," Anna said blearily, "there's a letter for you here. From Podge."

136

"Really?"

"Yeah, he wrote it last week. He was going to post it to you."

"OK, listen Anna, can you get into Podge's private chat messenger?"

"Yeah, he told me the password. It's –"

"No, don't tell me!" Karl interrupted, then looked up and whispered, "Good for you, Podge!"

"OK Anna," he continued, "I want you to log in there in about five minutes. I'll tell you how to get that letter to me."

"OK, I will."

"Thanks Anna. Now more than ever, let's free this world. But we'll have to play smart now. Keep a low profile OK?"

"Yeah sure."

"OK, and take care of yourself, Anna. We'll talk soon."

Karl shut off the phone and sat there in shock and disbelief for a while. Podge! My God! What a waste. Anna had told him everything that had happened. Someone must have cut in on the SWAT radio channel and given a fake order to shoot both men. But who? Could anyone just hack into the Police frequency like that? If it was someone else, then surely they must have planned the whole thing somehow? Podge must have known something. He had to get that letter.

He spent a few minutes googling addresses in his own neighbourhood trying to find the name of one of his neighbours. He found one, then cross-checked it and went for Podge's private chat account.

"Anna, when you get a chance, here's what I want you to do. Take a walk tomorrow and bring Podge's letter with you. If you're pretty sure no-one's following you, duck into a Post Office, buy an envelope and mark it to this address: Ken Waller, 41 Hyde Road, Blackrock, Dublin, Ireland.

"Then on Podge's envelope write '4Karl F-Day' on the back, put it in the other envelope and post it. But if you think someone's watching you or following you, don't send it! Wait until you're totally sure.

"Great thanks. Stay safe and stay low for a while. Please. Drop me a message just to let me know you got this. Ciao, K.

"Oh by the way, what was the name of the other guy they shot? The other protester?"

F·DAY -3119

Karl had spent almost two hours doing searches on Mattie Lynch. He had also started using an encrypted relay network for internet. He no longer had any irrational reason to feel paranoid. He knew he was now in danger and he had to start being extremely careful with all his actions.

Mattie, according to all the public profile information that he could glean from the social web, was obviously someone who suffered extreme paranoia, and according to Anna, had dabbled extensively in dangerous drugs like heroin and coke. It was pretty easy to make that assumption anyway by looking at his pictures. He was very skinny and his face looked at least fifteen years older than his real age of thirty-six.

He had a blog page but there was only one entry on it, which was an incoherent rant about how the military establishment was tampering with the water using satellite lasers, and how they were making everyone sick. It was pretty nauseating reading and Karl had to stop after a while. It was clearly a drug-fuelled tirade, mostly written in upper case, with almost no punctuation or paragraphs. Of course, Karl knew, as is usual with that kind of writing, the words had less to do with what was wrong with the world and more to do with the writer's own misery.

Anna had mentioned that Mattie's mother was very sick. Also, she had heard one of police officers mention that he told Podge he owed a lot of money. There was definitely a lot more to this story, so there was only one thing for Karl to do. Ring the man who knew everything.

As usual, Mike Ross didn't answer the phone, so Karl left a message. Within ten seconds the phone rang.

"Hi Mike, thanks for calling back."

"No problem, what's up friend?"

"I need to talk to you in a private channel. What's the best way to do that?"

"Em, Pidgin software? Have you got it?"

"Yes, is that OK for you?"

"Sure, er, get me at user name 'foxtrot14168', all lower case."

"OK I'll be on in five minutes."

Karl was not disappointed as usual. Mike really was a living oracle. If he didn't know it, he could find out within seconds. Whatever internet he was using, it was better than Karl's. Maybe he was trawling the so-called 'deep web', Karl mused. He imagined Mike walking along an ocean floor picking up long lost Spanish gold and tossing it aside in favour of an old photograph or long-lost letter. Information was Mike's real treasure, and in an age where some information was worth many times more than gold, he truly was a master diver.

foxtrot14168 is typing...

"...so your guy had a few possession charges, nothing too serious. Class C... Charges dropped in one, other two... got some community service... Don't see any relationship or social correlations, probably single...

"lives, sorry lived... with his mother Anna Jackson in 252 Mott St, Lower East Side...

"Mother has advanced Parkinson's Disease... scheduled for hospital care twice but cancelled both times. No reason given...

Let me check pharma records..."

Karl was taking some notes and doing some googling himself. It looks like this lady needed constant care and heavy meds. Maybe they couldn't afford the care so had to cancel. Looks like this guy had a lot going on in his mind...

foxtrot14168 is typing...

"interesting..."

"What?" Karl typed.

"Well, most advanced Parkinson's patients need heavy doses of a drug called Perodopa which she was taking along with other pain killers and occasional steroids..."

"Yup?"

"Well, she stopped taking them last year..."

"OK...?"

"Well, I mean there's no more prescription records after that time... She either stopped taking her meds which is doubtful... or..."

"or???"

"Or she was getting them on the black market..."

"Aha..."

"??"

"Podge's girlfriend Anna said that one of the officers who shot him heard Mattie say he owed a lot of money... maybe he was involved in some... prescription drugs gang? Is there even such a thing?"

"You bet. In fact, most of the meds you get in your spam box are the real thing. Most people don't know that... They pretend it's a copy so police kinda leave them alone. Usually, they are smuggled out of the big pharma factories."

"Ah, so maybe he got involved in the racket when someone offered him cheaper meds for his mother..."

"yup then probably started dealing and getting behind with payments..."

"Oh my god..."

"What?"

"It all makes sense now... Anna said that Mattie had said something like, 'If you kill me, she dies too.' He must have meant his Mom. She wouldn't get her tablets..."

"And?"

"And that's why they thought it was a hostage situation. They thought he had a girl with him."

"Ah right, but he was firing shots dude. There's even a video of him doing it."

"Yeah, but it just shows how the media twisted the story."

"Well not on my watch dude!"

"Haha, yeah sorry..."

"NP"

"OK, you've been totally awesome as usual. I'm gonna do a bit more digging on this."

"OK, but stay safe. Stay encrypted!"

"Sure, thanks!"

Karl closed the chat window. He opened Google again and typed the word 'perodopa'.

Lots of results came up, the third one obviously the manufacturer: Mendez-Long Corp. He clicked on it and looked for some details on the corporation. They were a US pharmaceutical and cosmetics company with offices all over the US and the world. He wasn't going to find out much more than that here.

Karl thought about it. So someone in Mendez-Long Corp. was taking medications out the back door and selling them on the net, or rather, selling them to dealers who sell them on the net. I guess Mattie had some dodgy website set up where he was selling all this stuff. For God's sake, he thought. He did all this to help his mom get cheaper medications but made a complete mess of it and got himself shot. And Podge too.

Podge! My god, he couldn't believe Podge was gone. He was such a great guy. A tower of a man, built like a cage-fighter, but incapable of harming a fly. He was such an incredible contact to have in New York too. He knew everyone and everyone knew him. What a fucking waste of life for this stupid fucking money charade. He could feel himself getting madder.

But much as he would love to expose some big corporate cover-up and pull some red-faced operatives out from their secret lair, it really wasn't a solution to anything except his own personal satisfaction. He had to keep his eye on the bigger prize. The reason for all this bullshit to exist would still exist: money. Money, and the individualistic craziness that was killing the planet.

Karl was one of the few people on that planet who was in a position of being able to make a big difference to that cause, so he even felt duty-bound now to follow through on it. Much as he would have loved to avenge Podge's death, his prime focus had to be to continue what he had started, and of course to take care of his own family.

He stood up and took the video camera out of the drawer.

"OK, show time..." he muttered to himself.

F·DAY -3116

www.bbc.com/world:

ICELAND REQUESTS 'TRADE-FREE' STATUS

Following on from the recent collapse of the Icelandic Króna, and the country's remarkable resilience in the face of what ECB director Michel Legrand termed a 'doomsday scenario', Iceland's President has formally requested that Iceland be granted what he called a 'Trade-Free' status from the UN.

Speaking earlier today at the UN, Iceland's President Reyksson told delegates of his country's 'miraculous recovery of the working spirit in the face of wage uncertainty', and described how all of Iceland's vital services and infrastructure have remained fully intact and operational.

"Naturally, there have been many difficulties," Baldur said from the legendary podium. "It looked for a while as though Iceland's electricity and water companies were going to suspend operations, until one young man, Mr. Anders Einarsson – an electrical engineer with one of our electricity providers – phoned up RÚV radio and announced his intention to return to work the following day on a pro bono basis.

"Thankfully his inspiration spread, and many of his co-workers and workers in similar companies also took the pledge to return to work. We estimate in all utility sectors that staffing levels are on average running about eighty to eighty-five percent.

"On meeting with the heads of Government departments, the chiefs of the main companies, and members of the newly-formed Voluntary Representative Committee, we are now in the process of agreeing on a formal strategy of Service Days, to define a recommended minimum number of hours per month that each citizen can spend serving their community.

"The Service Days won't be mandatory of course, and nor should they be, but they will soon become the normal way of keeping our society flowing freely once the public are fully educated in the benefits." The President continued in his calm confident voice, "We are beginning to learn the futility of attempting to measure our citizens by their input to society. This, we feel, is the one-dimensional view of the paid labour system which must now be consigned to the past.

"For example, a citizen may never once contribute to his local community for thirty years, then suddenly invent a cure for cancer in a flash of inspiration. Similarly, a citizen may work twelve hours of the day for the community, but actually be a hindrance to it. The society of the future will have moved beyond this primitive system of measurement.

"This is perhaps one of the greatest pitfalls with the money system, although it is not realised until you step out of it: the simple number scale of money causes one to apply basic arithmetic to the fabric of human life. Let me give you a simple example. The number twenty is greater than the number ten. Simple maths, but apply it to life: one job pays you twenty dollars an hour and another similar one pays you ten dollars an hour. Which one are you going to choose? We automatically believe that the twenty dollar an hour job is greater than the ten dollar one, but that is not the full story. Is the worker who gets twenty dollars an hour really twice as happy as the guy who gets ten dollars an hour? Or, more significantly, is the person getting twenty dollars an hour doing twice as much good for his community and environment than the one getting ten?

"Clearly not, yet we still live with this system whose arithmetic simplicity acutely blinds us to the complexities of human needs and relationships. We don't measure our happiness in a digital sense, nor our love for our children, nor our sense of fulfilment, yet this money-number system forces us to somehow shoehorn our feelings and experiences into this base scale."

He took a stately pause to let his words reverberate.

"Iceland is an experiment. An experiment in the future of human life on this planet. Our people have risen to the challenge and for that, I am immensely proud. However, promising though it appears, it's not perfect. Our capacity for energy and agricultural self-sufficiency is technically possible, but we are not there yet. It will likely take some years for us to get to that stage. So we cannot go it entirely alone.

"For this reason, today the Icelandic Government, on behalf of its people, have officially released a schedule of resources and skills of which Iceland is currently in short supply. If necessary, we are happy to engage in trade with other democratic nations in order to obtain them. Of course, it would be fascinating if other nations were happy to help us meet our needs without seeking reward – remembering, of course, Iceland's legendary hospitality."

There was a ripple of mirth around the chamber. In true leadership style, Baldur allowed it to propagate, then moved firmly back to business.

"But Iceland is an experiment which will succeed, and one which will, I hope, become the template for other countries to follow. I can tell you now that I have already received several high-level communications from the leaders of other nations who are exploring similar ideas. Countries who also wish to place their people's happiness and well-being above monetary concerns; countries who are being plundered and pillaged by untouchable corporations for their natural resources; countries who are witnessing massive losses of biodiversity; countries so crippled with debt that they cannot afford the luxury of supplying fresh water to their citizens.

"I am calling on the United Nations to officially recognise Iceland's unique effort towards this brave new world, and institute a globally-recognised Trade-Free Status to safeguard the internal interests of participating nations. A Trade-Free Status that affords each member the respect it deserves as a peace-loving nation. Iceland is currently the trail-blazer, but other nations are hot on our heels, so it would seem appropriate to create this officially recognised standard.

"In Iceland, we are creating a new way of life. A way of life that teaches us that freedom is not independence. Freedom is happiness, and happiness is interdependence. In the dark hours of Iceland's economic freefall, we discovered hidden riches. Those riches were each other.

"Thank you, ladies and gentlemen."

The room was filled with mixed applause. Cheers and high enthusiasm from some quarters, polite applause from others, and silent nonchalance from the larger nations, too busy discussing more important matters among themselves.

F·DAY -3111

Karl was rudely awoken by the phone going off right beside his ear. In his bleary struggle back to consciousness, he knocked the phone onto the floor. Now Abby was awake, the baby was crying and Kylie started barking.

"Fuck!" he swore, accidentally sliding the phone under the bed while trying to pick it up from the floor. Abby silently stormed out to tend to the baby. Finally, he found the magic button.

"Hello?"

"Hi Karl, it's Stef. Sorry did I wake you?" came the Dutch voice.

"Er, no. No, not at all," he lied in a sleepy voice. Why did he always do that, he thought to himself? So what if he was in bed?

"How are you Stef? What's on your mind?" he said while stretching a tee shirt over himself and propping himself back up in the bed with the duvet over his legs.

"I can hear the baby. Sounds like I woke up the whole house," Stef joked.

"No, not at all," Karl lied again. "Everything's good. How are you?"

"Not bad, thank you. Listen I rang you because I went through all those log files..." Karl was silent as his brain was still playing catch-up. Stef continued, "Remember? From the site crashes?"

"Oh! Yes, yes of course." Karl exclaimed. He was fully awake now.

"You remember we discovered that site attacks came from certain locations?"

"Yes," Karl said. "Egypt and the Philippines and er...?"

"Yes, also from South Africa, Canada and Indonesia," Stef finished.

"Right, yes," Karl remembered. "Go on."

"Well, there was no doubt about the coordination of the attacks. Probably they were servers set up to fire DDOS scripts..."

"DDOS?" Karl asked.

"Distributed Denial of Service attacks – basically, a group of computers ganging up on your computer," Stef said.

"OK"

"Well, remember we tried to trace back the IP addresses to see who owned the servers and we just met blind alleys. They all looked like sham companies?"

"Yes, I do."

"OK, so that wasn't working but it was bugging me for a while, so I tried some lateral thinking, and found some very interesting stuff indeed."

"OK," Karl said, sitting up now. "What did you do?"

"Well, I was looking through the times of each request in the logs, and it looked like there was exactly one request per second except for every ninth second which showed two requests. First I just thought it was a glitch in the server timings, but when I checked it was consistent all the way."

"OK..." Karl said, wondering where this was going.

"Well, it finally dawned on me that it wasn't a glitch but that the requests were spaced slightly less than a second apart, like around 900ms, so it only gave the appearance of one a second, except for every ninth second which got two requests, you follow?"

"Yes."

"Well, I ran a script over the logs, so I could get an even more accurate result – because there were so many entries. It turned out to be 920ms between each request exactly. I cross-checked this with all the other IPs addresses and they all checked out the same: 920ms."

"OK, so what does that tell us?"

"A lot actually," Stef said proudly. "First, it's pretty conclusive proof of a coordinated attack – not that we needed it but still it's good to be sure. Second, it means all those servers were running the same program file. The timings are so accurate that the servers must have been acting independently, not remotely."

"What do you mean?" Karl asked.

"It means the servers weren't relaying requests from another server, they were acting on their own once they got the instruction to start. If they were relaying requests, the timings would not have been so accurate, due to network traffic."

"OK, sounds interesting..."

"No, this is where it gets interesting Karl. I did a bit of fishing around in some hacker forums. It turns out that it's quite common practice among hackers to use their own unique numbers when coding. It's like their unique identifier – or a badge of honour if you like."

"Right, OK"

"So there was one forum I found that gives users tips for setting up a DDOS network attack, and you can download scripts and tools to do it. I had to be careful and go through a proxy network myself to look in the site. But one of the moderators on that site called themselves 'arbiter92zero' which caught my attention. He or she was the one giving out advice to other potential hackers.

"I googled around with that username and found other similar sites with the same information, but the last entry by him in any of those sites was over two years ago. So I stripped out the forums from the search results and then I struck gold," Stef said proudly.

"Really?" Karl laughed. Stef was so serious he thought, but he was having fun with this.

"Indeed. I discovered a small news article in a paper called The Inquirer, a Philippine newspaper. The story is about a hacker called Gani Aquino, alias 'arbiter92zero', who was arrested on multiple charges of cyber attacks and theft two years ago, and was due to be extradited to the US to face prosecution."

"Wow! You think that's our guy?"

"Well, I have his number. Why don't you ask him yourself?"

"Haha!" Karl burst out. "You have his phone number? What do you think? Should I ring him?"

"Well, why not?"

Karl couldn't really think of a good reason not to, so he took down the number and thanked Stef. Looking to the bedroom door and seeing that everything was quiet he decided to bite the bullet and call the number straight away. It would be evening time in the Philippines.

"Halo?" came the foreign voice.

"Hello is that Gani? You speak English?"

"Um, a little, yes. Who is this please?"

"My name is Karl. I believe you do some work in computers?"

"I'm sorry. Karl who?"

Karl knew he would have to be careful to gain Gani's trust, because he was probably naturally suspicious, If he hung up he would probably never get to talk to him again. Karl left a long silence, then decided to go for the gentle, direct approach.

"Gani, I need you to trust me for a minute and listen to what I have to say. My name is Karl Drayton from the Free Movement. I know you were behind the cyber attacks on my sites a few weeks ago..."

Gani burst in with something foreign and unintelligible to Karl.

"Please don't be alarmed Gani," Karl interrupted. "I don't want to cause you any trouble. I just want to know more about what you did."

"I don't know what you talking about... I'm very sorry..."

"OK Gani, let me explain a little of who I am and what I'm trying to do. I promise I am not looking for any trouble..." The line went silent, so Karl assumed Gani was listening but not wishing to incriminate himself in any way. Karl continued.

"I'm just a guy who's trying to create a better world for you, me and everyone else. That's all. No hidden agenda. The Free World Charter and F-Day Clock are part of our global initiative to rid the world of the market system and all the associated problems that it causes. Our planet is dying and people are suffering because of this way we run society. Unless we urgently start changing our behaviour, the future of our species and countless others is in doubt.

"The campaign revolves around several websites which are crucial to our operations. We do not do this for the money. We are all in it just to try to create a better world for all.

"Recently we discovered that there were some people – we don't know who – who are forcibly trying to stop us. A few days ago two of my friends were shot dead in New York because they belonged to our group. I'm guessing that the same people who were behind that may also be the ones trying to take down our websites..."

"But how..." Gani said suddenly.

"Our tech guy is a pretty smart guy too Gani. But only he and I know about this. It won't go any further I promise, but..." he paused, feeling himself getting emotional, "we need to know who's doing this Gani, because people are getting killed and what we're doing is... too important... for everyone."

"Listen man," Gani said. "I got some trouble a couple of years ago. Big trouble. The Police come one morning, trashed my place and banged me up in jail waiting for extradition order to the States..."

"OK," Karl said.

"Well, week later this guy shows up. I think he's from US Embassy, nice suit and talking. He says I in shit trouble and they going to put me in Guantanamo for terrorism. I scared like shit thinking of my little family, my woman and my boy. They will be in the street. So this man say his name is Jeff and can make all charges drop, you know, but I need to do some favours..."

"OK..."

"So he gives me card with like a code word on, and says when I get message with instructions and this code word, I have to do what they say. Otherwise they charge me you know? I say OK and they let me out. Then a few weeks ago I get message to bring down these sites, signed with code word..."

"What did the message say Gani?" Karl asked quickly.

"Shit man I don't want trouble..."

"I don't want trouble either Gani. For you, or anyone else, but if I can expose these guys who are trying to stop us doing our thing, it's going to be better for everyone. I promise I will never reveal what you're telling me, but I need to know so I can find out who these people are..."

"I don't know man. I read your sites before. They are very good. I think you are good person, but..."

"I give you my word Gani," Karl cut in. "I will never use any information they can trace back to you. Tell me the email address, the code word and what the message said."

"OK." Gani started tapping on his keyboard furiously. "OK here's the message: 'Important task request. Bring down all sites at IP address 171.154.28.310 for a period of 48 hours from 7/10 to 7/12. Yours, Bishopsgate,'" Gani read, then added, "'Bishopsgate' is the code word."

Karl was busy writing it down on the inside cover of a book beside his bed. "Bishopsgate," he repeated. "Hmm, that's in London I think. Or maybe there's more than one? OK, I'll check it out. What's the email address? And the sender IP address?"

"I looked up mail IP but it is proxy server in Canada: 21.128.151.57. The email is just Hotmail account, 'tiger7847@hotmail.com'. The only thing that matters is code word."

"OK," Karl nodded. He knew Gani was right. The email and the IP address were worthless. The only thing he had to go on was the code word. He thanked Gani and assured him once again that he would keep him safe.

He put the phone down as Abby walked in with their baby. Beautiful Eli, the second-most wonderful woman in his life. He was very proud. Abby had settled her down and they all curled up together in the bed for a mid-morning snooze.

Bishopsgate...

F·DAY -3110

www.grapevine.com:

WELL, THIS IS EMBARRASSING

So Captain Barley left his glasses at home and went shopping at the UN last week. Seriously? Requesting trade-free status on the one hand and handing over a shopping list with the other? Has our non-President finally dropped his last few remaining marbles? Well, you've got to hand it to him. He's either the bravest, smartest person that ever lived, or he needs to be led gently back to his barley farm where hopefully he won't injure himself.

Iceland has never been one to go cap in hand to our fellow nations. So what if we're running low on tomatoes when we can eat barley? And who needs bananas, when we have whole fields full of, er, barley? And as for condoms – yes we're running low on them too apparently – well, people will be too busy planting and picking barley to think about such base desires!

Is this Iceland Experiment going to end up becoming The Iceland Circus on the world's stage, and we the performing chimps, dancing to Ringmaster Reyksson's whip? Well, with no bananas, that's not going to end well!

<u>Reyksson at the UN >></u>

f-day.org/feeds/update:

UN TRADE-FREE STATUS GRANTED [-1000 DAYS]

The UN has officially recognised Iceland as a 'Trade-Free' country, leaving the way open for other countries to follow suit. The Trade-Free Status is an instrument to help respect borders and resources of countries who have chosen to devolve from a market and militarised system.

For this valuable precedent, 720 days have accordingly been deducted from the F-Day countdown, bringing F-Day to less than forty years away.

<u>F-Day.org >></u>

The next day Karl awoke suddenly to something he hadn't heard in a while.

Silence in the house. He turned his head and Abby was gone. He jumped from the bed and went out, calling her.

"Abby?"

He put on his dressing gown and ran out to Eli's room. Empty cot. He went downstairs, calling and again was met with silence. Then he stopped and smiled. There was a note with a heart drawn on it on the table.

'The girls have gone shoppies! Love you, see you later, x'

Karl couldn't help smiling. He felt truly blessed.

"Arf!" said Kylie suddenly through the patio door, looking up at him pleadingly and wagging her tail.

"OK Kylie. Didn't think I'd get off so lightly" He went to fetch the dog leash. "OK come on girl, we're going to get Uncle Podge's letter," he joked. Kylie was doing somersaults at the very thought of Podge's letter.

Fifteen minutes later he had the letter in his hand. His neighbour regarded Karl with confused suspicion and begrudgingly handed over the mis-addressed letter. He stopped on the street and opened it.

'Hey Karl, how are you brother?

'Shit is going down here and I wasn't sure if I could call or email, so I thought they'll never think of us messaging the old-fashioned way! Anyway, I'm going to seal this letter good, so if someone's fucked with it you'll know.'

Karl turned over the envelope in his hand. It looked intact apart from where he tore it.

'The other day you suggested I ask the neighbours if they saw anything weird around the time our passports were taken. Well, there was. There's a big fat man lives in the basement flat. He said a guy came around who was dressed in work overalls – like a cable guy. Said he was acting strange.

'Apparently this 'cable guy' said he was checking a line fault in flat 102 and went straight upstairs. The thing is flat 102 is on the ground floor in this building. When the fat guy realised the mistake, he expected the guy to come back down the stairs, but he never did – at least not until about half an hour later, then he was walking out the door.

'The fat guy shouted after him if he got himself sorted – thinking that maybe the guy didn't need to actually enter the apartment, then the guy just turns and says 'yes he got in OK – that the owner had given him the key' – but he wasn't anywhere near flat 102.

'The fat guy walked out after him and was surprised to see him get – not into a van – but into a brand new black sedan which drove off really fast. He couldn't get the reg or anything, but he said that it wasn't a NY reg. It was from out of town and it had a funny yellow crest on the side. He couldn't make it out, but said it was kind of like a cop car or something...'

Karl was feeling cold shivers – even though the sun was shining.

Kylie was looking up at him wondering what the actual delay was with the walkies.

Podge wrote this in fear of his life. And now he's dead. Karl's heart felt like lead. He wiped away a tear as he read on.

> 'I don't know what any of this means man, but it sure looks like someone's out to make things difficult for us – and they're not teenagers.

> 'Anna's scared and so am I. We're gonna scale back the burning protests. Also, I'm going to take Anna away out of here. (She doesn't know yet) I got us some tickets to Acapulco. They got lots of progressive stuff going on down there. We're going to check it out...

> 'Stay safe man. Don't be a hero. Be alive. Talk again when I'm in Mexico.

> 'Ciao, Podge'

Karl was weeping openly now. He felt somehow responsible. Poor Podge. Poor Anna. She still doesn't know he was planning to take her away for a better life. What a wonderful man.

As Karl started heading for home, it didn't take long for his sadness to become anger and resolve. This was now open warfare as far as he was concerned – and a war that he was going to win – not with bullets – but with pure weapons-grade common sense.

F·DAY -3109

That night Karl dreamt about Podge. He saw him and Anna on the train for Mexico, hurtling through the desert in an antiquated wooden train car – like something from an old spaghetti western movie. Podge was singing Auld Lang Syne in a kind of manic, high-pitched voice and slapping his thighs while Anna was begging him to stop.

Karl woke up with an aching emptiness inside his chest. He looked at the window. Dawn was breaking. The birds were stirring. He got out of the bed and tip-toed over to Eli's cot. Fast asleep. It immediately brought warmth back to Karl's heart. To see their perfect creation sleeping so soundly – oblivious to the everyday struggles of adult life.

The combination of sleeping Eli, innocent to the future world his fellow adults were busy destroying, the death of Podge that Karl felt responsible for, and a desire to avenge, filled Karl with renewed vigour.

"I swear you are never going to have to go through all this bullshit, little one," he whispered.

Eli kicked her leg in agreement. Karl smiled.

"Yes, exactly. Daddy's going to kick their ass!"

While the family was still asleep, Karl sat in the kitchen enjoying his coffee, reading through his normal news digest and checking his sites for any developments. Nothing special. Switzerland was about to embark on the Basic Income Guarantee system, despite much muted criticism from their EU neighbours. It wasn't popular for any politician to denounce the idea of course, but their 'warnings' to the Swiss Government were tell-tale enough of their fear of the knock-on effects that were inevitably going to find their way onto their doorstep.

In some ways, Switzerland had been like Iceland. Only a few key people in Swiss officialdom had commented on the B.I.G. idea, inadvertently setting an avalanche of public support in motion. Presumably, other leaders in the EU were deliberately keeping quiet too, sensing that the avalanche wouldn't just stop there and pressure might eventually mount on them to follow suit.

Many of Karl's friends in the Free Movement liked the idea, but Karl was not a fan. For him, it just meant prolonged enslavement to an imaginary control system – money. Like trying to give up cigarettes by using a nicotine patch – you weren't eliminating the dependence. He felt there was even a great danger here. B.I.G. perpetuated the myth that money was the only way to order society and disguised it as a give-away bonanza. It effectively amounted to paying people to continue believing in the myth.

Karl flicked on down when a familiar name popped out of the screen. Mendez-Long. He scrolled back to find the article.

'Mendez-Long, the American Pharmaceutical company, along with four other corporations, Milside-Jacks, Mykrochem, Sylvan-Parkers and Allisen Products have all been found in breach of US Environmental Protection Agency laws. Judge Merryl Candace, presiding over the Supreme Court case, ruled that each corporation would bear all costs in correcting the environmental damage caused by 'shamefully inadequate waste treatment policies' of the companies.

'It is the second time in five years that the same five pharmaceutical and chemical giants – known collectively as the 'Big Soaps' for their dominance in the US detergent market – have been before the supreme court in hazardous waste charges. Judge Candace handed down fines to the corporations totalling 1.9 billion dollars and ordered a Federal inquiry into work practices at all their factories.

'In a statement outside the court, Maurice Kay, CEO of Mendez-Long apologised unreservedly for what he called 'shameful practices' that went on at his company. Click for video >>'

Karl didn't bother. He knew the drill. Act humble and full of remorse when you've been caught. Give the cameras their villain, be dignified, vow to do better, say thank you, then get into the car, give your PA a memo not to let this sort of thing happen again, then carry on doing exactly what you were doing before. Whatever fines these companies got last time it obviously didn't stop them from re-offending.

Karl checked into his favourite Iceland site Grapevine to see what was going on there. Things were not going well. The 'Iceland Experiment', as the media had coined it, was on the brink of failure. With dwindling food supplies and commodities, many people had started trading again using US Dollars and international credit cards. Journalists were ironically referring to it as 'The White Market'.

Karl felt a pang of disappointment. He wondered whether to ring Baldur, but thought better of it. Maybe there was a better way to help. He opened a blank document and started typing.

'The Iceland Experiment Needs Your Help

'Friends, I have been saddened to see things in Iceland haven't been going so well. So I am asking for your help.

'There is much we can do, and there is a lot at stake. If Iceland fails, it will forever be held aloft by detractors of this movement as 'proof' that a moneyless society cannot work. We will forever be hearing the words '...but look what happened in Iceland!' We cannot let this happen. If we are complacent, we may cause irreparable damage to our cause. I ask you, please, to ACT and act now. Here is what we are going to do...'

Karl stopped typing for a minute, rested his hands on either side of the keyboard and closed his eyes.

Then it came like a burst of fire. He started typing furiously for ten minutes, then copied his words into every conceivable communication means at his disposal. He sent to his four mailing lists, he posted it to all the social media channels he could get his hands on, then, of course, reached for the camera and made a quick video.

He looked at his coffee. Untouched. He drank it up and chuckled. Let's see what happens he thought.

A few minutes later, he heard the first reply coming back.

'Dirk says: I'm on it!'

Then another,

'Jay C says: LOL. Great idea bro, doing it now...'

Then another,

'Margaret Farnell says: Yes of course. Will do.'

Karl had learned from all his campaigning activities that when you do something good, you always feel the love straight away. While most people in Karl's online circle were very supportive and enthusiastic, sometimes it was hard to tell the difference between the polite and respectful 'it's great,' and the genuine 'it's great'. The difference, he had learned, was time. When people respond straight away, you know you've touched them.

Another three replies came in.

Karl smiled.

Let's see what happens...

F·DAY -3109

Yawende Kone stepped out of the shower and back into her freezing cold Lewisham bathroom. Like a penance, she turned and wiped the mirror then looked at herself in shame. Fat, breasts hanging like empty socks, giant hips, thick legs, horrible wiry hair. It was like a sick ritual. She loved to look and hate herself. She wasn't sure why. Did she expect to look and see someone slim and beautiful some day, or did she just like to wallow in her own private bodily shame? She wasn't sure.

She dried herself quickly and got dressed. She walked out into the living room.

"Benjy! I told you to turn off that TV and do some homework" she shouted at Benjy, her twelve-year-old son, who sighed, flicked off the TV and stood up. "You're sick remember? And you got exams in two weeks. You need to get into them books boy, you hear?"

"Yes mum," Benjy replied with all the sigh he could muster, and reached down for his schoolbag.

"Mommy, look what I made," came another voice running towards her with an outstretched piece of paper.

"Cindy, were you in Momma's drawers again? I told you not to go in there, you hear?"

"Sorry Mom." Cindy lowered down the piece of paper and stood there crestfallen.

"OK, whatch you got there?" asked Yawende sitting on the couch and patting her knees. Cindy hopped up, confidence restored.

"It's a picture of Granny and Grandad," she announced proudly. It was drawn with lipstick. Two stick figures beside a mud house and a large incomprehensible scribble.

"Very nice. What's this honey?" Yawende asked, pointing at the scribble, thinking about where she was going to hide her lipstick from now on.

"It's a dead lion," Cindy proclaimed, proceeding to explain the whole scene, prodding the picture for emphasis with her red lipstick finger. "The big lion was running after Granny, who was in the jungle, then Grandad came along with his spear and killed the lion and saved Granny," she explained simply.

Yawende laughed and felt herself instantly transported back to Nigeria, to her Mum and Dad. She missed them so much.

Born in a humble village in central Nigeria, her childhood had been tough, but always happy. Every day she would meet the other kids in the village square and they would be dancing and playing games, under the watchful gaze of the old men sitting in the afternoon shadows. Some evenings they would be allowed to visit the Catholic priest's house and watch his satellite TV.

That was when she discovered London. She had been mesmerised by The Houses of Parliament, Tower Bridge, the London Eye – all so civilised, so proper and organised. That was the place to be – not here in the scorching outback, eking out an existence.

She remembered the day she left the village in a sheep truck, bound for Lagos, with nothing but a small bag and the money she had worked for and saved in the cocoa fields. She remembered how her mum was so teary-eyed, and her two best childhood friends Tia and Omoye had come to see her off. Their smiles were etched permanently on her memory...

"Mommy?" Cindy asked.

"Yes sweetie, I'm sorry," Yawende responded, coming back to reality.

"I said, have you ever seen a lion?"

"No sweetie. Lions come nowhere near where we lived." She ruffled her daughter's curls, who seemed a bit disappointed. "Saw plenty of monkeys though. And snakessssssssss..."

"Hehehe," Cindy giggled as Yawende tickled her tummy making snake movements with her hand.

"Now Momma's got to get ready for work honey, so you go play with your dollies, you hear?"

"Yes Mom," said Cindy and ran off to her bedroom.

Yawende sighed. She felt her smile subsiding and the same old dread rising up again. The children were great. She didn't know what she would do without them. She hadn't seen their father Lucas for over two years and sometimes she felt so lonely. She survived on a tiny welfare allowance and doing some late night work in the launderette. Everything was a struggle.

She was behind with her loan payment, and Benjy didn't even have enough books for school – never mind a laptop which all the other kids had. Keeping the kids' food interesting and wholesome was a constant challenge. Her credit card had long been cancelled and the local lender was beginning to put a little more menacing pressure on her now too. He was coming again tomorrow. She didn't know what to do.

From her high-rise she had a great view over the city and the beautiful winter evening sky. She could even see half of Tower Bridge from here – that icon of success that had breathed life into her dreams of leaving Nigeria as a young girl. Now here she was looking down on it from her home and desperately unhappy. How was it that she'd been happier with nothing in Nigeria?

Her phone suddenly vibrated.

An email from Karl Drayton? Oh yes, the Free World guy, she thought. If only...

She read the email. They were looking for some help with the Iceland project. She laughed out loud as she read.

'...Here is what we are going to do. I would like you to send something in the post to Iceland – it doesn't matter what. If you think it will help them, then send it, take a picture or video of what you're sending and put it anywhere you can on the internet with the hashtag #HELPICELAND. It's just a publicity exercise that will cost you very little, but will make a big difference.

'Please do it. I am doing it now and sending them a tin of pears! Use the same address as below.

'Best, Karl.'

She smiled, put down the phone, and had a look around the apartment bemused. What did people in Iceland need? She wondered. Well, they must be cold, she figured practically. She went to the drawer and pulled out a scarf and some gloves, then proceeded to make her phone video, posing with the scarf. She laughed to herself then went to find an envelope.

F·DAY -3104

Baldur Reyksson was no stranger to oddball things happening around him. Ever since he had become the first 'free' president, he had become used to receiving crazy emails and letters from both devoted fans and sworn intellectual enemies – who sent him megabytes of scholarly documents proving that everything he was doing would fail. Yet his 'failing' experiment was continuing on regardless. It's true they were having some difficulties, but really only as a result of their physical isolation and the way in which their situation had been forced on them with almost no preparation. All in all, they were doing very well considering.

Yet there were some problems that weren't going to go away any time soon. They were having to ration more exotic commodities like gasoline, tea, grain and coffee and lots of non-essentials like machinery and car parts. It was getting a bit like post-sixties Cuba, where all the islanders had been forced to learn to cope in the face of scarcity, but different from Cuba in the strong emergence of the so called 'White Market'. The trickle of trade with the outside world had grown but no-one knew to what extent. It certainly seemed that the main international couriers were still being kept busy.

His online appeal for aid had come to nothing, and he was bitterly disappointed. Of course, Norway and Denmark were helping them out with some supplies as best they could, but it wasn't enough. Iceland was beginning to look like some kind of 'beggar state', bothering other countries in their failure to solve their own domestic problems.

That was a cross that Baldur didn't carry easily. He had always looked after himself without being a burden on anyone else – even if it meant eating barley for weeks on end. He was a survivor, but now finding himself the housekeeper of a country that was scrounging off others was making him very uncomfortable.

There was a light knock on his door.

"What is it?" he snapped. His housekeeper popped her head around the door. "Sorry, Agnes, please come in," he ushered.

"Sorry to bother you Baldur, but there's some post for you..."

Baldur looked at her in surprise.

"So? Just leave it on the table, I'll tend to it shortly." he could feel himself getting irritated again.

"Er, no, sir, there's... quite a lot of post actually. Maybe you should come and have a look?"

Perplexed, Baldur stormed out the door and along the corridor to the front door. Outside there were two men talking. He pulled the door wide and was met with the angry face of the postman.

"What the fuck is going on Baldur? What's all this?" said the angry face.

"I... don't..." Baldur looked past the man and his jaw dropped.

There was a car-sized pile of small packets on the ground, and the other man was unloading hundreds more small packets from the back of the post van. Baldur stooped and picked up one of the packets. It was from Spain. He ripped it open. Inside were two tins of red peppers and a note which just said 'for Iceland'.

"Well, I'll be..." Baldur burst out laughing, then clapped the postman on the shoulder and went over to help them unload the van.

F·DAY -3103

The next day Karl and Eli were enjoying a wonderful winter stroll in the local forest when his phone started rattling in his coat. He braked the buggy, pulled off his gloves and was delighted to see an unknown Icelandic number looking for his attention.

"Karl, I don't know what to say..." Baldur started.

Karl burst out laughing. "Did you get my tin of pears," he inquired.

"Ha ha! Yes, we're saving those for next summer," Baldur quipped, then continued seriously. "Karl, I wanted to call and thank you personally for this effort. What you've done is amazing. We have a whole roomful of stuff now, but I know this is not the point..."

"Exactly Baldur," Karl said. "This is just a gimmick – a way of getting attention. It's been very lively on the net the last few days. We hashtagged it 'helpiceland'. Check it out."

"I already did Karl, and thank you once again for your efforts," Baldur said seriously. Karl was beginning to sense that something was not right. "Karl," he continued, "much as we appreciate this gallant effort from the Free Movement, unfortunately, it looks like it will be too little, too late for us.

"I'm not sure if you've been following Icelandic news reports, but we're getting pretty close to having another mini revolution on our hands – but not of the free variety! Our delivery and bus network is almost grinding to a halt. We've had to ration fuel drastically. All the fuel stations are now empty and we're now dispensing it only on a very select basis to those who need it most.

"Of course, you can imagine many people are not happy with that, and frankly, I don't blame them. Foods have already been severely limited with many popular items no longer available here. Some people have organised buying these products from outside and are selling them openly on the streets for US Dollars, or whatever they can get their hands on. The fuel shortage on top is now the last straw for most people. Don't forget we have lots of people living in very isolated locations here. Their fuel is their lifeline."

"Yes, I understand," Karl said.

"Of course, we have also had constant attention from the IMF and the European Central Bank. We've had two delegations here already. They are dangling the Euro under our noses, and to be honest, it's not a bad deal. I have no choice but to put it to a public vote next Wednesday and it will almost certainly be passed."

"That's only five days time. Dammit! What are the Euro conditions?"

"Ha! Well, first and foremost, to reinstate our sovereign debt which had been temporarily frozen – plus interest accrued of course – but at a slightly reduced rate than before. Also, the IMF are 'strongly recommending' – in other words 'do it or else' – that we immediately commence construction of the undersea electric interconnector to Scotland and of seven new geothermal power plants near Hvolsvöllur, as a way of stimulating the economy and creating stability."

"Hmmm."

"Yes, hmmm. Same old, same old. Economy first, atmosphere second. But really Karl, there's no way out of this now. This time next week I will probably be signing legislation bringing Iceland into the

Eurozone."

"And Icelanders?"

"They don't care any more. They just want their lives back. This is the only deal on the table that can guarantee them food and fuel security. I can't blame them for wanting that."

"True," Karl said. His heart sank. There really wasn't anything more he could say. The experiment was over. Iceland would fail.

He said his goodbyes and well-wishes to Baldur and hung up. He continued down the avenue of chestnut trees, pushing Eli along in her buggy. Karl looked down at her. She was very snug in her red anorak and boots. Karl found himself feeling a little envious of her. She had no problems, no worries. Someone else was always going to sort out her problems. Although, of course, at the expense of her independence, he conceded. Life really is a strange mix of paradoxes, he thought as they walked along. We can be independent, but isolated; popular, but dependent.

We spend most of our lives wanting something, then when we get it, it's not as good as we thought it would be. Or when we lose something that we don't care about, we start to miss it like hell. It's like everything has disappointment built right in. But then, maybe disappointment is just about having the wrong expectation. Expectation is based on our external perception of something. But if, as the Buddhists say, we expect and desire nothing to achieve fulfilment, are we improving? Are we progressing?

Is having a world without money actually progress? What is progress anyway?

Eli dropped her dummy on the ground, as if in protest at these thoughts. Karl stopped, picked it up and handed it back to her, which she took without even a word of thanks. Ha! Karl thought. We live in a world where people constantly expect reward or thanks, but probably neither is right. Eli doesn't have those filters yet. Maybe there's no such thing as helping – or even giving? Everyone is just doing what comes naturally to them and it all evens out in the end – until you throw monetary accounting and slavery into the pot of course!

If Iceland was to fail, what then? Would the other countries Baldur mentioned still proceed with trying to go money-free? What would happen to the Free Movement and others? Would people lose interest? Time would tell. It was going to be a major blow, that was for sure.

Karl knew more than most why Iceland failed. Really they had been dropped in the deep end with no preparation. Yes, they had the capability to be a one hundred percent self-sustaining community, but they did not have the time or infrastructure to make that a reality – not in the few weeks or months they had. Of course, this would not prevent the intellectual critics from berating the whole débâcle as 'irrefutable proof' that society falls apart without money.

Maybe they are right, and Karl and his contemporaries were all barking up a gum tree.

They came to the end of the chestnut avenue and veered left along a yellow path strewn with freshly fallen sycamore leaves. Karl's thoughts were silenced by the sweet song of a robin somewhere overhead. He knew the song immediately. He stopped to listen, straining to find the source of the exquisitely complex tweets and warbles.

The robin, as if suddenly realising he had a captive audience, went silent, fluttered down from his lofty perch, installed himself confidently on a low willow bough about three metres in front of them, eyed them up and down sideways, then launched into a full recital.

The song echoed so clear and true in the damp forest air, that both father and child were utterly mesmerised. Karl looked down at Eli. She was transfixed.

Wow, he thought, *what an amazing first music lesson!*

F·DAY -3100

President Carley's campaign director Oswald Moone was becoming a pain in the ass and a liability. Only four weeks left to election day and her re-election campaign was lacklustre to say the least. The Republicans had a very strong candidate in Pete Jefferson, she couldn't deny it. He had a good academic background, a highly successful Governorship in Massachusetts, and, of course – who could forget – lineage right back to the great Thomas Jefferson himself.

Maybe Oswald was just putting out half-hearted ideas to mark time and get paid, but Jean was a fighter and, having seen the latest polls putting her almost twenty points behind, she decided it was time to take matters into her own hands. She needed a trump card – preferably a spade to bury Pete Jefferson with – along with his precious ancestor who she was getting sick of hearing about.

She called for her ten o'clock coffee and fired up her screen. She was looking for something. She didn't know what, but she would know it when she found it. Lots of celebrity bullshit... royal wedding in Norway... bushfires in Australia... protests everywhere... Iceland voting on joining Euro... well that didn't last long, she thought, then stopped scrolling. *Wait, there's something funny with this story...*

Her old journalistic instinct was twitching. She did a search for Iceland news. There was some dissonance with the Iceland story – something didn't add up.

As a celebrity interviewer for twelve years, she could get under the skin of people with great ease and learn what made them tick very quickly. She had watched an interview with Iceland's President Reyksson some months ago and was supremely impressed by his determination, strength of character and candour. She admired his gutsy resolve in bringing about the pioneering moneyless idea in the face of public ridicule. So why was this man giving up so easily after just a few months? There was more to this story and she wanted to find out.

Her searches threw up the Free Movement's #helpiceland hashtag, and she saw hundreds of pictures of people holding up envelopes with tins of food. Hmmm. Her assistant arrived with the coffee.

"Thank you. What do you know about this Iceland thing, Barbara?"

Barbara leaned over the screen.

"Oh yes, it was going well, but they started running out of essentials like fuel. The ECB have offered them a rescue package to be voted on... next week I think."

"Hmm, but this guy Reyksson. What do you know about him?"

"He was a farmer as far as I remember, but is very popular. A colourful character – stubborn too."

"Yes, that's what I thought. Let me finish my coffee and get him on the phone for me, will you?"

"Yes, Jean."

Twenty minutes later, the President of the United States of America and the President of Iceland were chatting about the virtues of tinned Spanish peppers. It turned out that both presidents were very keen in the kitchen, and Jean had become so engrossed that she almost forgot the reason for her call. Almost.

"So tell me Baldur, what happened? Why are you backing down so easily?"

Baldur paused, as if wounded by her.

"With all due respect Jean, it's anything but easy. Maybe it looks like that from where you are, but we're almost at crisis point here."

"Well, you handled the first crisis pretty well." she persisted.

"Yes, but there was a sense of historic opportunity, and a momentum that was irresistible. Of course, we were too hasty but there wasn't really any time to think or plan it. We had to jump. If we hadn't forged ahead at that moment, it would never have happened. But I've no regrets about that. We did the right thing at the right time."

"Well, it's certainly been interesting watching you guys," Jean said warmly.

"Thanks, but unfortunately logistics and reality have caught up with us now. The idea of having a moneyless society was to improve lives, not to make everyone miserable – and the people are miserable now. As President, it's my duty to get the best deal for Icelanders. The experiment failed, so we have to settle for the next deal."

"Maybe," President Carley said. "Leave it with me Baldur."

They exchanged pleasantries, she put down the phone and buzzed Barbara.

"Get me General de Vries on the phone, will you? And send in Lee Harvey Oswald in about ten minutes!"

Barbara stifled a snigger.

"Yes, Jean."

"Oh, and pack up all his things outside, and set up a press announcement for this evening's prime time."

"Yes, Jean."

Within just a few hours, Jean had taken over management of her own campaign and was about to risk everything on a hunch.

General de Vries, the head of the Armed Forces had tried to talk her out of it of course, so she had to politely pull rank on him. The wheels were now in motion and she would soon find out if her gamble was going to pay off. She took to the podium in her usual casual style.

"Hi ladies and gentlemen, and thank you all so much for coming along at short notice. This evening I want to bring you a very special announcement.

"When I was young, my mom used to send me to the shops to buy bread or milk or whatever, which of course I was happy to do. But every time, just as I was on my way out the door, she would yell at me, 'Oh and see if Mrs. Jackson wants anything too'. That was when my heart sank.

"Mrs. Jackson was one of our neighbours who lived in a small trailer around the corner, with what seemed like hundreds of cats, and the smell of her home every time I walked in nearly choked me. She was an old eccentric lady and lived in her own way, but she was a good person and never caused any trouble. Luckily for me, every time I asked her she said 'no' and that was that.

"One day I asked my mom why I had to ask her, and she replied something that I didn't really understand at the time, but it stayed with me. She said 'because that's what we do honey. We are all here to look after each other'. It took me a few years to figure that out, but I figured it out.

"Too often in this world, we live separated. We are separated by wage class, religion, skin colour, culture etc. We tend to forget that we all inhabit the same space, drink the same water, breathe the same air, and have pretty much the same needs. Too often we fight each other for things that don't actually have any value."

Some of the President's aides were starting to shuffle uncomfortably now in the shadows. No-one had been briefed before the conference on the President's insistence. She continued.

"Sometimes, in a world ravaged by conflict and injustice, we lose sight of the many hidden corners of the world whose peoples are living quietly, and know only peace. One such country of which I speak does not even have a standing army. That country is Iceland."

A whispering hubbub flitted around the room.

"No stranger to pioneering ideas, two months ago Iceland decided to see if they could create a fully cooperative, open economic society, and move beyond the traditional market system altogether. These are noble ideas, and I'm sure many of you who have been watching Iceland's progress will, like me, have been inspired by their courage in the face of phenomenal international pressure.

"Iceland's people, with the strong leadership of President Reyksson, rose to the challenge. They shared their food, their land, their commodities, they worked without payment to keep their utilities and services open. Government departments and essential service providers remained almost fully staffed as the people joined in a massive community effort to keep their country going.

"Today that community effort is in trouble. Despite their grit and determination, Iceland is fast running out of fuel to power its infrastructure, and food supplies have also been strictly rationed. With winter fast approaching, Icelanders are now faced with a choice of a very bleak winter of rationed goods and an uncertain future, or to give up on their idealism and return to the market economic system as part of the Eurozone.

"Some weeks ago, the Government of Iceland launched a website with a schedule of resources they required to maintain their economy. America does not turn her back on her peaceful Atlantic friends in their time of crisis, so today we are answering their call.

"Today at four o'clock, I signed an executive order to divert US Navy surplus fuel and commodities to Iceland with immediate effect. The US Navy tanker *Beatrice* and cargo vessel *Liberty Bell* are now on their way to Reykjavik and should reach there in a matter of days."

There were strong murmurs from all around the room now. A single enthusiastic clap came from one side of the room but quickly fizzled out. The journalists' heads were in a spin. They knew their readers well. Amid America's own economic uncertainty, this was not going to go well. Was this just a total wide-ball from a desperate president, or some intentional political suicide in the face of defeat?

Jean looked out at the audience and could sense their minds buzzing.

"OK, let's have some of your questions...," she asked.

Jean spent the next few minutes fielding questions on the specifics of the order and shipments. Finally, one reporter raised a question on the wisdom of the move.

"Mrs. President, what do you say to the homeless people of America who are also facing a cold winter without food?"

Jean had seen this coming.

"Good question," she said. "The people of America can rest assured that this gift to Iceland from the American people will not impact in

172

any way on current welfare services. The shipments used have previously been earmarked for overseas US Naval defence use only. Homeland public services are unaffected..." She motioned to the next raised hand.

"You said this is a gift?" the reporter asked. "How do you justify giving away free oil to Icelanders while Americans still have to pay for theirs?"

Jean could feel herself tensing up, but her professionalism quickly kicked in and she gave a broad smile.

"Yes, this is a gift from America to the people of Iceland to help them out in a time of crisis. It's not even a small percentage of our nominal foreign aid budget. In terms of American productivity, this is really a very small token..." she looked for the next hand, but the reporter persisted.

"...but this is a crisis of their own making. Iceland will probably vote on joining the Euro next week, then they can buy their own oil..." A wave of silence passed over the room. Everyone wanted to hear the answer to this.

Jean took advantage of the moment to compose herself and decided it was time to push the 'America' button. She looked sternly at the plucky reporter.

"My friends, there was a time in this country when we didn't have it so good either. Our forefathers built America into the great nation it is today, brick by brick, rivet by rivet. We fought through a civil war, two world wars and a great depression. Our founding fathers came here with a dream, to build a great land where life and liberty were enshrined into the Constitution as sacrosanct.

"America stands for freedom. America stands for hope. We stand with those in need of protection from injustice, tyranny and terrorism. We fought for justice time and time again, and we won. America does not turn away from her friends in their hour of need.

"We don't know if our gift to the Icelandic people will even be enough to preserve their particular dream of freedom, but we will stand by them and defend their right to choose to live differently and in peace.

"We value and appreciate the lesson that Iceland is trying to teach us all. We have much to learn from them. They are showing us that sharing is caring and that it can work. We will not sit idly by while our peaceful Atlantic neighbours are going hungry. Thank you."

There was a burst of questions, but Jean just smiled and waved at the podium for a minute for photos, then moved swiftly back to the dressing room, where she knew she would be hounded even more. She waved her advisers aside, went straight into the toilet and was violently sick.

After a while, she wiped her face then sat down in the cubicle in silence.

"Oh Jeb, what the hell have I done?" she said quietly in the darkness.

A few moments later, the toilet door opened and she heard footsteps coming in.

"Jean, are you alright?" came the concerned voice.

Jean stood up slowly, opened the cubicle door and fell into Barbara's arms. They stood there in silence for some minutes until Jean's sobbing subsided.

"Barbara, sorry... I... I don't know what came over me..." Jean began.

"It's OK," Barbara said, patting her shoulder lightly.

"Please... don't tell anyone about this..."

"Of course not."

They turned to the sink for a while to try and make the President presentable again.

"OK, how do I look?" asked Jean at last in the mirror.

"You're good to go, Mrs. President!"

"Great! OK let's go for part two," Jean said ebulliently.

"Yes Jean," Barbara said and swung open the door to the madding throng of suits outside.

F·DAY -3087

feeds·grapevine·is:

HERE COMES THE CAVALRY!

...and always in the nick of time – or is it too late?

Just in case you fell down a lava tube last night, US President Jean Carley surprised us all with a magnanimous rescue gift for Iceland: a container boat of essential supplies, and – proving that America likes to do things big – a full US Navy surplus tanker of oil!

Happy days may be here again, but is it too little too late for Iceland's perilous dreams of freedom? While Icelanders are generally grateful for the gesture, many prominent freeworlders are criticizing the gift as a 'late, politically-motivated whimsy'. Mark Ericsson from Akureyri's Voluntary Representative Committee said: "Of course the gesture is welcome and much needed, but unfortunately it is probably not going to secure any lasting progress towards Iceland's future freedom. Iceland's problem is not just lack of basic resources, it is the lack of technological infrastructure to maintain our self-sufficiency."

As if that wasn't enough of a blow to Jean Carley's grand gesture, she received a double-whammy with an almost instant drop of a further five points behind her election rival Pete Jefferson. It looks like most Americans don't have much time right now for foreign-aid election gimmicks in the midst of their own economic storm.

Anyway, don't listen to them, Jean! A big 'Thank You' from all of us here at Grapevine HQ. We're off for a nice big slap up lunch – we haven't eaten in months! :)

Watch the Presidential announcement >>

feeds·nytimes·com:

CARLEY'S CAMPAIGN ON ICE

Usually when we talk about something being 'on ice', we conjure up graceful images of skating lions and dragons, but in this case, the image is of an embattled president who has never used a pair of ice-skates before, and frankly it's getting painful to watch.

Jean Carley, who, *NYTimes* has learned, sacked her campaign director Oswald Moone Jr. yesterday and launched a rescue package for Iceland's beleaguered free community, is today soaking up the wrath of the American polls, falling between 2 and 5 points behind her Republican rival Pete Jefferson, depending on which poll you listen to.

Pete Jefferson, who today paid a surprise visit to a derelict motor factory in Detroit said:

"Every country has their problems. Iceland has theirs, but America has her own. In our own time of greatest economic challenges, our current administration has taken their eye off the ball, and seem determined to bring this proud nation to its knees. Well, I say different.

"As I stand here in this factory, I can hear the ghost of the proud American worker, pounding their hammer, building their community, and building our great nation. Well, today I pledge to all proud American workers, past and present, that I, Peter Thomas Jefferson, will rebuild this country, this economy, and this factory. In three years time, I will stand with you here again, in this factory, and we will enjoy the fruits of our labour together."

Watch the Jefferson speech >>

f-day.org/feeds/update:

PRESIDENT CARLEY'S US ANNOUNCEMENT [-1500 DAYS]

In light of President Carley's generous announcement of support and recognition of Iceland's endeavours, two years have been deducted from the official countdown, bringing F-Day now to thirty-eight years away.

F-Day.org >>

Karl watched the Jefferson video and was very impressed by him.

Jefferson was a slight man – not your usual run-of-the-mill square jawed candidate. He was dwarfish, intellectual looking, with wireframe glasses and a bald head. He looked more like a gynaecologist than a politician. Perhaps this doctor image was what had helped him earn the trust of people.

What was perhaps most surprising about him was the loud, confident manner in which he spoke. His rhetoric and intonation had been finely honed no doubt, but Karl couldn't help being amused at the thought of him being a politician trapped inside a doctor's body.

He closed the window and saw there was an email waiting for him. He didn't recognise the sender which was strange since he had gone to great lengths setting up filters for his mailbox to deal with the tons of garbage he received daily. He opened the mail and it contained just one word: "Pidgin".

Karl started to feel a little uneasy, then went to open up his encrypted Pidgin messenger, where there was a long text waiting for him.

> 'Karl, it's Gani from the Philippines – the hacker guy remember? :)

> 'I thought you should know I had another message from 'bishopsgate''

Karl immediately went cold.

> 'here it is:

> "Insert into RSS feed of AP Newswire at 0100 UST on 10/22 the following: Freeworlder Karl Drayton implicated in allegations of child sex. Allison O'Neill, 23, a schoolteacher from Navan, Ireland, who waived her right to anonymity, has claimed that Karl Drayton, 46, founder of The Free Movement, had unlawful sex with her in 2004 when she was 13. Ms. O'Neill, whose allegations came to light in an emotional letter written to an Irish radio station yesterday, is reported to have been contacted by the Irish Police authorities who are currently investigating the

allegations. Mr. Drayton was unavailable for comment when contacted by AP.'

'More instructions to follow – Bishopsgate.'

"I don't believe this f..." Karl muttered and slumped back in the chair. He sat there thinking for a few minutes.

Arbiter920 is typing...

"Aha!" Karl sat back up.

'It's in two days time, man. I don't know what to do...'

Karl sat looking at the screen for half a minute, looking for inspiration.

Finally, he typed a simple question.

'What do you want to do?'

There was a long pause.

'I want my life back man. I don't want to do this shit, but if I don't, they come after me for sure. :/'

'OK. OK, no worries...'

Karl was trying to think.

'What if you leave? Can you leave?'

'Even if I get out of the country, they got me. My passport. They find me...you know...'

He was right. Karl knew that whoever was going to such lengths to destroy him and The Free Movement were anything but amateurs, and they meant business. Suddenly, Karl saw an opportunity.

'Gani, how easy is it for you to do this?'

'Do what?'

'To hack into AP and plant this story...'

'It's pretty easy... I hacked into news sites before but not to plant

anything. Will probably take me a few hours to break in. I got three PCs to crunch it... and it's a busy site, which helps. :) Why?'

'Well, what if we give them what they want? That will get them off your back for a start. ...'

'k...?'

'...then we use your skills to plant counter stories in other sites? :)'

'Er... like what...?'

'I dunno... Like, let's find out who these fuckers are and expose them to the world. If we can do that, we got them off both our backs forever...'

'Good plan man...'

Karl put his head to his hands in thoughtful prayer for a second.

'We got two days to find out who these guys are and get a counter story ready. – Or maybe we can plant a counter story even before the deadline... OK, let me have a think about a plan of action... I'll be back on in an hour and you try to think of some ideas to find out who these guys are...'

'Right on man... Let's do it. Talk in an hour...'

'Ciao.'

Karl knew the first place to look. Outside. He went to grab his coat and hat and went to Abby. She was in the kitchen feeding Eli.

"Hey you two!" Karl said good-humouredly, kissing Abby and ruffling Eli's thin red curls.

"Are you OK?" she asked, looking down at his coat concerned. Karl thought for a second.

"No, there's a little problem that needs sorting out. I need to go and clear my head and get some ideas..."

"Sounds serious..." she said.

"It could be – unless I come up with some good ideas fast. Anyway, there's no panic. I'll tell you about it later."

"OK."

"I'll see you in a while." He kissed her and went out.

Karl liked brisk walking. It made him feel alive – to pump his legs and get his blood moving again. He spent a lot of time sitting in front of a computer, too much time. Walking in the cold fresh air brought him back to reality. When he walked, he could think.

So, first thing. What did he have to go on? 'Bishopsgate'. What does it mean? Well, it's a place in London. It's probably in other places too. He could check when he got back, but let's say it's London. Well if these guys had some 'international espionage office' in Bishopsgate, London, maybe it wouldn't be very professional to broadcast their address everywhere? That would be terrible for business, Karl chuckled to himself.

So what else could it mean? Why would that place have a significance? Well, maybe Bishopsgate just has some personal significance to the particular guy sending the mails – and it doesn't really tell them anything. Karl was a little depressed by that, but it was a real possibility. If these guys are serious – which they clearly are – they're not going to risk being uncovered so easily.

Maybe Bishopsgate is just a way of signifying that the message is from someone in London where multiple global operatives use such names to identify themselves to each other? Although Gani said the guy was American. Hmm, well there's bound to be a Bishopsgate in America – or maybe Canada. Perhaps he was Canadian? Karl was always amused when Canadians recoiled in shock when he 'accused' them of being American. Canadians were always so indignant and surprised at the mistake, but for Karl, there was no difference in accent. Maybe you had to be locally tuned to notice it.

Anyway, what else did he have to go on? Obviously, these people – whoever they were – were behind the shooting of poor Podge too. Ah yes – and the way they were able to get Gani released from prison and temporarily exonerated from American extradition must mean they are American and have fairly close relations with people high up in the food chain.

Was it an American Government agency? Like the CIA or the FEDs? Probably not, he thought. If it was, he would probably already be dead. Anna said someone had hacked into the radio channel to order Podge and Mattie's death, and that the operations sergeant was totally shocked. If he really had no idea, then it was probably someone on the outside, but who had access to insider knowledge. A private company working for the Government maybe? But what kind of company would have it in for the Free Movement so much?

What else to go on? The server attacks. That was interesting in itself. They only asked Gani to take the sites down for 48 hours. Why? Why not just block them permanently if they could? Suppose it was just a warning? Or maybe it was a test of Gani. Ah, that was probably it. They were checking to see if their new guy was going to be complicit with their demands. So they were testing him for something else bigger. But what – this ridiculous slur campaign? Maybe. Or maybe this is just the beginning of it.

Karl shuddered a little. He only realised then that he had reached the forest and was walking through. He had been so deep in thought that he hadn't noticed. He always gravitated to nature. It felt odd to him now to be here walking alone, with no wife, baby or dog. But he needed time to think – and this was serious.

What about the slur campaign itself? Surely the truth of planting a story like that will come out in the end? Shouldn't it? Surely the story wouldn't stand up to any scrutiny at all. If the police got involved there would be nothing to investigate, would there? Or maybe this 'Allison' person was a real person who wrote to the radio for them. Maybe she was employed by them, or they had some power over her like they have over Gani. But then, if it's a 'real' story from a real person, why would they need Gani to plant the story?

It was starting to get confusing. Karl's mind was racing on empty now. There was really almost nothing to go on, except Bishopsgate –

and even that might just be another big smoke.

He tried to empty his mind and filled his lungs with the fresh, cold forest air. After a minute he started to slow down a little. Then he stopped, and let out a small gasp. A wispy cloud alighted from his lips. He started counting on his fingers and mouthing something.

"HOLY FUCK!" he suddenly shouted.

A woman who happened to be passing with her Pekingese dog jumped back in fright, and the Pekingese started barking furiously at Karl.

"Er, sorry, sorry, sorry..." he said, turning and laughing and trying to pet the dog. But to no avail. Both dog and owner had clearly made up their minds. He gave up.

"Holy shit!" he said again, turning back around with his hands to his head. "Bishopsgate! The Big Soaps! Are they fucking serious? A fucking anagram? Ha ha ha!"

He ran back the way he had come, waving another 'sorry' to the unfortunate lady and her dog as he passed.

"Arf, arf!" the Pekingese reminded him.

Twenty minutes later, Karl was back at his desk – a man on a mission, and time was against him. He rattled the keys of his PC furiously, soaking up information like a junkie.

'The Big Soaps – a popular name for five American corporate chemical giants: Allisen Products, Mendez-Long, Milside-Jacks, Mykrochem and Sylvan-Parkers, so called for being major US manufacturers of everything from cleaning chemicals to household detergent, cosmetics to toothpaste...'

"Allisen Products, Allison O'Neill. For fuck's sake..." he muttered sarcastically. "A product of their own imagination then..." He read on.

'The five 'Big Soap' corporations have been repeatedly indicted for

environmental negligence, most recently, two weeks ago, where they were collectively fined 1.9bn US Dollars by the EPA...'

He flicked on...

'Sylvan-Parkers Corp, chief suppliers of industrial chemicals to the US Naval Defence Dept... Mendez-Long Corp., specialising in pharmaceuticals and cosmetics... Allisen Products, leading US manufacturer of infant foods and care products... Mykrochem Corp, owner of over 60 separate brands of medical and sanitation products... Milside-Jacks, owner of 182 brands of soap, toothpaste and personal hygiene products...'

Karl decided he would dip into each of them later to see what he could uncover, but for now, he was only interested in what they all had in common. He checked Yahoo Answers:

'Where did the 'Big Soaps' get their name?' Best answer: The Big Soaps refers to five American corporations: Milside-Jacks, Allisen Products, Mykrochem, Mendez-Long and Sylvan-Parkers. All had factories that opened in the 1970s (Except Allisen Products which began as 'Allisen Care' in 1967). All five companies began with factories along the Colorado River in Southern Utah.

'In 1979, a major chemical leak from one of the factories resulted in a ten-mile foam slick that flowed through Arizona and the Grand Canyon. The leaked chemical was actually harmless, but local press in Arizona coined the term 'The Big Soaps' as none of the five factories owned up to the leak. It was later discovered to have come from the Sylvan-Parkers plant, but the name stuck to this day. All the companies still have factories there to this day except for Sylvan-Parkers which has its main operation now in Illinois.'

It was clear to Karl that they were all very large companies and presumably very influential in American affairs. He decided to try to do a bit of googling of each. Allisen Products brought up a ton of babycare sites and forums as you'd expect. Mendez-Long brought up a very sedate corporate site with shareholder information and two large medical informational sites. They were also the subject of a lot of attention and vitriol from animal rights organisations like P.E.T.A. He grunted and continued his searches.

Sylvan-Parkers brought up a very minimalist site. They were principally US Navy contractors, now based in Illinois, supplying industrial cleaning chemicals and petroleum products. There was not much more about it. Looking further down he noticed that they had a manufacturing plant in Iraq. It looked like they were also contractors to the Iraqi Government – presumably, they got a nice shoo-in after one of the Gulf Wars, he mused.

Milside-Jacks brought up a plethora of soap and hygiene product pages, advertisement videos and consumer advice sites. One site noted that they had twenty-four brands of toothpaste alone. What the fuck, thought Karl, doesn't everyone basically have the same teeth? Why do we need twenty-four types from just one company? Karl sighed. Last one.

Mykrochem owned several different medical and sanitation products. They also ran a 'young innovator' competition, for which there were plenty of videos on YouTube. He opened one which wasn't particularly interesting – a teenager receiving an award for some chemistry project relating to purifying drinking water. Karl couldn't understand it. On the right side of the screen, there were several other video suggestions of a very different nature. He clicked on the first one.

It seemed that Mykrochem were also one of the main offenders in environmental pollution and dumping of toxic waste. A little ironic, he thought, given the previous teenager's award. Presumably, they were trying to smarten up their image. They had been indicted and fined on at least three occasions, prior to the recent one.

There were videos of eco-protesters at the gates to their factory in Utah. In one of them there appeared to be violent clashes as security teams tried to remove the protesters. One girl had handcuffed herself to the fence, which the security team were cutting with bolt-cutters under heavy shouts of protest. Some of the protesters were hitting the security guys with sticks. Karl thought the security guys were being quite reasonable and professional actually – but perhaps that was just because of the camera. He paused the video, stretched himself and sat back with his hands on his head.

He couldn't glean anything much from anything so far. He wasn't even sure what he was looking for. If Gani's contact was referencing his emails with these five companies, then there must be something linking them all. But what?

All he knew was that they all had factories on the Colorado river. He looked again at the paused screen and noticed that he could actually see a river in the background behind the fence. That must be the Colorado, he surmised.

In the foreground was the frozen image of the bedraggled handcuff girl being led away from the fence by a security guard – who was eyeing the camera sternly. The guard was wearing riot gear – helmet with visor and all black body armour – pretty impressive kit for a factory security guard, Karl thought. He looked down and noticed the uniform had a small yellow insignia on it. He suddenly remembered Podge's letter – and the black car that his landlord had seen driving away from his apartment.

He made the video larger. Larger... Larger.

"Aha!" he gasped. He began pounding on the keys again, opened a page, then stood up from the chair.

"Holy shit," he said, then typed something else and banging 'enter'. "My god, that's it," he shouted then ran out of the room to find Abby. It was time to tell her everything.

On the screen was a very basic website. Very clean, corporate, with almost no colour or information. Clearly a website for a company that didn't need one. The page open was the company's client list. 'Proudly serving clients such as: Milside-Jacks Corporation, Allisen Products, Sylvan-Parkers Corporation, Mykrochem Corporation, Mendez-Long Corporation...' At the top of the site, the same yellow insignia with the innocuous name: 'Riverside Security'.

F-DAY -3086

Yesterday had been tough for the Drayton family. So much had happened that Karl's confusing account and confessions to Abby only added to the stress levels. Abby was furious with Karl, not just for leaving them in the dark about what was going on, but for putting them all in danger in the first place.

She was right. He felt terrible. Of course there was more he could have done to protect himself and his family but he hadn't. He explained his idea to plant counter stories in the media, but she was unimpressed, retorting with: 'trying to beat lies and dishonesty with more lies and dishonesty is not going to get you anywhere – and against a giant conglomerate with a limitless budget and a track record of murder?' He had no answer to that.

Now Karl found himself living in a bad atmosphere, with only one day before Gani was going to plant the story, and he was all out of ideas. Sitting at his desk at the window overlooking their wild back garden, Karl clicked the computer on, but for what he had no idea. He stood up and looked out at Kylie in the garden while the computer was whirring itself into action. Action for what? He contemplated another soul-searching walk in the forest, but his thoughts were smartly interrupted by Abby who walked in holding a cup of coffee for him.

"I had an idea," she said warmly, handing him the coffee. Karl smiled and remembered why he married her. They both sat down.

"Your friend Gani will be in trouble if he doesn't post the story, right?" she asked.

"Right," Karl said.

"And what if he can't post the story? I mean, what if he tries and fails?"

"Well, he told me he would be able, but I think I see what you're getting at..."

"Yes, what if we alert that media site so they can block his attack?"

"Yeah, I thought of that too, but it won't help anyone really. Gani will probably get into trouble for failing and they'll just try and do the same again later anyway."

Abby nodded.

"That's what I thought, so here's what I was thinking: these people want to spread lies about you, but this should be their problem, not yours. The way they are trying to blacken your name is horrendous, but if they are exposed for doing so, the damage to them would be colossal."

"But how can we expose them? Who will believe us?"

"Karl, you have a huge advantage here. This story about you hasn't even been posted yet..."

"...and?"

"and..." she was motioning him to think a little harder. Finally, it clicked.

"Ah!" he said.

"Aha!" she seconded.

"Shit, I have to get busy," he said looking up at the clock.

"Yes, you do," she said, standing up. "Don't forget your coffee."

"I won't."

He stood up, hugged her, and smiled.

"Thank you," he said looking down into her green eyes. She smiled back, winked and walked out.

"How the hell did I get that lucky," Karl asked himself, sitting down at the computer and calling up Rob.

"Yo big guy, what's up?" Rob said.

"Surf's up, dude! I hope you're not busy today, 'cause I need to send something out pronto to every media email address in your possession."

187

"Wow! OK. Always ready for action boss, what's on your mind?"

"Ha! That's what I like to hear. Listen, there's no time to explain now, but this is hugely important. I'm gonna send you an email now in a few minutes. I need you to brush it up and send it out straight away," Karl said, adding wryly, "read it and you'll get the idea pretty fast I think."

"OK, roger that. I'll call you back later when it's sent."

"Fantastic Rob, thank you."

"My pleasure mate," Rob said and clicked off.

Karl sat back in the chair, sighed, then waited. It didn't take long. The words filled his head like a mountain spring, gushed and poured through his fingers onto the computer. Within ten minutes it was written. He read through it four times, fixed all the typos and clicked send. He watched it go, then sat there staring at the screen for a minute. He was just about to get up when he got an email reply from Rob:

"Holy shit! Sending it now mate. Cheers."

Karl smiled and nodded.

"Let's hope this works," he said to himself. "Oh, one more thing to do..."

He opened the Pidgin messenger to Gani, and typed:

'Hey Gani, please go ahead and do what you've got to do. I understand your position. I think we've got it covered at this end. ;) Thanks and let me know if anything else comes your way, K.'

Mike Ross, media guru, fixer, oracle, was, as usual, doing several things at once on several screens. He wasn't just good at multitasking, he was uncomfortable not multitasking. Currently, he was typing up two news release documents, photoshopping a protester into the background of a picture of the Boston Mayor, and watching two videos.

It took only a little extra cerebral bandwidth to acknowledge the email that had just managed to tango through his myriad keyword filters enough to trigger a notification bell sound.

Mike was in the business long enough to know that when that particular bell sounded it was show time. When it sounded, it meant that he was ahead of the game, but perhaps only for minutes. If he didn't react immediately, it was lost earnings, lost reputation. It was failure.

He opened the email.

'A message to my friends in the media from Karl Drayton, The Free Movement.

'Friends, this is not a news release, but the information here is important. Please do with it as you please.

'It has come to my attention that a certain organisation is embarking on a vicious, personal smear campaign against me, presumably with the ultimate aim of bringing The Free Movement into disrepute and disarray. Tomorrow, this organisation will begin circulating a story about me through a network of hackers into mainstream media channels. Obviously, the story is false.

'The organisation in question is known to me, and they represent several other highly influential organisations within the US, who seem to have taken it upon themselves to try and destroy the Free Movement, and me personally.

'I have reason to believe this same group were also responsible for the shooting dead of two 'Free World Kidnappers' in Wall St, on September 14th, one of whom was a close personal friend. These men were not kidnappers as was previously reported. Both were peace-lovers and utterly incapable of violence. Their killing was, in fact, an assassination by stealth, as police received orders to fire on both men from an unknown radio hacker operating remotely. I heard this from someone who was at the scene that day.

'Myself and some of my colleagues have conducted our own investigations into this and other various coordinated attacks on our servers, and now believe we know the identity of the group in question. However, we do not yet have sufficient proof to name them publicly. Also, I am now in fear for my life, since they have killed before.

'I am using this opportunity to write to you now, as I know from my sources that these fabricated stories about me will begin being circulated tomorrow. I urge you to fully investigate these stories and their sources before publishing. Know that I will pursue to the last any slander or libellous accusations made against me to the full extent of the law, and I will win. You have been warned, so please investigate your sources with all stories hereon relating to me or to The Free Movement.

'Thank you for your understanding,

'Karl Drayton, The Free Movement'

Mike scarcely blinked. He was, of course, completely unshockable and sat back in his chair ruminating over the words for a minute. Two things alarmed him. One: that he didn't already know the story that was about to break, and two: why Karl had not contacted him before about this? Since everything seemed to happen Stateside, he was surprised Karl had not been in touch. He felt a great empathy for the Free Movement and the work Karl was doing, and would like to help – albeit in the background – if he could. It was time to punch some keys.

There was an FBI investigation ordered into the two Wall St. killings, but looking at the parameters, it was a pretty low-level internal investigation... Usually, these tended to turn up nothing except a tidy profit for the law firms involved... He zeroed in on Karl's friend Podge...

OK, Podge... Patrick Frattini... born in Italy, moved to New York with parents in 1980... parents still live in Queens... dropped out of Yale... studying to be a doctor... left and... left the country??... travelling I presume... girlfriend?? Ah, he's back... Tanja Schmidt... doctor in psychology... from Switzerland... died a couple of years ago from leukaemia... pictures of Podge at Wall St. money-burning demonstration with another girl... hang on... ah Anna... Vasquez from Cuba... wow... she's been deported seven times! Public order offences, nudity, graffiti, theft, auto theft... this girl really gets around...

So, if Podge was with Anna when he was shot, then she is probably Karl's eyewitness... Mattie's cries about saving 'her' probably relate to his mother... that might explain the kidnap mix-up...

Mike was getting the idea. If he knew one thing about Karl, he knew that he wouldn't have taken an action like this lightly, so presumably some humdinger of a story was on its way. By Karl's language, it sounded like the story was somehow going to be planted on a website. It wasn't the first time this had happened. In fact, Mike chuckled, he had done the very same thing himself in his younger years when he was hungry and trying to make an impression. And it had worked like a charm.

His story – at a rather unsavoury client's request – had been aimed at the then New York Mayor in relation to 'anomalies' in his expenses account. Mike had later watched open-jawed when the Mayor had as good as confessed on live TV to the entirely fabricated claim. It was spectacular damage limitation at work on the Mayor's part. He was happy to offer up one skeleton from his closet, when he must have really had a few dinosaurs in there!

No-one had ever traced that story back to Mike. But that was the day he truly understood and learned to respect the power of the media at his fingertips. He had learned so much from people in all those years, and in Karl, he saw a good, incorruptible man of high moral standards. Whatever the story was, if Karl had gone to all this trouble, it was going to be a big and bad one. He knew what he had to do.

First things first, he relaxed all the keyword filters on his live news feeds. He wanted to be ready for anything when it hit. Secondly, he wrote a short public release statement in Karl's 'own words' to be ready to fire out the moment the story came in. Thirdly, he forwarded Karl's email to everyone in his media contacts. It was battle-stations. Now all he had to do was wait.

He didn't have to wait long. AP lit up first with the story. It was long and it was sordid. Even Mike's finger hovered momentarily before pushing send on his 'rebuttal'.

"Jeez don't let me down man," he said to himself. Mike was putting his own reputation in the way now. If he got it wrong...

Then something extraordinary happened. Within sixty seconds after Karl's story, AP had another story:

'AP newswire is currently experiencing server issues. We apologise for the inconvenience.'

Mike refreshed the page and saw that Karl's story had disappeared.

"Yes!" he said, throwing his empty coffee cup triumphantly into the trash. The combination of Karl's pre-emptive strike and Mike's rebuttal had done the trick. AP had removed the story.

Mike might have been just one of a handful of people around the world who had seen the story come and go. Of course, there was still an outside chance that one of the majors would pick it up, but in Mike's experience, it was unlikely.

He searched back through his emails and found an old one from Karl with his user name and server for encrypted chats. He logged in. Karl was online.

'So what's this all about? (off the record) - Mike'

There was a momentary pause.

Freeworlder1 is typing...

F-DAY -3072

Karl was thirty-three thousand feet over the Atlantic Ocean when he got the message from Abby:

'We're here now! Talk later. X'

Karl smiled and put the phone back in his pocket. He picked up the in-flight magazine again and stared blankly at some article about a Boston Cajun restaurant, together with the standard short depth-of-field promo photos. He tossed it back on the table again and tried to find something to watch on his screen.

After the near miss with ridiculous sex allegations, Karl had felt very fortunate, but he knew whoever was seeking to persecute him wasn't going to go away any time soon. He had made the snap decision to leave, send Abby to a safe hotel, drive to the airport and get on the next plane to the States.

And it wasn't just a knee-jerk reaction either. He had to assume that these people may be watching his every move – so the best way of keeping himself and his family safe was to be unpredictable.

One of the things that Karl had spoken about many times in his interviews about the Free Movement was his radical proposal for conflict resolution and today he was going to put it into action. He had dubbed it 'Creative Arbitration'.

It was very simple: first, make sure that each party fully understands the concerns and the reasoning of the other, then second, ask each party to suggest a number of possible resolutions that would satisfy both parties – no matter how wild or improbable. Karl's theory was that by forcing each side to understand then create solutions for everyone, an empathy is created, thus leading to a potential outcome that neither might have considered.

Of course, it was just a theory. Now he was flying solo and about to be his own first guinea pig – and his life may well depend on him being right.

With some searching, he had a pretty good idea who from Riverside Security he needed to meet. He was very much looking forward to seeing the reaction on the face of James Carson Jr. in around twelve hours time, on the dramatic banks of the Colorado River.

F·DAY -3071

feeds.bbcnews.com/russia:

RUSSIAN GOVERNMENT UNDER PRESSURE OVER TAPAC MEMORIAL

Calls for the erection of a monument or memorial to Tapac Lagunov, the nine-year-old freedom protester who was crushed during the miners riot two months ago have reached fever pitch. While the Russian Government has backed the idea to build a monument in Donskoy, where Tapac lived, there have been widespread calls for the monument to be located in Red Square, on the site where Tapac was mortally injured.

The Tapac Movement, which has seen huge numbers of supporters since Tapac's death, is insisting that Red Square is the appropriate location. Andrei Lagunov, Tapac's father, speaking at the campaign yesterday said, "There is only one reason why the Government would refuse to site Tapac's monument here – and that is a shame. Shame that an innocent boy campaigning for a better future died less than a hundred steps from the front door of the Kremlin."

The Tapac Movement Manifesto >>

feeds.bbcnews.com:

ANTI-FRACKING DEMONSTRATIONS IN YORKSHIRE

There were violent clashes in Ebberston Moor yesterday as Yorkshire Police tried to move seventy-five demonstrators from blocking the entrance to the fracking site. On the foot of a court order, police moved in at 5AM yesterday morning to disband the group. However, events took an unexpected turn when one of the demonstrators, Helena Worth, 29, went into labour. She was quickly brought to hospital under a police escort.

The officer in charge praised the group and the police officers for their diligent handling of the situation and announced that they would put a moratorium on the eviction order on compassionate grounds in light of the events. He also offered his congratulations to Helena and her partner Steve on the arrival of their new daughter Hope.

Amateur video >>

It was only when Karl left the terminal building at Grand Canyon Airport that he realised just how ill-prepared he was for the Arizona desert scorch. His thick Irish jeans, socks, shirt, sweater and jacket suddenly felt as clumsy as a deep diving suit. He quickly jumped in a taxi to bring him to his destination, and shamelessly gulped in the cool climate control air while thinking about which clothes he was going to sacrifice for the meeting.

He had not made any appointment of course. The only thing he knew was that he was flying back in three days – hopefully alive, he joked darkly. If all else failed, he could at least spend a few days enjoying the sights of the Canyon.

A couple of hours later, he reached Riverside Security. He looked up at the building from the car window. It was not as he had expected at all. He had expected to find a black, featureless building devoid of windows and soul, where evil men sat around dimly lit board tables hatching evil plans. It was nothing like that at all.

Riverside Security looked for all the world like a Spanish villa. An impressive two storey dwelling painted in an ochre wash. Tasteful granite fountains, symmetrically appointed in a garden of orange trees, flanked a wide gravel path leading to the thick oak door. It was charming and peaceful.

Having divested himself of his heavy clothes, Karl stepped from the car and approached the building in his shirtsleeves. As he walked up the path, he reflected on the fact that he had almost no plan – except to use a pseudonym to get in the door. He pressed the buzzer.

"Hello?" came the friendly, efficient response.

"Hello, I'm here to see James Carson Jr... My name is, er, George Best." Karl smiled to himself. There was a long pause.

"I'm sorry sir," came the voice eventually. "Mr. Carson is not here today. Would you like to leave a message for him?"

Karl had been in business long enough to know that those long silent pauses are when the secretary and boss are busy conspiring excuses. He thought a little.

"OK," he said. "Can you give him a message that my client Karl Drayton and his team of specialists are arriving from Ireland tomorrow to meet with him. I believe Mr. Drayton is a friend of Mr. Carson's?"

There was another long pause.

The door buzzed.

Karl walked in to the wonderfully cool hallway and approached the desk. The young girl smiled warmly at him.

"Mr. Carson is in his office, Mr. Best. Last door on the left." She motioned down the corridor.

"Thank you," Karl smiled, marvelling at how wonderfully efficient the girl was at lying through her teeth.

The building was more modern inside than out but felt a little more like a dentist's practice than he was comfortable with. It was the first time Karl had actually begun to feel that rising sensation of dread within him. The man behind that door was capable of killing him. He might never be going home to see his family again. Eli might be growing up without a father...

He raised his hand to knock on the door, then paused.

He could just walk back to the door right now and leave. Say he had to leave unexpectedly. No-one would ever know... God...

He knew he wasn't going to do that. He didn't come all this way to back down. He had to face this. If he didn't, they would never stop until they finished him off...

"Sorry Eli," he whispered and knocked on the door.

"Come."

He pushed the door.

"Hello, Mr..."

The man behind the desk choked and went pale.

"Yes it's me," Karl said matter-of-factly, looking for a chair.

James Carson Jr.'s body language belied his conflicting intentions. He was halfway between standing up, sitting down, running away and reaching for something in the drawer.

"That's OK," Karl said firmly. "I just came for a talk, that's all." He showed his palms as if signalling that he had nothing to hide.

"Mr. Drayton..." James said in an effort to restore himself. He felt foolish now. Drayton had nothing on him and both of them knew it, yet he was jumping around like a child caught with his hand in the cookie jar.

James was young. Mid thirties, Karl reckoned. He was thin, pale and wore a nondescript stripe suit. Obviously his father's company – this guy looked clueless, Karl thought. On his desk, James had a picture of a beautiful young woman and two young boys.

"Your kids?" Karl said, nodding at the picture and sitting down.

"Er, yes actually."

Karl turned back and looked James levelly in the eye.

"I have a wife and a daughter."

"Oh, really?"

James totally overdid the surprise and enthusiasm for Karl. It was time to get down to business.

"So you recognised me straight away, Mr. Carson. How is that?" Karl quipped.

"Well... yes, I... I've seen you obviously... in the news and..."

"Don't sweat it, James," Karl raised his hand. He had seen enough squirming. "I'm just here to talk. No tricks, no hidden cameras or microphones, no bullshit. I've come quite a long way. I'm sure you can afford me half an hour of your time. Does that sound reasonable?"

"Yes," said James, visibly defeated.

"Good. You should know firstly then James that I am not your average person. I am not here to avenge the deaths of two innocent men who you had killed. I'm not here to get you in trouble. I'm not even interested in what you call justice – quote unquote..."

James looked from side to side. "So... why are you here, then?"

"First and foremost to get you and your henchmen off my back and away from my family, and secondly..." Karl searched for the words.

"Yes...?"

"Well, two things. First I want to explain to you what I'm doing and why I'm doing it, and second, I want to hear your ideas for resolving...our little situation," he said at last.

"Pardon me?" James said.

"Well, you can think about the second part while I give you the first..."

Suddenly the door burst open. Karl looked around to see a giant of a man filling the door frame.

"Jimmy, is this who I think it is?" the man demanded, gesturing roughly at Karl. He was a preposterous figure. Both square and rotund with an out-sized tweed jacket, wild grey hair and skin rough and burnt as a clay pot. Karl stood up.

"Yes, daddy. This is Karl..."

"Karl Drayton," finished James Carson Sr., regarding Karl up and down. "You've got some bottle showing up here, I'll give you that boy. Bourbon?" He walked over to the bar.

"Er, no, not for me thank you," Karl said offering his hand to shake, which was ignored.

"So let me guess," the big man said smiling wryly and pouring himself a drink. "You're here to cut some kind of deal to get us off your back, correct?"

James Jr. stifled a snigger.

"Actually no, I'm here to provide a solution," Karl said, sitting down again.

"Really?" James Sr. laughed. "A solution to what precisely? It looks very much to me Mr. Drayton that *you* are the one with the problem, not me..." He sat down his giant frame in the seat beside Karl.

"On the contrary, Mr. Carson, *you* are the ones with the problem. You and your organisation have taken it upon yourselves to destroy the Free Movement and the people who support it. Obviously, our organisation is somehow a threat to yours – in other words, your problem."

Carson gestured around the room. "We are a security business, Mr. Drayton. We solve other peoples' problems for them. That is what we do."

"Including murder?"

"I'm sure I've no idea what you're talking about, Mr. Drayton."

"Let's cut the crap, shall we?" Karl said sharply. "I know you are involved in several criminal acts against me, my organisation and my friends. As I explained to James Jr. here, I have come a long way to resolve your and your clients' problems and get you off my back. I am not interested in trying to prove what I already know. I don't give a shit about justice or revenge. I am only interested in one thing – creating a better world for the living, including me. For every one of us sharing this flying rock. If shooting me as well is going to make you feel a whole lot better, then let's get it over with, but not until you – or whoever the hell is pulling your strings – hears me out first."

Carson Sr. looked over at Carson Jr. and shrugged.

"Whatever problem you got, you want to solve it right?" Karl continued. "Don't tell me you're in business to kill people. That's too fucked up. You're in business to solve things for you and your clients – whatever it takes, right? So let's solve it?"

"I can't argue with that," Carson conceded. "What you got in mind exactly?"

"I've got two things to prove here. One, to prove that I can solve your problem, and two, to prove to myself that this shit works."

"OK, so let's have it then, Mr. Drayton," James Jr. chirped in.

"OK, so the first thing is understanding each others' objectives. My objective is simple. I want to rid the world of money and trade because I believe we can create a much better world for everyone by doing so. It's not about stealing wealth from anyone, it's about rendering the notion of wealth entirely obsolete. You don't miss something that you don't need, right?

"We already know it works. This system I am proposing is already working in Iceland, and beginning in other countries too. If you ask the Icelandic people if they miss their personal wealth, they will say no. There has been hardship there for some, but the acts of overcoming that hardship have actually strengthened community bonds. People are happier. People are more productive.

"The system is in its infancy. It's not perfected yet, but in general it's working. None of the things that people thought would happen like hoarding or laziness have happened. In fact, the opposite is happening. Productivity is higher. More people are working. More people are contributing things to the communities that they used to own exclusively.

"When we started in these countries, people were given assurances that no-one would ever have to surrender their personal wealth or possessions, yet this is what people are now doing – voluntarily. Why? Because it just makes sense. Your neighbour needs a tractor and you have one lying in the garage. Why not offer it? If he breaks it, the mechanic will fix it. Why? Because the mechanic enjoys his cereal in the morning! So it goes on like that..."

Carson Sr. was getting impatient. He waved Karl down.

"I get ya son. All is rosy in happy town. Everybody loves everybody," he gesticulated. "That's just beautiful, ain't it Jimmy?"

Jimmy smiled.

"Mr. Drayton. I've no doubt, and I'm sure my daddy agrees, that what you're proposing can work in some places with some people. That doesn't mean it's ever gonna work here..."

"And if your clients are so confident it will never work in America, then why are they shooting people who think it will?" Karl retorted.

"Listen, sonny," James Sr. said. "Maybe you're right. Maybe we can turn America into some commie paradise with everyone floating in bliss and smoking their brains out or whatever, but there're people – and I mean influential people around here who will happily shoot you, me and anyone else before they'll see that happen."

"OK, well have you got any influence over these people? You know how they operate. You know what they want. If I can convince you, can you convince them?"

"You've no idea who you're talking about sonny," said James Sr. smirking, "but hell I'll pass on your message if it makes you happy."

The two men exploded laughing.

"Great," said Karl unabashed. "So now you have the gist of what I want, why not tell me what they want?"

The big man straightened himself out.

"Simple. They don't want none of that shit here. These men and women have worked hard to get to where they are today and are not about to throw all that away on some hippie fantasy. They are just defending what is rightfully theirs."

"So they *are* threatened by the Free Movement. Good. At least that shows that they see it becoming a reality. Otherwise, they wouldn't be interested in us."

"Just because something can be made real, don't make it a good thing, son."

"That depends on whose point of view you're talking about. If I own a store full of grain and someone takes all that grain, that's bad for me, but it's not bad for the person who took it, right?"

"Of course."

"Now change that a little. If I have a store full of grain and I decide to keep more than enough for myself and my family and share the rest to whoever needs it, everyone wins. No-one loses. Also, it's future-proof for me, as the ones I'm helping now will be far more likely to reciprocate later on when I need something from them.

"If that is how we operate society, *no-one* would need to hoard anything – because hoarding anything that you can't consume yourself is just being wasteful and ignorant. Whatever you think about being wasteful, being ignorant will always come back to bite you in the ass some day when you need something."

He looked to James Jr.

"Hoarding is what we do when things are scarce and the future is uncertain. By creating a society where everyone's basic needs are met, hoarding resources would just be a stupid thing to do. The people you are working for, Mr. Carson, are pathological hoarders. They have long since passed the point of requiring wealth to meet their basic needs. They just never stopped repeating the behaviour. Now it's nothing more to them than an idle challenge to see how high they can go."

"You can dress it up any way you want, Mr. Drayton," Carson Sr. said, "but these people are just as entitled to their money as you are entitled to whine about it."

He pulled out a fat cigar and leaned in towards Karl.

"Yes, they are threatened by the Free Movement. Yes, they want to protect their interests. If my company wasn't fulfilling their needs, they would find someone else – and maybe someone far less scrupulous than me, if you get my drift."

He paused to light the cigar.

"Sure, we are not in the widow-making business here, but we're not here to negotiate world peace either. We are here to serve our clients."

"How well do you know your clients, Mr. Carson?" Karl asked, leaning in himself.

"Well enough..."

"Well enough to speak or act for them?"

"Yeah, I reckon so..."

"Good. So here's what I propose. I want you to do a little mental exercise – on behalf of your esteemed clients. I want you to think how they would think. Speak how they would speak. Can you do that?"

Carson waved his cigar nonchalantly. "I guess..."

"OK, so here it is. You know what I want, and you know what they want. Now I want you to propose a solution where everyone gets what they want."

"What?" the old man cried.

"You heard me. I want to hear *your* proposal for a solution where everyone goes home happy."

Carson looked lost.

"Well, I think that's not possible, Mr. Drayton," James Jr. said.

"Well then, humour me," Karl replied. "Even if it's impossible."

"But you can't solve that," the young man said. "You want one thing, they want the opposite."

"That's binary thinking," Karl snapped. "That's what school does to you."

James Jr. looked confused, but James Sr. had been quietly thinking.

"OK," the big man said at last. "A solution – though an impossible one of course – would be to create a second America. You have one and we have the other."

The two men exploded laughing again. This time Karl was laughing too.

"That's great!" Karl said. "That's a good start. Have you guys got any tea here by any chance?" he asked suddenly.

"Yeah sure," the young man said and buzzed the secretary in.

"And some biscuits?"

"Pardon me?"

"Cookies, Jimmy. Cookies," the old man answered.

Three hours later, Karl Drayton shook hands with both men and walked from the building to a waiting taxi.

"Where to sir?" the driver asked.

"Ha ha! I don't care," Karl laughed. "Show me around! Show me this big fucking hole in the ground you've got here..."

"Pardon me? The Canyon sir?" the eyes frowned in the mirror.

"Ha ha! That's the one," Karl shouted triumphantly, slapping the top of the passenger seat. "Let's go! Woohoo!"

The driver regarded Karl suspiciously in the mirror and decided just to keep quiet. Karl was sitting back singing now. He was totally ecstatic. The two Carson gentlemen had just kindly given him a taxi-cab for the rest of the day to take in the sights. Not only had he just completed the greatest deal of his life – but possibly the greatest deal in history!

He took out his phone and called Abby.

"Hey how did it go?" came the voice.

"Honey pack your things, we are moving to Iceland!"

"WHAT?" she screamed.

"Yep. You betcha!" he shouted. "I just done gone and cut the best deal ever for y'all!"

It was time to call in Reyksson's favour.

F·DAY -3065

Commander John Alton of the USS Liberty Bell was in the map room double-checking their course for the last 20 miles into Reykjavik harbour. Satisfied, he stepped out onto the bridge again to survey the Atlantic waters ahead of them. He was an impressive figure of a man, though short, he was stocky and had a large, bristling red moustache that gave him an air of authority. He took his job very seriously and had worked very hard to get where he was. Not one of his crew ever dared to question him or answer back – he just somehow gave the impression that something terrible would happen to them if they did.

"Sir, we got a blip, three miles at 11 o'clock," the radar officer piped up.

"Probably fishing," snapped the commander, as he took up the binoculars and went out on the bridge-wing. He could see a vessel, but it was too big for fishing, too small for a tanker, not on any ferry route, must be cargo from US or Canada probably...

"Call them up and get an ID," he ordered, stepping back in from the cold and closing the door.

"Aye aye," the radio officer said. "Hello, unknown vessel on heading 280, this is USS naval cargo vessel Liberty Bell on heading 290. Please identify yourself, over."

"Good morning USS Liberty Bell!" came a cheerful voice over the tannoy, "This is the Canadian Navy freighter Manitoba bound for Reykjavik. Are you bringing the sandwiches, over?"

The radio officer looked up at Commander Alton and shrugged.

"What the hell is he on about?" snorted the commander. "find out what they're doing here!"

"Aye aye sir."

"Sir, we got another couple of blips," cut in the radar officer. "One at 2 o'clock, seven miles, another at 3 o'clock, five miles."

The tannoy crackled again. This time a more distant Nordic accent.

"Hello USS Liberty Bell and HMCS Manitoba, this is cargo vessel MV Gallic Fjord out of Bergen, Norway, also bound for Reykjavik. It sounds like we are having a party, yes?"

The Commander said nothing and grabbed the microphone from the radio officer, "This is Commander John Alton of the United States Navy Vessel Liberty Bell. We are on a humanitarian mission, bringing vital supplies to the people of Iceland, under the direct orders of the US President and Federal Government. Please state your business in these waters."

There was a long silence. The radio officer shuffled his feet.

Finally, a tiny voice with a thick Scottish accent broke through on the tannoy. "Same thing as you my friend – but with a wee dram of whiskey to keep out the cold!"

Two hours later, the Liberty Bell entered Reykjavik Harbour and was met with the most incredible scenes. The harbour was full of boats of all shapes, sizes and flags – Russian, Scottish, Irish, Canadian, Norwegian, Finnish, Danish, German – even Greek. The piers were packed with people and what appeared to be market stalls. Large heated marquees were being erected, along with a fairground and big wheel too. It looked a lot like someone was planning a huge carnival.

Commander Alton expertly manoeuvred his ship himself into the berth that had clearly been reserved for it. The harbour was small and full, with boats tied three and four abreast. The Liberty Bell was a retired destroyer that had been converted to carry naval cargo and food supplies. Despite its small size, docking it in such a full harbour was no mean feat, and the multitude of tiny dinghies that had launched to meet it made it a slow, delicate process.

Leaving the gangway, the commander was met by Iceland's

President Reyksson, a few other dignitaries and the other commanders of the recently arrived flotilla.

"You are very welcome to Iceland, Commander Alton," the President said, shaking the commander's hand firmly.

John Alton couldn't help but shake his head and crack a big broad smile. "It's a real privilege to be here, Mr. Reyksson. A privilege indeed."

No-one could have predicted that such an act of human unity would ever have taken place in such a tiny harbour, in such a tiny country just outside the Arctic Circle. During the next days, all the ships' supplies were unloaded in record time by the extraordinary multinational harbour team made up of whoever was available – Icelanders and visitors alike.

On the final night, a giant carnival of music, fire and ice marked the end of an extraordinary event that was nothing short of historic. For the first time, countries were gifting their resources and labour unconditionally – not out of charity – but out of unity. What started out as simply a pre-election publicity stunt from President Carley became a worldwide historic event, later to be known and celebrated as 'Neighbour Day'.

While Iceland celebrated, four and a half thousand kilometres away, Jean Carley was sitting alone in the dim silence of the Oval Office putting the final touches on her election concession speech. She looked up at the portrait of Thomas Jefferson wistfully.

"Looks like it's gonna be a family affair around here for the next while. Congratulations sir," she said, raising her glass of Chianti.

PART 3
COUNTDOWN

*"It's no use going back to yesterday,
because I was a different person then."*

Lewis Carroll – *Alice In Wonderland*

F·DAY -3035

K arl and his family were welcomed personally at Keflavik Airport by Baldur Reyksson. Baldur gave Karl a bear-hug and welcomed his two ladies with a polite peck on the cheek.

"Welcome," he boomed.

"Wow, how times have changed already!" Karl exclaimed. "In what other country in the world does the President show up in person and offer hugs to his visitors?" Abby chuckled.

"Hahaha!" Baldur said and clapped Karl on the back. "Well, strictly speaking, I am not a president anymore. We have surpassed all that pyramid mumbo jumbo. I'm just a kind of familiar looking face around here..."

Karl laughed. "Great to hear it – and great to see you too," Then he took a more serious tone. "Thank you, Baldur, for what you have done for us. We are eternally indebted..."

"Nonsense!" the former president declared. "Besides, no-one is indebted around here any more."

Everyone laughed.

"Well, thank you again," Karl repeated. "There's so much we need to catch up on Baldur. I've been rather, er," – he looked at Abby and Eli – "busy of late."

"Haha, I'm sure. Well, there's plenty of time for that later." He gestured with open arms. "Welcome to Iceland, our beautiful country, our wonderful open society, and your new home!"

There was a small crowd of on-lookers who, sensing the excitement, were also shaking Karl's hand.

"We have organised a wonderful home for you just fifteen minutes

213

out of town and a little electric runabout to get around," Baldur said.

"Wow, that's extremely generous Baldur, but how..."

"More of all that later. We are not perfect by any means, but we aim to please our very distinguished guests..."

Baldur agreed to meet them the following day and bade them farewell outside the airport, pointing to something over their left shoulder. They both waved and turned around, and there, outside the airport door was a very new looking white electric car with the door open for them.

"Wow!" they said. They went over and Karl sat in the car. He turned the key, the instrument lit up silently, and the satnav sprang to life with the words:

"Home. Leave now?"

Karl and Abby smiled and loaded up the car with Eli, Kylie, their bags and themselves.

Within an hour they were on the far side of Reykjavik, when the satnav ordered them to take the next left. They turned into a lane way, rounded a bend, and were met with the most charming wooden cabin nestled in some trees, between two grassy hummocks and an uninterrupted view of the lava field.

"Wow!" Karl shouted. "It's like a scene from the Forbidden Planet," he exclaimed.

"It's beautiful," she said. "So, is this, er, ours?" she asked tentatively.

"Erm, I don't... actually know," he conceded. They stared at each other.

"I love you," he said. "This place is wonderful..."

"*You* are wonderful," she answered, hugging him. "I love you too. Let's unload?"

"Yup!"

F·DAY -3034

feeds·newyorktimes·com:

POLISH MILITARY RULE IN DOUBT

Poland's caretaker military government, led by General Brzezicki, is under mounting pressure to accede to what is now becoming known as 'Citizen Rule'. Protests against handling of the social and economic problems have not abated since the military took charge thirteen months ago. Riots have been ongoing and several attempts at curfew have largely failed.

Spokeswoman for the Citizen Rule Alliance, Cecylia Rudaska, told the rally yesterday: "Time was up for the centralised, military backed institutions of power. We, the people are more than capable of creating stability, peace and prosperity through self-determination and engaging in self-responsible acts. [...] We are wise. We are many. We are self-motivated. We are self-empowered. The persons behind these walls do not speak for us any longer."

Attendance figures for the CRA rally range from 250,000 to 1 million people.

See pictures and video >>

feeds·ft·com:

SWISS INCOME EXPERIMENT

Two months in and, frankly, it looks like Switzerland's basic income experiment has been disastrous, causing inflation to soar to 5% and unemployment figures to 21% – *and* a labour shortage in some sectors. Also, they have had to introduce tight border controls causing massive traffic delays in and out of the country to control the mass influx of immigrants desperate to cash in on the new deal.

The Government's move to foot the bill of the new scheme on the upper tax brackets has caused many companies and private individuals to begin taking their money out of Switzerland for the first time. Yesterday the Swiss Franc (CHF) closed down twenty cents on the Euro – an unprecedented drop as confidence in their future economy wanes.

Despite all that, it still looks as though no-one in the Swiss

Parliament is prepared to publicly oppose the basic income experiment as it has been considered a widely popular move by its citizens. That may be short-lived though as the economic side-effects might begin to soak through into peoples' daily lives.

The French, UK and German Governments – all of whom have been watching the Basic Income experiment are now distancing themselves from the idea. France's Prime Minister Pierre Ledoux called it a 'shambolic and ill-conceived economic suicide'. That said, protests against austerity in Paris are still on the increase and tensions are still high in the ongoing Camp d'Eiffel blockade now in its fifth month.

Swiss Basic Income has also created another monster in its wake: work inequality. Those in full time jobs were now demanding less hours for the same pay to seek parity with those who weren't working but enjoying all the benefits. Also, many people were leaving their lower-paying jobs meaning many vital utility services were not being delivered. Shops and fast-food companies were also having to increase their salaries to stop people from leaving, thus increasing prices and further exacerbating the inflation problem.

There have also been several calls for strike action in the civil service and among public health workers. It looks like the architects of B.I.G. were having an enormous job trying to keep all their balls in the air.

F·DAY -3033

Karl surveyed his new panorama with awe. The icy morning mist was beginning to dissipate, revealing the uppermost knobs of moss-carpeted rocks. He had risen early to cut logs for the day. Even though their new home was heated from the ground below, it was still nice to use the stove. Baldur – or whoever had organised their home – had seen to it that they had plenty of wood in the yard.

Yesterday, they had spent their time organising the house, now he was exploring the local landscape with Kylie. Reaching the crest of the higher hummock beside their house, Karl and Kylie had a fantastic all-around view of their new home. Their home was, in fact, sitting on top of a centuries-old lava lake, locked in between the heather hills on the left and steep rocky mountains on the right. Karl tried to imagine the same scene all those centuries ago, looking over a seething lake of boiling rock, hissing and spitting sulphur, methane and black smoke. He wouldn't have lived long standing here and would have asphyxiated in minutes. He marvelled at the power of nature. Closing his eyes, he filled his lungs deep with the crisp, pure air.

Looking over his shoulder, he could see the distant urbanisation that was Reykjavik. That was sufficient to jar him back to the present.

"Come on Kylie," he called. "Time to do what we came here for."

Kylie wagged in agreement and they made off back down the hill to the cabin with the white thread of smoke.

Karl arrived early to the office that was part of the old Alþingi. It was quite a surreal experience since there were no guards, no police and no security barriers on entering the building. There were some staff passing through the corridors, but no-one paid any attention to Karl. Obviously, this was still the logical place for organising national affairs, so he assumed that these were the voluntary admin staff Baldur had mentioned.

He helped himself to a coffee.

Baldur arrived a few moments later. The two men shook hands warmly.

"Great to see you. How's the house?" Baldur asked with a glimmer in his eye.

"It's... beautiful Baldur. We can't thank you enough..."

"Don't thank me," Baldur interjected raising his hands. "It was a house that belonged to my secretary's mother. It was her idea."

"Well, thank her, and thank you for helping us."

"It's our pleasure."

"OK Baldur, I've so many questions and ideas, but I think I need to explain myself a little here first..."

"Really?" Baldur raised his eyebrows. "How so?"

The two men sat down.

"Well, as you know, when I first met you, I told you I had reason to believe there may be a threat against me and my family."

"Yes, I know."

"Which is why I asked you to help us out in case we ever needed to 'disappear', remember?"

"Right."

"Well, it turns out that I was right, there is a very real and dangerous threat, but it's not the only reason I'm here."

Baldur looked puzzled.

"Let me explain," Karl continued. "A few months ago, I, or should I say we – the Free Movement, were having some... problems shall we say... I don't want to go into the details, but suffice to say I discovered there was a small group of very powerful individuals who were hell bent on destroying us and discrediting the movement."

"Yes... I think I know what you mean..." Baldur started.

"Well, things got so bad that I became afraid for my life. So I made it my business to find out who these people were and went to meet them face to face..."

Baldur's eyes raised again. He was clearly impressed.

"Haha, yeah!" Karl laughed, "So I had a very, er, strange meeting with these people in the States, but one that turned out very well – or potentially very well for all concerned..."

"Oh? How so?" Baldur asked.

"We both gave a frank account of our views and explained what we wanted and why we wanted it. I set about explaining how and why they would benefit from turning over their business and production processes to the commonwealth – that not only would they personally feel better for it, but that they could also maintain the lifestyle that they were accustomed to.

"Needless to say, they weren't buying that, but at least I got them to see it from my point of view which was important. That, for me, is the first objective of any negotiation – drawing out their empathy. Make them feel it too – even if it's disagreeable to them."

"Yes, my experience too," Baldur said. "So what happened?"

"So I decided to employ a little creative arbitration. I asked them to come up with a solution – however improbable – that would satisfy both parties."

"And?"

"Well, it made them think. They hummed and hawed and joked about for a while, then what they came up with blew my mind..."

"Yes?" Baldur leaned forward.

"Well, it turns out there's this billionaire guy living here in Iceland, Einar..."

"Einar Einarsson, yes I know," Baldur cut in sourly. "Yes, we are having some problems with him, but anyway, carry on with your story..."

"Yes, Einar Einarsson. Apparently, he is a close personal friend of one of my, er, friends..."

"OK..."

"So they proposed a wager."

"A what?" Baldur gasped.

"Yes, a bet. They said they would leave us alone and even consider de-privatising their companies in the public interest if we can prove that the money-free society in Iceland is better for billionaires like them, and their friend..."

Baldur was staring in disbelief now.

"And not only that," Karl continued, "they have even offered logistical support to our efforts here to bring it about."

"Well that sounds incredible," Baldur said. "But I think it's a safe bet for them. Einarsson is one of the most stubborn, obnoxious men I've ever met. What happens if you lose the bet?"

"Oh that's easy, they'll just go back to trying to kill me and disrupt the movement, while I race around trying to find evidence to have them all arrested." Karl laughed.

"Hahaha! Back to cat and mouse, eh?"

"Pretty much..."

"So? How long have we got before this, er... ceasefire ends?"

"They said one year, I said two. So, eighteen months or thereabouts," Karl said lightly.

Baldur stood up.

"Well. Let's get straight to it then, shall we?"

"Absolutely. I like living!"

"Haha! Me too!"

Einar Einarsson was called 'smiley' by everyone he knew. But never to his face. He had a face that could freeze a volcano at a hundred paces, and no-one wanted to fall into that icy stare.

He described himself as a 'humble businessman' – and one whose net value was last estimated at over four-and-a-half billion dollars. He had gotten into Iceland's aluminium smelting industry early on and owned three plants that were extracting the versatile metal from raw minerals twenty-four hours a day, availing of cut-price electricity.

He, along with several others among Iceland's elite, were, not surprisingly, vehemently opposed to the new money-free society and were thwarting efforts in any way possible. For the most part, Einar's compatriots in maintaining the status quo were being flatly ignored by the freeworlders, but not him.

Being the owner of the three largest aluminium plants, Einar was a vital link between Iceland and the outside world. Aluminium was Iceland's greatest export and had contributed greatly to Iceland's prosperity over the last thirty years. During the hazy days after the implosion of Iceland's economy, many rushed meetings and negotiations had taken place between the falling government and key business owners.

President Reyksson had insisted that Iceland needed to maintain a vital economic trade link with the rest of the world, and aluminium was the obvious choice. Their plan was to foster the community cooperatives on a local level, continue to provide national services and utilities freely to all citizens, while maintaining commerce with the outside world for money and commodities they could not themselves produce.

It seemed justifiable, but Reyksson had met obstacles on both sides – Einar Einarsson, and the local environmentalists who wanted the smelters shut down permanently. Hasty compromises had been made, but it was clearly not going to be a long term solution. The environmentalists detested the plants, Einarsson detested the environmentalists and the fact that the electricity supply had become frequently unreliable due to low staffing. There were regular outages to the plants as engineers diverted shortages to urban areas and hospitals.

Reyksson's deal with Einar was that he could make as much aluminium and money as he wanted with free electricity and zero taxes, but to reserve a quota of profits for the newly founded International Trading Fund. It seemed reasonable, but with the power outages it was turning out to be a much costlier arrangement than merely paying the taxes and electricity.

Baldur and Karl exited the building and got into a waiting electric car, which broached the subject for Karl.

"So Baldur, this car that you gave us. Is it ours?"

"Haha! Lots of things have changed around here, Karl. You'll get used to it." He said good-naturedly. "The car is yours as long as you have use for it. We call it 'usership'. If something is of use to you, it's yours. When you don't need it, you leave it for someone else."

"Ah."

"If you look around the town you will see many cars parked with the sign in the window saying 'Available'. All these cars are open with the keys in the ignition. You can just hop in and take one – keep it as long as you want – then leave it for someone else when you're finished."

"Of course, it makes sense."

"This is what the free world is all about."

"Yes, but to get to that level so quickly? Obviously, no-one vandalises or abuses the cars, right?"

"Of course not. There were a few incidents at the beginning of course, but people were only getting used to the idea. It's amazing how quickly people adapt to a new way of doing things."

"Yes."

"The same goes for your house. It's yours as long as you have a need for it. When you're finished, you leave it nice and tidy for the next person, then go to the Resources section of the Community Hub website and mark it as available. It's that simple."

"Wow! Incredible."

"It's amazing how frightened and brainwashed people had become over private property, but as you well know, it's all just about scarcity and jealousy. We're doing a great job here disposing of all that primitive behaviour," Baldur quipped.

"Thank God for that," Karl said.

222

"Come on, I'll show you all the other things we're getting up to."

He drove through the streets of Reykjavik, waving at the many passers-by who recognised him. The streets of Reykjavik looked different to Karl as he remembered them. Then it struck him.

"No advertising? Anywhere?" He looked all around. Baldur laughed. "Wow, what a difference that makes. Everything is so..."

"Calm?" Baldur suggested.

"Yes, calm. People look more relaxed. No-one rushing around. But what of the shops? Are all the shops still open?"

"Come, I'll show you," Baldur said and took a sharp left turn.

They left the car and walked through an alley that led on to the main shopping street.

"Laugavegar! Like you've never seen it before," Baldur announced, stretching out his arms.

Karl looked up and down the street. There were still many people, but something was different. Everyone was taking their time, there were no garish shop signs, noisy music or advertising trying to pull you in. They were standing outside a large shoe shop. Karl motioned to the door.

"Please," Baldur gestured.

They entered the shoe shop, which was very large but quite basic. It had rows of shelves containing lots of different men's and women's shoes arranged in pairs. Karl couldn't see any member of staff, but there was a till area at the back.

"Do you need shoes?" Baldur asked spontaneously.

"Well, yes actually. Some walking shoes would be great..." He went to look at the walking shoes and picked up a pair that he liked. He sat and tried them on.

"Perfect," he said. "What now?"

"Nothing. They're yours. You just need to scan the barcode and that's it."

Karl saw a familiar barcode tag on the shoes. He walked over to the till area where there was a small sign. 'Please remember to scan your items'.

"Ah, so this is how they keep an inventory and know what to order?" Karl asked.

"Yes, of course," Baldur replied. "It works the same as with money. You can see the demand and manage the supply, but just by people reporting what they are taking – no money required."

"Wonderful," Karl smiled and scanned the shoes. The screen returned the message:

"Thank you! Please remember to replace your item on the shelf for the next person."

Karl looked at Baldur who motioned at the door behind him.

"You need to take another pair from the store and put them on the shelf," he said.

"Ah, of course."

Karl walked into the back store, found the same pair of shoes and put them on the shelf where he had taken his from.

"That's the only price you pay," Baldur quipped. "The mild inconvenience of re-stocking the shelf."

"Haha! OK," Karl laughed, "That's the cheapest pair of walking shoes I ever bought."

"Come on, there's much more to see," Baldur turned and they walked back out onto the street.

"Many of these shops and offices have been converted into dwellings," he continued. "That's why it looks different. Shops with no window displays."

"Ah, that's what's different..." Karl said.

"Yes, we don't need twenty shoe shops obviously, and once it was decided which units were best suited to serve all, the smaller ones closed and became dwellings or apartments. This shoe shop provides all the basic types of shoes for everyday wear. Down the other end of the street we also have a shoe library for the more exotic designer shoes that people only use rarely."

"Wow, excellent."

"We have libraries for almost anything now. Shoes, clothes, tools, cameras, music equipment, etc. it's more of a depot than a library I suppose. You keep something as long as you need, then bring it back."

"But do people bring it back?" Karl asked. "It's obvious why they should, but do they actually do it?"

"Yes. Again there was plenty of stuff at the beginning that went missing and has never been returned, but, as I say, people change their habits quite quickly, when the benefits to themselves become obvious and they see others doing the same.

"Come on, I'll show you some more. There are also some things that we need some help on."

"Of course," Karl answered. They were sitting back in the car and Karl was looking proudly at his first pair of 'free' shoes. "Oh I see these are made in Germany," he noted. Baldur was driving back down the street and towards the outskirts of town.

"Yes, probably. We are not so advanced yet to have our own shoe factory, so we still rely a lot on imports – and our mutual friend Einar Einarsson," he said grimly.

"Can we meet him?"

"Yes, but not yet. It's better if you understand a little more about what we're doing first."

"Sure," Karl said.

Baldur looked over at Karl and could sense his worry.

"Don't worry. Iceland is going to succeed. You'll see."

225

They drove on and came to the motorway. Soon they had to slow down and came to a stop.

"What's wrong?" Karl asked.

"Road works. We're re-building an old bridge that was getting dangerous."

"Ah, interesting." Karl was heartened to hear Baldur use the word 'we' when referring to who was building the bridge. In every other country in the world, people would say 'they'.

"How are you getting on with finding workers?" Karl asked as they passed a man who was diverting the traffic. "Can we stop and take a look? I'm really curious."

"I knew you would be. Yes, we are going to stop and talk to the project director."

A few minutes later they arrived outside a temporary prefabricated office building. Baldur knocked.

"Come in," came the Icelandic voice.

Baldur walked in and the man behind the desk jumped up.

"Baldur!" he beamed with an outstretched hand.

"Dagfinnur!" Baldur said, taking the hand. "Great to see you. I would like you to meet my good friend Karl Drayton..."

"Karl Drayton, yes. Wow! Wonderful to meet you, Mr. Drayton. You are a local hero, no?" Dagfinnur laughed.

"Ha! Hardly," Karl said. "Just doing my bit to install some common sense back into the world."

"Ah yes, we need it."

"Dagfinnur," Baldur said. "Why don't you explain to Karl about our little building project here?"

"Yes, of course." The three men sat down. Dagfinnur pointed to a map on the wall which had some pictures pinned to it.

"Well, a few months ago, we discovered a large crack in one of the main concrete struts of this bridge. Our engineers had a look and found other faults in the structure too, so the decision was made to demolish and rebuild the entire bridge.

"Of course, in the old days, that was pretty straightforward. We would define the work we needed and companies would tender for that contract. But obviously with our new, er, economic situation, we couldn't do that – or at least, we wanted to explore all other options first. We were in uncharted waters and had no idea how we were going to convince seventy men and women to help in rebuilding the bridge without payment. It's a lot of people and a lot of work."

"Yes, of course," Karl nodded.

"So we contacted the old construction companies and unions and asked them for a list of their members. We drew up a proposal for the work we needed to do and sent it out to them, asking if they would help.

"We got back lots of positive responses – more than enough for what we needed..."

"That's fantastic, no?" Karl enthused.

"Well, yes, but we knew from other early experiences that it would probably not be enough. We have found that many people who might earnestly want to help would not follow through or stay the full distance of the job, which we estimated was around three months. So we came up with an idea..."

He pointed to a framed certificate on the wall.

"We got members to sign up to a pledge that they would see the job through to completion. That one there is mine."

Karl looked confused.

"But how would that compel them?" he asked. "You can't... sue them or seize their property, right?"

"Ha! No. But basically, it kind of does compel them through social pressure. We asked candidates if they would be prepared to publicly undertake a pledge to finish the project. We selected the best seventy who agreed and held a pledge-signing ceremony right here with locals from the area and their families etc."

"OK right," Karl was beginning to get it. "So the compulsion is actually emotional and social. No-one wants to be the one to let the side down after publicly taking a pledge, right?"

"Right. We call it the Project Pledge System."

"Brilliant. So the question is, does it work? Is it working?"

"Absolutely. Well, we lost two guys so far in two months but found replacements straight away. But the surprising thing is, usually staff losses on this kind of project are higher. They usually lose around five guys a month."

"That's incredible. It would be cool to talk to some of them."

"Absolutely," he said looking up at the clock. "They're on a tea break right now. Let's go."

Dagfinnur took them around the yard to the canteen area, where Karl could hear the familiar roar and laughter of men on their tea break.

"They certainly sound like happy workers," he remarked.

"Why not?" Dagfinnur said. "They have everything they need, zero stress and a great social experience – apart from the work. We are starting to confuse the boundaries between work and play now – which is as it should be. When work is fun, it's not work. Simple as that."

They entered the building and were met with a wall of hot sweat and hubbub. Everyone was too engrossed in their conversation to notice the ex-President and Karl walking in.

"Hey," a skinny, weathered man remarked as he was walking past them. "You're the guy from America with the Free Movement right?" he said to Karl.

"Yes, well, Ireland actually. Pleased to meet you."

228

"Good for you, sir. Are you coming to work with us?" he asked.

That was the last thing Karl expected to hear, but it was reasonable. And now, come to think of it, what reason did he have to say no? He looked at Dagfinnur.

"Well, if I can help out, then why not..." he started.

Dagfinnur rescued him.

"No, Mr. Drayton is just visiting and anyway, we have all the help we need right now.

That seemed to satisfy the man, so Karl decided to seize the opportunity of being a tourist.

"How long have you been working on this project?" he asked the man.

"A couple of months."

"Do you like it? How do you find it – not being paid?"

"Well, it's what I've always done anyway, and I know most of the guys here," he said looking around. "Yeah it's strange not being paid at first, but I have everything I need. No bills, no hassle – and we have good fun on the site. You get used to it, it's just like normal work – only better. We've a good team and everyone's happier."

"Yes that's true," Dagfinnur chimed in. "We are actually ahead of time by two weeks on this project which is remarkable. I've worked as a foreman for civic contracts for twenty years and we always went over time – and over budget." He smirked.

"Guys," shouted the skinny man. "Look who's here. Reyksson and the guy from the telly."

Some men looked up but most were far more interested in their tea and chat to pay any attention.

Baldur shrugged and laughed.

"Sorry Karl, show business ain't what it used to be."

"Haha!"

Ten minutes later, Baldur and Karl were back driving on the motorway.

"You know, that guy was right," Karl said suddenly.

"Who?"

"The guy in the canteen just now. I need to make myself useful while I'm living here."

"Yes, of course, Karl, but you've just arrived, so relax and soak it up for now. But it's a good chance to explain our next little invention..."

"Oh really? Yes please," Karl said. He was loving this. Iceland was like a whole new country-sized toy.

"Well it's really simple. Instead of work or jobs, we now have community service..."

"What, like criminals?" Karl joked.

"Yeah exactly, but without the crime bit," Baldur quipped. "But of course, it's all voluntary. It's a way of being better organised and focussing peoples' attention on what needs to get done."

"OK, go on..."

"So a lot of our community organisation takes place online as you can imagine. We have a great team of programmers here who have built us a pioneering Community Hub.

"Everyone on the island registers once on the platform, then they can input data directly on what's needed where, what needs to be done where, what skills they have to offer, what resources they have etc. So, say for example you live in the North in Akureyri and you notice that there are some trees overhanging the road dangerously. Well, you can input that information into the website and the location.

"Then that becomes a community service task for that area and alerts go out to all people who would be matched with that task in that area. Everyone on the island is encouraged – and now feels a duty – to perform a minimum of thirty-six hours a month of community service. We worked out that this covers most of the more mundane tasks that need to be carried out, but in reality, most people contribute much more than that."

They were now passing through a small village on the main road north out of Reykjavik.

"You can see just how clean and tidy all these villages are now. The unexpected gain from the community service system – as opposed to the paid employment system – is that people's pride comes to the fore. In many ways, the money system over-shadowed that drive to make our communities better, because people were just so absorbed in making ends meet and paying their bills. Now the heat's off, and that drive to make your community better is the only motivator to make your community better – if you know what I mean..."

"I certainly do." Karl said, then added wistfully, "Money masks so much and separates us from our true desires by stealth over the years. We don't even notice how our dreams are drained slowly from us in the clamour to pay bills."

"Well said!" Baldur enthused. "Now, through the community service section of the website, people can browse the list of tasks that are applicable to them according to their skill, preference and location. Then they just claim a job and do it.

"Last week, for example, I cleared the bottom part of a field of brambles to make way for a new potato crop that's going in there. I also sowed an entire plantation of tomatoes in one of our heated greenhouses. I'm probably already well over my weekly recommended nine hours, but no-one cares. No-one is counting anymore and there's an enormous sense of liberation in that."

"Oh, that's fantastic Baldur. This is what I have been dreaming about for so long. I can't believe it's actually happening, and I'm here, being a part of it..."

"Yes, I'm sure you're anxious to get onto the system and start contributing to all this. It really makes you feel great." Baldur was really puffed up now, more than Karl had ever seen him.

"I can't believe, Karl," he said earnestly, "that we put up with all that money business for so long. How we were so blind and sleepy to it all. Everyone here is becoming much happier and more liberated. It's a real privilege for me to have been a part of it too."

"Yes, it is. Me too." Karl paused. "Actually, Baldur, speaking of liberation, that's something else I've been meaning to ask you," he said, turning in his seat.

"What?"

"The criminals? The prisons. What happened with Iceland's prisoners?"

"Ha! Well, fortunately, we didn't have that many," Baldur laughed. "But yes, that was one of the first tough things we had to solve."

"What did you do?"

Baldur sighed. "Well, we obviously gathered them all together and explained exactly what was going on. Then we gave them a choice: take a public pledge to leave prison, rejoin society and behave themselves, or..."

"Or what?"

"Or stay there," he shrugged.

"And what happened?"

"Well, some took longer than others, but they all took the pledge. Every one of them."

"Well, it's a no-brainer I suppose, but how has it worked? Any problems?"

"Hmm, well yes and no," Baldur said thoughtfully. "In general, there have been no problems, but we did have a situation with one particularly unsavoury individual. He was a big guy – in prison for rape. He took the pledge like the others and we let him out in good faith."

"Go on," Karl said, interested.

"Well, as you probably know, Iceland officially disbanded its police and prison force when we adopted the free society, but of course, these men and women didn't just disappear, or forget what they were trained to do..."

"OK."

"So a few of us decided that being a free society was one thing, but being stupid was quite another. So we put together small covert teams of ex-police members to monitor the prisoners who we thought were high risk re-offenders..."

"And...?"

"And one night this guy was hassling a girl in a bar in Akureyri. He started tugging her by the wrist and pulling her outside..."

"Shit..."

"Yes, well thank God we had taken precautions. Two of our guys were also at the bar and they tasered him down, cuffed him and brought him to the police station while we decided what to do with him."

"You did right. Just because a society has no laws doesn't mean you abandon common sense and reality," Karl laughed. "So what did you do with him?"

"Exactly. Well, here's the thing: nobody wanted to put him back in prison because he would have been the only one in there, and that would make unnecessary extra work – so we did one better!"

"Oh?"

"Yes, so we handed him over to our toughest team of counsellors for rehabilitation." Baldur winked with that mischievous twinkle in his eye.

"Really? Who are they?" Karl looked at him, perplexed.

"You'll see," he said smiling.

"OK." Karl laughed. They drove in silence for a while and Karl took the opportunity to soak up some more wonderful scenery. In the distance, he could see yet another of Iceland's spectacular waterfalls – a crystal thread plunging down from a precipice into a misty rainbow.

"What about tourism?" Karl asked suddenly, waving at the waterfall. "Or tourists I mean. I presume you still have tourism? Do the tourists all get stuff for free too?"

"No, hardly," Baldur laughed. "That was one of the first things we instituted because tourism is big business here. All the tourists coming in to the country now have a choice. They can either pay a visitor's fee to the International Trading Fund, or they get a work card where they are required to work a certain number of hours for a portion of their stay."

"Great. Makes sense. And do people take advantage of the work card? I mean, get a card but don't do the work?"

"Yes, we've had plenty of those, and we've had to be very strict. From the outside world, Iceland looks like a free-for-all, so it's not surprising people come here with that intention. They are asked to pay to the ITF or we deport them straight away. As you correctly say, having no laws doesn't mean being soft and stupid."

At last, Baldur took a right turn.

"OK, this is what I want you to see. This is where it all started."

They were driving up a rocky avenue for a few minutes then arrived at what looked like a giant industrial plant. There were great steel pipes snaking all around the grounds and a concrete building with several large chimney towers that were blowing white smoke high above.

"Welcome to Hellisheiði Power Station," Baldur announced dramatically.

"Wow, it's huge," Karl was getting out of the car, looking up at the giant spaceship-like structure.

"It's our biggest. Come, there's someone I want you to meet."

They cracked across the lava gravel path and into the wonderful, warm glass atrium. Baldur smiled at the girl who was on the phone behind the desk.

"Is he here?" He mouthed to her. She nodded and waved towards the door. Baldur gave her a friendly thumbs-up.

Inside the door was a long corridor and lines of rooms. Baldur walked along looking in the windows of each of the doors as he went . Eventually, he found a door and knocked.

"Come in," said the voice.

Baldur leaned his head in. Karl could see that there seemed to be some kind of class going on. The room was filled with people of all ages. He was confused. A school? In a power station? The man excused himself to the class and left the classroom.

The man came forward to Karl, beaming with hand outstretched.

"I've been dying to meet you, Mr. Drayton." He was mid-thirties, dressed in his shirtsleeves, with neat black glasses and a very positive manner.

"Karl, I'd like you to meet Mr. Anders Einarsson."

"Er, delighted to meet you Mr. Einarsson," Karl said, more as a question than a greeting.

"Karl, Anders here is something of a local hero," Baldur explained. "He was the first man who rang into the radio station during the utilities crisis to offer his services freely to the power company."

Karl got it now.

"Oh wow, yes, I heard. The electrical engineer. Sorry, I didn't recognise your name... My God, you really are a hero, sir. You totally put yourself out there."

"Well, it wasn't exactly a difficult choice," Anders said bashfully. "It was either that or read in the dark," he chuckled. "I've been dying to meet you. And here you are at last..."

"Yes, I'm finally here and hoping to stay for a while," he glanced at

Baldur. "Tell me Anders, why is... why is there a classroom in a power station – if I may ask?"

Anders chuckled again.

"Well, it seems the good people of the Voluntary Representative Committee decided that we needed to, er – how shall I say – 're-purpose' people in light of the radical changes that took place? Most people took to the new way of doing things like a duck to water, but many didn't. So, Baldur and the other good people of the committee thought that I would be a good candidate to help with the re-learning program."

"Re-learning program?" Karl repeated.

"Education, Karl," Baldur said, "– the most important tool we have to shape our society. We only interact with the world based on what we know. Change what we know, and we change society."

"Yes, exactly," Anders said. "Education has always served no other purpose than to funnel people into careers and profit, rather than teach them valuable life skills. That's why the world is full of reckless, irresponsible people. They were never taught how to live properly.

"This is an adult teacher class," Anders motioned to the door. "They are the most important ones now as they are re-shaping their own ideas, so they pass it on to the kids at school. It's pretty intense, if you think about all the stuff that we need to be teaching, but never were."

"Like what?" Karl asked.

"We call it 'Life Education'," Anders replied. "It includes stuff like the ecosystem, cycle of life, how communities work, respect, sharing, trust, empathy, being responsible, leadership, team-work, resolving disputes, self-anatomy, nutrition, hydration, breathing, meditation, massage, self-acceptance, self-respect, relationships, effective communication, coping with negative emotions, problem solving, critical thinking, creative expression, food growing and preparation, sex, parenting and family... I could go on and on..."

Karl was speechless.

"Yes, a little bit more important than 'now I know my ABC', wouldn't you say Karl?" Baldur mused.

"You bet! So what age do the kids start in school?" Karl asked.

"Whatever age they want," Anders said. "Some schooling is definitely recommended for Icelanders, but it's not compulsory. We leave it to the parents to decide when the time is right. There are skills and lessons open for kids of all ages from two to twelve. And we don't worry too much about dividing into age categories. Everyone has something to learn from an educational experience."

"What? So you put two-year-olds in with twelve-year-olds?" Karl asked incredulously.

"Yes, of course. Because the twelve-year-olds can help the two-year-olds, and they learn from that experience too. We are learning that age is not necessarily wisdom, nor youth stupidity. We all have wisdom to gain from each other, whether intellectual, emotional or physical. Also, having different ages reduces competition and envy between students."

"Of course..."

"Our classes are more like meetings," Anders continued proudly, "and the role of a teacher is less like a dictator of facts, and more of a navigator. It's group learning. Everyone learns from each other. The teacher – or navigator – is just there to propel things forward."

"Wow, it all sounds..." Karl began.

"Revolutionary?" Baldur offered.

"I prefer 'evolutionary'" Anders quipped. "We are just improving things. It's all perfectly normal."

"Haha!" Karl laughed.

"Anders, is Eymar here today?" Baldur enquired.

"Yes, he is," Anders replied, then leaned in the door of the classroom. "Eymar, someone to see you!"

Karl watched as a giant man came forth from the class – nearly two metres tall, with a round unshaven face, wearing death metal jeans and jacket.

"Eymar, this is Karl Drayton from the Free Movement," Anders announced, "and Karl, meet Eymar Eriksson, ex-prisoner, now one of our finest kindergarten teachers!"

Karl beamed and offered his hand.

"Nice to meet you, sir," the giant said, faintly embarrassed by the introduction.

"And you too. Thanks for your work here." Karl said.

"What Anders is doing here Karl," Baldur said, "is reshaping our education system at its root level – and safeguarding the future of our endeavours. In my opinion, this is the most important work being carried out on the island today. We are, literally, creating better people."

Anders looked a little modest.

"But," Karl asked. "Why here? Why in a power station – in the middle of nowhere?"

"Context," Anders said. "The symbolism in this building is hugely significant to Icelanders. This is the closest thing we have to a temple. We are drawing free energy from the ground here that drives our community, and it is also the place where our social revolution turned around. To be immersed in this environment while learning the new skills that support it strengthens the learning."

"And anyway, this is Iceland," Baldur finished. "And we do what the fuck we want around here."

F·DAY -3032

Karl had a fitful sleep, interspersed with flashes of power stations, shoes lying in the gutter with 'available' signs attached to them, the overly happy face of Anders talking endlessly about sex, parenting and ecosystems to Eli, and the grim face of Einar Einarsson standing in the background, ready to throw a dark blanket over everybody.

Karl pulled himself from the bed in an effort to get away from the cacophony of images that were bubbling over in his head. He went to the kitchen and prepared a coffee.

As he became more awake, Karl began to realise why he hadn't slept so well. He had been dreaming and talking about just such a free world scenario like this for so long, and then to see it all happening around him was like a sensory overload.

He took up his wallet from the table. There was a hundred Euros in it. He felt strangely forlorn – like he had lost that money. It was incredible to think that here, in this place, these were literally just pieces of printed paper – and not even particularly pretty ones at that. Even he was going to need a little time to adjust.

And there was still Einar Einarsson and his capitalist – but necessary – enterprise. Karl recalled the image in his dream of Einarsson ready to throw the blanket. Baldur said they were having some problems that they needed some help with. Was Einarsson one of the problems?

Happy as he was to see all this fruition of the free world with Baldur, it had been exhausting and he was glad to be home. Baldur had dropped Karl home and told him to register on the Iceland Community Hub and have a look around. Last night he had been too tired, so he fired up the laptop and decided to check it out.

The site opened up with an interactive map of Iceland. He couldn't click on anything until he signed up. Karl didn't hesitate to sign up, putting in his location, age, skills, aptitude, work preferences, physical condition and availability. Next, the site asked him if he had access to any potentially useful resources at his location. He looked around and drew a blank. He could fill it in later if he thought of anything. He confirmed all his contact details and then he was set.

Immediately he received an email welcoming him to the service with a link to his own personalised community service board. The page opened with three sections: matching specialist jobs in his area, non-specialist jobs in the area, and specialist jobs in other areas. There were many jobs listed – each with an urgency rating and estimated time required. He clicked the first specialist job in his area.

> 'Web-developer required for integrating environment control system with live climate data. Urgency: 5/10, Distance: 7Km, Est. completion time: 7 days'

This matched Karl's criteria and was definitely something he could do. He added it to his 'interested' list. He wondered how, if anyone put in a low urgency rating, it would ever get done. He checked the site help. Ah, the urgency was automatically incremented over time, so the longer the job was available, the more urgent it became. That made sense. He checked the non-specialist list.

> 'Today! Help required for house move, Þjóðvegur 2576. Urgency 7/10, Distance: 2Km, Est. completion time: 0.5 days'

Perfect. That sounds easy, he thought and went to contact the owner. He noted that five others had already expressed interest. He sent a message saying that he would be there in an hour.

"Haha!" he laughed. "This is great. That's my job for today sorted."

He went to look at the other areas of the website.

"Wow, this is totally awesome," he whispered to himself. He clicked back to the main map page and could see it fully functioning. A 3D interactive image of the island covered in little markers. He clicked on a few to see what they were.

> 'RESOURCE: Large amount of wood available – suitable for burning, Þjóðvegur area'

> 'RESOURCE: Cut steel sheets. 0.5CM x 2M x 2M. 47 available'

> 'SKILL: Carpenter, Mechanic – Anders Tomasson – H223 – Reykjavik area'

> 'SKILL: Jeweller – Repairs – Anna Blake – H72 – Reykjavik area'

> 'REQUIRED: Martial arts instructor – Akureyri area'

The map was covered in markers like this, and there were buttons where you could limit results to what you were interested in offering or receiving. Karl was curious about one thing. Each person had a number after their name beginning with an 'H'.

He checked his own profile and saw that he was also marked 'H0'. Ah, he thought. It must be a reputation score or something. He clicked on it and learned about the Iceland Honor System.

> *"The Honor System is a way of showing appreciation, respect and trust. If someone has done a good job or helped you out, you can choose to send them an Honor. Every islander has an Honor Record which helps other users decide who they think is best for the task."*

"Wow, they've thought of everything here." The Honor System looked like a way of paying someone for a good job – without paying. He checked the main menu again and clicked on something else called 'Open Proposals'. A page opened with listings of what looked like motions proposed by members of the public. He scanned the top ones:

> *'Extend Akureyri hospital. 125060 YES | 159 NO | 161763 UNKNOWN, Proposed by Dr. Ísleifur Gíslason H210. 5 days left to respond. Quota reached'*

> *'Re-build the central R26 road. 74221 YES | 2028 NO | 210733 UNKNOWN, Proposed by Gunnar Armannsson H143. 13 days left to respond. Quota not reached'*

> *'Re-develop Reykjavik harbour. 1070 YES | 64223 NO | 221689 UNKNOWN, Proposed by Janís Ulvarsson H88. 2 days left to respond. Quota not reached'*

Abby walked into the kitchen with Eli.

"Hey sleepy girls," Karl joked. "You've got to check out this Iceland community website Abby. This is incredible! Self-determination in action – and it's working! Well, you have to sign up for community service anyway..."

"Community service?" Abby replied sleepily.

"Yes. Where I'm going now. I volunteered to help with a house move down the road here. Want to come?"

An hour later, Karl, Abby and Eli were driving along slowly looking for the house. It soon became obvious which house as there were many cars parked outside.

"Hello? Is this the moving house?" Karl enquired, knocking on the open front door.

There was an eruption of laughter inside, then a lady shouting, "Yes, yes come in..."

The Drayton family walked in, past all the half-filled boxes of the living room and into the back kitchen, where they were met with a packed, hot room of around forty people having tea and biscuits.

Karl put his hands on his hips.

"So this is where the party is at?"

"Haha! This always happens," the woman who had invited them in said. "Welcome to our new business as usual!" she said, gesturing to all the helpers around her.

F·DAY -3030

feeds·rt·com/us:

JEFFERSON UNDER FIRE OVER TAPAC REMARKS

President Jefferson came under intense pressure from the international community over his remarks on the controversy over the placement of The Tapac Memorial in Moscow. Yesterday, during a press conference, he said, "We all love Tapac and the ideas he stood for, but he was not a leader. You can't put a statue of a child beside the founding fathers of a nation. It's just not appropriate."

Enraged Tapac followers began demonstrations and burning American flags in Red Square in protest at the comments. Andrei Lagunov, Tapac's father said, "I wish President Jefferson's famous ancestor was alive today to hear those remarks. He, if anyone would have understood the importance of civil struggle against oppression to improve the lives of ordinary civilians. Shame on you, Mr. President. Shame on you."

See video >>

feeds·bbcnews·com/southamerica:

BOLIVIA IN CRISIS

Bolivian banks remained closed today for the second day following their economic turmoil of the last week. The Finance Minister Alberto López ordered the banks to remain closed until further notice. The trouble began when Bolivia officially defaulted on its debt for the second time since last January. Confidence in the Boliviano currency evaporated overnight in light of the default and the Government's mishandling of the country's economy.

Minister López announced that they were in discussion with the IMF, and that "other options" were also being discussed.

Bolivian crisis in pictures >>

HOLLYWOOD'S FINEST PRODUCE OPEN ECONOMY VIDEO

Some of Hollywood's top actors have joined forces in an amazing promotional video, depicting themselves as you've never seen them before. Without make-up or special lighting, the video shows each of them working and interacting at an OE food store and restaurant, partaking in normal activities, sweeping the floor, emptying bins and stacking shelves.

The video 'Opening Up Time', was shot with a phone camera to highlight how real life could work in an American Open Access Economy, and depicts Sandy Stone working with friends in a bagel bar in between movie shoots, finishing with the slogan, 'Do what you love. Love what you do!' Movie director Sammy B. Taylor has publicly criticized the ten-minute promo as irresponsible and unrealistic. The movie has already been watched over a billion times.

Watch 'Opening-Up Time' >>

f-day·org/feeds/update:

ICELAND ADVANCES + OPENING UP TIME VIDEO [-1200 DAYS]

Owing to real world success on the ground in Iceland and the timely promo 'Opening Up Time' video from Sandy Stone and other famous actors, no less than 1200 days are being deducted from the F-Day countdown, bringing F-Day to just thirty-four years away.

F-Day.org >>

F·DAY -3026

Karl was amazed how quickly he had assimilated into Iceland's Free Society. In less than a week, he felt like he had lived there for years. He had met so many people, made new friends and had great fun. Since arriving he had helped with a house move, done house deliveries, helped out at the local grocery depot, been part of a sewerage works team and helped with repairing street lights in Reykjavik.

Abby had gotten involved with the local school group and was now almost becoming a full time teacher. She loved being around children – and, of course, Eli came too.

And none of it seemed like work, even though they were both already over their recommended weekly nine hours. There was no onus on them to do anything. No feeling of dread going to work, no mindless repetition of tasks, no stress, no bills, no worries. Neither Karl nor Abby could begin to imagine going back to the 'normal' world of drudgery and bills. This dream society was like a one-way ticket.

Karl and family were just returning from the depot with some groceries and were planning to take a day off to roam their local countryside when Karl got a call from Baldur.

"Karl, I see you are settling in well," he said.

"Er, really?" Karl asked.

"Haha, I just checked your profile and see you're already an H10!"

"Ha! Oh really? I didn't even realise. That's nice."

"Listen Karl, we need to meet today if that's OK. We have some visitors coming that I'd like you to meet. Can you come to Reykjavik?"

Karl looked at Abby who shrugged her assent.

"Yes, sure thing. I'll be there in an hour."

"Wonderful, see you then."

An hour later and Karl walked into a very busy administration office. There were photographers, admin workers, onlookers and lots of dark-skinned people, some dressed in suits, some in military uniforms, and some in bright traditional costumes. These were clearly not locals. Fighting through the crowd, Baldur shouted to Karl.

"Karl, come on through," he shouted.

Karl pushed his way through into the back room which was full of more foreigners. Baldur was standing beside a gentleman in a neat green military uniform.

"Karl, this is Pedro Gómez, the Foreign Minister of Cuba."

Karl offered his hand.

"Very pleased to meet you, Mr. Gómez."

"It's a privilege to be here in this wonderful country, Mr. Drayton. Mr. Reyksson tells me that you have just recently arrived. How are you liking it?"

"It's... it's incredible here." He looked to Baldur. "It's like being in another world."

"Mr. Gómez," Baldur said, "please explain to Karl why you are here."

"Yes, of course. Mr. Drayton, we have been sent here by His Excellency the President of Cuba to learn about Iceland's new socio-economic model. We are exploring the idea of bringing the same system to Cuba."

"Wow, that's incredible," Karl said looking at Baldur.

"Yes," Baldur said, "and there is also a delegation from Haiti and the Dominican Republic arriving tomorrow night. It looks like we are going to start experiencing a whole new kind of tourism around here."

The Minister laughed.

There was a sudden loud rumble and hiss as two buses pulled up outside.

"This way please," a young admin worker beckoned the delegation towards the exit.

"Well, goodbye for now, Mr. Gómez," Baldur said, shaking his hand. "Enjoy your tour and I shall meet you again in a few days."

Baldur turned to the delegation.

"Thank you, ladies and gentlemen. Rest assured you are in capable hands. Laura here will bring you to all our various projects on the island and explain the work that is going on. I think you will be suitably impressed. I will join you in Akureyri in three days time."

Finally, when the hall was clear and silence returned, Baldur turned sharply to Karl.

"We've got problems."

"Oh?"

"Yes, big problems. Come with me." Baldur turned on his heel and went briskly back to his office.

A few minutes later he was sitting at the computer and turned the screen around for Karl to see. Baldur was scrolling through a gallery of photos of what looked like a building site.

"Don't understand," Karl said at last. "What am I looking at?"

"This is one of Einarsson's smelting plants."

"OK... is he extending it? Looks like a building site to me."

"No, he is not extending it," Baldur snapped. "He is building a geothermal power plant."

"Ah. Oh," said Karl when the penny dropped.

"Yes, exactly," Baldur said. "Like him or loathe him, Einarsson is our vital link with the outside world. We give him a tax-free haven, electricity and he supplies money to the International Trading Fund. Without that fund Karl, we are fucked – pardon my English."

"But the tourists..."

"It's buttons, Karl. That tourism money wouldn't even cover our gasoline, never mind other imports..."

"OK."

"When President Carley sent us that shipment – and all the other countries too – we were spoiled. We have enjoyed abundance since that time, but that is almost exhausted now and I was pinning my hopes on Einarsson to make up the shortfall.

"But of course, he has quibbled over every last detail of the ITF quota and we have relied mostly on his good will to reach the agreement. We are not really in the business of police and handcuff-type law around here any more. We rely on people's good will."

"It's ironic," said Karl, "that the only place on the island where good will disappears is where capitalism still reigns."

"Hmmph, yes exactly."

"Do you think you can bolster up the tourism sector or increase the daily visitor charges to meet the shortfall."

"Not a chance – unless we increase them by about twenty thousand percent!" he snorted. "No, Einarsson and that damn aluminium is our only link with the world. We don't have the resources to build our own, and we can't sit around and wait for the charity of other nations either. That's not sustainable. Bottom line, if we can't convince Einarsson to play ball with us, this experiment has failed."

"Hmmm. Maybe I can talk to him."

"Yes, I think you should. It's time for that now. This is not just about Iceland any more."

F·DAY -3023

Through the rain and windscreen wipers, the sudden sight of chain link fences and coils of barbed wire stretched out against the sky seemed so incongruous to Karl now, having experienced the familiar openness of Iceland's new way of life. A guard motioned to him to roll down the window and asked Karl something in Icelandic.

Karl shrugged, then the man repeated. "What is your business here?"

"My name is Karl Drayton. I'm here to see Einar Einarsson."

"Is he expecting you?"

"Er, no," Karl shouted. "But he will see me," he chanced.

The guard walked back into his booth. A few minutes later he waved Karl through.

Karl had underestimated the size of the complex. Through the misty rain, he could see the building works going on in the distance as he drove the long avenue that led to the main smelting plant. On his right-hand side was the North Atlantic and a small harbour where presumably the raw aluminium ingots began their journey to whatever corner of the world they were headed.

Ahead was the smelting plant itself, a series of long, low profile buildings. Presumably, raw minerals in one end, purified aluminium the other. The buildings looked around half a kilometre long, with several chimneys rising along their length. At one end was what looked like offices, so Karl headed in that direction.

He was starting to feel a sense of déjà vu with his visit to the Carson family of Colorado. Well, not quite, he placated himself. He was pretty sure Einarsson was not going to try to kill him, but, indirectly there was a threat. If his meeting with Einarsson took a bad turn, it could cost heavy in the long run.

Karl had to admit that he didn't really fear for his life anymore. He felt very safe in Iceland, and would be more than happy to see out his days here without the Free Movement and all the responsibility that went with it. If Iceland failed, then so be it. He would lose his wager with the Carsons, and maybe the whole Free Movement effort would fail too, but at least he would be safe.

"Well, nothing like the weight of the entire world on your shoulders going into a meeting," he joked grimly. Then shrugged at the idea. "Whatever happens happens, and so be it."

He arrived at the front door of the grey factory office. He entered, and was met immediately with a block of a man wearing a grey suit with his hands on his hips.

"What do you want, Karl Drayton?" he said coldly.

Karl nearly fell backwards. The last thing he expected was for him to be waiting for him. Einarsson was heavy set, with a face like a stone block, grey eyes, cold and unforgiving. Clearly, a man who wasted no time.

"Er, Einar... Einarsson? He fumbled. The man didn't answer, or acknowledge Karl's proffered hand.

"This is private property, Mr. Drayton. Unless you have some important business or news for me, I suggest you leave, as I have better things to do with my time."

"I... well yes, actually I do have some important business," said Karl, finally starting to gather himself. He looked at the receptionist who avoided his gaze. "But I need to talk to you in private."

"Hmmph," said the man and turned on his heel toward the door. Karl stood there wondering whether he was meant to follow. The receptionist barely nodded to him. He followed.

Einarsson walked through the factory ahead of Karl without

speaking. The factory was huge, eerily silent, and decidedly hot. There was a very low rumble of machinery, but mostly this place was nothing more than a giant oven – making aluminium cakes, Karl mused.

Finally, Einarsson ushered Karl into a side office.

"You've got three minutes, Mr. Drayton," Einarsson said sitting down and looking up at the clock.

Karl had been glad of the walk through the factory as it gave him time to compose himself. He decided to do as Einarsson and dispense with the pleasantries.

"Apparently, you are building a private power plant here..."

"What of it?" Einarsson cut in.

"What of it? Well, presumably your reasons for doing so are to do away with the need for power from the national supply, and thus your responsibility towards the Trading Fund?"

"Mr. Drayton, not that it's any of your business, but I have a responsibility to my company, my customers and my workers to have a reliable power supply and to cut my costs."

"So, you regard your input to the International Trading Fund merely as a cost?"

"According to that idiot Reyksson, it is a voluntary contribution. Presumably, if I stop contributing voluntarily, quote unquote, pretty soon all the lights will go out here, would I be correct?"

"No, you would not be correct, Mr. Einarsson. You would not be correct, because you are not even asking the right question." Einarsson glanced up at the clock.

"The question," Karl continued, "is not what's best for the company. The question is simply what is best. Your company is not an island or a separate rock in space. You are not a lone person. You – and your company – are a part of this community, whether you agree or like that or not. That's just physics. The people around you support you. They are not your customers. You are not their supplier. They are living, breathing beings like you – with needs like you.

"They too want to eat, drink, breathe, laugh, fuck, be happy, feel satisfied. You don't have to be fucking best friends with everybody or all lovey-dovey with your neighbour just to give people the basic respect of your support as a fellow being."

Einarsson was getting uncomfortable now. Karl went for the jugular.

"You build as many power stations as you want, Mr. Einarsson. Forget the Trading Fund. Cut yourself off from the rest of the island. You know that Iceland and its people will suffer greatly as a direct result of that, but know this, they *will* recover.

"You see, there's no going back for Icelanders now. These people have tapped into something that is more precious than aluminium, more precious than gold or oil. They have tapped into an ancient kinship that has been gradually suppressed over thousands of years – and the wealth they have found there is infinite. There's no stopping them now."

Karl stood up.

"I suggest, Mr. Einarsson, before you decide to live out the rest of your days as the ugliest, most unpopular man on the island, to take a walk outside in your local community. Do some community service, see the way people are living now. Talk to them. Ask them if they are happier. Ask yourself if you are happier. Because at the end of the day, happiness *is* an option. It really is. And so is being an asshole. You get to choose. And every morning you get to make that choice." Karl leaned over. "Which option do you choose today, Mr. Einarsson?

"I'll see myself out, thank you."

Karl walked back through the hot factory and back out into the cold misty rain. He held out his hands and opened his mouth to the rain.

"Man, I love this place," he said.

F·DAY -3011

`feeds·grapevine·is:`

LOOK OUT, THE COMMIES ARE COMING!

And not just the reds. Or even pinkos! Iceland looks set to become the multicultural capital of the world! Last week, four foreign government delegations arrived from Cuba, Haiti, The Dominican Republic and Vanuatu. (Say what? Yeah, Vanuatu. We had to look it up too — a beautiful Southern Pacific archipelago between Australia and Fiji)

This is tourism with a difference — to sell a way of life! All foreign dignitaries — including the Foreign Minister of Cuba — were treated to a full-on round tour of the island and met some of our communities face to face. Culminating in a conference held in Akureyri, each of the country's representatives gave a rousing tribute to the people and their efforts to co-create a beautiful society.

Well, we kind of agree. Shucks.

See pictures >>

`feeds·bbcnews·com/world:`

CITIZEN VICTORY FOR POLAND

General Brzezicki has stepped down as caretaker military commander in Poland, bowing to what he called 'immense public pressure'. The speaker for the Citizen Rule Alliance, Cecylia Rudaska, told journalists: "History has been made. I would like to applaud the courage and integrity of Commander Brzezicki who has made history possible. Poland's government is no longer for the people. Poland's government *is* the people."

There were jubilant ceremonies held throughout Poland's major cities to commemorate the event. It is widely expected that the Citizen Rule Alliance may propose a motion for an open economic society similar to Iceland.

SWITZERLAND PROTESTS

There were violent clashes last night in Zurich and Berne, Switzerland, as protests over the scrapping of the basic income have swelled over the last few days since the announcement last Monday that the scheme may be dropped in the next budget.

Opposition parties have called for the Swiss Government, led by Hans Schwimmer, to step down over the débâcle and to hold fresh elections. In a press conference, Mr. Schwimmer insisted that abandoning the scheme was only one of a "range of options" being considered. He was also quick to point out that all the opposition parties had originally voted in favour of the BIG scheme.

Hans Schwimmer statement >>

F·DAY -2990

It hadn't taken Karl very long to eventually seek out the people behind the wonderful Iceland Community Hub website. There was a team of four guys dotted around the island who had put it together. Karl had now offered his services as well to help maintain and improve the site. He felt he had given Einarsson his best shot, and now the best thing he could do was just forget about him and concentrate on improving the community, and, most importantly, plan for whatever challenges lay ahead.

With the International Trading Fund now dwindling away – despite all of Iceland's best fund managers trying to keep it buoyant on international currency markets, they were now very much into the plan B stage. Karl and two of the web team had joined Baldur and several other admin people at the Alþingi to discuss the situation.

Baldur was grim – more than Karl had ever seen him.

"Ladies and gentlemen, I have to report that we are bracing ourselves for another even bigger crisis. Our public inventory now shows that we will run out of gasoline in seven weeks. Despite our best efforts in agriculture, we are still consuming far more food than we produce. Without further imports, we estimate a crisis in basic food stuffs in around three months.

"Of course, we can economise and we all will, but that only prolongs the inevitable. We need lasting solutions – and we need them quickly, otherwise..."

"What happened with Einar Einarsson?" Karl cut in.

"Nothing I'm afraid. But we do know his new power plant is fully operational and his power consumption from the national grid has dropped by at least fifty percent. He is still technically committed to make another payment, but these figures I am giving are taking account of that.

"So, we have limited choices now. We can ride it out and see what happens – which is not my favourite option. We don't want to look like a charity case, begging the world for supplies. We must now present viable solutions."

"There is only one solution, Baldur."

"What's that, Karl?"

"We do whatever it takes to become a hundred percent self-sufficient – and do it quickly."

There were murmurs of approval around the room.

"That is not a single solution," Karl said. "It's a range of small solutions, and we can all do our part to make it happen. If we can't get gasoline, then screw gasoline – or we start making hydrogen and convert our vehicles. If we need tropical fruit, let's build more heated greenhouses. If we need milk, let's grow rice or soy. Let's get serious about being self-sufficient – whatever it takes.

"Also, let's talk to the other countries who are thinking of going this route. Let's free-trade with them? I don't know – Cuba sends us bananas, and we'll give them aluminium – or, or..."

"Rocks?" someone humorously suggested.

"Yes, rocks! Why not?" Karl said unperturbed, "Let's turn these fucking rocks into something we can export. Bricks or slabs or gravel, whatever... The point is, let's take action. Whatever happens, it's better if we are self-sufficient, and the sooner we start, the better."

Everyone cheered.

"Agreed," said Baldur. "Let's create teams and tackle this from all sides. Food, fuel, exports, etc. We need to step up the community involvement. Maybe increase the recommended minimum to seventy-two hours a month?"

"No," Karl advised. "Just send them a message outlining the plans. Be honest. Tell them what you told us. Tell them of the urgency. This is an open society. There are no secrets here. Let's pull together. Outline a plan of action and appeal for their help. Let them be motivated themselves."

"Good point. I'll put out a video tonight."

F·DAY -2986

news·cnn·com:

CUBA FOLLOWS ICELAND

Cuba has become the second country after Iceland to declare itself trade-free. In an announcement that was widely anticipated, Cuba's President made a televised address to the nation, stating that Cuba had applied to the UN for Trade-Free Status, granting it immunity from outside market forces and assisting in border security.

Cuba's president Alvarez said "Cuba, as a sovereign nation, affirms its commitment to make the necessary changes in society, a society that must regard nature and the elements that sustain life for all species as cherished above all else, and that mankind must dispense with any and all means of incentivizing the destruction of our natural habitat as a matter of urgency."

Other countries which also look like following suit are Greece, Estonia, Ireland & Haiti.

Watch the video >>

POLISH CITIZEN MOVEMENT SPREADING TO RUSSIA

In a significant development, the burgeoning Citizen Rule Alliance group in Russia has united with the Tapac Movement and members of the Russian and Ukrainian Free Movements. Yesterday saw the first combined March of Movements on Red Square in Moscow, where citizens placed millions of wild flowers at the Tapac Monument.

Russia's leaders are appealing to citizens for calm. With elections due next spring, it is likely that the new Russian CRA will enter the political arena with a strong campaign.

The story of Tapac >>

f-day.org/feeds/update:

CUBA GOES OPEN [-1000 DAYS]

Following on from the fantastic announcement of Cuba adopting the open economy, 1000 days will be deducted from the F-Day countdown, bringing F-Day to less than thirty years away.

F-Day.org >>

feeds.bbcnews.com/openeconomy:

NEW OPEN ECONOMIC ADVISORY PANEL

The administration panel of Iceland has announced the creation of an Open Economic Advisory Panel, whose purpose is to advise other nation states on the feasibility of adopting their open economic model.

The new panel of twelve, headed up by Stef Gruber of the Free Movement will travel to candidate countries and consult foreign Government agencies on best practices to make a smooth transition to an open economy.

"Iceland has had a baptism of fire where the bringing of an open economy is concerned," Stef told our reporter. "But it has learned the harsh lessons, gaining it the experience that it can offer to other states now."

"We have been approached by seventeen countries in total and are currently in high level consultations with them. Many of them are small island nations like Iceland, but there are also a significant number of large 'Western' states who we are currently consulting with too."

F·DAY -2985

Karl had just returned from the airport after seeing off the small Irish delegation that he had spent the last couple of days showing around. It had been quite a surreal experience, showing around the politicians that he only knew from the TV. They were nothing like that in real life, Karl noted. Very normal, reasonable, smart people. Whoever trained them to talk like that on the telly, Karl thought, was frankly a menace to society.

Baldur had put all his teams in place, and Karl had opted to join the agricultural initiative. It would be nice to work in the fresh air again. There was something deeply visceral about working with clay, Karl felt. It stirred something inside so deep that it made you feel wonderfully connected to the Earth.

He got a call from one of the Community Hub team, asking him to come to the office. It was on his way, so he headed there straight away. Joe, the web guy, met him at the door.

"Sorry Karl, I knew you were passing. I couldn't resist. You have to come and see this – maybe history in the making." Karl was confused.

They went into the back office and three others were gathered around one of the screens. Karl looked over and could see a live web cam from one of the schools. All the children were singing Old McDonald Had A Farm. He looked in closer and could see a large man in the centre of the gathering, playing a keyboard with one hand and conducting the kids with the other.

"Oh my god, it's Einar Einarsson!" Karl laughed, putting his hands over his mouth.

"And that's not all," Joe said, opening another screen. "We just received a very large transfer into the ITF this morning."

Karl was amazed. "Oh my god, that's incredible," he shouted.

"AND..." Mikkael, the other web guy, said. "Check this out."

257

He opened up the Icelandic Honor System page and pointed on the screen. Einarsson had suddenly become a very respectable H5.

Karl smiled. "Oooh! Good for you, sir!" he said.

Mikkael clicked on one of the awards.

'Thank you Mr. Einarsson for your wonderful advice and help with my begonias. I never knew you were such a flower expert!'

F·DAY -2917

news·bbcnews·com/us:

JEFFERSON ANNOUNCES BETTER WELFARE DEAL

President Jefferson's announcement of a better welfare deal for low waged and unemployed American families was met with mixed reactions. Last week Jefferson had announced that he would be making a 'significant economic announcement', driving speculation wild all week, with some pundits thinking he was going to announce a basic income scheme similar to the one which failed spectacularly in Switzerland two months ago, bringing down the Government. Many left wing organisations also speculated that America would follow the lead of Iceland.

Expectation was such that many felt the better welfare deal of an extra $45 a week for unwaged and low income families was a huge disappointment. Social Equality USA called the move "an insult to struggling families", sparking a massive backlash to the announcement on social media.

In New York, protesters once again filled Wall St., with some groups taking to the infamous money-burning rituals of two years ago.

Listen to Jefferson's speech >>

AMERICAN OPEN COMMUNITY HUB

An enterprising Silicon Valley start-up called 'Hubus' has stolen a march on the global economy by launching its own 'unofficial' US version of the Icelandic Community Hub website. The service Hubus

(hubus.org) was launched just two weeks ago and is effectively a replica of the Icelandic Community Hub – the central organisational platform of Iceland's Open Economy.

The founder, Jason Sigurdsson, 27, himself a second generation immigrant from Iceland, told the BBC why he did it. "I know this is coming to the US. It's only a matter of time. Already we have nearly twenty thousand users in the first two weeks and loads of good stuff going on there already. Why wait around?"

Hubus.org >>

HAITI ADOPTS OPEN ECONOMY

Following in the footsteps of its Caribbean neighbour Cuba, the Haitian Government last night announced that they had sought Trade-Free Status from the UN and were now in what it called 'monetary wind-down'. President Jan Wilhali called on the people to follow the example of Cuba and Iceland and to help "co-create a living paradise for everyone". He also announced that Haiti, Cuba and Iceland have entered into a special international arrangement of mutual support.

After making the announcement, there were many unconfirmed reports of panic and looting with illegal border crossings from the Dominican Republic. Amateur phone footage shows what is apparently a small town near the border being overrun with 'economic refugees' from the neighbouring state, looking to find a new life in Haiti.

IS POLAND CONSIDERING AN OPEN ECONOMY?

The Citizen Rule Alliance who ousted the Polish Military rule have made their strongest hint yet that they are seeking to engage an open economy. Cecylia Rudaska, the acting spokeswoman, gave a conference yesterday saying that Poland had made history in becoming the first ever entirely citizen-ruled country, and they had a duty to explore every avenue that could improve the quality of life for her citizens.

EU leaders have warned that if Poland adopted OE, it would create a 'nightmare scenario' for trade and the economy throughout the Eurozone, Baltic States and Russia, and may result in Poland being disqualified from the EU.

HAITI GOES OPEN, DOMINICAN REPUBLIC LIKELY TO FOLLOW [-500 DAYS]

500 days deducted. Welcome Haiti!

F-Day.org >>

F·DAY -2916

"OK. Ideas please?" Baldur said as he paused the video.

There was a silence in the room.

"Where did you get that?" Karl asked.

"The President of the Dominican Republic sent it to me. It was taken by one of their military helicopters yesterday. As you can see, ladies and gentlemen, they have a big problem on their hands. Tens, if not hundreds of thousands of souls trampling the borders, looting and destroying anything in their path."

"It's like the Berlin Wall all over again," Stef observed.

"This was obviously handled badly," Karl said. "What happened with the Dominicans? I thought they were going to jump at the same time?"

"Yes me too," said Baldur. "Well, two things happened. The Dominicans hesitated too much and the Haitians hesitated too little."

"There's only one thing to do here, Baldur," Karl said.

"What's that?"

"Nothing."

"Nothing?!" Baldur demanded.

"He's right," Karen, one of the admins, said. "This is not pretty but it will sort itself out..."

"Are you serious? There have already been reports of some fatalities and countless reports of violence and looting. We can't do nothing."

"OK, well here's a suggestion," Stef said. "Let's send a delegation to both countries, assess the problem and try and meet some of the local villagers."

"Er, do you want to go?" Karl asked Stef.

Stef didn't answer.

"He's right Stef. I think it's too dangerous," Baldur said. "But I see where you're coming from. Create a photo op to make it look like we are working on it, yes. But that is deceiving. The truth is, there is nothing we can do. This is ugly, but it's no more ugly than a group of lions devouring an antelope. We have to let nature take its course."

"And hope that the Dominicans will see sense," Stef finished.

"Just give it time to settle," Karl said. "If there's one thing we absolutely must do, it's learn from this." He waved at the frozen screen. "We need to do everything to make sure this never happens again."

"Agreed," Baldur replied.

F·DAY -2900

STATE-LEVEL MARKET DEVOLUTION PROCESS

A living document from the Open Economic Advisory Panel

Monetary and market devolution should be a legal process, undertaken with due process within the traditional framework of Law and local Government. This is the currently recommended mechanism by which Government should responsibly undertake to offer the greatest security and smoothest passage to a fully open, marketless economy, while also maintaining reasonable safeguards.

Since every State and economy has its own unique qualities and challenges, great care must be taken to adopt *and adapt* these steps according to local conditions and customs. Once there is a willingness of Government to begin the devolution process, these are the recommended steps:

1. Do <u>NOT</u> publicly disclose the intention to devolve in the early planning stage, due to high risk of public disorder. Preparation before public engagement is vital.

2. Identify key problem areas such as loss of imports, border hazards, potential social side-effects, interruption in essential state services. Plan solutions and contingencies for these problems.

3. Draft a bill to enshrine the new economic measures into Law.

4. Draft a bill to 'freeze time' on private property ownership rights and the instruments of Government at the date of referendum, to be re-enacted in the event of any later decision reversal.

5. Draw up a strategy for implementing a later decision reversal.

6. Draft an emergency bill to freeze all sale and transfers of property and natural resources on the day of the first public release of information.

7. Plan a national re-education program to aid the public in understanding the changes and re-organising their priorities.

8. Engage with large companies – especially food, drink and utility suppliers. Identify their key problem areas and work with them to ensure non-interruption of vital services.

9. Contract a software development team to create an online National Community Hub, for optimising community operations and the delivery of labour, skills and resources.

10. Plan a recommended community service schedule to meet perceived labour requirements.

11. Plan a democratic referendum to adopt the new Laws and Open Economy.

12. Plan a national awareness campaign to lead up to the referendum.

13. Choose dates for the announcement, the referendum, and a proposed date to devolve. One month between announcement and referendum, and three months between referendum and devolution are deemed reasonable, once sufficient preparations have been made.

14. Make a nationwide broadcast and news release announcing the intention, the date of the referendum, the proposed date of devolution, and the immediate enactment of the Bill freezing all property transfers until either after the referendum (if not passed), or date of devolution (if passed).

15. Transparency is vital once the announcement has been made. Create an ongoing media campaign outlining the reasons, the potential problems and their solutions, and the community and personal benefits that people will enjoy.

16. If the referendum is passed, enact the Bills to enshrine the Open Economy into Law, and to freeze property rights.

17. Activate the National Community Hub and invite citizens to join, offering appropriate education to use the platform where needed.

18. Any later public desire to reverse the decision can be made through the Community Hub's Open Proposal system.

F·DAY -2152

Abby couldn't believe how quickly the two years had passed since their arrival in Iceland. Both she and Karl were almost unrecognisable to themselves. They were different people and now had quite a vibrant circle of friends – each of whom they were sharing duties with in some way or another. Abby was now in the school full time with Eli about thirty hours a week. Karl was busy in the nearby permaculture food factory and had become quite an expert on tropical fruit trees. They had had quite a party when the first Icelandic bananas had been born.

To them, the outside world really seemed other-worldly now, and neither could imagine for a moment going back to a life of debt, rent, mortgages and working fixed hours a week. The free world was a one-way ticket – that was for sure. But things had changed a lot even in the last two years.

Abby had been to Ireland twice to see her father, and it looked like Ireland was also on the verge of going OE. Sharing a land border with the UK, however, made things a bit more complicated for Ireland. Hopefully, they would never see a repeat of the scenes that had overrun Haiti and the Dominican Republic before, but there would undoubtedly be some problems. The Haitian problem had resolved quite quickly once the Dominicans adopted OE themselves shortly afterwards, but that was unlikely to happen in Ireland. The UK was a much bigger economy and showed no signs of making the change.

There were now officially nine countries using the open economy. Iceland, Cuba, Haiti, Dominican Republic, Vanuatu, Fiji, Bolivia, Uruguay and Paraguay. There were strong hints that other South American countries would soon follow, the most significant being Argentina. In Europe, Poland, Portugal and Greece were on the brink as well. Both Argentina and Poland were seen by many freeworlders as 'dam-pluggers'. They believed that when those countries went open, the ripple effect in the surrounding areas would be enormous.

The hard core capitalist countries like UK, America, Germany, Japan and China showed no particular signs of budging, even though the number of visible protests and acts of civil disobedience were sharply on the increase. The German Government was perhaps the most stoic and vocal against the open economy, with the Chancellor describing it as a "wave of hysteria and freeloading that would not end well."

Karl had put up a world map in their family room with markers for each country that had gone OE. Eli loved to ask questions about all the different countries – and Karl loved nothing better than to explain. She was going to be an explorer some day, that was for sure.

Abby had been at home preparing the lunch when Karl arrived.

"Hey, how's all my girls?"

"Daddy!" Eli cried and ran to hug his leg.

"Hi, lunch is almost ready," Abby said, kissing him.

"Wonderful! I'm starving", he said, plucking Eli up from the floor and raising her over his head.

"Oh, you had a missed call earlier on the house phone," Abby said. "A very strange number. No idea from where."

Karl's stomach twitched a little with dread. He still felt a mild, distant threat against him from unseen forces, and had been very careful who they gave their home number out to.

He picked up the phone. He had no idea which country the number was from either. He shrugged and dialled the number.

"Hello?" came the distant voice.

"Er, hi this is Karl Drayton. I missed a call from you earlier?"

"Karl Drayton! Hey, it's me, remember," shouted the excited voice. "It's Gani. Gani from the Philippines."

Karl went cold.

"Gani! Why the hell are you ringing me on my private number? How did you find this number?" he shouted.

"Haha! It's OK my friend. I find everything, you know."

Karl was panicking.

"Gani, if you want to talk, talk to me on private chat. We agreed remember? I'm hanging up now..."

"No, wait!" Gani shouted. "It's OK. It's good news!"

Karl said nothing.

"They release me, man."

"Who released you?"

"Yesterday I got a message, from our friend? Bishopsgate? And today the police come to my house and tell me all charges against me are dropped."

"Uh-huh," Karl said non-committally.

"They say this: 'Tell KD that the North Winds have blown in his favour and the glacier has melted! You will not hear from us again, Bishopsgate.' I don't know what it means but..."

Karl exploded laughing so much that he couldn't hear Gani talking. Eli started laughing too. Abby looked on perplexed. Karl mouthed 'We won the bet!' Abby's eyes widened and she started dancing with Eli on the spot. Now Kylie was in on the act. If everyone else was going to be dancing, she wanted in on the action too.

Karl wished Gani well for the future and hung up. He was almost tearful with relief. He had no idea until that moment just how much tension had still been pent up inside him over the Carson bet. He felt lighter than he had felt in years. No-one could touch them now.

"We are free," he said to Eli, swinging her by the arms.

"freeeeeee," she repeated.

F·DAY -2100

news·cnn·com:

OPEN AMERICA? WHAT WOULD IT LOOK LIKE?

For many years, fringe organisations like Truthfest, The Free World Charter and F-Day have been calling for an end, not just of capitalism, but of the entire market system. In other words, no money or trade. Even Hollywood actress Sandy Stone got in on the action with the 'Opening Up Time' video. Usually, these ideas have gone ignored as most people just think it's too crazy – but is it really that crazy? CNN has been looking into it.

Many countries like Iceland, Cuba and Bolivia have already adopted or are in the process of adopting an open economy. So what is an open economy? We spoke to Stef Gruber of the International Open-Economic Advisory Panel.

"An open economy is primarily about connection. People living in an open economy use the connection and collaboration of people to create prosperity. They are liberated from the requirement of working to survive, which, given how technically easy it is to provide for ourselves now, is kind of an old-fashioned idea.

"Having that liberation from the usual long hours and stresses of daily life gives each person the freedom to engage more in improving their community's needs and reach their full potential.

"Everyone comes to the open economy with the knowledge that their needs are met by that community and that they will also play their part in making that happen."

"So is that not just some form or Marxism or communism?"

"No, not at all. We are talking about an entirely self-organising, self-regulating system. There is no coercion to comply, because every person is given an in-depth understanding of how communities work and why certain behaviours are optimal and some are not. In communism – as in capitalism – money has always been the control system which, along with government, attempts to constrain human behaviour. But as we have seen, what is still effectively a fight for survival creates too much temptation to gain self-advantage."

"So, you're saying that education is the new government?"

"Yes, you could put it that way. So far in western civilisation, we have busied ourselves teaching our children about religion, reading, writing and mathematics, but almost nothing about life, or how to get along with people, or how to deal with your own emotions. It's like we don't think that's important, but actually, it's the only stuff that matters. We have set up all the schools in Iceland now with our new Life Education program. Sure, we teach maths and writing too, but eighty percent of the program is focussed on how to be the best person you can be. The results are astounding. Our studies have already shown that these students excel at maths on average fifteen percent more than their traditionally-educated predecessors.

"In short, teach a person how to live and you never have to tell them what to do."

"Do you think this kind of open economy could work in America?"

"Well, have you got humans there?"

"Haha! Yes, well mostly..."

"Well, then it should work there, yes."

Watch full interview >>

f-day·org/feeds/update:

US MAINSTREAM MEDIA COVERAGE [-1200 DAYS]

Miraculously, the mainstream media has suddenly come on board with news of the imminent Open Economy. This is fantastic news! Thank you, Media Gods! :D 1200 days deducted.

F-Day.org >>

The sky was open.

She spread her wings and flung herself upwards. Soaring high, she looked down on her tiny island – her home of millennia – placid in its sapphire waters. Suddenly she felt the upsurge, the rising hot wind of hope – accelerating, pressing on her fickle wings, burning at the edges. The friction of heat, diving into flames, through the sonic barrier and into a great arc.

She is outside time, a free spirit. Beyond the trouble and travesty of animal existence. An idea, non-dimensional. She embodies hope and joy, carrying knowledge from one aeon to the next. Yesterday a reptilian bird, today a butterfly.

Swooping suddenly now, she turns her head to see a great land, a land of desert and beauty. The red rock they call Uluru – a timeless holy place. Where elders walk among their ancestors. Where natural wisdom is stored and never spoken. One of many ancient gathering sites. Immutable. Steadfast. Incorruptible. Gently landing on its scorching surface, her heart sings as she draws in its wisdom.

She moves to the edge a little. A coral reef whispers to her. She dives into her deep, azure domain, meeting a riot of colour and fleeting life. Her tropical brothers and sisters, playing from sunshaft to shadow, competing for diversity and oddity. But she senses an uncertainty among the elders. There is a smell of death. She fixes herself to the giant coral mother and feels her yawning waves of sadness. Weak and drunk from the intoxicating currents. She draws in new knowledge.

Rising again, she crosses the immense silver blue plateau and enters the world of men. A gathering of leaders, clad in worm silk, sheep wool, cow skin. Clothes tight and constricting – a thick padding. They sit in a large chamber, gasping words into the dead air, shouting, angry, bored, indentured by countless sheets of dried wood pulp, black with words and numbers. They are empty and sad. Alive, but not living. She goes outside. There is a city – a city of man. She feels the upsurge of hope again.

There is a magnetism. Many people are gathering – like the elders of yesterday. They have found the old knowledge. They have found community. They have discovered their disconnection – and are reconnecting again. The rocks and the earth are unbending, and they never forget. The trees never stopped broadcasting it. The birds never stopped singing it. The flower never hid her colour, no matter how many times they cut her.

For men of simple aptitude know that nature is their master. Though his ingenuity outgrew his common wit, this left him lost and without direction – forgetting his place within the cosmic community. His ideas are futile who tries to control that which does not belong to him.

She is flying now at incredible height and speed. Now she knows what she is looking for, and she sees it everywhere: in the hearts of common people – the knowledge that was never far from the surface.

She sees the gatherings growing. She sees places where the gatherings have drowned out the men without answers. She sees the ancient wisdom that must surface again as part of mankind's learning and maturity:

To become responsible custodians of Nature's Empire. To grow. To transcend. To seek out the stars.

F·DAY -109

Poor Kylie was having trouble keeping up with Eli as she whizzed by on the road on her new bike. Karl had picked up the old bike from a neighbour and brought it to a metal-shop to get it reconditioned. He had done most of the sanding himself, but Thierry, the local metal guy had done the more intricate work like realigning the frame, balancing the handlebars and adding the electric motor.

It was another misty grey day and Karl was already in trouble as Abby had expressly asked him to keep Eli indoors because she had a temperature.

"If she comes home now, we are all going to be grounded," he said to Eli as she whizzed by again, then thinking to himself how much trouble he really would be in if she fell off the bike now.

"Don't be silly Daddy," shouted Eli. Then continued, as if explaining to a tiresome child, "Mummy won't be home until seven o'clock at least because she went to get the car repaired after school, and the man at the garage yesterday said it would be five o'clock at least before he could take a look."

"OK smart ass," he said. "Why don't you do some pedalling for a change?" he shouted as she flew past him again.

"Because I want to see how long the battery lasts at this speed. It's only gone down by two percent in the last five minutes, but I need to wait and get a better average."

"OK, so my child is a genius," Karl told himself. "What did I expect?"

He was quite impressed with the new battery. It was the latest technology from Ireland. Encased in a solar surface, the flat battery pack was very light, sat inside the bike frame and was apparently infinitely rechargeable. Theoretically, this bike should never need another battery.

This technology is unbelievable he thought. The solar surface was nothing more than a cheap plastic roll that stuck to anything. It was easy to produce and boasted sixty-five percent efficiency. How much more proof do we need? We can power the whole planet with this stuff alone. Billions of micro power stations everywhere working constantly in the sunshine. There was even talk now of a high efficiency solar concrete. You just plaster it on your building and you have free power forever.

Eight years since Iceland declared itself trade-free, lots had happened. Fifteen countries in all had adopted OE, including Poland, Portugal and Ireland in Europe – though at the expense of their EU benefits. Many of those countries were still struggling and the 'white market' still operated, but Karl and the Open Economic Advisory Panel had visited all countries more than once and they were getting to grips with it.

As more countries came on board, avenues of 'free-trade' between OE states were making things considerably easier, and new import and export opportunities were presenting themselves all the time.

New Zealand and pretty much all the Pacific Isles were on board. Spain was in limbo with many areas becoming autonomous and turning their back on the central authority. Austria and Italy were using a kind of hybrid system. They were giving free electricity, phone and internet and a basic income which was being paid for through taxes. They were having more success than Switzerland had years ago, but for Karl, it was not an open economy until the country's labour market was fully dismantled. Presumably, it would not sustain itself and would come to a head soon enough.

It was amazing for Karl to see how an idea so alien a few years ago could suddenly seem so commonplace and obvious, once you saw it in action. For that reason, Iceland's Economic tourism was booming, with many official delegations and universities coming to study their methods.

The media in many countries were portraying island life in Iceland and other OE countries as harsh and arduous, which, coming from an outsider's point of view of paying someone to polish your shoes was an easy mistake to make. The problem was, as always, how monetary economics reduced all aspects of life to the arithmetic of cost, and thereby avoidance of responsibility. What OE gave people was an unbridled sense of happiness and fulfilment which even the greatest billionaires had difficulty finding. Einarsson was living proof of that. Let's hope he has plenty more friends in moneyland, Karl thought.

The last country to declare itself trade-free had been St. Maarten – a tiny island nation in the Caribbean. But that was almost two years ago. It looked for all the world like everyone had settled for the situation, and no-one was pushing for OE any more. The Euro-Atlantic Trade Alliance were apparently considering a new deal that would restrict economic trade with OE states, with German Chancellor Braun calling the move "regrettable but necessary". What a joke, Karl had thought. The only possible reason they could have for not wanting to trade with OE countries was that they were afraid of contagion.

Well, maybe it was working. Protests in the UK, Germany and France were relatively low. But America was different. There was now a hugely significant minority of people who said they would opt for Open Economy given the chance. This was thanks in part to how much the liberal US media had opened themselves up to the idea. Karl had no doubt that his friends in Colorado had been more than instrumental in removing the blanket ban on the topic.

Karl felt that maybe things needed a kick-start. Maybe it was time for him to do something. He felt a revelation come over him. He had no idea why or from where it had come, but it told him that he needed to go to China.

"Come on Eli, we'd better get in," he said. "It's going to bucket down any minute."

"And?" Eli said, defiantly pedalling in circles. "It's only water Daddy."

"Yes, I know but if you get any sicker, I'm going to be sleeping on the couch tonight."

"Four hours," she said succinctly, alighting from the bike.

"Pardon me?"

Eli sighed. "The bike will go for four hours at a steady ten kilometres on one charge."

"Wonderful. I can use it to escape to the airport when your mother comes home."

Eli stopped and looked at him. "Sadly no, Daddy. Not with your weight."

"Thanks, chicken!"

After settling Eli inside near the fire in her pyjamas, Karl opened his computer and looked up his Chinese freeworlder contacts. He was surprised. He hadn't expected many, but there were quite a few. Just over twenty-two thousand in fact. He zoomed in on Shanghai and found around eight thousand contacts there. OK, he thought. He selected the contacts, opened up the mailer and wrote the simple message: 'Hi, Karl here. Give me a good reason to go to China...?' He pressed send.

F·DAY -108

The next day Karl had just forty replies – Most of which were along the lines of 'great country, you are very welcome', 'best country in the world', 'for the tea...'. But one message stood out from the others. It simply said, 'You know why, Karl.' And he did know why.

As the world's largest economy and industrial nation, China was the heart of the global monetary machine. If someone was going to stop this machine, the best place to be was in the engine room.

Karl checked the International Trading Fund to see if he had enough allowance to make the flights. He did.

"Woohoo!" he said. After eight years, Karl was coming out of retirement for one more campaign.

F·DAY -69

Karl arrived in Shanghai and was greeted by Sun Qi-Ru, or 'Sun-Ray' as he preferred to anglicise himself. Sun-Ray was a physicist for the giant engineering firm Sheng-Pan Inc. He was an active member of the Free Movement and also very wealthy due to a number of quirky patents that he owned. He invited Karl to stay with him and his family, which Karl warmly accepted.

One of Sun-Ray's patents, Karl learnt, was a device which filters almost any water to a clean, drinkable standard without expensive or replaceable parts. It did it using a simple bio-plastic micro-mesh that regenerates itself entirely on contact with a mild alkali.

"It's so simple and cheap to make," Sun-Ray told Karl, "but because I work for Sheng-Pan, they own the rights to the patent. But here's the crazy part: one of our competitors pays Sheng-Pan a large exclusive licence fee *not* to make it. Effectively, they are silencing the invention."

"Seriously? That's totally nuts," Karl said. "This invention could save lives..."

"Yes, and who do you think is the company who are paying the exclusive licence?"

Karl shrugged.

"Mykrochem Corporation."

"Fuck! One of the Big Soaps! I don't believe it!"

"I think we should do something about that, don't you?"

"That's exactly what I'm here for," Karl announced proudly. "To screw the system that is screwing everyone else."

Karl and Sun-Ray decided to go public with details of the device. They released the schematics on Twitter, and Karl recorded a video of Sun-Ray showing exactly how the device is made, and how it had been in existence for the past sixteen years, but held in abeyance due to monetary restrictions.

"How many lives could have been saved with this simple technology?" Sun-Ray said, "I can't guess. But the company who bought the licence did not want the world to see this – because they make too much money from selling products related to sanitizing dirty water. Does this sound right to you?

"Here is a direct example of profit over lives. It's time to stop this madness. Find out how to build this device yourself at the link below. Thank you."

The exposé was thrilling, but Karl couldn't help feeling a little uncomfortable.

"Why didn't you want to name the company, Karl?" Sun-Ray asked afterwards.

"It's a long story, Sun-Ray." Karl said. "In Ireland, we have a saying, 'let sleeping dogs lie'."

"I know. You got it from us," Sun-Ray laughed.

Karl spent the next few days learning about Chinese culture, but in particular, how the wheels of industry move to make the world's largest economy. It became immediately clear to him how this was achieved – through the expendable use of people and natural resources. Working and living conditions for most Chinese factory workers were appalling.

In Sun-Ray's Sheng-Pan factory, Karl saw some of the hundreds of women and men in their thirties who looked well over fifty due to overwork, bad diet and smoggy air. Most seemed happy enough, but did they even realise how much better their short lives could have been? Was ignorance bliss? If he could convince them of another way, would they even be interested? Humans are such habitual creatures, he mused. They keep doing the same thing over and over, even if it hurts them or doesn't make sense anymore. Why is that?

Leaving the factory one day, Karl spent a few moments pondering to himself on the steel bridge outside. Looking down at the vile, brown water passing below, he immediately began to think back to his eureka moment at the beach stream back in Ireland.

How long ago that seemed. An idea that had done a lot of good in the world and that had brought him many great adventures. He was immensely proud of that. He hadn't even checked how many signatories of the Charter he had lately, but the last time it had been around eighty million.

But despite his successes, he had felt a little hopeless these last days. Seeing the vastness of China, the problems, and the enormity of what he was trying to do. He felt like an ant trying to carry a skyscraper up a hill.

His thoughts were suddenly broken by the drifting corpse of a small mammal in the water below.

Damn! He couldn't quit. He couldn't un-know what he knew to be right. Even if it all came to nothing, he had to keep trying.

F·DAY -64

feeds.bbcnews.com/world:

UKRAINE'S BID TO AID POLAND BACKFIRES

Yesterday evening at 5PM, the Ukrainian Government closed all borders with Poland to stop the flow of Ukrainian and Russian economic refugees to Poland. Under the UN Trade-Free Pact which recognises Poland as a trade-free state, Ukraine was coming under increasing pressure by other nation members to do more to alleviate the extra burden on Poland's newly formed open economy.

However, there was a strong backlash from both the Ukrainian and

Russian people, reigniting the Tapac Movement, with reports of over a million children countrywide holding vigils at Kiev, Moscow and many border posts in the country.

Looking like something from a scene from World War II, there were many instances of Ukrainian and Polish children talking and sharing jokes through chain-link fences and razor-wire.

21st Century Border Children >>

Karl and his free world contemporaries were suddenly hot media property again. Karl received ten messages from major news channels seeking interviews and comment on the unfolding Russian-Polish drama. He arranged to do a satellite interview with the BBC from Sun-Ray's house in China.

The BBC interviewer suddenly cuts in on Karl's earpiece: "...and is with us now to talk about it. Good afternoon Karl and thank you for joining us."

"And good morning to you, Brian," Karl said good-humouredly.

"Karl, what do you think of the unfolding situation in Russia and Poland? It seems like the Open Economy idea creates problems and tension wherever it goes. I'm thinking of the narrowly averted human catastrophe in Haiti and the Dominican Republic, and the ongoing difficulties we are seeing at borders in Northern Ireland and South America. What have you got to say about that?"

"It's true there are many problems and difficulties when moving from one diametrically opposite system to another. You will, of course, remember that the main problems are caused by people who are trying to take advantage of a free system – as in, they are trying to escape the not-free system...

"So logically, you have to ask yourself what is the problem with the incumbent system that everyone wants to get away from? Perhaps your questions should be directed at the head of the World Bank, not me?" Karl quips wryly.

"Indeed. Some people have criticised the Free Movement for involving young children, some as young as three, in getting involved with complex world issues that maybe they don't really understand? What would you say to them?"

"Firstly, The Free Movement has never coerced or enticed children to take part in rallies. This is a campaign for human society to grow beyond the use of money to create a fairer, freer and more sustainable world for all species. It's about the future of all of us. These kids are clearly picking up on this and acting for themselves. I think they're incredibly brave and smart kids..."

"...But some of these children are as young as three," Brian cut in. "Are they really the genuine wishes of these children, or maybe the parents pushing their agenda perhaps?"

"Well maybe in a few cases, but most of these kids know exactly what they're doing. Why do we adults consistently underestimate our kids, or treat them as stupid? Kids are not stupid. Adults have a lot to learn from children. In fact, we adults spend most of our lives *unlearning* all the important stuff that kids already know, like basic empathy and respect."

"Karl, you are talking to us today from China. Can I ask why you are in China?"

"Sure. I came here to unfuck the world," Karl said defiantly. "Everywhere the Open Economy system has been able to operate with minimal interference from the outside world, it works. Iceland, New Zealand, Fiji are perfect examples. Where there are land borders or strong trade ties, things get messy. Why? Because everyone is trying to escape from the bullshit alternative.

"The so-called Euro-Atlantic Alliance have been sitting on their hands too long on this issue, and economically, China is cowing to their continual consumption of garbage. I'm here to put a spanner in the spokes of this greed machine. Yesterday we released details of a Chinese patent that could save millions of lives but has been brushed under the carpet for decades. That's not the kind of world I want to live in, and I'm not alone.

"Everyone in the established OE countries can't believe how much better off they are, having stopped putting blind faith in abstract ideas and institutions, and putting real trust in each other, their neighbour, their friends, their community. *This* is how we are meant to live. This is true wealth and prosperity. For too long we have associated prosperity with objects, but prosperity is actually just happiness.

"The Euro-Atlantic Alliance needs to listen to their people. The economists, politicians, bankers don't have any answers. They can't produce happiness no matter what they do. Happiness comes from each other. It's a shared experience.

"Let's open all the borders. Let's open our minds. Let's open our hearts. Let's open up ourselves and our world to its infinite possibilities. Let's jump together. Now. All of us. It's time."

And that was the moment everything changed.

What Karl did not realise, having made no preparations, was that the live video was being syndicated not just on every major news channel in Europe and the States, but also on Chinese TV that was relaying it all across the Far East. The effect was astounding.

First, all Karl's Free World websites crashed with too many requests. The last statistics showed over a hundred thousand new signatories an hour before crashing. Open economy was trending all over the net. The F-Day Clock crashed. Luckily the Freeworlder tech team had everything back up and running very quickly.

Karl got prime time news coverage on every major channel in Europe, carrying segments of the interview and footage of thousands of people taking to the streets, some in celebration, some in protest. In Europe, the Middle East, Africa, Asia and the US. It seemed like the world had forever altered.

Abby rang him laughing and saying there were journalists and photographers at the door looking for him. They had obviously forgotten in their excitement that he was in China! The next few days were a complete haze to Karl. He soaked up as many interviews as he could for every major global news channel.

Later Karl was watching the unfolding of global events. New countries declaring themselves free. In South America, every country apart from Brazil had gone OE, without border complications. It was only a matter of time for Brazil.

Almost every country in Asia was in turmoil. Widespread looting, protests and celebrations. In many countries, the police had abandoned their duties and joined in.

In Europe, France declared a state of emergency with protests out of control. Germany and UK were dealing with mass protests and money-burning everywhere.

Later, sitting in Sun-Ray's house video-chatting to Abby and Eli, Karl was exhausted. He told them he loved them and was coming home. Eli showed him her picture of Daddy on the TV. Underneath she had written the words 'Daddy, unfucking the world'.

He smiled, told them he would see them on Thursday, blew them a kiss, turned off the screen and went to bed.

F·DAY -63

feeds.bbcnews.com:

CHINA ON STRIKE!

For the first time in China's history, many state services have called strike action. Bus and train drivers, airport staff, maintenance crews and cleaners joined the unprecedented strike action, refusing to return to work this morning. It is widely believed the action was instigated by the obscure Nat-Cha anti-government organisation who posted on their website warning state workers of repercussions for not participating in the action.

China's military have been drafted in to keep state services functioning. Speculation continues on whether the strike action may have been called on foot of an interview with Karl Drayton, leader of the Free Movement who is currently in Shanghai, China.

See the Drayton interview >>

Karl was sitting on Sun-Ray's front porch enjoying his breakfast outside in the front garden. Sun-Ray's house was in one of Shanghai's most select suburbs, with a private garden that boasted a large oak tree as its centrepiece. There was even a tree house in it where Karl could hear Sun-Ray's children giggling high above.

He was reading the news on his tablet with amazement. He was just about to shout when Sun-Ray walked over without a word, took the tablet, typed something in Chinese and handed it back to him.

"Look," he said. The page was mostly in Chinese.

"What is this?" Karl asked.

"This is the Nat-Cha page – China's ruthless underground anti-government movement."

Karl looked bemused. "And?"

"It's bad," continued Ray. "They are threatening to kill anyone who does not support the anti-Government movement. They are citing the Free Movement as the coming new order and are trying to mount a coup on the Government."

"What?" Karl shouted, "that's totally fucked up! They're using us for their own agenda, whatever that is?"

"Karl, I think it would be best if..."

Suddenly their thoughts were interrupted by two large grey cars that had raced around the corner and came screeching a halt outside Sun-Ray's gate. Six men jumped out and started unholstering their hidden weapons.

"That's the special police," Sun-Ray gasped.

Karl felt dizzy. A million things went through his mind. For an instant, he thought about running back into the house and out the back window, but then thought better of it. This was no movie. They would just shoot him and go off to their next job.

"OK, let's do this..." he stood up slowly and raised his hands.

They cuffed Karl and bundled him into the back of the car without a word. Sun-Ray stood helplessly and watched as his friend sped off down the road.

"How many people have gone off like that and never returned," he said to himself. He prayed inwardly.

F·DAY -56

feeds.grapevine.is:

HANG ON, DID AUSTRALIA REALLY JUST SAY THAT?

Does anyone know if Australia is actually an island? Cos I thought I just heard something about Oz adopting an Open Economy. Was that not a luxury reserved for, like, real islands – ie. not massive land masses with gazillions of people? Well, we're about to find out. The Australian Open Economic Committee just announced that they are shortly going to make an announcement. How cool is that?

Call me superstitious, but when someone from an Open Economic Committee announces that they are going to make an announcement, I don't think they are going to announce the winners of the local donkey derby, do you? And according to their latest Government polls, it looks like people from the Land of Opportunity are going to be hopping with joy when this announced announcement is finally announced.

OE Australia? What the polls said >>

f-day.org/feeds/update:

CHINESE NATIONAL STRIKE & AUSTRALIA [-800 DAYS]

In light of the extraordinary events in China and the recent Australian polls, 800 days will be deducted from F-Day countdown.

F-Day.org >>

In what was possibly the most cut and dried Presidential campaign ever, Jean Carley effortlessly swept aside all before her and strode back into Office after an eight-year hiatus. So much had changed in the world. So many people had discovered she was right. Iceland had become a shining beacon of peace, freedom and equality like no other place on Earth, and much of that was thanks to her actions at the right time.

In her acceptance speech, she dispensed with the normal rhetoric, instead paying a moving tribute to her late husband Jeb.

"Corporal Jeb Carley, my husband, and the father of my two children was killed while trying to defuse a sand mine in Northern Kuwait. He was hailed a hero who had selflessly saved others and paid the ultimate price himself.

"But I say he wasn't a hero. Jeb was a pawn who died because of someone else's greed. Because of a resource war, planned and executed by powerful people from their air-conditioned war-rooms – far from the blood, the madding cries of children and bone-shattering explosions.

"This is the politics of the old world. I stand before you now as the new President with a simple message: that our Government will no longer stand by and allow wars and disputes over resources to wreak havoc among our species and our planet.

"My Jeb died in ignorance, but not in vain. He was killed as part of a great and cruel learning curve of our species. Without mistakes, we cannot learn. Without learning, we can't progress.

"Now a great era of change is upon all the people of the world. America is ready to embrace different ways of doing business – to face new challenges, put away tired old ideas, spark new thinking and move fearlessly into the future.

"Our disconnection with each other, with our fellow species from other countries, with our planet, with the results of our actions – no longer applies today. No more excuses. We are all in this together. We are the generation who are going to take responsibility," she finished.

The crowds gathered at the Washington Monument erupted.

The speech is hugely well received. Afterwards, in the make-up room her chief adviser jokes on the way by.

"Nice one chief, you missed a great job in sales. They'll buy anything from you out there now!"

She smiles half-heartedly, but catches herself in the mirror. She stops undoing her neck-tie and looks at herself for a moment. Suddenly, she knows exactly what to do about the Free Movement.

"Where's Barbara?" she shouts suddenly. Her PA, sitting right behind her, nearly chokes on her sandwich. "Get me the Irish Ambassador!"

"Yes, Jean."

F·DAY -53

Sean Quinn, the Irish Ambassador to America, liked his job. He didn't really like work very much as a rule, so this suited him perfectly. He had to give a few speeches, cut a few ribbons, smile for some photographs, in return for which he got a giant salary, a giant house with staff, lots of free gala dinners and all the wine he could drink without falling over. He figured falling over was a sackable offence, and especially inappropriate for an Irish dignitary whose job it was to deflect Irish stereotyping.

He was a round man, originally from Miltown Malbay, County Clare, in the south-west of Ireland. He loved golf, but his body had other ideas – which usually involved an impromptu game of find-the-ball in the adjoining fields. It didn't bother him though because what he lost in his swing, he more than made up for in his raconteuring at the nineteenth hole. He was very popular, having been an amateur boxing champ back in his days at Yale, but these days he used jokes rather than jabs to disarm and win over his opponents.

This day had been troubling him. He had just returned home from opening a school in Brooklyn, to find a mix-up in the roster had left him without a chef for the day, and it was almost lunchtime. Lucky for him, one of the cleaners apparently had a knack for such things and kindly agreed to cook something for him. He mopped the sweat from his brow, poured himself a small whiskey and sat out on the porch. It was a beautiful spring day in DC. His gardener had cut the lawn this morning and there was an intoxicating smell of fresh grass in the air, blending in very nicely with the faint aroma of boiling potatoes. He smiled to himself. Then things got weird.

He turned on his phone and had two voice messages. The first was from the Whitehouse, saying that they wanted to organise a private meeting with an Irish citizen, one Karl Drayton. The second message was from the Irish Ambassador to China saying that an Irish citizen, Karl Drayton was currently being incarcerated in Shanghai for treason and it was likely to cause an international incident without diplomatic intervention.

"Bollocks!" muttered Sean as he drained his glass. This day wasn't going to get any easier.

Some seven thousand miles away, Karl Drayton was having a better day – relatively.

Since his farcical interrogation last week by two belligerent security chiefs and a meek, apologetic interpreter, Karl had been confined to a solitary cell while they decided what to do with him. He was sure whatever accusations of treason they had levelled against him would have well evaporated by now.

Admittedly his cell was reasonably comfortable. Perhaps this was a tourist cell, he mused. It was fluorescent bright and clean, with an ensuite toilet, shower and a proper bed. Room service consisted of a hatch in the wall where a light would come on indicating that something had been left for him. The food had been pretty good too, but Karl secretly vowed not to eat rice again for at least a year when he got out.

This time, the light came on and he opened the hatch to find a small note. It read:

"You have phone call."

He was turning the note over in his hand when the door made an electronic clunk. He went over and tried pulling it. It swung heavily inwards and outside there were two small guards with a black and red uniform waiting for him. One of them motioned him outwards and Karl began walking down the long corridor flanked by his two diminutive friends who, he decided, looked a bit like tin soldiers.

Karl hadn't spoken to anyone in a week. He hadn't even been allowed to make a phone call. He wasn't worried about Abby though. He knew Sun-Ray would have rung her and explained the situation and she was well able to take care of herself. He wondered who the phone call was from. He guessed that probably Sun-Ray had organised an English-speaking attorney for him and maybe this was him or her on the phone.

The tin soldiers finally ushered him into a small white room in which there was a chair and a table with a phone sitting on it. They moved over and stood opposite him without saying a word. Karl sat down and picked up the phone.

"Hello?"

The two guards looked at each other.

"Hello?" Karl asked again, but there was nothing but silence. He looked up at the guards. They looked at each other again and finally one of them shouted.

"You have phone call!"

"Ah right," Karl said, then laughed. "I can *make* a phone call?"

The guard nodded stiffly.

Karl put down the phone and thought to himself. He didn't know anyone's number. They were all in his phone.

"I don't know anyone's number," he shouted to them. They looked at each other but didn't appear to understand. Karl sighed. What to do, he thought. There was just one number he knew by memory so he decided to ring it.

"Hello?" came the distant voice.

"Dad! Hey, it's Karl!"

"Karl! My god. Are you alright?"

"Yes, I'm fine, I'm fine. Sorry, I was allowed one call and your phone number was the only one I knew."

"No problem..." Karl could hear his mother talking in the background.

"Karl," she said, obviously grabbing the phone off his father. "Are you alright, love?"

Karl smiled.

"I'm fine Mum. This place is pretty good. I've had no problems. I'm feeling well and getting lots of bed rest," he quipped.

"It's wonderful to hear your voice," she said. "We are so worried about you. Abby and Eli are here in Ireland. She just went out for a walk with Eli. She is very worried but they're ok. She has been ringing everyone." Karl smiled again. That was Abby – ever the fighter. God, he missed her.

"OK, I think I only have one call. I don't know when I might get another."

"OK"

"OK, so here's a few things I want you to do... Have you got some paper? First, tell Abby and Eli that I love them very much and will be home very soon..." He felt a huge lump rising in his throat which made him pause.

"Yes?"

"OK, tell Abby to ring Mike Ross in New York and tell him what's been happening. His number's on my computer.

"OK..."

"And tell her to contact Stef..." Suddenly there was a rumble and the sound of other voices in the room.

"Hello, Karl?" It was Abby.

"Abby! My God! It's you!"

"Yes, of course, it's me. Your father just rang me on the mobile and I came straight back... How are you, my love?"

Karl was suddenly filled with emotion.

"I'm OK," he sobbed, then recovered himself. "I'm OK... This place is pretty comfortable but I know nothing, no-one has spoken to me in a week. I don't know what's happening except they gave me this phone call..."

"Don't worry my love, I've been in touch with all the embassies and they are trying to work something out. They all know about you now. Don't worry, they will get you out..."

"That's fantastic. Yes, I know, listen I love you very much and will be home soon OK?"

"I know."

"How's Eli?"

"She's perfectly fine. She's looking for you though, so hurry home, please! I love you so much..."

"Yes, I will. Listen, please ring Mike Ross in New York too. He can help us. I know he can..."

The phone went dead. Karl looked up at the guards. They both stood out from the wall and motioned that it was time to leave.

They walked back down the long grey corridor. Karl was smiling so much after the call. He felt lighter. He looked at one of the guards and contemplated making a joke with him, but thought better of it. It would be an enormous pity to be shot dead now over some jokey misunderstanding.

He arrived back at the cell and the door clunked closed again. He lay back and relaxed on the bed. The phone call had really achieved almost nothing practical, but he felt so much better, and probably that was all he could hope for at this time.

F·DAY -51

Sean Quinn had known Jean Carley for many years but had never warmed to her. Perhaps it was because she was so powerfully efficient in her manner, and he was so fuzzy and imprecise. He was more interested in raising a smile or two – and maybe a glass – than solving diplomatic incidents if he could help it. He and Jean had crossed paths many times during their campaigns and had both gristed through their disapproval of each other for the sake of the cameras, before quickly going their separate ways.

This was, however, the first time he could recall that they had ever had a private official encounter. He sighed a little and knocked on the door.

"Come."

"Ah Mrs. President, how are you this afternoon?" Sean smiled as he swung in the door.

"Cut the crap Sean and take a seat," the President replied looking up only momentarily from her papers. The Ambassador found the most comfortable chair, not too close, and rested down his over-indulgent frame with a sigh.

Jean took her time to finish what she was writing then put down her glasses and sat back.

"What do you think about the Open Economic movement, Sean?" she asked.

"The Iceland people?"

Jean shrugged. "Iceland, Poland, New Zealand, Cuba, all over South America... It's popping up everywhere. They're even starting it in Ireland. What do you think of the idea?"

Sean inwardly panicked. It was a loaded question. He knew that whatever he offered as an answer would probably be wrong. The trick, he thought, was to get it wrong as little as possible.

"I admire what they are trying to do, but it's impossible of course."

"Really? It's working well in Iceland, by the looks of things." She said, nodding to a newspaper on her desk which presumably had some favourable story about Iceland.

"Well I'm sure that will implode in due course and will all be forgotten about," Sean said quickly, hoping that she wasn't going to quiz him on the front page article that he hadn't read.

Jean stood up from her desk.

"That's what I thought too Sean," she said as she walked over to the window. Sean had to admit she was an impressive figure of a woman. She had managed to be an aggressive Commander-in-Chief while still retaining her femininely wiles and a deeply compassionate air. He wasn't sure any man could actually achieve all those qualities in one. Perhaps this was why he was a little afraid of her. She had power in more ways than just her office.

"But as far as I can see it's not going away any time soon," she said. "And in the meantime, we've also got ourselves a little problem," she announced at last.

"Oh? And what's that?" Sean enquired.

"This Karl Drayton fellow – the leader of the Free Movement. He's gone and got himself landed in jail in Shanghai..." Sean looked at her quizzically, as if waiting for the punch line. Jean caught his blank expression, then continued abruptly. "He's *Irish*, Sean. Yesterday I had a call from the Irish Prime Minister looking for help."

"Ah..." Sean finally realised why he was there. He had no idea Karl even existed before now but decided not to divulge that for now. "Yes, er, from Dublin, wasn't he?" he chanced.

Jean looked at him sternly. "Yes, he *is* from Dublin."

Sean was starting to see where this was going.

"So we kind of have a mini international drama going on that could potentially get ugly," Jean continued. "According to my office, the Free Movement's social networks are all lit up demanding Karl's release. Also, NBC has already run a story..."

"But this is an Irish problem surely," Sean interrupted. "Why the hell would the US get involved?"

"It's more than an Irish story, Sean." She offered him another newspaper. "It's an Icelandic story, it's a Cuban Story, it's a Bolivian, Venezuelan, Chilean, Greek and Estonian story. All of these countries are devolving from the market system and moving to the open economic model."

Sean took out his glasses and started skimming the story.

Jean continued. "This movement could possibly be bigger than any of us. And the more this story grows, the more sympathy and air time this Free Movement gets, you follow me?"

Sean nodded. They sat in silence.

"OK, I'll see what I can do," he said at last, standing up.

"You know how relations are with China at the moment," Jean added. "If this story blows up in everyone's faces... well... we don't want to turn this into a hostage trading exercise, you follow?"

"Yes, I know," Sean admitted. Everyone knew the US was now in so much debt to China that Karl could end up being used as a pawn to give China even more political leverage.

"Go gently," she advised. "If China thinks Karl Drayton is important to us..."

Sean nodded.

"Leave it with me," he said and went for the door.

"Oh, and Mr. Quinn..." Jean said.

Sean stopped and turned.

"Tell Mr. Drayton I would like to see him, will you?"

F·DAY -50

Abby, finally back in Iceland, had just spent the last hour looking for Mike Ross on Karl's computer. She had often heard Karl talk about Mike, but didn't really know who – or what he was. At last, she managed to get into Karl's email account and did a search for 'Mike'.

"Gotcha!" she exclaimed, and took up the phone.

Of course, Mike didn't answer, but Abby, not realising this was normal just hung up without leaving any message. She put down the phone and started to see about writing him an email. She hit 'compose' and the phone rang.

"Abby," the voice said sharply.

"Er hello yes, this is Abby, who..."

"It's Mike. You rang me a second ago. Karl asked you to ring me I guess, right?"

"Mike! Thank God. Yes, I only spoke to him for a few seconds and he asked me to call you..."

"How is he?" Mike cut in.

"Er, he's... OK, at least he sounded OK..."

"That's great," Mike said, not wishing to waste any more time. "Listen, I've already been doing some work on this. I got a twenty-second spread on the main NBC news. I've also been in touch with some friends in China, and..." he paused.

"Yes?" Abby asked.

"I have to tell you it's not gonna be easy. The current government in China are arresting hundreds of people every week for anti-Government activity. Once you get picked up by the Special Police, you automatically bypass any hearing and are incarcerated indefinitely..."

"Oh my god... so he could be..."

"Abby I gotta tell you straight. There's guys in that same prison Karl is in that were arrested just like Karl in the 1990s. None of them ever got a trial. None of them have been seen since." Abby was putting her hand to her mouth. Mike went on. "If Karl sounded fine to you, then great, but it probably also means he doesn't know how serious this is."

"But that's crazy... there must be something we can do."

"Well that's kind of the problem actually," Mike continued. "There are things that we can do, but this is not America or Europe we're talking about..."

"What do you mean?"

"We can actually get good coverage on this story in the media if we push, but..."

"But what?!"

"Well, it might make things worse," Mike said flatly. "If China thinks they have an important political prisoner, they will exploit that situation to the hilt. They did this in 1994 with a Dutch investigative journalist who was also a prominent member of the South African

Parliament. When she disappeared, the world media lit up demanding her release.

"Well, suddenly the Chinese Government realised then they had something of value. It turned into a kind of bizarre hostage situation with teams of South African officials going to Beijing to negotiate."

"So, what happened? Did she get out?"

"She got out about six months later, yes, but not without the Dutch and South African Governments making huge concessions to China. There was no official story of course, but pretty soon after lots of heavy industrial or civic contracts in those countries were being moved to China. Four factories in South Africa closed down. It got so much bad press in the South African media that it eventually brought the Government down."

"My God, that's horrible..."

"Well, that's the good news Abby, I'll be honest," Mike said frankly. "Almost all these kind of prisoners are still in there somewhere..."

Abby nodded.

"And if push comes to shove, we don't have that kind of bargaining power where Karl is concerned." he finished darkly.

"So what *can* we do?"

"My advice is tread very lightly. If Karl sounds in good spirits or healthy at least, that's great, because it gives us more time to try to figure this out."

"Yes."

"I have some good contacts in the Chinese media who have dealt with this kind of story before. Sometimes you can get lucky with the local arresting officer in these cases, but..."

"What can I do?"

"Being honest, just sit tight Abby. Let's try to figure out what we're dealing with here and see what's the best approach to play..."

"OK, my god. Is he going to be OK?"

"Well, if it's any consolation, China's human rights have improved dramatically over recent years, so he's probably going to be just fine, but listen as soon as he rings again, ring me immediately. I'll email you my cell number."

"OK."

"And one thing very important Abby..."

"Yes?"

"When he rings you have to ask him this one simple and clear question: 'Are you in danger?' OK?"

"OK."

"How he answers that will affect our actions dramatically, so don't forget."

"OK, I got it. God, thanks, Mike, I don't know what I would have done. I spoke with the Irish consulate in..."

"You already contacted the authorities?" Mike interjected.

"Well, yes of course. I didn't know what to do..."

Mike sighed.

"OK," he said. "Well let's just hope they have the brains to handle this right. I'll see if I can find out what they're doing about it..."

"Thank you Mike, and sorry... I..."

"No don't be. I can only imagine what you're going through. Leave it with me for now."

After the call, Abby was starting to feel a lot better. At least now, she knew everyone was doing their best. She sat for a while looking at Karl's computer. She couldn't help chuckling. Seven hundred and twelve unread emails and counting. She looked through the window at Eli who was playing in the garden with her friend Simon and Kylie.

"Your daddy's going to be camping in this office for days when he comes back," Abby said.

Eli was so big now. It seemed like only yesterday that she was throwing her bear on the ground and giggling, playing fetch with Daddy. Now someone had to fetch Daddy!

F·DAY -48

Both Mike Ross and the US Government knew that Karl was a hot potato. The US administration didn't want to start making private petitions to the Chinese Government, as to show they had a special interest in the case would put them in a compromising position economically. Similarly, Mike was reluctant to push all the media buttons as it could make life worse for Karl. Everyone knew it was better if Karl was just some foreign nobody.

Mike had tickled all the Government resources he had to see what information they had. The only reliable thing he found was that the Irish American Ambassador was now involved. Clearly, the US administration was, like him, treading carefully.

Usually, Mike's first call with any problem was to first search everything about the person in question. This time, it was Karl himself.

It took him only a minute until he burst out laughing. It was time to send a text.

🦋

Ambassador Sean Quinn had just got off the phone with Carley's secretary who was checking on his progress and was pretty sure she had seen through his rambling, mumbling excuses. As a seasoned raconteur, he knew the key to unlocking any problem was through people, but this time, he was all out of ideas – and all the thinking and stress was making him thirsty.

He headed to the nearest hostelry, took a seat and ordered a whiskey soda. A quick gulp later and his resolve returned.

"Same again," he snapped. The barman nodded mutely.

Beside Sean was The Washington Post. He picked it up and scanned the headlines. He flicked through and eventually found a tiny article about Karl Drayton with the droll headline "Jail for the Free Man."

> 'It has been confirmed that Karl Drayton, leader of the Free Movement, has been arrested and detained by police of Shanghai where he has been travelling. A statement issued from his family said that Karl was taken in for questioning by police over two weeks ago and has not returned to where he was staying since.

> 'Police in Shanghai have not released any details, but have confirmed that Mr. Drayton is currently being held on criminal charges. Karl Drayton, widely considered to be an anti-government activist, was a key proponent in bringing about the open economy in Iceland.'

"Bollocks," he said and tossed the paper aside.

And, as if he had just uttered a magic Irish spell, the answer came in a fairy-like tinkle.

A text from an unknown number. First a picture of a man that he didn't know, but who looked vaguely familiar, followed by a very short, rude message. Indignant, he was about to report the text as spam when suddenly the TV in the corner exploded into an obnoxiously loud TV show.

He looked up at the TV, then back at the text. Then he knew.

Sean Quinn, like every good politician, knew that when it was time to act, it was time to find someone to act for you. He dialled the office.

"Hi Shelley, I want you to make a call to a company called 'Shout Productions' in New York please."

F·DAY -45

www.bbc.com/openeconomy/latest:

BRAZIL AND PORTUGAL DEVOLVING

In a timed statement, the leaders of both Brazil and Portugal have announced they are devolving to an Open Economy in light of the overwhelming public support. Ending weeks of protest and speculation, the devolution will be carried out on a phased basis starting with free food basics and utilities.

More >>

FRENCH OPPOSITION HAVE CALLED FOR OE

The leaders of the French opposition parties have issued a formal letter calling on the Government to accede to public pressure and devolve to an open economy, stating: "unless we listen to the people, we become the detached villains and no better than the failed monarchy our ancestors fought so hard to overcome."

Full statement and march videos >>

CANADIAN PARLIAMENT ISSUES 'STATEMENT OF INTENT'

In a national broadcast yesterday, Canadian Premier Elizabeth Canten announced that Canada has made preparations for the devolution process and, as per the OEAP guidelines, has declared a referendum to be held in 30 days.

Full press statement >>

f-day.org/feeds/update:

BRAZIL / PORTUGAL ANNOUNCEMENT [-1200 DAYS]

A further 1200 days will be deducted from the countdown in light of the historic announcement from Brazilian and Portuguese Governments, potentially bringing F-Day to just seven years away!

F-Day.org >>

F·DAY -42

Karl was meditating in his cell when the guard opened the door with a single word, "Visitor!"

Before Karl even had time to react, there, filling the room with his tall square frame was the last person on Earth he expected to see, and the one he was most glad to.

"Ben!" he shouted and ran to hug his brother.

"I came here to free the freeworlder," he boomed. "you're one of the last few free people on the planet..."

"Haha! How the hell did you end up here? Am I being freed?"

"Yes, you are free to go, bro," he said ruffling Karl's hair. "In China, everything is easy – once you're talking to the right people of course. Turns out my TV show is watched by almost a billion people here. A billion people, can you imagine? Watching that shit?"

Karl laughed.

"So you decided to come and put your face around the police station, huh?"

"You bet. I even signed the captain's wrist so he could show his wife tonight."

"Whoa! Lucky her!"

"Lucky you, bro!"

"Yeah. Lucky me. Thanks, man." He clapped his hand on his big brother's back and they walked out from the cell.

As they left the building, Karl had to stop and adjust his eyes to the strong daylight. He took in some deep lungfuls of the muggy Shanghai air. It was better than the stale air he had endured for the last three weeks. He suddenly felt a little dizzy and weak. Ben put his arm to support him.

Sun-Ray walked up the steps to meet them and gave Karl a hug. He had Karl's suitcase with him.

"It's wonderful to see you again Karl. But my advice gentlemen, is to leave now. Go straight to the airport, get something to eat, have a shower and leave on the next flight."

"Yes, he's right Karl," Ben said. "Maybe my celebrity will wear off around here as quickly as my scrawl on the captain's wrist."

"Haha, yes," Sun-Ray replied. "Or maybe captain's wife will be in bad mood. Best get out of here."

"Thank you for everything Sun-Ray," Karl said shaking his hand warmly. "We'll see you on the other side when all this nonsense is over."

Sun-Ray handed Karl the case and the two brothers got into the taxi.

"Phew," Ben said. "Let's get the fuck out of here."

"Agreed. Hey, can I use your phone?"

He rang Abby to tell her the good news and that he was on his way home. He was just about to hand Ben back his phone when he had an idea.

"Mind if I make a quick video?" he asked.

"Fire ahead!" Ben said.

Within minutes the video of a bedraggled looking Karl was going viral on the net.

"Friends, just to say I am safe and well and just got released from Shanghai prison, where I have been held hostage for the last three weeks.

"I have to say that the guards in the prison treated me well and respectfully and the cell that has been my home for all these weeks was comfortable and the food was good. However, despite that, I have been held against my will in a foreign country, without questioning, without reason and with no leave to appeal.

"Obviously the Chinese Government sees anyone who threatens

their precarious position as a potential terrorist. One has to wonder how justifiable *any* government is that needs to defend its position with violence against any citizen. True leaders are leaders because they are widely respected and admired. Enforced leadership by any means, whether without the express consent of the people, or through the limited choices of sponsored elections, is a dictatorship.

"China looks like a dictatorship, but the only difference between China and America is China are more honest about it. All Western monetary states are dictatorships. You choose a leader based solely on their publicity dollars. The richest candidate wins, not the best one. And when they win, you have almost no control over what they do when they get into power.

"Western Governments are a scam. The Chinese Government is a scam. Monetary economics is a scam. Self-rule is happening already – and it's working. People are leading happier, more fulfilled lives. Isn't that the whole point of living? Just to have the best life possible? To live in peace? To reach your full potential with no-one forcing you to do shit you don't want to do?

"We have all been *conned* into believing that when you take away government all hell breaks loose. Ask yourself, just who is perpetuating that message? As someone who has seen both sides of the story, I can tell you that something else entirely waits on the other side. All *heaven* is gonna break loose, once we release control of the people.

"If you're out there, and you give a fucking damn about anything, you need to know this. The emancipation of humanity from monetary slavery is coming. Withdraw immediately all support for government, for banks – for any agency that does not have the interest of all life on this planet as its *primary* objective. This lie is over. The hurt is over. The wait is over. Freedom, abundance and fulfilment is within our sights. Let's jump together, now. For all our sakes. For our children's sakes."

Karl was shaking when he stopped the recording and was violently sick in the taxi. The driver started shouting, but Ben waved him down.

"Eli," Karl was saying weakly. "Where's my Eli?" He was delirious.

"It's OK," Ben said. "We're going home now."

F·DAY -14

feeds·bbcnews·com/openeconomy

RUSSIAN GOVERNMENT COLLAPSES

Russia's parliament collapsed in disarray last night as hundreds of leading politicians walked out. Protesters, including police, military and many children had stopped work and flocked in their millions to Moscow City yesterday demanding Government step down to make way for an open economy.

As Parliament came into session, parliamentarians began filing silently out of the chamber one by one in solidarity with the protesters, leaving just twenty-four members in the chamber, including the Prime Minister.

Prime Minister Ivanov told the almost empty chamber, "Ladies and gentlemen, the hand of history is upon our shoulder. We are no-one to deny the people, nor ignore the great wheels of change. I hereby resign as Prime Minister. It has been an honour to serve, but an even greater honour to be alive to witness the arrival of this new chapter in our colourful history. Thank you."

Watch video >>

EURO-ATLANTIC TRADE ALLIANCE IN DOUBT

Following the mass demonstrations that took place all over Europe last night with widespread work stoppages and protests, many Government services failed to open today. In Germany, France, Spain and the UK, millions of people took to the streets to voice their dissatisfaction and reclaim their freedom.

The centre of Paris is at a complete standstill with an estimated 3-4 million people having blockaded the Eiffel Tower, the Champs-Élysée and Parliament Buildings.

In the US, there have been large protests and work stoppages in all major cities. New York was brought to a standstill when millions of workers, police and military flooded the streets to declare their freedom. Wall St. remained closed as international markets continued their erratic behaviour of the last two days.

President Carley addressed the nation in a live TV broadcast, thanking people for their peaceful protest, and to remain calm and steadfast in the face of uncertainty. "Rest assured," she said, "my administration will do everything in its power to seek a positive resolution, and get our proud nation back on its feet."

Watch video >>

HISTORIC SCENES IN BEIJING

Last night, Beijing's Tiananmen Square began filling up with child demonstrators. In a rehearsed display called 'The March of the Children', the children, all wearing red costumes, arrived to lay flowers on the steps of the Great Hall of the People to commemorate the people murdered or who have gone missing at the hands of the Chinese Government.

It is estimated that between four and five million people descended on Beijing's city centre to take part in the mass demonstrations, with many reports of police and military joining in the demonstration. The children and parents who participated in the ceremony have set up temporary dwellings on the square.

f-day.org/feeds/update:

HISTORICAL MILESTONES [-1800 DAYS]

1800 further days to be deducted on foot of recent historic events. Protests epidemic throughout Europe and US, the gracious dissolution of the Russian Government, Chinese marches. F-Day estimated now at just over two years away!

F-Day.org >>

F·DAY -1

There was an eerie silence in the Oval Office. Karl and Abby were sitting at Jean's desk, feeling a little like expectant parents visiting an obstetrician. Eli was very busy on the floor, drawing with the coloured pencils and paper that the concierge had given her. Jean was pacing around the room, lost in thought.

On the President's computer screen sat the F-Day Clock, still ticking inexorably away to its projected destination two years away.

"You know what I'm going to say, right?" she said eventually to Karl.

Karl laughed. "Yes," he said.

"...and?"

"Yes," he said. Then looking at her, "Of course."

Jean continued pacing.

"Can someone please tell me what this is all about?" Abby burst in.

Karl and Jean looked at Abby and laughed. Abby slowly put her hand up to her mouth. "You mean..." They were already nodding.

Suddenly Eli jumped up from the floor, holding up her paper triumphantly.

"Look!" she said gleefully.

On the paper was a beautifully drawn picture of the Statue of Liberty, but instead of the flaming torch – an open hand releasing a butterfly.

The three adults gasped in shock.

The next day America was set to enjoy her most historic Independence Day celebration ever.

F·DAY 0

High above the carnivals and confusion, the Commander gently cleared his throat and steadied himself with the rail. He dropped the camera and it floated gently away from him. He cursed, buckled himself in, then took another look up at the giant blue planet over his head.

"This one's for you mama," he said quietly, then reached out to retrieve the runaway camera.

"We are standin' at the crossroads
of planetary fate
where the power of humanity
has never been so great.
But with all this might and power,
comes responsibility.
We alone are the keepers,
but first we must be free.

On this day, we will be free
from the lines dividing you and me
In a universal day of love,
soon we will be free, soon we will be free...

We are livin' in the shadow
of what this world can be
with amazing new technology
we're waking up to see
to a world full of plenty
where you can be just what you want to be
where the greatest gift is laughter
and everything is free...

NOTES & ACKNOWLEDGEMENTS

The Free World Charter (p.20)

The Free World Charter is a real movement, endorsed by over 55,000 people as of this publication. If you like the ideas expressed in this book, then please consider giving it your support and learning more at:

www.freeworldcharter.org

The F-Day Clock (p.42)

The hypothetical F-Day Clock is also real, counting down the days, hours, minutes and seconds until the world moves beyond the market system into an Open Economy:

www.f-day.org

Iceland: The World's First Open Economy (p.40)

There is already a growing movement suggesting that Iceland could be a contender for the first Open Economy. Check out:

www.facebook.com/icelandfree

The Zeitgeist Movement (p.12)

The Zeitgeist Movement and Zeitgeist movie series are loosely represented in the book as 'Truthfest' and 'The Truth Movement', who also promote a post-market system:

www.thezeitgeistmovement.com

The Venus Project (p.13)

The Venus Project and the work of futurist Jacque Fresco are also loosely referenced in the novel as 'The Earth Project'. For more, visit:

www.thevenusproject.com

HonorPay (p.241)

An Honor payment system such as described as part of Iceland's Community Hub already exists at:

honorpay.org

Freeworlder.com

This is the author's personal blog and Open Economy information site.

freeworlder.com

Author's note:

There are many characters in this book which may vaguely resemble real people I've had the pleasure to meet during my travels on this whirling rock. If you recognise yourself among them, then take a bow. You obviously made an impression!

However, please remember that this is a work of fiction and some details and characters have been embellished for the purposes of the story.

I've had great fun writing this book. I hope you enjoyed reading it as much I enjoyed writing it – but hopefully in considerably less time!

Colin R. Turner,
Málaga, Spain,
July 2016

freeworlder.com

19575436R00176

Printed in Great Britain
by Amazon